*the* SILK HOUSE

D0208452

27134

Daughter of *Silk*

*Romance, adventure, danger. Young Rachelle Dushane-Macquinet
finds them all in the court of the evil Catherine de Medici.*

LINDA LEE CHAIKIN

ZONDERVAN™

GRAND RAPIDS, MICHIGAN 49530 USA

ZONDERVAN.COM/
AUTHORTRACKER

ZONDERVAN™

Daughter of Silk
Copyright © 2006 by Linda Chaikin

Requests for information should be addressed to:

Zondervan, *Grand Rapids, Michigan 49530*

Library of Congress Cataloging-in-Publication Data

Chaikin, L. L.
      Daughter of Silk / Linda Lee Chaikin.
        p.   cm.–(The Silk house; bk. 1)
      ISBN-10: 0-310-26300-X
      ISBN-13: 978-0-310-26300-5
      1. France—History—Francis II, 1559–1560—Fiction. 2. Catherine de Medicis,
Queen, consort of Henry II, King of France, 1519–1589—Fiction. 3. Courts and
courtiers—Fiction. I. Title.
PS3553.H2427D38 2006
813'.54—dc22   2005031947

Interior design by Beth Shagene

Printed in the United States of America

---

06 07 08 09 10 11 12 • 20 19 18 17 16 15 14 13 12 11 10 9 8 7 6 5 4 3

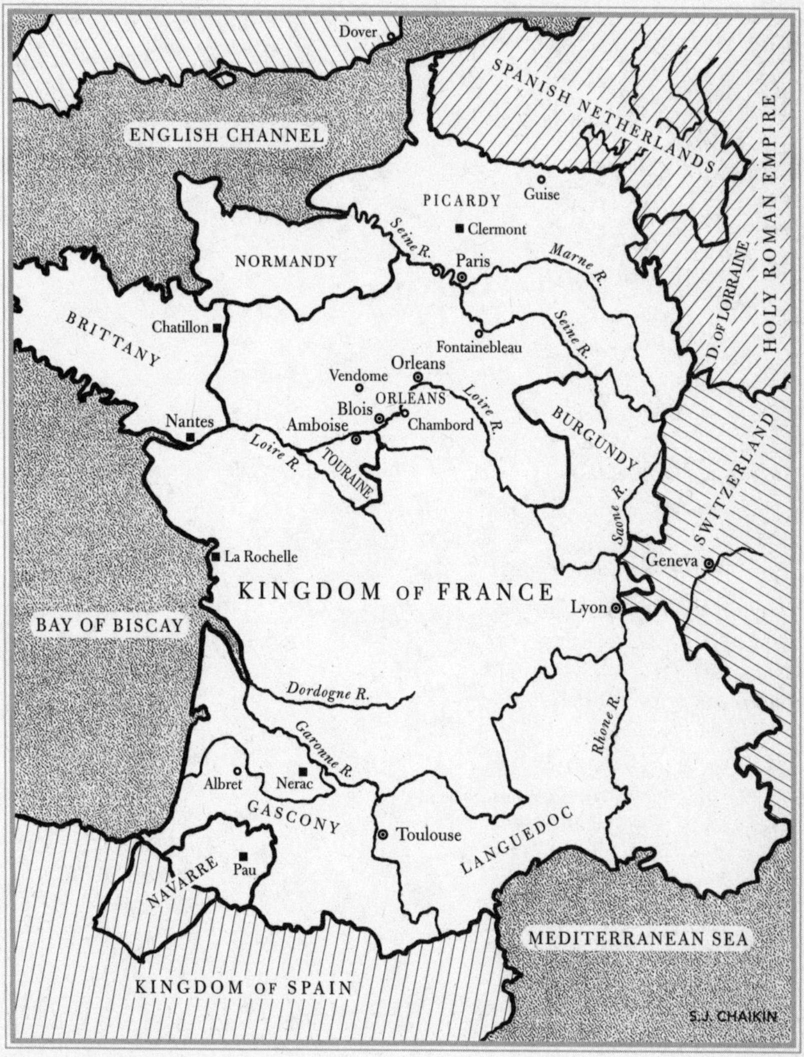

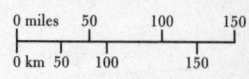

Dover

ENGLISH CHANNEL

SPANISH NETHERLANDS

HOLY ROMAN EMPIRE

D. of LORRAINE

PICARDY

Guise

Clermont

NORMANDY

Seine R.

Paris

Marne R.

Seine R.

BRITTANY

Chatillon

Fontainebleau

Vendome

Orleans

ORLEANS

Loire R.

BURGUNDY

SWITZERLAND

Nantes

Blois

Amboise

Chambord

Loire R.

TOURAINE

Saone R.

La Rochelle

KINGDOM OF FRANCE

Geneva

BAY OF BISCAY

Lyon

Dordogne R.

Garonne R.

Rhone R.

Albret

Nerac

GASCONY

Toulouse

LANGUEDOC

NAVARRE

Pau

MEDITERRANEAN SEA

KINGDOM OF SPAIN

S.J. CHAIKIN

FRANCE IN THE 16TH CENTURY

(showing prominent provinces and cities for this series)

■ Huguenot center

| 0 miles | 50 | 100 | 150 |
| 0 km 50 | 100 | 150 | |

Glossary of French Terms

a bientôt — so long, see you later

adieu — bye

affaire d'amour — love affair

affaire d'honneur — duel

ah, ça non — definitely not

allon bons — oh dear

ami — (m) friend

amie — (f) friend

amour — love

amoureux — to fall in love

amoureuse — enamored, affair

appartements — apartment

atelier — shop, workshop

au contraire — on the contrary

au revoir — good-bye

avoir la foi — to be a believer

beau — (m) good looking, fine looking, beautiful

bébé — baby, very young child

belle — (f) beautiful

belle dame — painted lady (unflattering)

bien — good, well

bien entendu — as a matter of course

bien joué — well played

bien sûr — of course

bel ami — (m) lover

belle des belles — the most beautiful

bon — (adj, nm) good

bonhomie — friendly, warm feelings, camaraderie

bonjour — good afternoon

bonne — (adj, nf) good

bonne chance — good fortune, good luck

bon vivant — vibrant

Bourbon — kingly family, of royal blood

ça alors! — good grief! (exclamation)

calèche — carriage

carrousel — carousel

casques — helmets

cercle — group of close associates, often the Queen's

c'est bien compris — Is that clear?

c'est bien le moment — (irony) great timing

c'est bien promis? — Is that a promise?

c'est charmante — (f) That is charming.

c'est magnifique — That is magnificent.

c'est sotte — (slang) That is silly.

ceux de la religion — those of the religion

chaise longue — reclining chair

chambré àcoucher — sleeping room

charmante — (f) charming

cher — dear, darling, cherished

chevalier — the lowest title or rank in the old French nobility, also *cavalier* or *chivaler closet* — a small room, for sleeping, dressing, writing letters, reading, etc.

coif — stiff ruffle around the neck (period clothing)

comte — nobleman, count

comtesse — countess

coterie — clique, group

coucher — go to sleep

Cour d'Honneur — Court of Honor

courtier — agent

cousine — cousin

couturière — designer, expert in sewing

coup de foudre — love at first sight

Corps des Pages — School for Pages

cuirasse — breastplate

décolletage — bodice

déjeuner — midday meal

delicieuse — delicious

demoiselle — young lady

dépêchez-vous — hurry up

dernier cri — last word in fashion

diables — devils

diner — evening meal

divertissement — entertainment, amusement

docteur — doctor

duc — French spelling for English duke, the highest ranking noble except for a prince of the blood

duchesse — duchess

duchessina — duchess, Spain

duchy — the territory ruled by a duc or duchesse

eau de parfume — perfume

elegante — elegant

enceinte — expecting, pregnant

enfant — child

escadron volant de la reine — Catherine de Medici's ladies-in-waiting and maids-of-honor; forty immoral women of beauty who served her political intrigues

espèce de pestes — special nuisance

enchantee — enchanted

en memoire de — in memory of

fanfaronnade — fanfare

faux pas — false step

fait accompli — an accomplished fact

fête — party

fleur-de-lys — lily flower

forte — accented, loud

frère — brother

galante — a chivalrous man

grand prieur — head man, head of an abbey

grisette — a seamstress specializing in dress-making, embroidery, design; usually still under training

grandes dames — great ladies

gaucherie — awkwardness

grande salle — large room, salon

haute monde — upper class fashion

honneur — honor

ingénue — a naive girl

infirmière — nurse

Institutio Christianae Religionis — (Latin) Calvin's *Institutes of the Christian Religion*, doctrinal writing

jennet — a small Spanish horse of the time

joie de vivre — joy of life

Huguenot — French Protestant, of Calvinistic doctrine

laissez faire — noninterference, tolerance

la gloire de la France — the honor of France

le misérable — the poor

le moment — the moment

lettre — letter

ma belle — my lovely

ma fleur — my flower

ma foi — my faith

ma petite — my little one

mais certainement — but surely

maitre — form of address for a doctor or an advocate

magnifique — magnificent

maman — mother

Marquis — highest ranking nobleman next to a duke

marquisat — the territory ruled by a marquis, including land estates, wealth, future title of Duc

merveilleux — marvelous

messire — an honorable man or a knight

messieurs — plural of Mr.

mesdames — plural of madame, or of Mrs.

merci — thanks

merci mille fois — thank you a thousandfold

mes petits — my children

mignon — cute

mille pardon — thousand pardons

mille diables — thousand devils (slang)

Mlle. — Mademoiselle

Mme. — Madame

Monseigneur — Lord, addressing someone of high rank or respected office

mûreraies — a grove of mulberry trees for feeding the leaves to silkworms

naturel — natural, natural-looking, casual

nenni — slang for no

neveu — nephew

noblesse oblige — nobility obligates

non — no

oncle — uncle

on est très ami — We are very close friends.

Oriflamme — the red banner of St. Denis, near Paris, carried before the kings of France as a military ensign; a rallying or symbol

oui — yes

palais chateau — palace, castle

pardon — pardon

par excellence — archetypal

par exemple — for example

père, mon Père — father, my Father

parterre — an ornamental arrangement of flowerbeds and bushes; an area under the galleries in a courtyard

Pasteur — Bible pastor, teacher

petit noir — coffee

petit dejeuner — breakfast

petit — (m) little, small, young, humble

petite — (f) little, small, young, humble

petite reinette — little queen

petite sœur — little sister

peste — (nf, slang) a nuisance, a pest

poppinjay — (slang) puffed up, proud

portier — gate-keeper

précisément — precisely

quivre—alertness

quelle stupide—how senseless, how foolish, how idiotic

reinette—young girl-queen

salle—hall

salle de sejour—living room

salle de garde—guard chamber

sang-froid—(nm) poise, self-control, calmness, indifference

savoir-faire—knowledge of what to do, know-how

se depêcher—hurry up

sil vous plâit—please

surement pas—certainly not

sœur—sister

soirée—fancy party

sotte—silly, inane

tante—aunt

tarts aux cerises—tarts, chicken, or sweet-filled pasties

tenez ferme—stand firm (as in Ephesians 6:14)

tête a tête—head-to-head, conversation

toilet—washroom

toque—cylindrical hat

tout a fait—entirely

tout de suite—at once

toute la nuit—all night

un non categorique—an emphatic no

vive la Reine—Long live the Queen

vive le Roi—Long live the King

Historical Characters

Alessandro — Alessandro the abuser, a brother of Catherine de Medici

Anjou — Henry of Anjou, third son of Catherine de Medici and King Henry II

Avenelle — Maitre Avenelle, betrayer of the Huguenots

Bourbon — Prince Antoine de Bourbon, older brother of Louis. He later became King of Navarre through marriage to Huguenot Queen Jeanne d'Albret.

Bourg — Anne du Bourg, a Huguenot man sent to the Bastille by Henry II. He was burned at the stake under the Cardinal de Lorraine when boy-king Francis ruled with Queen Mother Catherine. The Huguenots then felt betrayed and planned the Amboise plot.

Calvin — M. John Calvin, writer of Calvin's *Institutes* (*Institutio Christianae Religionis*)

Chatillon — Cardinal de Chatillon, (Odet Coligny) brother of Gaspard and Francis Coligny

Coligny — Admiral Gaspard de Coligny, protected Huguenot provinces

Condé — Princesse Eleonore Condé, a niece of Admiral Gaspard Coligny

Condé — Prince Louis de Condé

Este — Cardinal d'Este, from Ferrara, Italy

Este — Anne d'Este, wife of the Duc de Guise (Francis)

Guise — Charles de Guise, the Cardinal de Lorraine, younger brother of Duc Francis de Guise

Guise — Duc Francis de Guise, of the infamous Borgias family from Florence, Italy

Guise — Monsieur Henry de Guise, later a duc, younger son of Duc Francis de Guise

Lefevre — M. Jacques Lefevre, translated first Bible into French

Machiavelli — Niccolo Machiavelli, a cunning and cruel man; he was associated with corrupt, totalitarian government because of a small pamphlet he wrote called "The Prince" to gain influence with the ruling Medici family in Florence.

Madalenna — Italian serving girl of Catherine de Medici

Medici — Catherine de Medici, Queen and Regent of France over Francis II and Charles II Valois

Montpensier—Charles de Montpensier (the Duc de Bourbon), had rights to the throne that equaled or exceeded those of the Valois

Montpensier—Duchesse Montpensier, of the House of Bourbon, a Huguenot

Navarre—Prince Henry of Navarre, son of Antoine and Jeanne of Navarre

Nostradamus—a soothsayer in the Roman Catholic Church

Paré—Ambroise le Paré, physician and surgeon to kings, a Huguenot

Poitiers—Mme. Diane de 'Poitiers, mistress of King Henry

Renaudie—Messire de la Renaudie, a leader of the Huguenots, a retainer of Prince Louis de Condé

Ruggerio—Cosmo and Lorenzo Ruggerio, brothers from Florence, Catherine's astrologers and poison makers

Rene—Perfumer, also Catherine's poisoner

Ronsard—Poet who served the Valois Court, Chatelard

Sadeleto—Jacopo Sadeleto, Archbishop of Carpentras

Stuart—Mary Stuart (la petite reinette), married Francis Valois, King Francis II

Tasso—Poet from Italy

Valois—Princesse Elisabeth Valois, daughter of Catherine and Henry Valois, married Philip II of Spain

Valois—Princesse Marguerite Valois

Valois—Hercule Valois, the fourth and youngest son of Catherine and Henry Valois, little is known of him

Author's Note

DEAR READER,

Writers who enjoy researching history generally accumulate far more information than can normally be incorporated into a novel of this size. In this series I have occasionally found it practical to compress a decade or more of significant historical events into a manageable time period for my characters. In *Daughter of Silk*, I was therefore able to include more of the key events that portray the Huguenots' great struggle under persecution in France, Spain, and Rome. Indeed, the half has not been told, and the history I have incorporated is accurate and representative, and the characterization of historical individuals is based on careful research. As always, I have created fictional characters who are representative of the time in which this history takes place.

As to particulars, the majority of historians agree with the view that Catherine de Medici did use poison to rid herself of enemies, and that the Duc de Guise and the Cardinal de Lorraine were lecherous in their deeds (which they always claimed to be doing in the name of Christianity) in order to maintain the power of the House of Guise.

Let me also say that I have nothing but regard for those with a Roman Catholic background, and in fact, my husband's family on his mother's side is such, and is also French from those who migrated to Quebec at a later time in French history.

You may contact me through my website at *www.lindachaikinbooks.com*.

Thank you for your correspondence, and may our wonderful Savior continue to give you His joy and peace in the darkening times in which we live.

LINDA CHAIKIN

Daughter
of
Silk

Chapter One

Marquis Fabien de Vendôme stood on the open balustrade of the royal palais chateau at Chambord, resting his muscled shoulder against the broad marble embrasure. He fixed his attention below in the courtyard where voices shouted and horse hooves clattered over stone.

Another burst of activity erupted near the gate. The king's *cuirrasiers,* garbed in black and crimson, sporting brass and steel, threw open the double gate. Riders thundered into the courtyard as though pursued by fiendish gargoyles.

Fabien recognized le Duc de Guise mounted on a black charger with a jeweled harness and gold velvet housing edged in green braid. Guise's men-at-arms followed, bearing the flag of the House of Guise from the duchy of Lorraine.

Fabien straightened from the embrasure, clamping his jaw. The secret rumblings of hatred smoldered in the rocky caverns of his soul at the sight of the duc.

Le Duc de Guise looked up toward the balcony. His gaze appeared to search, as if he could sense a burning pit of hellish emotions attacking him from somewhere, as if he was a jackal smelling a rotting carcass to feed upon.

Then le Duc de Guise locked gazes with Marquis Fabien.

Guise's lips turned into a hard, faintly mocking smile. Fabien smiled in return and offered a bow.

Guise turned his head away and peered over his shoulder toward the gate. He raised a gloved hand whereupon a masked, black-cowled rider burst through the turret gates, dusty, his horse sweating. Fabien tensed.

Who was this? A moment later the duc's men-at-arms tightened their escort around the mysterious rider, encircling him within their midst.

Is Guise protecting the masked figure or confining him? Why the cowl and mask? Fabien narrowed his gaze, as if by staring he could bore through the mask to identify the *messire*.

He was here at Chambord at the invitation of the boy-king Francis and his *petite reinette*, Mary of Scotland, but not to become ensnared in whatever ongoing intrigue the House of Guise was presently hatching.

Fabien left the balcony. Patience, he reminded himself. The long-awaited hour to apportion revenge upon the head of le Duc de Guise would eventually dawn.

The marquis pulled his brows together as he walked along the gilded *salle* in the direction of his chambers. If anyone at court understood the reasons behind the unexpected arrival of Guise, it would be Comte Sebastien Dangeau, a member of Catherine de Medici's privy council and Fabien's relative through marriage.

Sebastien's position was a precarious one since the House of Guise might discover he was of the Huguenot faith. There were other Calvinists at court, and they too walked the edge of a precipice. One *faux pas* and they would slip from the slope into the bloodied clutches of the Guise brothers' inquisitional penchant.

COMTE SEBASTIEN DANGEAU, upon hearing that le Duc de Guise had ridden into the courtyard with a masked rider, joined other esteemed courtiers on one of the balconies. He held back, keeping behind the others so as to not be seen, as he managed a survey of the courtyard.

Sebastien's gaze stumbled over a masked figure cowled in black, being escorted by some dozen men-at-arms under the proud flag of le Duc de Guise. The duc himself led the way into the palais. *No doubt on his way to see the king. Ah but yes, there is something familiar about the hesitant gait of that hooded figure —*

Footsteps pattered up behind him, the scampering feet reminding him of a mouse — or a rat?

Sebastien turned sharply. His gaze lowered to rest upon an expressionless face with brown eyes. The Italian *demoiselle* stared up at him. She was Madalenna, the young servant girl in bondage to the queen regent, Catherine de Medici. The Queen Mother had brought Madalenna with her from Florence, Italy, when Catherine first came to France to marry Henry Valois II. Madalenna, secretive, spying; Madalenna, always approached in a whisper of movement, emerging from some shadowy corner where one least expected to see her. Madalenna the spy.

Madalenna curtsied. "Monsieur le Comte, my mistress, Her Majesty the Queen Mother, bids you come to her state chambers *tout de suite*."

Sebastien glanced again toward the courtyard, then turned and departed for the chambers of the Queen Mother, known by those who knew her best as *Madame le Serpent*.

MADEMOISELLE RACHELLE MACQUINET felt her heart thump and a trickle of perspiration ran down her rib cage. This was to be the telling moment. All she had labored for these many weeks, sometimes working twelve hours a day, would be held to the crucible of scrutiny. For this day Princesse Marguerite Valois, the youngest daughter of the Queen Mother, would try on the unfinished gown. The cut and flow, the stitching, all must be exact. Rachelle would measure and tack the hem with a steady but feathery hand and bring the gown back to her chamber to complete tomorrow. The gown was but one of several in various degrees of completion, however this particular gown was mostly Rachelle's work, and her future as a *couturière* depended on the princesse's pleasure.

Rachelle, a *grisette* from the Chateau de Silk in Lyon, was yet under the supervision of the grand couturière herself, Henriette Marie Loiselle Dushane, otherwise known to Rachelle as her adored grandmère, a dainty widow in unrelieved black satin, with silver hair and sparkling dark eyes. Rachelle knew her to be no easy mistress with the needle, nor did Rachelle wish her to be otherwise. It was her desire to follow in her steps.

Rachelle stood on the terrace of the royal chambers facing Princesse Marguerite and her ladies-in-waiting. Her wine velvet pincushion with her initials, *R.D.M.*, was strapped to her wrist with a black velvet band, while a pair of specialized Dushane scissors swung from the chatelaine. Her measuring strip draped about her slender neck. She took the widths of sheer burgundy silk, draped gently over the cloth of gold, and with trembling fingers allowed it to fall gracefully over Marguerite's dark hair. The garment settled softly around her feet, shimmering.

"Ooh . . ." came the sigh of the ladies-in-waiting.

"*C'est magnifique,*" Marguerite purred, holding a section of the silk to her cheek. "It is perfect. La, la, Rachelle, you will always do my gowns. I insist. You and your famous Grandmère."

"Merci, Mademoiselle Princesse." Rachelle curtsied, dipping her head and offering a quick thanksgiving to God. "But the work, it is not yet finished. If it please my lady princesse, I would measure now for the hem and the addition of the Brugesse lace."

Marguerite stepped onto the small stool, and Rachelle knelt to smooth out the folds on the bottom of the gown.

Marguerite spread her arms gracefully, lifting her face toward the March breeze and allowing the sparkling material to float. "Monsieur Henry should see me now," she whispered, drama in her voice. "Ah, but he is not here . . ."

Her ladies uttered sounds of sympathy.

Rachelle admired Grandmère's embroidery work on the burgundy silk. The tiny gold rosebuds were sewn with a secret stitch Grandmère had perfected at the Macquinet Chateau de Silk, and Rachelle was determined to master the stitch as well. She was already practicing on leftover sections of silk. Each section of crafted rosebuds left a glittering mound of gold thread, yet the silk material around it lay smooth and unpuckered, a most difficult technique to master. Rachelle could only marvel. Not even Maman could make a perfect rosebud, and Maman too was a seasoned couturière.

The gown shimmered with Princesse Marguerite's every movement. Diamonds could be added to the bodice after the gown was finished, but only under the watchful eye of a guard. Rachelle had no desire to handle the diamonds. A tale had circulated at court of a certain grisette, who during the reign of King Francis I, had stolen rubies meant for the queen's bodice. The grisette, believed to have swallowed them, was sent to the Bastille. Rachelle shuddered, imagining what had befallen the woman. As for Marguerite's gown, Rachelle was of the opinion that any addition of diamonds would add little to its beauty, but the princesse insisted on jewels, jewels, and more jewels.

To Rachelle, Grandmère represented the heart of the family silk enterprise, for she had carried with her all of the prized secrets of silk weaving, when as a Dushane, she had married into the Macquinet family, who had been their competitors.

Rachelle was thrilled when Grandmère had first been summoned to court by Queen Regent Catherine de Medici to design and oversee the intricate cutting and sewing of gowns in the new shades of Macquinet lavender blue, rosy pink, and the deep burgundy that was Rachelle's favorite. This newer cloth had been developed in Lyon, known for the finest silk weavers in France, a matter of which Rachelle was most proud.

Princesse Marguerite desired a dozen new gowns, and eighteen-year-old Mary Stuart of Scotland, the new Queen of France through her recent marriage to seventeen-year-old King Francis II, wanted two gowns and a farthingale. The queen regent, Catherine, however, wore naught but black since the death of her husband.

Rachelle shuddered suddenly. She remembered what Grandmère told her and her sister Idelette after meeting with the Queen Mother in her state chambers. Catherine, after asking Grandmère questions about silk in general, had then casually inquired about its possibilities as a medium.

"I have heard of a certain deadly poison being used in silk undergarments in the twelfth-century Moslem East by harem women wishing to remove a dangerous foe. Is this so, Madame Henriette?"

Grandmère, the emissary for the Dushane-Macquinet Chateau de Silk at court, had confessed to the Queen Mother she had heard such things but knew naught how such murders of ancient times were committed. Afterward, Grandmère returned to the Macquinet chamber looking troubled. She had commented: "Remove a dangerous foe, she said, I vow! Such liberty these royal persons take with the French language. Her study of my person after I deliberately interchanged the word *murder* gave me a tingle, I assure you. Murder, or if you prefer, assassination, continues unabated in the courts of Europe, not merely among the Moslem Turks."

Rachelle was helping with the cutting and sewing of the princesse's gowns while Idelette, more advanced than she, was assisting Grandmère with Mary of Scotland, now Queen of France, everyone's *charmante* darling—except the Queen Mother's.

The Macquinet women, entitling themselves the Daughters of Silk, had departed Lyon two months earlier by *calèche* and wagon for the journey to the Louvre Palais in Paris. However, soon after their arrival the boy-king's health had so deteriorated that the doctor had advised the royal family to leave the unhealthy air of Paris in search of fairer weather in the French countryside, where fragrant greenery and flowers adorned the region of Touraine.

So once again the Daughters of Silk had overseen the tedious packing of their supplies, which included large rolls of various cloths wound on smooth ash wood lined with velvet to protect the filaments, and they had traveled to Blois.

Rachelle and Idelette had assisted the younger grisettes-in-training to pack the Genoan velvets, the brocades with interwoven threads of gold or silver, and of course, the Dushane-Macquinet silk. They had carried lace of every variety: ivory Alençon with tiny rosettes, the heavier Brugesse so wonderfully used for ruffles and clusters in diagonal shapes, the princely Burgundy style used for softer draping of waterfalls at the throat, and edging that was gathered on cuffs.

So also had many of the sewing and design instruments journeyed with them in wagons, for Grandmère insisted the equipage used at court was not as fine as her own.

The large trunks were a sight to behold and always thrilled Rachelle. They were embossed, either in gold or silver, with the famous name Dushane-Macquinet emblazoned with artistic flair.

Upon their arrival here at the Chambord palais chateau, she had been amused to see wondrously garbed servants bearing the trunks on their shoulders in a long, somber train as though they carried the remains of a king. "A flurry of trumpets would be a pleasant touch," Rachelle had whispered with a subdued laugh to Idelette.

Each of the Daughters also carried a personalized hand case: Grandmère's was gold-embossed Italian leather; Idelette had chosen a deep rose brocade; and Rachelle, who had recently received the *honneur* of becoming a full-fledged grisette before departing Lyon, had chosen the burgundy velvet out of a secret infatuation for the good-looking Marquis Fabien de Vendôme, born of the princely Bourbon blood.

Each of their names was inscribed in gold on their small case, which contained all manner of sewing equipment. Rachelle and Idelette were in the process of earning additions to their treasure of special needles, pins, cutting instruments, and spools of colored silk thread — some from Italy, Spain, and the Netherlands.

Presently, as she knelt before the stool where the princesse stood in pose, Rachelle considered her work as anything but *elegante*. She was perspiring beneath the direct sunlight which blazed down unsparingly. Her undergarments were binding tightly about her middle, and an annoying section of her thick auburn hair had come loose from its pins to hang across her damp cheek and neck while she stooped, bent, and crawled around the princesse, gauging the hemline on the draping cloth of gold for accuracy. She slipped her highly sharpened Italian pins into the cloth of gold as sparingly as possible so as not to leave marks. It would be to her shame if she snagged a single filament of this costly material with one of her pins.

Rachelle was paying scant attention to Princesse Marguerite's maid-of-honor, Madame Charlotte de Presney, who stood near the balustrade, peering below and commenting on an arrival in the courtyard.

"Le Duc de Guise just rode through the gate from Paris. Ah, what a worthy retinue rides with him," Charlotte de Presney was saying in her indolent voice.

"I care naught except if the duc's son is with him, ah my darling Henry de Guise," Marguerite said. She snapped her fingers at one of the ladies to hand her a sweetened glass of lemon water.

"The duc brings a stranger, Princesse. How curious, I promise you. The stranger hides behind a mask." Charlotte leaned against the balustrade.

Rachelle, interested, glanced toward Charlotte.

"Your *joie de vivre* will soon return, Princesse, for I see your monsieur Henry de Guise among his father's entourage."

Marguerite gave a shriek at the name of her lover and jumped down from the stool, spilling some of the lemon water.

Rachelle groaned. Did any splash onto the dress?

"And why did you not tell me at once?" Marguerite rushed toward the balustrade to see for herself. Rachelle, gritting her teeth, scrambled after Marguerite in desperation, trying to keep the half-pinned hem from dragging.

"You did not tell me Monsieur Henry is here? Perhaps you have designs upon the prince yourself, Charlotte?" Marguerite accused her in a warning voice.

"Monsieur Henry de Guise is loyal to you, Mademoiselle Princesse. I am sure of it ... just as loyal as you are to him," Charlotte said too quietly.

Rachelle held her breath. She watched the princesse's dark eyes turn upon Charlotte, then flash with molten rage. She reached over, cuffed her, and grabbing her earlobe between her thumb and forefinger, she drew Charlotte toward her.

Rachelle winced along with Charlotte.

Marguerite glared as she pinched Charlotte's earlobe. "Careful, little fox, or I will have you beaten."

An uneasy hush descended over the ladies.

Charlotte, stoic as always, gave a submissive curtsy to the princesse. She then turned her attention once again to the courtyard.

Rachelle, having made certain that the silk was neither stained with lemon water nor the hem stepped upon, stood with Marguerite's ladies at the balustrade. Her gaze sought the masked rider, but neither he nor le Duc de Guise was in sight.

"Ah, but how *galant* is Monsieur Henry," Marguerite crooned. "Look how tall he is. And that golden beard, look how it curls just so and shines with just enough auburn to make him look angelic."

Rachelle pressed her lips together to keep from laughing. Angelic! That varlet?

"See how Monsieur Henry looks up toward your chambers?" Louise de Fontaine told Marguerite.

She is trying to please the princesse.

Marguerite, clasping her bejeweled white hands together in exaggerated happiness to make her ladies laugh, sighed deeply and dropped a flower over the rail. Henry doffed his hat, and a page ran to retrieve the flower and take it to him. He lifted it to his nose and held it high toward Marguerite. Rachelle wondered what the Queen Mother would do if she saw this forbidden display?

"Look, ladies—Marquis Fabien de Vendôme. But how *beau* he is appearing this day," Louise said.

"He is always so," another replied.

Rachelle's heart tripped for the first time at the mention of Marquis de Vendôme. Her gaze sought him across the way where he stood on the opposite balustrade, but he was not looking in their direction.

It was true, Fabien de Vendôme was by far the handsomest man at court, exceeding Henry de Guise. The marquis had captured Rachelle's interest from the first moment she saw him. Yes, his *savoir faire* had been, and was, impeccable. But then, after the death of his father, he had been raised for some years at court with the present King Francis II and Mary of Scotland.

Marquis de Vendôme appeared oblivious to the ladies watching him, including Princesse Marguerite, and instead stared below into the courtyard.

Rachelle took in Fabien's virile build, housed in velvet and rubies, the handsome features, and fair hair. It was no marvel to her that most every woman at court was aware of him. Someone of high title such as he would surely marry a future duchesse. Perhaps a princesse? Rachelle was related to a dowager duchesse, but she was not in line to inherit. The title would rightly go to a blooded niece.

"Athenais has already conquered the marquis's heart," Louise said with an exaggerated sigh.

Athenais? Rachelle wondered. She had heard her name before, but not her family name, nor the region of France from whence she came.

Charlotte de Presney clicked her fan open and swished it rapidly. Rachelle glanced at her and saw that her painted mouth was tight.

"If Athenais is spreading such lies as you have just spoken, Louise, then she deserves Marquis de Vendôme's scorn, and so do you for repeating such rubbish," Charlotte said. "I did not see Monsieur Fabien paying Athenais any undue attention last night at the play, I assure you."

The play! Rachelle recalled this with renewed disappointment. She had thought Marquis Fabien would attend, and she had been right, he had.

When the invitation arrived for the Macquinets, Rachelle had suggested the three don their silk gowns and go, but Grandmère had gently refused Rachelle's plea.

"Such plays are oft immoral," Grandmère had stated.

"But Grandmère, after all we have seen here at court of the *escadron volant*? I am no longer an *enfant*, I know of these vices."

"It is one thing to *know* of them, *ma petite*, but quite another to laugh and be entertained by them. How can one find amusement in what offends the holiness of God? Surely you understand the difference?"

Rachelle had no experience with French plays by which to judge, but she had suffered more disappointment over the denial than had her sister Idelette, who had not protested. It was not that Rachelle had wished to see the play as much as she had wanted to make an appearance magnificently gowned in hopes of being noticed by the marquis. But she dare not admit such a thing.

Madame Clair, their maman, before sending them off with Grandmère to Paris, had warned them not to become enamored with the *galantes* of high title — "Because they must, and will, of necessity, marry titled mademoiselles. You will be pained by the outcome of folly, I promise you."

Rachelle's *père* had also warned of these matters when learning his two daughters would be journeying with Grandmère to court to work as grisettes. The "wisest" husbands were to be found in Reformational Geneva, not in Paris.

She and her sisters had grown up in a warm, loving Huguenot home where Arnaut Macquinet made yearly visits to John Calvin's Reformational Geneva. On his return home to Lyon, Arnaut always brought two or three scholars from the theological academy to the chateau with him. For a few days there would be nightly discussions on the politics of France, followed by Bible studies and discussions of important Christian doctrines. Other Huguenots came quietly to the Dushane-Macquinet Chateau de Silk from as far away as Moulins to learn. After a tearful *adieu*, Arnaut traveled with the scholars to other areas of France, especially Languedoc and La Rochelle, Huguenot strongholds. There, these same Geneva scholars taught and encouraged Huguenots in their house-churches.

Rachelle knew too well the consequences if ever it became known that her family was aiding the propagation of "the religion," as it was often called.

Rachelle wondered about Charlotte's curt remark concerning Athenais. Her obvious jealousy told Rachelle she was casting eyes toward the marquis. It was troubling that Charlotte was one of the most belle-looking women at court, with her golden hair and blue eyes. She was a member of the infamous escadron volant, a clique of some forty compromising belle dames, married and unmarried, who served the Queen Mother's political intrigues with all manner of vice, sparing no scruple. Rachelle had struggled to like Charlotte from the moment they first met in Paris, and now, months later, she was losing the battle.

"Never mind the marquis," Louise de Fontaine said. "What of the masked stranger? Did you see him?"

"He is gone now," Charlotte said.

"I can see for myself he is gone, but I was asking if you might know him."

"How should I?" With shimmering skirts, Charlotte brushed past Louise, pride in every gilded step.

Rachelle wondered at this odd exchange. Was Louise questioning Charlotte for some reason? Why? Could Charlotte know the identity of the rider wearing the mask after all?

"Do you suppose, ladies," Louise said sweetly, "that the masked rider is but one more *bel ami* of Madame Charlotte? Perhaps to avoid her, he chose this desperate way to slip past her lest she capture him at once?"

Several of the younger ladies snickered, but Rachelle suspected Louise's original intent when she asked Charlotte if she knew the man had been more serious than the suggestion of *amour*.

In all of this Charlotte showed no rise of emotion over her rival's remark. She merely surveyed the less attractive Louise with a languid dip of her feather fan, as a sprinkling of sapphire chips reflected the sunlight.

"That you would recognize any possible bel ami, in or out of the palais, is a wonder to me, I assure you, Louise. You have been at court now for a year and have failed to attract the attention of even a page."

Louise de Fontaine turned a ruddy color which appeared to please Charlotte, whose lips formed a faint smile as she turned her attention back onto the courtyard.

Rachelle glanced in sympathy toward Louise. The daughter of Comte de Fontaine was a pleasant girl who had showed friendliness to Rachelle when first arriving to serve Princesse Marguerite. Rachelle disliked seeing needless embarrassment.

She wished to say that it was wiser to wait and attract one man of character than to collect a pack of drooling wolves, but Rachelle knew her position at court. Already Charlotte de Presney did not look upon her with favor. Any ill-chosen remark to defend Louise would turn Charlotte into an enemy. She was powerful at court and could do harm to Rachelle if she wished. Rachelle was relieved when Marguerite turned her attention from Henry de Guise to what was happening around her.

"*Espèce de pestes!*" Marguerite snapped her jeweled fingers at Charlotte and Louise. "Have I not worries enough that you must yowl like two discontented cats?"

Marguerite left the balustrade and stepped firmly back onto the stool, leaving Rachelle to claim her own position of kneeling before her, her knees on a pillow. She turned her gaze with deliberation back to the burgundy silk. Now that she had finished pinning the hem on the inner cloth of gold, she began gauging seven widths of Brugesse lace to be tacked three inches above the hemline.

"Have none of my ladies any affection for me?" Marguerite scolded in an injured voice. "I am most unhappy, and do any of you care? You make jest with one another and speak in excited words about plays and balls. Is there not one loyal *amie* among you who feels sympathy for my plight?"

Her ladies again assured her with soothing words that they were most sympathetic. Charlotte brought her a Viennese glass plate with dainty bonbons.

Marguerite touched her hand to her forehead. "To think my brother the king wishes me to marry that boorish Huguenot prince from Navarre. *Non!* I will not marry a heretic."

Heretic. Rachelle stole a glance upward at Princesse Marguerite. *Does she know I too am a Huguenot?* The crown prince of Navarre was also of the Protestant belief. Marguerite and the Navarre prince were too young to marry, but marriage contracts among royalty were oft settled during childhood or even at birth! Rachelle could hardly imagine such a fate. Why, a princesse might become the bride of an old man in another country, or a man looking like King Henry VIII of England, who was known as a food glutton with a passion for easily tiring of his wives. Rachelle wondered what she would do if, like Marguerite's sister Elisabeth, she had been sent to Spain to marry Philip II.

King Philip, that unsmiling religious fanatic, called himself the Sword of the Lord so as to render the Inquisition against all who questioned the traditions of Rome.

Marguerite oft moaned she had heard discussion of her coming marriage to the future King of Navarre, which she considered an insignificant kingdom, and a Protestant one at that — located in the south of France near Spain.

"And I will not marry him," she said again.

Marguerite, called Margo by her friends at court, was plumpish, attractive, and sensuous, though some called her licentious. Her hair was full and dark, her black eyes yielded to mischief, and she sought relationships with men as though motivated by an inner need to be valued. Though reckless, she had not inherited her mother's propensity for cruelty or the occult. Marguerite was considered to be one of the most learned young women in France, but her lack of wisdom in moral decisions was pointing to a future downfall, and this concerned Rachelle.

Rachelle kept herself aloof during conversations that somehow seemed to always turn sensual. She did not know why, but these women at court seemed worse than the men in their discussions of bed chamber interests — but then, how would she know if they were as ribald as men?

She therefore found herself an outsider, a pilgrim in a strange and foreign city. Her two months here at court proved startling, many times, embarrassing. She had no desire to follow their wayward steps, but after sharing company with them she was also affectionately attached and sympathetic with their burdens, though often those burdens seemed shallow and devoid of eternal value.

Rachelle was especially sympathetic toward Princesse Marguerite. It was easy to see that she was frightened of her mother. When the Queen Mother sent her maid Madalenna to call Marguerite to her royal chambers, Marguerite visibly trembled. Louise had told Rachelle the Queen Mother beat Marguerite until she fainted. "Licentious harlot," the Queen Mother was known to call her when she was angry. Rachelle could not imagine such abuse, having such a gracious maman of her own, but she believed these tales of Marguerite's treatment to be true. On one occasion Rachelle had seen bruises on Marguerite. If Catherine discovered the *affaire d' amour* Marguerite was now indulging in with Henry de Guise, Rachelle shuddered to think what would befall her.

Marguerite stood like a statue in the sunlight, the folds of burgundy silk and the cloth of gold catching the sun and gleaming. But with the breeze continually moving the cloth, Rachelle sighed and again ceased her work. She requested they work inside the chamber but Marguerite would have none of it.

"I feel imprisoned here at Chambord. Oh, that I were in the garden now with Monsieur Henry. Oh, I must be outdoors to breathe."

Charlotte drifted back to the balustrade. "Marquis de Vendôme knows Monsieur Henry de Guise well." She was looking toward his balcony again. "It may be, Princesse, that he can arrange a meeting for you both tonight in the garden. Then you shall be happy again. Shall I ask the marquis?"

Rachelle pricked up her ears. She glanced across the terrace at Charlotte. Scheming again, the minx.

Louise laughed coldly. "How unselfish of you, Charlotte, to risk the ire of the Queen Mother by arranging such a meeting. What will you tell her Majesty the next time you report to her?"

Princesse Marguerite shivered at the mention of her mother.

Charlotte ignored Louise. "Now there is a man for you, I assure you." She could only be speaking of Marquis Fabien.

Charlotte breezed on with calm confidence: "I shall have him for my own before the season is over."

Princesse Marguerite laughed scornfully. "Do not imagine you will prevail. You will never have *him*. He is too shrewd for even you, Charlotte. Even I could not capture him. Now he is my *ami*."

"It is Athenais who has his interest," Louise said, "no matter what you say, Charlotte."

Charlotte lounged seductively against the pillar on the balustrade, hands behind her. Her blue satin dress with Oriental pearls showed her curvaceous body. Her *décolletage* continued to get lower with each gown she wore. *It would not trouble her to run about naked,* Rachelle thought wrathfully.

"Athenais is a mere child, and she will not hold his interest. There are ways to end even that," Charlotte said.

Rachelle blew away the strand of hair that tickled her cheek, and once again, would like to have jabbed a well-spoken word into Charlotte's pride. Charlotte was older than the rest of Marguerite's ladies. Perhaps she thought her experience would appeal to the marquis? Rachelle felt confident the *belle dame* would not suffer a wounded conscience for tempting a man. She did so deliberately. *She's had too much experience,* she thought, then was ashamed of her own gaucherie. After all, except for court gossip, what did she truly know about Charlotte?

"Ouch."

Princesse Marguerite looked down at Rachelle, who put her finger to her lips.

"Pricked yourself, m'amie? Do not get any blood on my hemline, or I shall give you two pricks."

"Fear not, Princesse, I should sooner leap from the balustrade as to spoil this silk from my own home in Lyon. Only I know the labor my family went through to bring it here to you, an honor I assure you," Rachelle hastened.

Marguerite laughed and reached over to playfully tug at a strand of Rachelle's hair.

"And such wondrous silk," Louise said with a renewed sigh, and the others agreed there was none like Macquinet silk.

"Mademoiselle-Princesse, you shall show yourself the most belle of all your ladies when you wear *this* gown, for there is none like it, I assure you." Rachelle gave the princesse a tired smile, taking refuge for the moment in the praise of her work.

Marguerite stepped down from the stool. "Enough for today, Rachelle. I have grown restless. Come back in the morning." She wandered across the terrace, allowing the breeze to lift the material like butterfly wings. "I am expected to wear this gown for the King of Portugal at the banquet in his honor when he comes to Chambord this summer, but I will not. I shall wear it only for Monsieur Henry, I swear it."

Her ladies helped Marguerite remove the gown and fold it carefully for Rachelle to take with her to the Macquinet chambers where the final work would be done.

Marguerite now seemed interested in nothing more than sending a secret message to Monsieur Henry de Guise to meet her in the garden that evening.

"I will send my message through Fabien and—" she turned and fixed her vibrant gaze on Rachelle—"and you, m'amie, will deliver my message to him."

Rachelle's heart thundered. *At last ... a reason to meet him—*

Charlotte moved closer. "I shudder to think what Madame Henriette Dushane would say to her youngest granddaughter wandering about the corridors unchaperoned, Princesse. I shall see your message is securely delivered, as always, if it please la Princesse."

"Oh, as you wish ... come then, while I write it. Deliver it at once."

"Of course, my lady."

Charlotte walked past Rachelle without a glance in her direction and followed Marguerite into her chambers.

That notorious cat!

Louise caught her eye with a look of sympathy, and Rachelle felt herself flush. She did not wish for even a friend to realize her disappointment.

Louise walked closer as Rachelle gathered her sewing goods and placed them inside her case.

"Madame de Presney is jealous of you. Be careful of her," Louise said, then joined the other ladies to prepare for Princesse's *déjeuner*.

Rachelle snatched up her case and left the terrace calling adieu to the ladies.

"Adieu, Rachelle," they called in return.

Out in the corridor, Rachelle hesitated, tempted to wait until Charlotte came out and burn her ears with what she thought of her. Non! She would not give Charlotte the satisfaction to see her flushed of face and in an irritated mood.

Rachelle lifted her chin with practiced elegance and walked down the corridor with her skirts swishing, her eyes straight ahead, pretending not to notice the approving glances thrown her way by guards strolling the gilded halls.

Chapter Two

RACHELLE MACQUINET, HAVING DEPARTED THE ROYAL CHAMBER OF Princesse Marguerite, carried the burgundy silk and cloth of gold draped carefully over her arm and her sewing case in hand. She entered the oak-paneled salle on the second floor of the palais chateau, where the Macquinet chambers were located. One of the rooms had been turned into their *atelier*, where the bolts of cloth and tables were located for sewing and cutting. Her sister Idelette was at work there now.

Before entering the family chambers she paused in the salle, glancing to the far side where a broad embrasure of an oriel window looked toward the quiet verdant forests. Here, wildlife roamed, and the marvels of God's creation drew her, as always. She walked to the window to gaze out, to refresh her tired spirits before Grandmère inspected her work on the burgundy gown. She drank in the view of the surrounding sage-green forest and searched for a glimpse of the stag that she had seen early that morning. The stag would not likely reappear until eventide, but there were a good many colorful birds flitting in the branches and a large number of game fowl as well, including peacocks, all belonging to the king's table — *bien sûr!* She hoped the stag evaded the king's archers.

Wispy clouds of a pearl-like sheen settled gently over the treetops. How restful the beauty of the wooded Touraine appeared at first glance. She was temporarily soothed by it, though lasting peace was an illusion concealing mysterious, even dangerous, events. Thinking so brought to mind her arrival here from Paris, and what she had learned from her Cousine Claudine. The first two weeks she arrived were spent in *bonhomie* with her Dushane cousin, before Claudine had returned to Orléans to the estates of her aunt, Duchesse Xenia Dushane. Claudine had whispered to Rachelle the uneasy details about the spying closets and many other listening devices in the various chambers here at Chambord. "All were put here by Catherine de Medici, I vow it."

Claudine, a lovely girl Rachelle's age, had been one of the Queen Mother's ladies-in-waiting. She had returned to Orléans near Fontainebleau at the personal request of her blood aunt, Duchesse Dushane. Madame Dushane had requested the Queen Mother to release Claudine from her "favored position."

"Non! It was a frightening position," Claudine had whispered to Rachelle before she left Chambord. "I shuddered whenever I was in her presence."

Rachelle never fully learned the reasons for Claudine's unexpected departure for Orléans, except that she had become frail in health — a curious incident over which Rachelle sometimes pondered, for Claudine had been robust in health.

Rachelle entered the Macquinet chambers.

Her older sister Idelette was sitting at the long cutting table. She looked much like their maman — tall, fair, with a slender, pious face, and pale blue eyes. She was working on a difficult sleeve for one of reinette Mary's white satin gowns. The upper sleeve near the shoulder needed to be bunched into a pleated fan, and it took masterful fingers to manage it with artistic perfection. Idelette was two years ahead in the steps to becoming a couturière, and Rachelle had not yet progressed so far.

Idelette turned her head toward Rachelle. "Oh, Grandmère is not with you?"

"Non. I have just left Princesse Marguerite's chambers."

Idelette set aside her work and stood up from the chair and table, with hand at her lower back. "I shall grow old very quickly, I vow it. One would think I was old and vagrant at twenty."

Rachelle proudly displayed the burgundy gown on the mannequin and arranged each fold with her fingers, smoothing them.

Idelette nodded approvingly. "You did well, ma petite. Oh, I shall never weary of gazing at those colors. I think of sparkling grapes effused with golden sunshine."

"Mmm. It looks well on the princesse with her dark hair." She glanced about the busy-looking chamber with its work materials here and there. "I am anxious to win Grandmère's approval. My hem and the gauging of my lace is perfect."

"La, la, so you think. It is Grandmère's eye that is perfect. Wait until she gauges your lace."

Rachelle frowned critically at the hem, though she could find no fault in her work. "It was most difficult measuring the princesse. I have never seen a mademoiselle more restless, I promise you. She talked incessantly of Monsieur Henry de Guise. It was not until he rode into the courtyard with his père, le duc, that the princesse grew happy."

"Pouf, happy for *le moment*, that is all. It is the mind of the *haute monde*. Wanting more, always more, and never satisfied. What is the verse in Ecclesiastes? 'The eye is not satisfied with seeing, nor the ear filled with hearing'?"

Rachelle turned her mouth in rueful agreement. "It is sad, but Marguerite will never be satisfied with *one* man."

"It is so with all of them, all the girls. The nobility are notorious for their greed."

I, myself, would be happy with one particular man, Rachelle thought.

"I do not envy you working with Princesse Marguerite," Idelette said.

"And la Reinette Mary?"

"So charmante, and so generous in her behavior too. She talked of the masque that was to be held tomorrow night, but she believes it might be put off until later, though no one knows when."

"But how strange. I was musing over how entertaining it would be for us if Grandmère would attend."

Idelette laughed. "Grandmère ... or you? I vow, sister, you never give up on these matters of frivolity. It is all such nonsense." She drew her brows together and jabbed her sewing needle into her pincushion.

"La, la. I should still like to go but once, if only to see what it is like."

The court, consisting of ducs and duchesses, comtes and comtesses, had assembled here at Chambord for several months of entertainment.

The courtly elite were expecting a time of bonhomie among themselves, of *fêtes*, musicals, royal hunts, and even a *carrousel* in the courtyard of the palais chateau in which the *grand prieur* was to ride disguised as a gypsy woman, carrying a monkey on his back that was dressed as a child.

Idelette nettled her at times. "Do you never wish to wear a silk gown like those we make for others and attend a gala?" Rachelle asked.

Idelette shrugged. "It does not matter what I wish. Even if the masque goes on tomorrow, Maman told Grandmère not to allow us to attend without a male chaperone."

"Such an excuse. There is Comte Sebastien, our brother-in-law, is there not? He is here, serving the Queen Mother."

Idelette's face grew serious. "That woman, I vow she frightens me. Does she not you? Her eyes, they do not blink but stare deeply, cold like a snake."

Rachelle forced a mild laugh because the thought gave her a chill. "*Allons bon!* Such words as these will prompt me to look beneath my bed tonight with the lamp."

"I imagine the monkey would be very amusing to see all dressed up in clothes, but it is quite silly, that. A waste of time."

"But to see the costumes would be valuable. Such entertainment. We might become inspired with a new dress design. And—" Rachelle glanced toward the empty tea table and remembered how hungry she was—"I imagine the sweetmeats and pastries would be wondrous to taste."

Idelette laughed. "You and your bonbons. It is a wonder you are not fat instead of possessing a figure that makes royalty jealous. There is no good to your wishing, *petite soeur*. Grandmère sent Nenette an hour ago to say la Reinette Mary wishes for accessories to go with her gown. You know how tedious it is to make accessories of the finest sort? How long it takes? It is an art in itself."

Rachelle absently flipped a curl at the side of her sister's cheek and walked over to the long trestle table. She began arranging her sewing equipment in her case for the next day's work.

"There was a flurry in the courtyard this morning. Did you see it by any chance?"

"I was too busy and did not wish to interrupt my work to go to the balcony, but I heard the confusion."

"Le Duc de Guise arrived with his men-at-arms. There was someone with them, a dark-hooded stranger wearing a mask."

"I do not suppose it means anything."

"Do you not? I find it all most odd."

Grandmère Henriette Dushane entered the chamber, followed by Nenette, one of the grisette novices from the Chateau de Silk and also their serving girl. She was carrying Grandmère's personal case. Her bright carrot hair was awry as usual, and her thin, immature figure was lost to her blue cotton dress.

Grandmère, at seventy, looked as fresh as when she had emerged from her *toilet*, with every strand of silver hair in place, and her crisp black dress with white collar showing not a wrinkle. She stepped sprightly to the mannequin displaying the burgundy silk gown, and using her round eyeglass, lifted the hem for inspection, scanning for any bunched thread or pulled cloth.

Rachelle held her breath. Grandmère took an extraordinary amount of time, or so it seemed. *My nerves will curl with agitation at any moment,* she thought.

Grandmère turned to her with a satisfied twinkle in her dark eyes.

"*Ma cherie,* you have done fine work with your needle. I am most proud of your ability to concentrate on such stitching, but, and only here and there — " she spread a gracefully wrinkled hand against her small bodice and tipped her head, pursing her lips. "The thread, it is in a few places pulled a fraction too tight, as though *ma belle* Rachelle was oh so tense."

Rachelle took her evaluation with calm repose, but inside she was jubilant. Grandmère came to her, smiling, and patted her cheek.

"Ah, but it will pass. *Oui,* it is fair enough. But remember what I taught you? The nimble fingers, the relaxed wrists. These you must have. But? I am most pleased with your abilities! Yes, you will do well. Tomorrow you will be permitted to try your hand at the gold tassels for the sleeves."

Grandmère's approval was a balm to Rachelle's tired knees, and well worth having crawled about Marguerite all the morning long. Rachelle's slow smile broke into a laugh, and she planted a kiss on Grandmère's cheek. *"Merci,* Grandmère." But she thought: *Ah, making the tassels from bright gold thread will take all my concentration.* Could she pass another of Grandmère's inspections? Even so, she found herself deliriously pleased to have passed this one test of the hem. And, *mais certainement* it was an honor to have been chosen by Grandmère to undertake the tassel making. *I am now on my way to becoming a couturière.*

There was, however, another of her desires that was least discussed. That dream was to *design* the gowns, to become *le dernier cri* in fashion, and to open a dress shop appealing to the haute monde of London offering ready-sewn gowns carrying the family label of the Dushane-Macquinet Chateau de Silk in Lyon. Such a dream must wait, loitering in the misty future.

Rachelle went off to her private closet to freshen herself before tea. She found her mind wandering again to Marquis Fabien de Vendôme. She had written to her eldest sister Madeleine, in Paris, who was married to Sebastien Dangeau, inquiring about Marquis Fabien. Since Sebastien was his oncle by marriage, Madeleine was well acquainted with Monsieur Fabien. What interesting morsels would Madeleine pass to her?

Chapter Three

"When the house of Guise is plotting, be assured it will mean trouble and woe for all those of the religion," Rachelle's père often said. She frowned as she readied herself for tea. Was the duc plotting?

She was in her private closet with gold satin bed cushions and light blue draperies. Removing her soiled cotton work dress, she put it aside to be cleaned and poured cool water from the urn into a large white bowl with painted pink rosebuds sitting on her vanity stand. She washed herself, her mind finding no rest over the morning's happenings. She used fragrant powder to dry and used her pearl-handled hairbrush on her wealth of long, titian hair.

The Queen Mother had left le Duc de Guise behind at Paris when she gave orders to travel here to Chambord. Rachelle believed Catherine had sought to rid herself of Guise's influence upon the boy-king Francis and had not expected Guise's arrival this morning. Yet he arrived boldly with his brother, the cardinal, bringing the masked figure. Why?

She chose her new mint green silk and cream lace dress to wear and arranged her hair in a fashionable new style which Louise de Fontaine had shown her. A knock at the front chamber door drew her attention. It was followed a moment later by Idelette's voice calling for Grandmère.

Rachelle strained to hear the hushed voices in the front chamber while she quickly finished with her hair. Perhaps it was Comte Sebastien coming to inform them of the messire in the mask. Sebastien, highly positioned in the Queen Mother's council, would know much of what was happening at Chambord and elsewhere.

Rachelle was adept at discerning people's moods by voice inflection and when, a few moments later, Grandmère's became taut, Rachelle set her comb down on top of the blue and gold marble vanity table and went to the closet doorway. She peered into the main chamber.

Rachelle expected to see Sebastien or another visitor and was surprised when the only two people standing in the middle of the chamber were Grandmère and Idelette. Rachelle entered and glanced about.

"Did I not hear someone at the door?"

Grandmère and Idelette turned to look at her. Rachelle felt her tensions rise. How pale Grandmère had become. Her black moiré dress emphasized this. Idelette's lean face with its noble bone structure looked as though she had applied two circles of pink rouge.

"What is wrong?" Rachelle asked.

Grandmère lifted the fine silver chain from her shoulder on which was hung a round looking-glass and fingered it absently.

"Ma cousine, Duchesse Xenia Dushane has sent her page Romier. We three are to come to her chambers for tea at once."

Rachelle lifted her brows. She would have expected Grandmère to be pleased, for it was not often the duchesse called for their company in a spirit of bonhomie.

"Allons bon!" Grandmère said. She paced the rose-colored Aubusson rug, the tall, square heels on her pointed black shoes making no sound as they sank into the heavy pile. "At such news as this I despair."

Rachelle exchanged a questioning glance with Idelette.

"Despair? Over tea with le duchesse? Did you not tell us you were pleased when we arrived at Chambord and discovered she was here?" Rachelle asked, confused.

"But yes, yes, *pardon,* Rachelle ma cherie, I have not explained." She lowered her voice. "It is not Madame Duchesse, but le Duc de Guise and the cardinal of whom I despair."

"La duchesse is assured of coming trouble," Idelette said. "Her page has informed us of certain concerns she has."

"We are to go to her chambers tout de suite," Grandmère said. "And on the way we must show ourselves of casual countenance, as if thinking of naught else but having tea with her."

A short time later Rachelle and Idelette walked with slow and dignified carriage close behind Grandmère, who led the way through the salle on the south end of the palais chateau. Approving heads turned their way as they passed. Bows from the many messieurs passing them in the salle came like tossed blossoms to sweeten their path. Rachelle was pleased she had taken time before tea to freshen herself and don a clean, becoming frock. She cast casual glances here and there in the hope of meeting Marquis de Vendôme, but fair fortune did not call upon her. *It is trouble that comes to knock*, she thought. *Allons bon! Not him. Anyone but that messire!* Rachelle saw the young Comte Maurice Beauvilliers, the blood nephew of Sebastien, looking toward them from where he stood on the upper gallery near a stairway. His gaze found her and attached itself.

"It is Monsieur Maurice," Idelette whispered toward Grandmère. "What should we do now? How can we ignore him?"

"Say nothing. Leave this to me," Grandmère hissed back.

"It is your fault, Rachelle," Idelette said.

"My fault!"

"Oui. He is always looking at you. He has romantic plans, I promise you."

"Fie! I cannot endure the pestilent conceited fellow."

"Shh, both of you," Grandmère warned. "He is coming."

Maurice Beauvilliers overtook them and paused ahead in their path with a sweeping bow.

"*Bonjour*, Madame, Mademoiselles."

"*Bonjour*," they echoed.

"Monsieur le Comte," Grandmère said, "your Oncle Sebastien left his hat in our chambers yester evening when he called. I have not seen him this day but wish to speak with him. Will you mention it when you see him?"

His inky brows shot up. "Fate! It was I, Madame, who was going to request such information from you *belles* ladies." And his languid pearl gray eyes wandered first to Idelette, then to Rachelle. "I am seeking mon oncle. One wonders where he has gotten himself."

"Ah, then we have foiled one another, *bonne* sir. If you will pardon us we must be on our way. Merci, Monsieur-Comte, bonjour." With a nod of her silver head she was moving on her way.

Rachelle smothered a smile.

"Did Sebastien truly leave his hat?" Idelette asked.

"Oui. Most assuredly, ma petite. It is black satin with a peacock made of red and green gems."

AT THE FAR END OF THE SALLE they came to a curving stairway, and at the top, on either side of the gallery, priceless tapestries in burgundy, blue, and gold caught Rachelle's attention. When she reached a painting of King Francis I, grandfather of the present boy-king Francis II, which was displayed in a place of prominence, she slowed her ascent, her emotions awakened by the sight. She wondered what Grandmère and Idelette might be thinking as they too looked up into the face of the past king.

The painting caught the light from the upper diamonded windows. Rachelle noticed the king's eyes were too close together and looked falsely humorous with a touch of sly mirth on his arrogant face. His hawklike features and sensuous lips bore, in the flickering March sunlight, an enchanted look as though he had just come awake from a spell in the magic forest. This, Rachelle reminded herself, was the king who was hailed for introducing the French Renaissance, who had brought Leonardo da Vinci from Italy and established him in the Chateau de Clos near the king's own castle of Amboise. Rachelle had heard how Francis I never wearied of da Vinci's company, and da Vinci was said to have died in the king's arms.

As Rachelle beheld the artist's masterpiece of the king, she did not remember Francis Valois the *man* of kingly elegance or civilized kindness, but saw him for quite another legacy: a selfish, ravenous character who had thrust the tortuous flame to the faggots of persecution against French Protestants, burning them at the stake in order to pacify intolerant Spain. Rachelle remembered from her childhood the stories Maman had told her and Idelette of how Francis I had vented his wrath against Jacques Lefèvre d'Étaples, who had first translated the Bible into French, and who was hunted as a heretic until he escaped with naught but his life to Strasbourg. This beau Renaissance king with his smiling little eyes, his long nose, and his passion for art, beauty, and literature, had also made it necessary for John Calvin to flee France for his life.

Rachelle raised her head and continued climbing the stairs, lifting her skirts as she went, meeting the painted laughing eyes with her own calm and quiet confidence.

Here I am, sire, in one of your many chateaus — the niece of one of the lovers of Scripture whom you killed. You are gone too — you await the day when you must come before the Judge of all men to answer for your rule over the French people. What will you tell him? That you blessed France with great paintings but murdered the true Sovereign's children?

Rachelle thought of the quiet trips to the Lyon square with her parents and Grandmère to remember the day of the burnings. Even John Calvin had written from Geneva to the five martyrs encouraging them for the ordeal that awaited them.

Now, fresh sparks of persecution were about to reignite the commencement of the demonic dance once again throughout France.

Duchesse Xenia Dushane was a secret ally of the Huguenots and an amie of the Bourbon leaders, Prince Louis de Condé and Admiral Coligny. Rachelle knew her to be a woman of esteem within the inner echelons of court life and one of those privileged few of high title who belonged to the Queen Mother's afternoon *cercle*. Accordingly, la duchesse possessed much knowledge of the happenings at court. On a number of occasions she had warned Huguenot nobles of the dangers hatched at court to destroy them.

Rachelle and Idelette arrived with Grandmère at la duchesse's chambers where tea was waiting. Grandmère entered first, introduced by the page Romier. Rachelle and Idelette followed, each curtsying in turn to the distant kinswoman from the Dushane family of La Rochelle, a Huguenot bastion and the town for which Rachelle had been named.

Of recent days la duchesse had been obliged to use a cane as some malady had weakened her, for which she was being treated by the king's own physician. She was several years younger than Grandmère, and both Dushane women wore a crown of silver hair, but their likeness ceased there. Madame Dushane was large boned and tall, and her flesh was firm, for until her illness she was fond of riding, hunting with the king's royal party, and walking in the woods with her retinue.

She pushed herself up from her *chaise longue*, favoring her weight on the black cane sprinkled with red gems. Her white cat, Pandy, leaped away from where it had been lying on a red settee and escaped the nuisance of guests by slipping behind the gold satin draperies.

"Ah, Henriette, ma petite cousine, bonjour."

"Bonjour, and may it please Madame Duchesse to soon find herself in fine fettle again."

Madame's eyes were brown and lashless, her angular nose pleasantly aristocratic, and Rachelle noted that she had marvelously retained her teeth, which were white and polished. When she smiled, her nose inevitably crinkled in a most *bon vivant* way that never failed to pull a smile from Rachelle no matter her mood.

La duchesse, after greeting Grandmère and dismissing her attendants, turned full scrutiny upon Idelette and Rachelle. Rachelle was never certain whether she passed Madame's inspection. It was Comtesse Claudine Boisseau whom she favored these years, for Claudine was of closer blood and in line to inherit. Rachelle was pleased when, on this occasion, her great-aunt took special notice of her.

"*Ça alors!* But you have matured into a woman in your own rights now, Rachelle. I am pleased to have been reminded of it, seeing you again. Not to say how Comtesse Claudine oft reminds me of it and says you are of no silly mind and worthy of serious camaraderie."

"*Merci bien*, Madame Duchesse."

Duchesse Xenia then made kind remarks about Idelette and how she reminded her of her mother, Madame Clair. She lowered herself into a chair and signed them to be seated opposite her with a marble table between, holding sweetmeats and hot and cold refreshments of tea and honeyed lemon water.

Rachelle grew tense, wondering what would be said. The duchesse, she noticed, had weary marks of faintest violet beneath her eyes and her cheeks sagged.

"I could but wish your daughter, Clair, were here now, Henriette. I could always depend on her cool head when action was needed. And where is she now, Geneva, is she not? And with Arnaut?"

Grandmère lowered her voice. "Arnaut will soon return to Lyon with Bibles in the forbidden French language and copies of Calvin's *Institutio Christianae Religionis*. Clair wished to attend him this time."

"A worthy endeavor. My prayers are with them. The Huguenot households in France need doctrine, for they are like restless children tossed to and fro, weighed down with religious traditions that do precious little to break the binding chains. Even so, the danger Clair and Arnaut place upon themselves on these secret journeys terrifies me. And petite Avril?" she asked of Grandmère.

"My youngest granddaughter remains at the Chateau de Silk under care of our family governess."

La duchesse nodded her approval. "It is a grave time in the history of Christ's body, his true church. One wonders what will become of us all here in France."

"Madame Duchesse, our Lord has encouraged us to fear none of those things that shall come upon us. With his strength girding our minds, and his assured amour warming our quavering hearts, we shall yet be his overcomers," Idelette said. "If God is for us, who can prevail against us?"

A tender smile spread across the older woman's face. "Fitly spoken, ma cherie, yes, fitly spoken." She lifted a white hand sparkling with jewels in Idelette's direction.

Rachelle watched her sister respond as was the custom, by standing and approaching to offer a brief kiss.

"You bring me bonne cheer, Idelette. With young Huguenots such as yourself and Rachelle to lead the Reformation on its continuing way, we shall indeed overcome our national trial."

Idelette lowered her head. Grandmère, too, looked tenderly pleased.

Rachelle knew her sister had meant every word. A prick in her own heart made Rachelle uneasy. She was not as knowledgeable as Idelette who studied the French Bible every morning and evening before bed. Even here at court, in the very nest of serpents, Idelette read the Scriptures, which if it were known, could mean imprisonment in the Bastille or even death, especially now with the arrival of Cardinal de Lorraine. Yet her sister persisted, and none could quell her.

"Here, *mignon*," la duchesse said to Idelette, suddenly removing a pearl ring set in gold from her little finger. She placed it on Idelette's palm.

"Oh, but Madame Duchesse, I could not—"

"A mere token of my affection."

Idelette dropped a curtsy and murmured her delight.

Rachelle looked on. Such actions as la duchesse had just taken were oft done at court by members of the highest nobility, who sometimes were extravagantly generous with those who pleased them in some way which they deemed should be publicly rewarded. Since Duchesse Dushane was a great-aunt through marriage, her presentation was all the more venerable, so Rachelle believed.

Idelette took her place again. Rachelle noticed that she avoided looking her way. Idelette embarrassed easily when praised.

"You hinted coming adversity, Madame Duchesse. A scourge upon Christ's own sheep here in France," Grandmère said in a quiet voice, her fingers intertwining tightly on the lap of her black moiré skirt. "What convinces you it is so?"

Duchesse Dushane's broad face tightened, and she glanced about the *salle de sejour* as if making certain they were alone, though she had dismissed all of her retinue. She leaned forward in her velvet chair, hand clasping the head of her cane, and whispered: "Henriette, I saw who was behind the mask. This messire's cooperation with le Duc de Guise brings danger and possible death for Huguenots here at court."

Tension dried Rachelle's throat. She leaned forward to catch every word.

"Ah!" Grandmère breathed. "I see, yes, I see ... a Huguenot then?"

A Huguenot! Rachelle opened her mouth to protest and ceased when she saw la duchesse nod her head affirmatively and shut her eyes against obvious disappointment.

"A Huguenot," la duchesse repeated, "one of our own. A messire who knows the names of those among us who are under-shepherds of Christ. How much else he may know — who can say?"

"But is he a betrayer or a prisoner?" Rachelle inquired.

"One wonders ... but even if he is not a betrayer, the cardinal will gain the information he wants at the *salle de la question,* the place of inquisition."

Grandmère groaned. A small intake of breath came from Idelette.

"I confess, Madame Duchesse," Idelette said, "I was of a mind to think the mask was but a humorous ruse for the ladies of court, stirring up their festive spirit for the upcoming masque."

"A jester, you thought? If only that were so, ah, but no. The *divertessement*, it has been canceled. Messire's arrival with the duc and the cardinal is not at all benign. No such comfort can be taken."

"And what messire is this, Madame?" Grandmère asked, pale and worried of countenance.

"Maître Avenelle. A trusted messire among the Huguenots in Paris. His arrival is a harbinger of sinister treachery. Would God I knew precisely what it is that he has told the duc and the cardinal."

"But why would they bring him here to Chambord?" Idelette whispered.

La duchesse widened her eyes. "They brought him to Catherine de Medici for some dark reason, bien sûr! What that is?" She shook her head. "Ah, that is what we do not know, mignon Idelette. We must find out." She looked evenly at each one of them in turn. "Yes. We must discover what is being planned."

Rachelle struggled to keep her own fears from surging forward like a pack of foxes.

Grandmère sat with her back erect, her frail hands still clasped together. "We know the House of Guise is our enemy; Arnaut believes they are legates of Spain."

"And they are," Duchesse Dushane said. "The Guise brothers are two of the most powerful men in France."

Rachelle recalled that both her père and his cousine Bernard had oft spoken of the House of Guise and their misplaced religious zeal in wishing to kill "heretics."

"Since the death of King Henry, with his son Francis on the throne, and Mary a blood niece of the Guises, they grow more powerful. I have sat in the Queen Mother's cercle and seen her eyes turn cold when either monsieur walks into the chamber. She knows they are using Mary to influence Francis in ways she cannot. Already, the duc has appointed himself head of the military.

"Appointed *himself,* Madame?" Grandmère cried. "It is unthinkable. The gall!"

"And that is the beginning. The cardinal has appointed himself head of the treasury of France."

Rachelle lifted her brows. "The treasury? But—"

"But! That too is fitting." La duchesse's lips curled. "He will doubtless profit from his action—again, for he is already one of the wealthiest men in all of France. The state church is rich, and he sits in control over it."

"And the Queen Mother?" Grandmère asked gravely.

"Catherine plots her Machiavellian intrigues, waiting in silence for her day of dark revenge. That is my perception."

Rachelle believed her, for the duchesse was exceedingly well situated to know this.

"All of this, and Maître Avenelle, what does it mean?" Grandmère furrowed her brow.

"There is a balance of power presently at court between Catherine and the Guises. Catherine fears them because Philip of Spain supports them in all they do, as does Rome. Both have given a command to Catherine to rid France of her heretics, else they will do it for her. That would mean her removal as regent, but far worse, the removal of her sons from inheriting the throne of France in favor of le Duc de Guise. If Maître Avenelle knows of some cause for which the Guises can move against the Huguenots and their political defenders, the House of Bourbon—then Guise may have brought Avenelle here to reveal the matter to Catherine."

Rachelle's heart was thumping in her ears. "Then Her Majesty would be forced to move against us."

"Such is my belief—and it is the belief of the Bourbon princes and nobles."

Rachelle, who had heard details of the tortures inflicted upon the Protestants in the Netherlands through the visiting theology students from Geneva, found the thought of Spain ruling France horrifying. She saw the same thoughts reflected in the attentive face of Idelette.

"You see, mes amies, do you not, where this brings us as Huguenots?" la duchesse said.

"These matters are debated and discussed fervently at the Chateau de Silk when Arnaut and Clair are home, I promise you," Grandmère said. "I lost my son Louis to the flames. He was one of the Lyon martyrs some years ago."

"Ah—yes, yes ..."

"Père's cousine Bernard Macquinet was trained as a minister under John Calvin at the Geneva Theology school," Idelette said, "so we know of these things, Madame Duchesse, yet we never cease to marvel at the ways of the Evil One."

Rachelle leaned forward, heedful, adding: "Students from Geneva oft come to us at the chateau on their way to edify the small house-churches throughout France. The brothers stay and rest with us a few days before going on their way. But we must not forget we have friends in France, the vassals of Prince Condé, our Huguenot army, who, at a moment's call from the prince and Admiral Coligny, can form a strong defense."

"Ah yes, and have done so in the past," the duchesse said. "Yet, do also consider the even larger army available to le Duc de Guise. My spies tell me the Spanish ambassador has promised him several thousand experienced soldiers from their wars of inquisition in the Netherlands."

"I hardly fathom it, Madame." Grandmère shook her head in obvious dismay. "It is not pleasant to think of, but we must, I know."

"We live in trying times, Henriette."

"Indeed, Madame, and may God grant us grace."

Moments of silence followed in which Rachelle saw each of them locked in their own thoughts, perhaps wondering what the future might ask of them in the battle for truth.

Duchesse Dushane sighed at last, looking thoughtfully from one to the other. "I think, *cher* ladies that this generation of God's people will not escape the fiery trial. We will follow the sanctified footsteps of the early Roman Christians. We must prepare our minds to accept suffering. If not …"

Rachelle glanced at Idelette, whose determination reflected in her blue eyes. Grandmère looked tired. Rachelle longed to plant a kiss on her cheek and throw her arms protectively around her. Grandmère had already experienced too much suffering in her years. But who was Rachelle to say it was too much? How much was too much? *Be thou faithful unto death, and I will give thee a crown of life …*

Do I have the grace to lay down my life if it is required of me? Rachelle shuddered inside, but outwardly she kept her hands folded, partly to keep her trembling from being noticed.

"Madame, if the House of Guise has its way, then the wars of persecution ordered by Spain and Rome will prevail," Grandmère said. "But perhaps Maître Avenelle is not our betrayer. There is a bonne chance he will give forth no incriminating evidence against the Huguenot shepherds."

"We may hope, Henriette, but we dare not suppose. My concern is for Sebastien. If he is named to the duc or the cardinal, then the Bastille or even death may await him."

Rachelle's alarm leaped to the forefront. Sebastien! "Oh Madame, this is most distressing."

"And with cher Madeleine soon expecting her first child." Grandmère groaned.

"Ah! Ah! Most distressing to be sure," la duchesse said.

"Apart from the good grace of our Defender, there is naught any of us can do to thwart the deeds of our great enemy. We must pray; we must take upon us the whole armor of God," Grandmère said.

"How true, Henriette! Catherine will question Maître Avenelle this very afternoon in the council chambers. If one could hear what Avenelle said—"

"Then we must warn Sebastien immediately," Idelette said.

"If I called for Sebastien to come here, the news would be known by the Guises and Catherine before sunset. Nor can I go to him. It would draw attention. All of my retinue are well-known and watched. I cannot but wonder if somehow my last letter to Prince Condé was discovered, in which I warned him he should not come to court if summoned, for his life is in danger. That is why I called the three of you here to tea. It is most *naturel* that I should receive kinswomen. It is you who must warn him of Maître Avenelle. He will know what to do to warn the others."

"*Précisément*. We will do what we must," Grandmère said. "We Macquinets go unnoticed. We have come to court from the Silk House for the one purpose only, of sewing for Reinette Mary and Princesse Marguerite."

The duchesse lifted a sealed envelope from beneath her satin pillow fringed with gold. "I had thought to send this to Sebastien naming Maître Avenelle, but it is too risky."

Rachelle watched in silence as she took a lit candle and set the letter aflame.

"Should we not go to Sebastien at once?" Idelette asked.

"It is wiser to wait until we return to our own chambers," Grandmère said. "We desire no connection with Madame. If only we could think of a reason to call for Sebastien."

"But Grandmère," Rachelle said, "we have the perfect reason. You mentioned it on our way here. Sebastien forgot his hat last night."

"Ah, *c'est bien le moment*, Rachelle," la duchesse said approvingly. "But wait, Henriette, it will appear far more innocent if your granddaughter returns the hat."

Grandmère was obviously reluctant.

Rachelle and Idelette looked at one another. "We will both go together," Idelette said.

"One of you will draw less attention, I assure you. Let it be your youngest granddaughter," she said to Grandmère, "who would be least suspected."

Rachelle stood to her feet. "But yes, I will go. As soon as we return to our chambers."

"Bien," la duchesse said. "First, we have our tea. We must not give even a feeble reason for any to say the tea for which you were invited was left untouched. Who will pour?"

"I will, Madame," Idelette said.

No one now appeared to have an appetite for the delectables on the tea table, and they drank their refreshment and ate their pastries out of duty. They soon departed the chambers of Duchesse Xenia with the elder woman's warning ringing in Rachelle's mind. *And do you be cautious as well, m'amie. One can never be too careful with the enemy on satin-slippered feet.*

Chapter Four

Rachelle made her way to the lower floor and to the chambers of Comte Sebastien Dangeau. The peacock of precious gems on the black satin hat she was returning to him caught the midafternoon light from the windows and winked up at her with a flash of red, blue, and amber.

Arriving, she expected the page to receive her and announce her presence.

She glanced about, and finding herself alone and unwatched, she entered by means of the common passage door. After all, Sebastien was her brother-in-law.

The *salle de garde* was empty. Where was the page? The other servants?

Rachelle waited in the servants' chamber, looking about, noticing that afternoon tea, of which Sebastien was known to be fond, had not been served. That too was odd. Was he not here? Where had he gone?

She tried the door into her brother-in-law's private chambers and found it ajar. She pushed it aside and passed through, holding the hat.

The gaudy appartements of blue and gold were wrapped in stillness. Rachelle was ill at ease. A sense of something amiss was in the atmosphere. She crossed the floor, thick Eastern rugs of gold flowers on burgundy, to the windows that opened onto the balustrade. She stepped out, facing the courtyard below where earlier that morning le Duc de Guise and le Cardinal de Lorraine had ridden in with the secretive Maître Avenelle. The soldiers' activity appeared to have increased since her arrival at Chambord weeks ago. Soldiers ... and Sebastien. If he had already been taken somewhere, who could she appeal to?

She knitted her brows together, watching the soldiers below the balustrade as her fingers tightened around the rail. Marquis Fabien de Vendôme? But yes, and why not? Was he not Sebastien's nephew and of high title in the Bourbon clan? She could not think of anyone better. Her heart quickened. *It is for Comte Sebastien and for Madeleine that I wish to contact him, not for my self-interests,* she thought defensively. *Fabien de Vendôme will know exactly what to do.*

The March sun was nearing the western hills of the Touraine countryside. A chill wind and clustered clouds over the distant hills promised a spring storm. The wind rustled her light green skirts and chilled her face and throat. She hunched her shoulders against it and turning, went back into the salle de sejour.

Her gaze swept the chamber and lingered upon Sebastien's desk. A clutter of papers were scattered, as though he had been in a hurry — or perhaps searching. Had he been interrupted?

She went to the desk and searched quickly to make certain he had not left a message.

She paused, lifting her head from the desk, whiffing a fragrance coming from somewhere. Musk? The smell filled her nostrils and prompted her to a shudder. She did not find it pleasant —

Hesitant footsteps came from one of the other chambers. She turned swiftly.

From an inner chamber door, a slim, dark-haired monsieur stopped and stared at her. A pleased look came across his dark saturnine face, like a cat approaching a trapped mouse. With graceful movements he came toward her, holding a goblet of wine in one hand, the other laid against his frilled silk shirt.

Maurice Beauvilliers. She tightened her mouth and straightened from the desk, throwing back her shoulders.

"What bonne luck. So we meet once again, Mademoiselle Macquinet. May I suggest, ma cherie, I call you Rachelle and you call me Maurice?"

She lifted a brow. "I think not, Monsieur le Comte."

His sensuous lips turned upward in a narcissistic smile, his almond-shaped eyes wandered over her. "I am devastated, Mademoiselle."

"I hardly think so, Monsieur."

Rachelle could not fathom why the belles dames at court found him attractive. She was sure the attention he received harmed him, and with his mother, Marquise Françoise Dangeau de Beauvilliers, adding reinforcement, Maurice expected that such attention was wholly deserved and should be returned by all mademoiselles, including herself.

"You do not approve of me, Mademoiselle. Why?"

"I assure you, Monsieur, I have not considered one way or the other —I have too many important matters on my mind to attend to such thoughts."

"Mon Oncle Sebastien is someone we share in common, is that not so? Then should you not be ma petite amie?"

Rachelle ignored the underlying suggestion. "I am looking for Comte Sebastien. Is your oncle resting perchance?"

Maurice sprawled into a brocade chair and sipped his wine. He held up the goblet and peered at the ruby color through the light.

"Non. He is not here, I confess. I do not know where he is."

How much did he know? Was he aware of Maître Avenelle?

He looked at the hat she was returning to Sebastien. He grimaced.

"Such weak taste in fashion, do you not think so, Mademoiselle Macquinet?"

She did not particularly like Sebastien's hat, but she would not agree with Maurice. "Who can say? It is for him to choose."

Maurice touched lean, tanned fingers glittering with jewels to the Alençon lace waterfall at his throat. His gaze roved over her.

She narrowed her eyes. "Then, Monsieur, since you do not know where he is, or when he shall return, I shall bid you my *adieu*."

Maurice straightened swiftly from his chair.

"Na, na, na. Ha, m'amie la belle, do not run away." He waggled his long fingers, his polished nails catching the light. "I have my suspicions of where *our* Sebastien may be. I may confide them in your petite ear, ma cherie, if you will but trust me."

"*Ah, ça non*! Monsieur, I bid you adieu." She whirled on her heel and made her exit, shutting the door firmly behind her.

That rapscallion Maurice!

THE NEWS THAT SEBASTIEN appeared to be missing evoked consternation when Rachelle returned to Grandmère and Idelette.

"The fact that Monsieur Maurice is also looking for his oncle does not bode well," Idelette said.

Grandmère turned again to Rachelle. "You are most sure Monsieur Maurice gave no hint of what may have happened to his oncle?"

"He admitted his suspicion, but he would not speak plainly. He does not appear to take the matter seriously, I assure you. He is a wastrel."

"Where might Sebastien be?" Idelette said.

"And what if he has already been arrested by le Duc de Guise?" Rachelle said.

Grandmère clasped her hands as though in anxious prayer. "We cannot risk sending a message to Duchesse Xenia. She will hear of this soon enough, but somehow we must notify Prince Condé."

"Prince Condé is in Moulins at the Bourbon palais," Rachelle said. "Or even as far north as Chatillon with Admiral Coligny. Even if we managed to send a messire with a letter, it would take many days."

"Still, we must do something. Who could go to Moulins without detection? Perhaps Andelot?" Idelette looked from one to the other.

Rachelle's heart warmed affectionately at the thought of Andelot Dangeau, whom she knew from the silk chateau at Lyon. Andelot was also a nephew of Sebastien, but one in poor stead with the Dangeau family due to the scandal surrounding his mother, a harlot who had followed the French soldiers to war. She had died giving birth to Andelot on the field. For reasons unknown, Andelot had been brought here to Chambord to meet "secret" kinsmen that he would not divulge to her. Most surprising of all was that Marquis Fabien had befriended him.

"I do not think Andelot is the one to help us now," Grandmère said thoughtfully. She rubbed her temple as Rachelle had seen her do so many times when considering the outcome of a worrisome matter. She arose and walked about again.

"I think ... oui, it is to Marquis de Vendôme we should turn at this moment."

Rachelle managed a demure expression.

"The marquis is the highest Bourbon at court, related to Prince Condé by blood and to Sebastien by marriage. It may be that Marquis

Fabien can allay our fears on this matter. He may even know of Sebastien's whereabouts. And if Marquis Fabien believes the information Duchesse Xenia gave us on Maître Avenelle is wont of Prince Condé's attention, then the marquis is the one to contact his kinsman. We must inform him at once, but without drawing undue attention from the court spies."

Grandmère exchanged bright glances with Rachelle and Idelette.

"We will invite the marquis to tea. Here, we may speak to him freely, and who will suspect?"

"To tea!" Rachelle cried, embarrassed.

"But yes. Why not? I assure you such behavior is most naturel. What ambitious French Grandmère with two marriageable granddaughters at court would fail to hope that the marquis's heart would not give birth to amour? She would wish to invite him to a *soiree*."

"But the marquis knows what it is to dine with King Francis and sit in royal presence," Rachelle said. "Whereas a mere tea —"

Grandmère's lips quirked with amusement, but her dark eyes studied Rachelle with sympathy.

"Ma cherie Rachelle, and how would it appear if we, without title of our own, should invite a Bourbon to anything *but* a simple tea? It is what the *courtiers* would expect of us, surely not a banquet!"

Idelette drew her fair brows together above her trim nose. "Grandmère is right, Rachelle. But Grandmère, could we not send a message to the marquis by way of Nenette?"

Rachelle turned to her sister. "Nenette is sweet, but unreliable; you know it as well as I. What if Grandmère's message fell to the wrong hand?"

"It would only be an invitation to tea," Idelette protested.

"Non, if that is all Grandmère tells him in the message, he would ignore the invitation. He must receive dozens of them, I assure you."

"Think you so?" Idelette asked with a bit of a smile, her eyes teasing. "One wonders if he would ignore it. He may have seen you with Princesse Marguerite."

"*C'est sotte*. Non." Rachelle turned to Grandmère, feeling the flush on her cheeks. "Marquis Fabien will come if he knows of the danger of Maître Avenelle and that Sebastien is missing."

"Yes, we must not neglect Duchesse Xenia's warnings," Grandmère said. "I know such a task will pain you, ma cherie, but do take Nenette with you, for two are better than one, and I would not have you risk your reputation going to his chamber unescorted."

Idelette laughed. Rachelle ignored her.

Grandmère looked at the desk, her expression serious and determined. "Yes, this is best," she murmured, as if to reinforce her decision. "I shall write him at once. I never thought the day would come when I would be urging my granddaughter to take such a bold initiative. Ah, well. The gravity of the times …" She walked to the desk, pulling out the cherry seat and sitting gracefully. She drew stationery and inkwell toward her. "You have asked your sister Madeleine about the marquis so many times in your letters. Now fortune has it you are given a respectable opportunity of meeting him," Grandmère said lightly. She looked over her shoulder at Rachelle who felt her gaze go deeply. "Your grandmère herself sends you to him. And, it is favorable to us all."

So Madeleine had informed Grandmère of the questions she was asking about le Marquis. *Just wait until I correspond with Madeleine again.*

Rachelle convinced herself it was worry that caused her heart to beat so quickly and not the feminine excitement of confronting the marquis face-to-face, alone, for the first time. She straightened the Alençon lace on her bodice. Ah, lace … how she loved to run it through her fingers.

THE CREAM LACE on the cuff of the blue velvet sleeve of Marquis Fabien de Vendôme was not Alençon but Burgundy lace, with woven threads of gold and purple representing the blood royal. This lace originated in the region of Burgundy that had once been the powerful duchy of his kinsman of two generations ago, Charles de Montpensier, le Duc de Bourbon, one of the most powerful men in France whose rights to the throne equaled, if not exceeded, those of the present Valois royal family.

Fabien's late mother was Marie-Louise de Bourbon, and his father, Marquis Jean-Louis de Vendôme, had been the Duc of Bourbon, until his death — *assassination*, Fabien thought coolly. Fabien had lost the title of duc to a kinsman, Prince Antoine de Bourbon, the brother of Prince Louis de Condé. Antoine was presently the king of the Huguenot kingdom of Navarre. In respect to Fabien's ancestry, however, he was granted the marquisat in Vendôme, also his mother's family estate and some of his father's lands.

Now within his chamber in the palais chateau of Chambord, Fabien stood before a Venetian mirror mulling over the arrival of the cowled stranger who had been ushered into the palais beneath his very nose. He was angry with himself for not having expected the arrival of le Duc de Guise and his brother, le cardinal. They had followed the Queen Mother from Paris with a rather belligerent attitude. Due, no doubt, to the fact that their blood niece Mary of Scotland was married to King Francis II. Francis and Mary were as much under their influence as the queen regent herself. A matter that Fabien knew infuriated her.

Something unpleasant was hatching. He sensed it had something to do with the arrival of le Duc de Guise and the messire in the hooded cowl and face mask. Fabien decided to discover more about both.

Le Duc de Guise, known as *le Balafré* for the military victories he had led for France, had more recently turned his relentless hatred against those of the religion, the French Protestant Calvinists or Huguenots.

Thinking of Huguenots brought Fabien's master swordsman to mind. Chevalier Nappier was a secret Huguenot, an expert with the rapier, and Fabien, from his youth, had befriended him. Fabien knew a man of iron when he met one. He admired men of conviction, for most could be trusted once they had made the decision of loyalty. He had a number of such Frenchmen serving him. There was much about Nappier that reminded Fabien of the stern French pirate, Capitaine l'Olivier, who with one swipe could remove a head.

Now there was an arrogant galante for you! The cold-blooded Protestant liked to hunt and capture Spanish galleons and take no quarter. It was said he had his reasons for hating Spaniards, not the least of which was that he had been a prisoner under their torture for several years. That Fabien was baptized a Catholic and attended Mass with the king's royal household each noon in no way altered Fabien's respect for the pirate, though l'Olivier would certainly find that plaguing.

Had Nappier noticed le Duc de Guise and the messire with the mask riding into the courtyard? Guise's men-at-arms would of necessity take food and rest near the armory and barracks where Nappier might catch a snatch of verbal exchange between them that would prove interesting. Fabien made up his mind to go there as soon as he located Sebastien.

Fabien straightened his light blue velvet jacket and tried on his hat, the wide-rimmed style so fashionable at court, this one with a white feather. He had heard women describe his hair as the color of sun-ripened wheat, his eyes the hue of violets. He was admirably handsome, he knew this by the response cast his way from delectable feminine creatures who, if he chose to, he could collect like sweet plums on a silver plate. Ah ... but he was no fool. He had seen the fall of his kinsmen, the Princes Antoine and Louis de Condé. He knew the biblical story of Samson well.

He drew his straight brows together. He had his doubts the ladies at court would be able to capture Capitaine l'Olivier with their schemes as they had attempted with him. Several ladies-in-waiting and maids-of-honor had set about to trap him with their allurements. Not that all the belle dames at court wanted marriage. Nor did age matter to many. He had been but sixteen when the wrinkled old Duchesse la Belangée had tried to bribe him into an affaire d'amour while her husband was away from court on business. La Belangée had shown him a large ruby which had been given her when she was young and beautiful by Charles V of the Holy Roman Empire.

"It is yours, mon petit. Just lie with me this night."

Fabien had acknowledged the ruby as fair but admitted he had too many rubies and diamonds already. The duchesse had not appeared offended or embarrassed by his inadequate refusal.

"Are you then a sober Calvinist?" she had inquired suspiciously.

He had offered a deep, elegant bow. "No, I am a Catholic, Madame. Am I to assume there are no Catholics sober?"

Her silver brows had lifted. Then she had thrown back her head and laughed.

It was well-known that the recent *maitresse* of King Henry, Diane de Poitiers, had been old enough to be his *maman*. Fabien, because of his position at court, knew that Catherine had despised her, and no sooner did Henry II lie dying from his ill-fated joust, than Catherine sent a message to Diane to return all of the jewels Henry had given her and to vacate the palais of Chenonceau.

Yes, it was dangerous at court. There were more ways than one to spend the night in a lion's den. The image of the belle Charlotte de Presney came to his senses—again. She was a physical temptation he found difficult to resist, though he felt an equal amount of contempt for her lack of fidelity to her husband. Fabien knew her husband, a sound monsieur, a soldier. Fabien did not fear his jealous rage, for he could well handle himself, but he feared for the foolish Charlotte, who did not perceive how near she played to the edge of a boiling pit.

A light tap sounded on the door and his page, Gallaudet, entered, bowing. His page was unsmiling as ever, yet patient and dedicated. He was young and wiry, with hair as fair as platinum. His red, white, and blue Bourbon livery fit him well, as did his rapier, a gift from Fabien who had made certain he knew how to use it with expertise.

"Monseigneur, a royal missive is sent to all courtiers. All festive events at Chambord are canceled without explanation."

Fabien took the missive and read the brief message:

> *His Majesty and his Court will depart Chambord in early morning to journey to the fortress-castle at Amboise.*
> *The Marquis de Vendôme will please have his personal retinue prepared for journey in the morning.*

The change in royal plans confirmed his suspicions. "When was this missive sent out, Gallaudet?"

"Not more than ten minutes ago, Marquis."

"Interesting, I assure you. So soon after the arrival of Guise with his cowled stranger. What do you make of it, Gallaudet?"

"Trouble afoot, Monsieur."

"Go and see what else you can learn from the other pages, especially Guise's page. Also, go to the armory and tell Nappier to see what he can discover from Guise's men-at-arms."

Gallaudet bowed his head and turned to leave, but Fabien stopped him.

"Have you seen Comte Sebastien Dangeau this day?"

"No, Monsieur, I have not. Shall I inquire?"

"You have enough to keep you occupied. I shall seek him out."

Gallaudet bowed and departed, followed a few moments later by Fabien.

Fabien strode down the corridor deep in thought. He could go straight to the young, ailing Francis Valois, newly declared King of France since his father Henry's death in the fatal joust at the palais Les Tournelles. Fabien could ask the reasons behind the arrival of Guise and the masked messire among his men-at-arms. Francis Valois and his recent reinette, Mary Stuart of Scotland, had been Fabien's acquaintances since childhood. He could solicit an audience with the king, but it would necessitate secrecy, since neither the Guise brothers nor Catherine would of late permit Francis many, if any, visitors. Even Marguerite Valois told him she felt a prisoner here at Chambord.

"His Majesty must rest," the word persisted. "The king's strength must be preserved and guarded."

Guarded, yes; but guarded so Francis could be better manipulated by Mary's shrewd oncles? Fabien was sure these two brothers cared very little about Francis, or even Mary. They had connived through Diane de Poitiers, the late king's mistress, to arrange the marriage to advance their own political power.

Fabien could also appeal to the king's younger brother, Charles, next in line for the throne, but he hesitated. Just thinking of the boy Charles Valois brought Fabien a scowl.

Fabien walked through the lower salle toward upward steps to the second floor and the royal chambers.

It would be a great risk to entrust his suspicions to Charles. Catherine controlled her young son through fear. Therefore he would tell her whatever she asked. It was most unfortunate that Charles lived on the rim of an abyss of mental hysteria. Part of the reason for his near madness was Catherine herself. Just as the Queen Mother had specific astrologers and mysterious perfumers that did her nefarious bidding, so also she had certain instructors brought over from her home in Florence, Italy, to teach Charles. Fabien believed that Catherine, who was of the blood of the infamous Borgias, maneuvered in the realm of the diabolical. For murky reasons of her own, she had set about to pervert Charles. For what purpose? Fabien often wondered. He now believed it was Catherine's objective to have absolute control over Charles, who was next in line to become a boy-king should anything happen to Francis—who was of such weak health. Unlike Francis, however—who was manipulated by the power of his beloved Mary's oncles, the duc and the cardinal—should Charles come to the throne he would be free of any manipulation by the Guises, whom Catherine feared of plotting against her wishes. Charles would bend to the will of Catherine alone.

The very idea brought uneasiness to Fabien. And what was the old parable—*uneasy lies the head that wears the crown?* Would Catherine set about to remove one son to place another on the throne? Fabien deepened his frown. He believed she had used poison before in her extended family and would use it on others she deemed a threat to her power.

As for Francis, it did not require foresight to see that the boy-king—so frail with a sickness of the blood like the grandfathers on both sides of his family—would never reach an old age.

Fabien had been out with Francis just yesterday, riding in a joust with other young galantes at court. While Francis insisted on joining in, he had attempted to mask his weakness to impress Mary that he was as masculine as the best of his courtiers. Fabien had deliberately lost to him to terminate the charade and return him with Mary to their royal chambers for rest. Francis was still recovering today, trying to recoup his strength. What had disturbed Fabien most was the smile on Catherine's face when she thought no one noticed her. Fabien had the impression she desired her son to wear himself out in order to free herself from the restraints of the Guises through Mary.

Should Charles come to the throne before reaching maturity, Catherine would rule France as regent for many years. This was where her Florence instructors came in; she was using them now to terrorize him, to saturate his young mind with frightening, debase images, also attempting to bend Charles toward homosexuality. Fabien fought his own anger in thinking about it. Her reasons? Undoubtedly she wanted to keep Charles from producing an heir to follow him, and for that matter, neither did she want Francis to produce an heir through Mary, for Catherine desired her favorite on the throne, her petit Henry Anjou, the younger son after Charles, and the only son she adored.

No, it was wiser to avoid Charles for information, even though he was a spy in his own perquisite and likely to know as well as anyone who the mysterious visitor was.

Fabien climbed the broad stairway on his way to seek access to his boyhood friend, King Francis Valois II.

Chapter Five

RACHELLE MACQUINET DEPARTED FROM THE FAMILY CHAMBER ON HER bold quest to deliver the family message to Marquis Fabien. Young Nenette, fourteen, a student grisette and serving maid combined — also Rachelle's loyal ally and amie in many predicaments — came with her, scurrying along just behind Rachelle's heels as though held on a gilded tether.

Rachelle's skirts of mint green silk and lace swished with each step taken across the shining parquet floor, while the salle with its marble statues formed a silent guard.

"Mam'zelle, where is Marquis de Vendôme's chambers?"

Rachelle, having reached the landing on the broad stairway, now came to an abrupt halt.

Nenette squeaked, clasping hold of her shoulder to keep from colliding.

Rachelle realized that no one had explained just where Marquis Fabien's chamber should be.

"Now what?" Rachelle muttered. "Go back, Nenette, find out where the marquis is situated lest we wander aimlessly."

Nenette flitted back in the direction of the Macquinet chambers, and Rachelle stood on the top landing, one hand on the banister, absently aware of the carved *fleurs-de-lys* pressing against her palm. At that moment, unexpectedly, as though Providence were indeed on her side, the marquis himself appeared below in the salle, coming around the elbow of the stairway and boldly climbing up.

Rachelle realized that this was le momente she had been waiting for, and her heart thumped and her breath came quickly.

Marquis Fabien could be described as elegante, but unlike others she had seen at court, especially Comte Maurice Beauvilliers, Fabien was without a trace of effeminateness. Rachelle had first noticed Monsieur Fabien in a friendly jousting game with the other galantes at Chambord. His expertise with sword and horse had impressed her, as she suspected it had the other mademoiselles gathered on the balustrade. Now, though wearing the exquisite fashion expected of a marquis in the presence of royalty, he clearly retained his masculinity.

Monsieur Fabien came up the stairs with a faint scowl between his brows as though his thoughts worried him, then looking up, he noticed her and paused.

He took her in slowly. As their gaze met and held, Rachelle stood perfectly still.

He doffed his hat with its feather and bowed, hand resting on his light blue velvet jacket encrusted with diamonds.

"*Enchantée*, Mademoiselle."

She felt her knees turning into warm, melted wax. A curtsy was called for. He was a *marquis*. Good breeding took over and she did so flawlessly, but then his deep violet-blue eyes warmed her with a confident spark of interest that sent a strange tingle down her neck, and heat scorched her cheeks. She felt exasperated with herself. The emotion grew until his slow smile crumbled her confidence. She turned without thinking, her skirts swishing, and walked briskly away. She clenched her fists.

"*Quelle stupide*," she whispered to herself. "You did well until the end. Now what does he think of you? A comtesse would have carried on the encounter with *sang-froid*."

Nenette was coming through the Macquinet chamber doorway as Rachelle came toward her. Nenette's small mouth opened with surprise.

"The marquis is coming this way now," Rachelle told her in *sotto voce*. "Quick, to the stairway. Signal when you see him nearing."

Nenette darted ahead to keep watch. Rachelle loitered in the doorway watching. Nenette stood near the landing with her back and palms pressed hard against the wall. Now and then she would lean her head forward to steal a glance.

Nenette squeaked again and came flying toward her, her red curls bouncing, hands twittering.

"He comes!"

"Inside." Rachelle pushed her into the chamber and drew the door partly shut. With her ear to the crack she heard his steps coming down the salle. Then she saw him again.

As yet he had not noticed her behind the partially open doorway, and it seemed as though he would walk past.

"Monsieur de Vendôme!" she called.

FABIEN HEARD A VOICE, paused, and turned toward an elaborately carved door that stood partly open. Beside the door stood the same mademoiselle he had encountered on the stairway. She looked at him intently and beckoned.

He masked a smile. He knew many lovely women, but this one caught more than his usual interest. He assumed her coy behavior was deliberate and playful, rather than an *ingénue*. He wondered who she was. With so many mademoiselles hoping to win him for his title and wealth, it became more difficult for any one particular woman to make a memorable impression. They were all belles, too willing, and too much the same.

This mademoiselle was oddly different. He sensed it the moment their eyes met, though he could not have reasoned why.

He had not seen her before; he would have remembered. This had to be her first season at court. She must be a daughter of one of the ducs, sent to become a lady-in-waiting. How long would her innocent charm endure among so many wolves? This one would be snatched up quickly, he thought, feeling cynical. If *he* had taken note of her that quickly, then so would every other messire at court. He often thought that if he had a daughter he would hide her away until he could arrange a marriage to a lad like the guileless Andelot Dangeau, the nephew of Sebastien.

As the mademoiselle continued to beckon him, he tapped his chin. She had a wealth of titian hair, auburn — no, not exactly auburn, there was more dark brown in it.

She stepped out and curtsied again. The belles at court dressed in ornate gowns and jewels, and this one had style and charm, with some narrow lace at the neck and wrists, but no jewels. He also noted that the bodice line was well covered. A rare sight ... intriguing, so was the dimple at the corner of her well-shaped mouth. Her eyes he described as honey-brown, with thick, alluring lashes.

"Monsieur de Vendôme," came her overly stiff voice. "Please enter, I beg you. It is important."

Was this sweet little drama of hers a ruse? Ah! Maybe she was not the innocent he had thought. He might be entering the chamber of a woman belonging to the Queen Mother's *escadron volant de la reine*.

The Queen Mother's maids-of-honor consisted of a bevy of some forty amorous women who were treacherous spies. Perhaps not all would go so far as to sell their virtue and honor for the Queen Mother of France, though most did. Catherine had once said of them, "They are the best allies of the royal cause."

He could believe it. The royal cause was merely her own intrigues, and her escadron volant proved useful to fascinate and ruin Huguenot and Catholic alike.

Catherine had tried to trap him a few months ago in Paris by using Comtesse Soulier, though Catherine's motive was as yet unclear to him. After the death of his mother and father, both deaths questionable, Fabien told himself he was far from being a fool.

Was this demure and delectable rosebud yet another attempt?

He regarded her thoughtfully.

He stepped toward her chamber, pausing to lean in the doorway. He smiled. She blushed. Belle dames in the escadron volant did not blush. He casually rested his hand near his scabbard, not that he expected that sort of danger, but with the masked messire and recent events, he, a Bourbon, could not be trusting.

He pushed the heavy wooden door aside wide enough to glance inside. He saw no one else in the chamber, and it did not appear to be a trap.

His gaze came back to hers.

"Did the Queen Mother tell you to invite me to your *chambre à coucher*, Mademoiselle? A plan, perhaps to search my mind and heart by the application of your charms?"

She sucked in her breath.

"Granted," he said, "I find your charms alluring, ma cherie, but your plan will avail you of no information. I have no political secrets to share; my loyalty is sworn to King Francis."

"Monsieur de Vendôme, I blush for shame that you would think such of me, I assure you. I confess I have gone about this task most foolishly. I must appear very bold."

"Hardly bold, Madame."

"Mademoiselle," she said with uplifted chin.

He gestured his head in brief nod. "An error, Mademoiselle," he said indifferently.

"A grave error, Monsieur, I promise you."

He looked at her again, noting her discomfiture, but a quick flash of anger as well. His interest only grew. He wondered about her motives and was now at a loss, even experiencing a faint prick of conscience. *Surely this one was as fresh and untouched as any I've seen.*

"Though I quite understand your suspicions, I assure you," she said. "The Queen Mother has not sent me, nor does she know we planned to talk to you."

"*We,* Mademoiselle?"

"Madame Henriette—my grandmother. Ah," came her relieved voice. "Madame is here now." She turned, looking across the chamber. He followed her gaze.

Fabien, now thoroughly curious, saw an elderly woman wearing an elegant but plain black dress with a touch of white lace.

"Marquis de Vendôme happened to be passing in the outer salle, Grandmère," the younger mademoiselle explained. "And I did not need to seek an audience at his chamber. Though I fear I have caused him ... um, some confusion."

Fabien hid a smile at that.

Madame Henriette bowed with grave dignity in his direction.

"Monsieur de Vendôme, merci. I see you have met my younger granddaughter? Mademoiselle Rachelle Dushane-Macquinet. We are here at court as couturières, Marquis, called here from Lyon by royal summons from the Queen Mother herself."

Fabien began to understand. He had heard of the Macquinets, the famous silk couturières.

"Bien sûr, Madame."

Madame came toward him now. "My daughter, Clair, is not here, but she met you before in Paris, Monsieur, but you may have forgotten her? Clair Dushane-Macquinet, the mother-in-law of Comte Sebastien Dangeau. His wife, Madeleine, is my eldest granddaughter. She remains in Paris."

"Ah, but yes, pardone, Madame."

It was clear to him now that he had misjudged the mademoiselle with the magnificent auburn brown hair. One thing was settled; he would not forget meeting Rachelle. He looked down at her again, tasting her name as he studied her once more. She turned away. He found her profile exquisite ... yes, this one must be watched before some duc snatched her. A duc or a greedy comte like his cousin Maurice Beauvilliers. That, he suddenly decided, he would not permit.

The Macquinets of Lyon were known for their silk. Now that he was inside the chamber he saw their bolts of material. But of course! He vaguely recalled that Margo had mentioned having new gowns made here at Chambord.

Fabien offered a deep and elegant bow. "The pleasure is mine, Madame Henriette. Dushane, is it not, Madame?"

He saw the slight sparkle of pride show in her dark eyes. "Oui, Marquis. Madame Duchesse Xenia Dushane is a distant cousine of mine."

"A woman of merit, to be sure. I have met her on many occasions at court through the years." He wondered if this meant that Rachelle could be in line for a title. He thought, however, it was Comtesse Claudine Boisseau who would inherit.

Fabien would not admit he but vaguely remembered having met Madame Clair in the royal appartements of Sebastien at the Louvre some two years ago.

"I knew your père, Marquis Jean-Louis," Grandmère said. "A galante of the highest order. I grieved when he was slain in the war with Spain and le Duc de Guise took his position as France's general."

He thought his smile might have frozen at the mention of his father and Guise. His main reason for disliking the duc was rooted in the death of Jean-Louis.

Fabien bowed but kept silent.

Madame Henriette smiled, yet he noted gravity in her eyes. Maybe she too was aware of the arrival of le Duc de Guise and Cardinal Lorraine.

Fabien bowed over her small, veined hand, then turned as she said. "My granddaughter Rachelle is working with me here at Chambord gaining further training as one of my grisettes and as a future couturière."

Rachelle was dignified now, showing there was Dushane blood in her after all, but some color remained in her cheeks after their misunderstanding. *C'est charmante*, he thought. Her manner was refreshing for a change.

He lifted Rachelle's hand and bent over it. "*Mille pardons*, Mademoiselle."

Her eyes came up to meet his and a spark showed in their depths over her vindication. *Ah,* he thought. *Mademoiselle has a penchant for standing up for herself.* That too he liked.

"Merci, Marquis," she said with a sudden elegance.

He restrained a smile and affected gravity, willing his gaze to silently speak of his respect and growing interest. He wondered if she knew the confusion of their meeting had made her unforgettable. Had she done so on purpose? No, and in thinking so he realized he had become accustomed to the belle dames at court. He was cynical.

Madame Henriette spoke as Idelette entered: "My other granddaughter Mademoiselle Idelette, also in training."

Another beauty, Fabien acknowledged her sober curtsy. He thought her wan compared to the flushed liveliness of her younger sister, like a serene lily.

"Honored, Mademoiselle."

Inside the chamber his gaze fell on bolts of crimson, gold, and blue silks, burgundy velvets, gilded brocades of verdant greens and rose pinks. There were smaller bolts of lace in various shades of the rainbow beside the staple ivory. He took in the cutting instruments, spools of silk threads, and then—across the chamber, he saw gowns in the process of being finished. The burgundy silk over cloth of gold he particularly found attractive.

"I would not have requested my daughter to ask you here were it not that I have important news, Marquis, and it is a matter of trust."

"Am I to assume your reason for placing trust in me rests on the reputation of Jean-Louis?"

"Sebastien and Madeleine have spoken well of you, Marquis."

"Knowing you are related to Sebastien gives you my undivided attention, Madame."

"Merci, Monsieur. We are pleased the Bourbons have risen to defend our cause as Huguenots at court, for we of the Protestant belief have many enemies."

"You speak of my kinsman Prince Louis de Condé, also Admiral Coligny," he said, for he did not wish to include himself as a swift defender of Calvinism.

"Yes, Monsieur. We know you are a kinsman of Antoine de Bourbon, now King of Navarre."

Navarre was the mostly Protestant realm under Queen Jeanne who had married his kinsman Antoine.

"You too, Monsieur, are a Huguenot, are you not?" Rachelle spoke for the first time.

He turned to look at her. He would not be trapped into saying he was a Calvinist.

"*Au contraire,* I am a Catholic, Mademoiselle, as I think you already know."

"I did not know. I thought ..."

Madame Macquinet stepped in quietly. "Ah, so be it, Marquis de Vendôme, we already know we can trust you and that you are a good Catholic."

"Merci, Madame." He bowed casually, then continued in a quiet voice. "You may confide in me your troubles, Madame, I will do all I can to help you. What is it you wish to tell to me?"

Madame Macquinet released a breath and her shoulders sagged. He took her arm.

"Do sit. Are you certain we can talk freely here?"

Rachelle had come swiftly to her Grandmère, assisted her to a chair, then stood behind her, resting her hands on the backrest.

"Yes, it is safe. This chamber has no listening holes."

He tilted his head. "Is there something, Madame, you have learned, that I should know?"

"Madame Xenia Dushane has imparted to us information of utmost interest, Monsieur Fabien. She has also intimated you are trustworthy."

"Ah, the duchesse," he said. "Yes, that explains this meeting well enough then. She has proven herself a friend on many desperate occasions. I pray you proceed without further delay."

Madame Henriette sat straight in the high-backed chair, hands folded in her lap. Rachelle looked on with flashing eyes, while Idelette stood to the side with her hands calmly folded before her skirts, also watching him.

"It concerns the masked figure le Duc de Guise brought here to Chambord this day to meet with the Queen Mother," Henriette said.

He narrowed his gaze. "Yes?"

"Duchesse Dushane fears Sebastien is involved in something that may put his life at risk if it is known."

He waved a hand and the jewels sparkled. "Sebastien is a secret Huguenot, Madame; I am aware of it. You need not tread cautiously where he is concerned. I have known him and Madeleine since I was but twelve." And he could have added that they had introduced him to the Reformation which, had Fabien not found worthy of the highest intellectual pursuit, could easily have landed them in the Bastille dungeons. "I am no ami of Guise, nor of his fanatical zeal."

"There is more to Duchesse Dushane's fears, Marquis. Sebastien is missing. We fear his absence is connected with le Duc de Guise and the masked messire he brought here this morning. He is a spy — the duchesse is most sure of this — and a betrayer of the Huguenots."

There was a momentary silence.

He looked at her sharply. "How do you know this?"

"La duchesse saw his face — she was not supposed to, but he removed his cowl and mask as she was stepping out of her chambers. He and the duc were entering another chamber nearby."

"And who is he, Madame?"

"Maître Avenelle."

"*Mille diables*! She is certain of this?"

"She vows it, Marquis."

Maître Avenelle came from the Bourbon districts, near Moulins and Berry. Moulins was the very seat of Bourbon authority in the days of Duc Charles de Bourbon. Many of Fabien's kinsmen lived in the Bourbon Palais at Moulins. The forested area of Berry was not far away, nor was his marquisat at Vendôme.

"Avenelle …" he repeated, trying to piece together reasons for his being with le Duc de Guise. "What more did la duchesse tell you?"

"She is most certain that Maître Avenelle, a Huguenot, has become an ally of Duc de Guise."

"Madame, you are certain you did not perhaps misunderstand the duchesse?"

"Ah, Monsieur, I vow it."

"There is more," Rachelle spoke up. "Madame sent me to Sebastien to warn him of all this, but Sebastien is not in his chambers. Neither has he been seen by others. Your cousine, Comte Maurice Beauvilliers, told me so."

Fabien looked at her. "You have met Maurice, Mademoiselle?"

"I found him in Sebastien's chambers. He was seeking him also."

Fabien paced, one hand on his hip, the other tapping his chin. "If this Avenelle is to take counsel with the Queen Mother, one could ardently wish to hear what he has to say about the House of Bourbon."

Madame Henriette leaned forward anxiously. "Our fears are as yours, Monsieur, that some doom may be planned against the Bourbon-Huguenot leaders."

Rachelle said urgently: "And this Maître Avenelle knows all the nobles who secretly support Prince Condé. What if he names Sebastien?" Her eyes flashed as she boldly looked up to meet his gaze. Then she lowered her eyes to her Grandmère.

"If Sebastien is missing," Idelette said, "could it not suggest he has already been named by Maître Avenelle? And who may be next at court?"

"We must find Sebastien, Monsieur Fabien. My granddaughter, Madeleine, is *enceinte*," Madame Henriette said with delicate pronunciation. "If anything should happen to Sebastien — she is most delicate. She might lose the *bébé*."

"Forbid, Madame. Do not fully despair. There may yet be something we can do."

He felt Rachelle's quick, appreciative glance.

Idelette tried to comfort her Grandmère who appeared to have succumbed to anxiety. Fabien pondered the information, his chin resting on his doubled fist, pacing slowly. He knew Avenelle could endanger the Huguenots at court. There were others, including the king's royal physician and surgeon, Ambroise le Paré. But how could Avenelle be a danger to his Bourbon kinsman?

"Knowing Guise as I do, there is more to Avenelle's betrayal than having individuals at court exposed as sympathetic to the Reformation. There was a reason for Guise needing to disguise Avenelle. Guise will not be easily content with merely apprehending a Huguenot duchesse like Dushane or Sebastien or even the royal physician. Despite caution, I assure you that many of us already know of their religious leanings. Le Duc de Guise, though scornful, has more on his mind. In my opinion, there is some matter of greater importance."

But why would Guise need to bring Avenelle here to Chambord to have audience with Catherine?

"Maître Avenelle must know something important. Somehow, I must discover what it is before I contact my kinsmen." His pondering stride had brought him to the burgundy silk dress on the mannequin. He reached absently and lifted a fold of silk, feeling it.

"If there is some way to learn what Avenelle and Guise told Catherine," he murmured to himself.

Madame Henriette turned in her chair, alert. "Ah, Marquis, but the meeting has not yet taken place. Madame Dushane informs us they will meet this afternoon in the state council chambers. Le Duc de Guise and le Cardinal de Lorraine will be there as well as Maître Avenelle."

Fabien turned sharply, fixing his gaze upon her. "Madame, you are certain of this?"

"The duchesse was adamant, Monseigneur."

He heard Rachelle's breath catch lightly. Her eyes brightened, but tension also showed on her lovely face. She started, as if to suggest something, then seemed to restrain herself.

"Yes, Mademoiselle?" he encouraged.

She walked toward him. "Monsieur Fabien—pardon, Marquis de Vendôme—"

"*Fabien* will be sufficient." He bowed.

"Ah, Monsieur, I would address you by what your noble title deserves." She curtsied with such grace as to render her a princess.

"We shall see," he said with a smile. Then, aware of her Grandmère looking on, he glanced to see her reaction, but she wisely appeared not to notice. A master stroke on her part. She could not help but be aware of the interest that had flamed between them.

"But you were going to tell me …" He lifted a brow and waited for Rachelle to proceed.

"Marquis, there is a secret closet … a secret step, a listening hole, into the state council chamber."

Grandmère stood. "Rachelle!"

"It is true, I promise you, Grandmère."

"*Bien entendu*!" Fabien said. "I, myself, should have remembered this. I know of it—but the precise location escapes me. Catherine has such closets in most of the chateaus."

"Ah, Monsieur Marquis, I know where it is located."

"You know?" he asked, raising a brow.

"It was told to me by a kinswoman when she was here at court, Comtesse Claudine Boisseau."

He knew of Claudine. She had indeed returned to Orléans.

"I can take you to the listening closet," Rachelle said. "There you may hear all."

Fabien fixed her with a judicious gaze. "If you indeed know of this listening step, then it is one of many such devices the Queen Mother avails herself of in all the castles, though few know where they are located. May I ask how Claudine discovered it?"

"From the Queen Mother's Italian servant girl."

"Madalenna?"

"Oui, Madalenna. A child to be pitied, used as a slave by the Queen Mother. She became frightened and told Claudine."

"An error indeed, and if Catherine knew, it would mean the maid's swift demise, to be sure."

He saw Madame Henriette throw a worried glance toward Rachelle, who appeared not to notice. Idelette too drew nearer as if to protect her younger sister.

"Will Mademoiselle explain?" he asked.

Rachelle looked at her Grandmère and then back at him.

"Claudine was in the queen's royal chambers bringing fresh flowers as expected when she caught the demoiselle in the queen's chest. She questioned her sternly, thinking she had done some mischief, but now we know that was not the situation. Madalenna must have been so anxious to secure her lack of guilt she showed Claudine the very key she had been sent by the Queen Mother to retrieve."

"Here is a piece of fortune to be sure. Where is this listening closet you speak of?"

"I can bring you there now," Rachelle said boldly.

Fabien turned and looked at Madame Henriette. "You will allow this, Madame?"

"The answer, in this situation, is yes, Marquis. The matter of Maître Avenelle and Sebastien may be dire, so we must all take our risks and leave the harvest to the care of our kind Savior."

"You speak well, Madame."

"It will bring far less attention for my granddaughter to walk with you there than for me to escort you."

"My exact sentiments, Madame." He smiled.

Fabien turned to Rachelle. "Then take me at once. If Guise is to see Catherine about Avenelle, it will be after the déjeuner. We have but a short time."

Fabien reminded Madame Henriette to keep all of their words close to her heart. She assured him their secrets were secure. A moment later, after bidding Madame and Mademoiselle adieu, he and Rachelle left the Macquinet chamber together.

Chapter Six

RACHELLE MACQUINET WALKED BESIDE MARQUIS FABIEN DE VENDÔME along a section of stone promenade shaded on one side with a row of lime trees. The trees were in blossom as spring had come early this year, and the air was heavy with a sweetness that drew bees.

"It is so wondrous here at Chambord." She wished this moment in his presence among the blossoms would never end. Her feelings, however, warned her of unrealistic dreams concerning the marquis. "And even though there is beauty here, yet great woe may be in the planning behind these walls and gardens." She gestured toward the lime trees and myriads of blossoms that had fallen to the path after only a few days of bloom.

"Like the garden of Eden, Madame le Serpent is about, but hardly a topic suited to your company, which is most charmante, Mademoiselle. As for the beauty you mention, Francis had an appetite for building. He insisted on turning Chambord, which was merely a gloomy hunting lodge, into a palais amid the flat and dusty plains of Sologne. Here the Renaissance was to achieve its purpose."

"I believe he accomplished it, Monsieur."

"It is no surprise. He amassed every device, decoration, and eccentricity of his favorite style, as you can see."

The royal fortress chateau was one of several near Blois, and one of many throughout France to which members of royalty took their leisurely pleasure; this chateau was marked by numerous towers, turrets, broad flat roofs, painted windows, and ample courts.

Rachelle could well understand why Monsieur *le docteur* had recommended the boy-king come here for health reasons. From the moment she arrived she was impressed with the sunny little town of Blois that sloped sweetly downward toward the river Loire.

"And yet this king, who appreciated art, killed ma oncle," she said. "It took place before I was born at Lyon. Maman has told me of it. Oncle was one of the Reformers burnt in the Lyon square."

His mouth turned with some bitterness. "I am not surprised. I do not wish to sound hard, but kings — *and* queens — have a penchant for eliminating vexatious Huguenots."

She kept silent. "This way, Monsieur."

"Ah, the stairway. Catherine would have wanted some listening closets near at hand. I recall a time years ago when her Italians, the Ruggerio brothers, visited here. Now I can imagine the reason for their visit —" His steps slowed to a stroll. "Do not hurry so, Mademoiselle. We are being watched. That unshackled fop near the fountain is the Spanish ambassador."

Light pressure of his fingers on her arm told her to pause. The Spaniard removed his sombrero with gold fringes and rubies and bowed in their direction. Fabien returned the acknowledgment and Rachelle offered a curtsy. Fabien drew her away, and she smothered a laugh.

"What would Monsieur Ambassadeur do if he knew you called him a fop?"

"I might also have called him a *spy*, which would not have endeared him to us."

"I doubt not that you are right, Marquis."

"As for what the fellow would do, I have not a clue, though I have heard he is a laudable swordsman."

She threw him a glance. "I have heard you are also, Marquis, a swordsman *par excellence.*"

"With much credit due my master swordsman, Chevalier Nappier."

"But I doubt the day will come when you will have reason to use your skills against the Spaniard."

He lifted a brow. "This Spaniard? You are right. Ah, my disappointments are many."

She widened her eyes. "Marquis!"

"Why so shocked? Spain is the mortal enemy of every Huguenot. I would think you might look with favor upon certain Frenchmen deciding to take a few Spanish heads. I myself would not object unduly to harrying a few now and then. They are most annoying in insisting upon their divine right to light faggots and chain heretics to galley oars."

Rachelle sobered at the thought of the terrible religious wars led by le Duc de Guise and sanctioned by his brother the cardinal. In response to this divine right granted by Rome to rid France of its Huguenots, many had at first gone to their deaths meekly, singing hymns from the *Geneva Psalter* while being readied for burning at the stake. But when these burnings increased, women and children were added, followed by an entire Huguenot village; they rose up and appealed to their Bourbon princes and nobles ruling the districts where they lived. The Huguenots appealed to the Bourbons, who were themselves mostly Protestant, to come to their beleaguered cause and defend them from the wrack, the flames, the hangman's noose, the hatchet, and the molten lead poured down their throats. All because the Huguenots would not recant of justification by faith alone in the righteousness of Christ apart from any religious laws, rules, and traditions of the state church.

The Huguenots pleaded for their rights to be represented before the King of France by Prince Louis de Condé, Admiral Gaspard de Coligny, and the other Bourbon nobles. The Bourbon princes, sympathetic to the Reformation, honorably picked up the gauntlet of responsibility saying that *noblesse oblige*.

Civil war threatened if King Francis and the Queen Mother continued to allow the relentless attacks by Guise and his mercenary army financed by Spain's treasure ships.

"Rome has agreed that the wealth of the New World belongs to the King of Spain, who calls himself the Sword of the Lord," Fabien said. "The King of Spain was blessed by Rome to rid France and Europe of its heretics."

"You sound as though you may know something of this wealth of the New World, so freely bestowed by Rome to Spain."

"I assure you I am learning quickly enough. It is all so fascinating, is it not? This question of the divine rights of kings to become a sword in the mighty fist of religious Rome? Allowing no authority but their own, granting the holy right to torture?"

She hid a shudder. Much blood had been shed in the last decade, many short-lived truces, many edicts signed, but the Guises cared not for truces, and Rome encouraged the breaking of them to rid France of its heretics.

"As you say, Marquis, the sweetness of the lime blossoms beg a far different discussion." She smiled.

"Pardon! But the sharp weapon of Rome interests me, this Sword that sits in Spain. Spain's galleons, her wanton treasure ships, return yearly to Madrid bringing great chests of gold, emeralds, and pearls." His violet blue eyes hardened like jewels. "Do you know what Philip does with most of this bounty?"

Rachelle looked at him dubiously. "I suspect he gathers it together with his other bounty, and showers it upon his numerous wives. I have heard he has had many, besides our own Princesse Elisabeth Valois."

"Now called *Isabel*, Mademoiselle. But no, that is not his purpose ... though he no doubt tosses them baubles now and then. Philip uses the wealth of the Main to fund his wars of religion. Le Duc de Guise's army is mainly financed by Philip through his treasure galleons. Philip collects the treasure of the Americas to feed and arm his soldiers and to pay his mercenaries to wage battle in the Netherlands, and yes, here in France."

"I have heard of men from England who attack these treasure ships and take the gold to the English queen."

His hand waved an airy dismissal. "Have you not heard of the Frenchmen who command their own ships?"

"Corsairs, yes?"

"Corsairs indeed! And they are not all English, many are French. They are galantes, Mademoiselle."

"My père would agree with you, Marquis. He has spoken of such Frenchmen."

"Do you know what would happen in Europe if Spain did not take gold from the Americas and from what some in England now call the 'Caribbean'? Spain's ability to buy mercenary soldiers and pay kings and queens to wage war against its Protestant subjects would shrivel and die. Without its treasure galleons, Mademoiselle Rachelle, Spain would come to naught. Yet, I am amazed our royal and princely families who fear Spain do not consider this and take action."

"Do you intend to enliven the interest of our king?"

"With the House of Guise as Spain's legates, I doubt the king will have opportunity to seriously consider it." He looked at her. "Your leader, Coligny, knows the importance of France taking an interest in the Americas. He is sending men by ship to the Americas to begin a colony. They call it Florida. But we must keep our real intention from reaching the ears of the Guises."

"We? You are then, Marquis, interested in this colony?"

"The voyage, Mademoiselle. As I say, it is intriguing. I will help sponsor the venture."

She glanced at him, thinking it was Fabien who was intriguing. The diamonds on his blue velvet jacket sparkled in the sunlight, and she noticed the armorial emblem of the House of Bourbon on his gold bracelet. Here was a man of the blood royal, and she found it exciting to be engaged in discussion with him on a matter that obviously held his heart.

His gaze came to hers as though about to say something more on Spain. When he noticed her watching him, she flushed and looked away quickly.

"The sculptured staircase, Monsieur," she said.

She had brought him by a somewhat indirect route to a double staircase under the central tower. The staircase appeared to be a giant fleur de lys in stone, where those who ascended were hidden to those who descended.

"Another glimpse into the artistic side of King Francis I," he said.

She noticed, as he pointed it out, how the same design was in concealed doors, sliding panels behind the arras, and the many double walls and secret stairs.

They passed by into a wide salle that was open to the second floor. Above them was a balustrade and a gallery displaying the masterpiece of the Labors of Hercules, which was placed there at the wishes of King Francis I. Fabien commented that it had captured his imagination since boyhood.

"Then you have come here often?"

He hesitated. She guessed that he debated how much he should explain.

"After my parents' deaths I was taken to Paris. I was one of several who lived at court with the Valois children and Mary Stuart. Much of the year was spent journeying from one palais to another, including coming here to Chambord. It was a satisfaction to me when King Henry allowed me to return to my Bourbon kinsmen at Moulins and Châtillon, and recently, I gained possession of my marquisat at Vendôme."

Rachelle withdrew into silence. He had been raised with the royal princes and princesses, a Bourbon by birth, with Vendôme and his family estates and lands under his own rule. With the reminder of his position — a jolt that brought her back to the reality of her own lack of blooded status — she did not pursue the reasons for his presence now at court. Perhaps she had been foolish to dare allow herself to imagine his interest, or that it could ever progress beyond a flirtatious affaire d'amour. She had not thought of where her infatuation would lead. She had not seen beyond the next corner, wanting to trade the probable result, for the desires of the moment.

Although she had lapsed into thoughtful silence, he went on talking casually of the chateau's history, explaining how Chambord was once a mere royal hunting lodge, a small one at that, lying low on the banks of the river Casson. Francis I began an ambitious building program and had hired renowned architects. "As all kings do," he added dryly. "As you see, it is now a fair-sized palais."

It amazed Rachelle when Fabien pointed out how the king had his builders divert the path of the Loire River some fifteen miles away so it would flow by the walls of the chateau.

They entered the chateau salle from the garden walkway. All the windows were diamond shaped and set in painted arches. Rachelle led him to one of several stairways leading into the palais, and they climbed to an upper gallery. He seemed not the least surprised to be walking this direction. Her mouth turned. But of course he knew quite well where the state council chamber was located. Why then had he allowed her to lead him on this tour?

THEY WENT UP LEISURELY, showing themselves to any who noticed them as enjoying one another's company, a display which came naturel to him.

"Will you and your family follow the court to Amboise?" He looked down at her as they ascended the stairway side by side.

"Amboise? I did not know the king was leaving Chambord."

"Francis has sent a royal missive to all the nobles not more than an hour ago to prepare for the journey. We leave in the morning. I find the matter mysterious, as he came here to Chambord for his health. I was at my own estates in Vendôme when I was summoned. We have been here for but how long? It seems like weeks."

She laughed. "No more than a week for you, Marquis de Vendôme. I can see you did not wish to leave Vendôme."

"You are right. In my mind Vendôme is equal to anything here at Chambord."

"Does time here then go too slowly for you?"

"I find that it is moving more quickly now that I have met you. Your company, Mademoiselle, captivates me."

She fought against the flush of pleasure overtaking her cheeks. "Monsieur, you flatter me."

"I *insist* you address me in a less formal manner. When we two are together alone, Fabien will do for a start."

Her heart raced.

His smile was devastating. "I shall soon enjoy calling you Rachelle. And, I do not find it necessary to flatter you as I do others. You are, as you should know, charmante."

"I know nothing of the sort, I assure you."

"I insist you come and visit Vendôme."

She smiled. "You have set aside your serious mood, Marquis."

"I do not humor you? With proper chaperone, bien sûr," he added with a tilt of his head. "Tell your Grandmère you will journey there with Mademoiselle Claudine. She is a cousine of yours, is that not so? You will both be my honored guests."

Her head turned and she glanced at him. "You know Claudine?"

"I know her well," he said smoothly. "She is ailing now I am told. I was pleased to see her called home from the position of maid-of-honor to the Queen Mother."

Did she imagine the hardened altercation in his voice? She studied the masculine profile and decided he was far from underestimating the web of intrigue that Catherine de Medici wove in secret.

As for Claudine, who could inherit the title from her aunt, Duchesse Dushane, it was natural that he would know her. What titled family in all of France would not be looking in the direction of Marquis de Vendôme for their marriageable mademoiselles?

"As a fact, Marquis, I will be visiting near Vendôme. I have been requested to come for a visit at Duchesse Dushane's estate at Orléans. Claudine Boisseau has asked I come for a month."

"I shall remember, I promise you. When will you be there?"

She drew her hand along the polished banister and glanced sideways at him. "July. The exact dates I do not yet know."

"I shall learn them from Claudine. And any other secrets she may tell me about you."

"I have no secrets."

"It is just as well. When I want to learn about someone who interests me I have my ways. We in the nobility can be relentless, so I warn you now, Mademoiselle. You have intrigued me."

She laughed. "I am not so foolish, Monsieur, to believe everything a man of your appearance and stature may tell me. Once you leave here for Amboise, Grandmère and I will not follow the court. We will return to my home in Lyon, and after that you will forget you met me here. There will be so many belles about you, all clamoring for your slightest favor. I know, for I have seen them doing so here at Chambord. And many of them are highly titled and from powerful families."

"In speaking so, I almost believe you are challenging me *not* to forget you, Mademoiselle. Well, have no alarms about that," he said lightly. "My memory is most excellent, and be assured I have no wish to forget. Therefore you may be certain I will come to Orléans in July."

"Then I shall look for you."

"How is it we have been here at Chambord this entire week and I have only now the opportunity to meet you? Why have you not come to any of the divertissements so I could have noticed you earlier?"

She smiled. "I can see I shall need to be on guard so as not to permit myself to be overwhelmed by your compliments."

They had climbed the stairway to the second floor landing. Rachelle paused, her excited mood changing to one of uneasiness. "This is the place," she whispered. "Do you see that oval door engraved with the fleur de lys?"

"Yes, I know of it, but do not draw attention to it. Catherine has spies everywhere. We will need to convince her we have developed an affaire d'amour."

As though to reinforce his decision he drew her toward the gallery rail. His touch awakened all her senses.

"Grandmère would disapprove of our standing so close —"

"Tell me about this door at the end of the hall."

"The Queen Mother uses it," she whispered. *He must be aware of that.* He had more experience at Chambord than she had. She went along with his affected innocence, noticing that the violet blue of his eyes could be mesmerizing.

"If you follow the steps to the top, you will come to an observatory for stargazing, Monsieur . . ."

"She is a firm believer in the zodiac and the dark arts. She consults Nostradamus. He has made a chart for her, foretelling her sons' future reigns on the throne of France."

Rachelle searched his face. "You do not believe such things, Marquis, surely not?"

A brow lifted. "Mademoiselle, do you think I would?"

"Non . . . Monsieur John Calvin speaks hotly against the idolatry of stargazing and fortune-tellers."

"It appears as if Monsieur Calvin and I are in some agreement, Mademoiselle. But is it Calvin who speaks against the potions and mutterings of soothsayers, or is it the Bible that does so?"

Her heart lightened. "Ah, you are wise to ask that, Marquis. If it were but Calvin it would not matter so, would it? I take it that is your point? Though Monsieur Calvin, like Monsieur Luther are firebrands for God. Non, it is the Bible that forbids looking to the zodiac for wisdom." She gave him a cautious glance from beneath her lashes. "There is a Bible in our French language now, do you know of it?"

He appeared to take the charming bait. He smiled, lifting a brow, and leaned against the balustrade beside her.

"There is, Mademoiselle?" he asked innocently. "In *French,* you say? You do not mean it!"

"It is so, translated first by Lefevre d'Étaples."

"Lefevre d'Étaples, oui. I faintly remember the name ..."

"Why do I suspect you know *well* his name?"

"I cannot guess." A smile loitered around his mouth. "Lefevre d'Étaples was protected by another Marguerite Valois, this one the sister of King Francis I. Had it not been for her they would have burnt him. He escaped eventually and went to Strasbourg. That is where your John Calvin met him."

"Then you know more than you pretend, Marquis."

"Pretend? Perhaps. Do you have one of these forbidden Bibles in French?"

She smiled nervously. "Non, I do not—but we have one at the Chateau de Silk. My Cousine Bertrand works with Calvin in the free city of Geneva."

FABIEN REGARDED HER SOBERLY. "Fortunately you were wise enough to leave your forbidden Bible back in Lyon, hidden I hope."

"I would let you see this Bible if you like sometime, if you wish to read it. I could bring it with me to Orléans."

"Merci, Mademoiselle — but I doubt I will have the time for such reading. And you, do you read this forbidden Book in our mother tongue?"

"Yes, and not as often as I should, unlike Idelette."

"I reproach myself to even speak the horrors that will come your way, and your sister's, if this becomes known."

She was sober, and he saw her shoulders straighten perceptibly, as though reinforcing some decision in her mind.

"Yes, I am aware, Marquis. I shall be most careful, I assure you."

"You should not be so trusting. You have told me you have heretical writings." He looked at her, but when her eyes widened, he smiled disarmingly. "Not that I would sit in judgment on Calvin's writings, or of the Bible in French, but others would." His smile faded. "Learn to be cautious in sharing such secrets." He frowned and warned himself that he as well must be careful. A relationship with her, however attractive, would broaden his circle of enemies.

"I mentioned my beliefs only because you are a kinsman of the Huguenot Prince Condé. You yourself are from the House of Bourbon."

"Come," he said, and they strolled down the gallery until she whispered: "Over there, Marquis. There is a hidden stair within that wall — concealed by that tapestry, the one of King Francis I."

"Do not look there. You are certain it is the tapestry?"

"Mais certainement. It is the one Claudine mentioned. Behind the tapestry there is a small door built into the wall, one you must stoop to enter ... Claudine saw the Queen Mother do so. She is tall, but she was able to enter. The tapestry simply falls back into place."

"The door would be locked — "

"Yes, but — I know where the key is kept. I can locate and bring it to you, I am sure of it."

Dangerous.

He regarded her, frowning. "Non."

"Monsieur Fabien, it must be. Others are at risk."

"Why should I risk you?"

"You — have only now met me, Marquis."

"*Le coup de foudre.*"

His RESONANT VOICE sent a chill along her spine. She tore her eyes away, feeling a warm flush coming to her cheeks.

"Could you then claim this key without endangering yourself?"

"I am sure of it." She sounded more confident than she felt.

"You are right then. She will hardly take the key with her into the state council chamber to interrogate Maître Avenelle this afternoon. Be careful of Madalenna. She must not see you. What excuse do you have for getting past the guards at the door?"

"Princesse Marguerite's gowns. I shall take one with me as though she had inquired something about it. It will convince the guards."

"I will do something to call the guards away."

Something moved above them on the other side of the gallery; her eye had just caught a slight movement, like dark wings. She tensed, but it appeared he too had noticed. She saw his alert gaze flicker up to the third floor where a diamond-shaped window let in the March light.

Unexpectedly she found herself in his arms. He held her in a passionate embrace, his lips brushing her temple. She stiffened, drawing in her breath, heart pounding. "Marquis!"

"Hush," he spoke into her hair. "It is Catherine de Medici. She is watching us. She must think we are having a secret *tête-à-tête*." Then his lips sought the tenderness of her throat sending her heart reeling.

Footsteps on stone echoed from the gallery of the floor above them. When the sound stopped, a commanding voice called: "Who is there?"

"Be brave, ma cherie," Fabien whispered. He released her suddenly, as though startled by the voice, and looked up toward the dark figure.

Catherine, standing behind the railing, stared down at them. Always in black since the loss of her husband, King Henry II, she stood with arms folded across her front. Her farthingale reached to her heels. Her black pointed cap rested on her forehead. Her prominent eyes sometimes stared unblinking, earning her the whispered name Madame le Serpent. Her face was broad and round, and she had the unnerving habit of suddenly bursting into bold laughter.

Rachelle surprised herself with her poise. She took a few steps forward and dipped a low regal curtsy, her skirts going out around her in a shimmer of butterfly wings.

"Your Majesty. It is I, your servant, Rachelle Macquinet. Pardon, Madame."

Catherine's look of sternness turned slowly into a smile, one that showed amused contempt at embarrassing two lovers.

"So it is you, ma petite Rachelle. A tryst, is it? And with Marquis Fabien de Vendôme! The most sought after and difficult beau in my court!" And she laughed.

Fabien stepped forward and gave her his most dashing bow, hat at heart. "Your humble servant, Your Majesty."

Catherine's throaty laughter bubbled in a manner that was bold and vulgar.

"Ah, ma petite lovebird has finally won the heart of the illusive Marquis." She then turned her smile on Fabien. "Have you at last found one of my demoiselles to your liking? I am pleased. I had begun to wonder, Marquis, whether you have Bourbon blood after all. Alas, I see you are indeed like your father."

Fabien despised hearing his father's honorable name being slurred. He had heard talk of his père and one of Catherine's daughters but he believed it not. The daughter, Elisabeth, had been sent to become yet another bride of Philip II of Spain.

"Ah, how we miss the great Duc Jean-Louis," Catherine continued in a sad voice, but Fabien knew this woman well enough to recognize mockery. He kept an immobile face.

"A man most esteemed at court and among my maids of honor." And with an amused smile, she turned to walk away, then paused to look toward Rachelle.

"La Macquinet," she stated. "I wish to inspect the gowns for Princesse Marguerite. Bring them to my chambers — that is, when you have said your adieu to Marquis sufficiently well." She laughed.

"Oui, Madame."

The Queen Mother walked the corridor and disappeared. When the last of her steps faded, Rachelle appeared as if she were about to sink to the floor. Fabien held her, steadying her.

"It is well. She suspected nothing unusual."

Rachelle tightened her lips. "Now she will question Grandmère. She will ask about you, and tell Grandmère how she caught us here together."

"There is but one thing to do. Tell Madame Dushane to satisfy Catherine's appetite."

"Monsieur!"

"Do as I say, Mademoiselle. She will tell Catherine how I am enthralled with your beauty, and your Grandmère must express her deep concerns over your reputation. And — " he bowed lightly — "while we remain here at court, I shall do my best to portray my ardor toward you. Hopefully, she will be convinced."

She looked at him evenly. "I understand all, but for one thing, Marquis. Was the kiss truly necessary?"

He feigned surprise. "Sainte Barbe, yes, most assuredly." He grinned at her display of affected offense. *"C'est bien le moment!* I assure you. And now. There is no time to lose. The meeting with Avenelle will be this afternoon. Can you gain the key by then?"

"Mais certainement, Marquis. As soon as Her Majesty leaves her chamber to keep the meeting."

"That she has asked to see Margo's gowns will serve you well."

"When I arrive, the guards will think I am most anxious to display them for the Queen Mother's approval."

"Then I will await you in the salle. Be calm, ma cherie. She believes we are smitten by one another's charms."

"It was very believable, Monsieur Fabien."

"Ah yes . . . it was, was it not? We will speak of it again later. Go now, cherie. *Au revoir.*"

She looked at him evenly, then bowed her head, and turning, picked up her skirts to proceed back down the stairs into the salle. She hurried on her way down the hall to the steps.

Fabien remained in the upper gallery a moment, thinking, tapping his chin. Outside the diamond-shaped windows he heard the crows. He glanced toward the upper balustrade where Catherine had been standing in the shadows, watching. Was she suspicious? Did the Queen Mother know the girl was a Huguenot?

Overhead, from the salle de garde, heavy footsteps passed by the state council chamber. If only he could discover what the Guises were planning with Avenelle. It must be urgent if it could not wait until the king returned to Paris. Francis was ill. Mary would not appreciate her Oncle Guise upsetting him now.

It was important to be inside that secret closet this afternoon.

GRANDMÈRE ENTERED THE CHAMBER with several more of Princesse Marguerite's gowns. She and Idelette began to work as efficiently as they could to fold them for Rachelle to take to the Queen Mother's royal chamber.

After Rachelle had told Grandmère and Idelette of the meeting with the Queen Mother on the upper balustrade, a cold realization of terror had gripped her. Could she get hold of the key successfully? The Queen Mother was intelligent, coldly so. A dangerous risk must be taken; Marquis Fabien was right about that, but Rachelle must enter the serpent's den.

Rachelle found Grandmère's worried gaze upon her.

She smiled, hoping to look confident. "Grandmère, do not worry. Only I know where the key is placed. All will be well."

"We will pray before you go," Grandmère said again.

Rachelle's mind plodded along as she oversaw the folding of the mounds of rainbow silk dresses for the Queen Mother's inspection. Princesse Marguerite was known to prefer daring gowns with a low décolletage, but Catherine disdained this and had once called Marguerite "wanton and wicked" in front of Rachelle.

Soon a young man by the name of Gallaudet, a page who served the marquis, brought a brief message.

"The Queen Mother has left her chamber. She has gone with Maître Ambroise Paré, the royal surgeon, to visit His Majesty, Francis. Now is the moment."

After the page left there was a nervous flurry in the Macquinet chamber, but Grandmère insisted on their sobriety and silence. "We will remain here, ma Rachelle cherie. We will be on our knees for you."

Idelette had called for the assistants, the grisettes belonging to the court, and the dozen gowns were carefully laid over their arms. They followed as Rachelle led the way to the appartements of the Queen Mother, located on the first floor.

Rachelle approached the royal guards and pages with an outward calm intended to portray confidence and dignity.

"Her Majesty, the Queen Mother, has called for me. I am to arrange these gowns for her inspection."

There came not a breeze of doubt. They permitted her and the court grisettes carrying the glittering gowns to pass.

Next came the antechamber where Catherine's pages and some of her ladies-in-waiting gathered. Several women sat in window boxes embroidering and gave deep sighs of appreciation as the grisettes entered with the silks of blue, gold, ruby, and a stunning ivory with rich mounds of lace. Rachelle smiled. "Merci, *mesdames*. Should you want Macquinet silks you have but to see me or one of my entourage before our departure for Lyon."

They all assured her they desired new gowns and each hoped for a unique design to benefit her figure.

Rachelle passed into the royal chamber of Catherine, holding her breath.

The marquis had been careful with his information. The chamber was empty. Rachelle took new courage from this. Briskly she ordered the grisettes to leave the princesse's dresses on the table. She alone wished to arrange them just so for Her Majesty to inspect. Assured by her dignified manner, her unwillingness to chatter and gossip, they appeared to accept her decision with disinterest and left.

When the last grisette departed, Rachelle stood alone in Queen Catherine's inner sanctum. She bit her lip. Perspiration dampening her forehead. Her stomach fluttered. She looked about her, making as certain as was possible that she was alone *and* unobserved.

She heard what sounded like wood creaking beneath someone's tread. A tickle of alarm crept down the back of her neck. Her hands trembled. Her gaze slowly traveled the chamber. If she had secret listening closets in all her chambers as some claimed, then would there not be one here in her private chamber? A peep hole in the wall, or in the ceiling?

She moistened her lips. She must not delay. She threw herself into the work arranging the gowns on the table. During these minutes she heard nothing more except the rustle of Macquinet silk and her own light tread as she moved around the table.

She could delay no longer. If she were to take this risk, now was the time. The Queen Mother could return, or Madalenna, or one of the ladies.

Her gaze raced through the chamber again, taking in the diamond-shaped windows set in arches overlooking the town of Chambord. The walls were of dark wood, decorated with a crowned *C* and a monogram in gold. Catherine's oratory had a large oval window where the light poured through upon an altar. Rachelle wondered about the altar. Sebastien had told her that Catherine was not a Catholic, not Christian, but placed her trust in soothsayers and dabbled in the dark satanic arts.

Her writing closet had many concealed drawers and there were secret entries in the walls — including a stairway leading to an observatory. Rachelle wondered if the Queen Mother had not followed those stairs up to the third floor gallery where she had watched Fabien and her on the gallery one floor below. There was a small room for her sleeping chamber with a built-in recess for her bed. The same gold monogram was embroidered in stunning work on the coverlet.

With every muscle tightening into knots, Rachelle made her move. So much depended on this success.

She went into the closet to the multitudinous sets of intricately carved drawers. There was a tall bureau. With clumsy, shaking fingers she counted down — one, two, three, four — seven, eight — Rachelle opened the drawer. A petite box of filigree gold that looked to be from Florence, Italy, stared at her. Rachelle opened it, saw the key, took it, and dropped it down her bodice. It might have been a dagger, so startling did the gray metal feel against her sweating skin. Breathing tensely, she shut the drawer and rushed back into the main chamber. She pushed a strand of hair away from her forehead and gathering her things, glanced back at the shimmering gowns, then walked out, head straight.

"Merci, mesdames. I shall return to my chamber and await Her Majesty's decision. Adieu."

"Adieu, Mademoiselle Macquinet."

Rachelle left the antechamber and entered the gallery salle once more. She walked slowly back toward the stairway and ascended. Now to take the key to Marquis Fabien.

Chapter Seven

FABIEN WAITED IN A LITTLE-USED ANTECHAMBER ON THE FIRST FLOOR OF the Chambord chateau, directly across from the stairway where he was to meet Rachelle Macquinet. He left his page, Gallaudet, on watch near her approach by the entry arch in case something went wrong.

Fabien paced. Rachelle was late. He bludgeoned himself with rebukes for even considering her entry into Catherine's private chambers. Had he been mad?

Some minutes later he heard heavy footsteps and peered through the crack in the partially open antechamber door. He saw the small entourage with le Cardinal de Lorraine, the younger brother of le Duc de Guise, making lofty progress up the stairs toward the state council chamber. Swiss guards in and around the guardroom fell back as the handsome cardinal swept past with crimson and black cloak floating behind. The cardinal entered the salle de garde to the state council chamber.

Some minutes later, his older brother, le Duc de Guise, followed with his loyal bodyguard of ten men. The duc had many enemies, some who might wish to place a poison dagger through his heart. Fabien's anger began to trouble his mind, making him restless. *You have no proof of his involvement. He may not have had Jean-Louis assassinated. There is only the word of Messires Gaston and Nappier.*

At times like this he felt driven to frustration that he might never know the truth about his father's death. Years had slipped by. As a boy he could do little except wait and plan. Now he wondered if those involved, except for the Guises, might all be dead. Who was there to verify what Nappier thought happened on that day so long ago in the war with Spain when Fabien's father was killed — non, murdered? Nappier, a corsair who had sworn allegiance to Fabien, was now master swordsman in the Royal Armory at the Louvre in Paris, and Gaston was with Admiral Coligny.

If either of the Guise brothers discovered Nappier had spoken to him about Jean-Louis de Vendôme, their lives would be in danger.

Minutes lapsed. Fabien left the antechamber, and crossed the salle to the stairway. When he reached the upper gallery, he stood behind a latticed alcove. He was now closer to the state council chamber where Avenelle would be brought to Catherine and the Guises. Beside him in the alcove was a white marble bench from Florence, veined with gold, and great gilded urns of trailing greenery.

Then, through the lattice, he saw Rachelle coming up the stairs to the second floor where he waited.

He saw no one following her, nor had Gallaudet signaled danger.

Fabien looked for posted guards, saw none, and left the alcove to meet Rachelle on the top of the wide stairway.

He admired her sang-froid. Anyone seeing her would have thought their meeting a chance encounter. He bowed, she curtsied.

"All is well?" he asked in a low, urgent voice.

"All went as planned, Marquis."

"I commend you, Mademoiselle. *Bien joué.*"

"Your page Gallaudet has a message for you," she whispered. "The Queen Mother has left the king's chambers and is on her way now, alone, to the state council chamber. She has taken the main stairway, so you will not see her pass this way."

"Do you have it?" he said urgently.

She casually opened her palm, revealing the key.

Fabien caught up her hand and bent over it. "Merci, ma cherie. I shall return it to you before Catherine misses it."

"Adieu."

He watched her depart down the stairs. Gallaudet would be waiting to follow her at a discreet distance to see her safely returned.

Fabien turned, holding the key, then his gaze rammed into an intruder. Saintes! He was being observed.

Comte Maurice de Beauvilliers, Sebastien's nephew, loitered at the far side of the gallery near the very steps Fabien must take to the listening closet adjoining the state council chambers. *Catherine might even at this moment be preparing to bring Avenelle into the council.*

Fabien bit the bridle of impatience. In a concealed movement he slipped the key into his pocket. His manner must portray his usual confidence. He walked in a leisurely pace toward Maurice.

FABIEN HAD BEEN BUT TWELVE YEARS when his widowed father Jean-Louis de Bourbon married Sebastien's younger sister Antoinette, making Fabien and Maurice cousins. Although he and Maurice were near the same age, they were not close; they did not share comaraderie of souls. *No David and Jonathan, to be sure.*

Thinking back, Fabien told himself he might have been kinder to his stepmother. She had been much in love with his father and had tried to win Fabien's amour, but he had held back, angry that his father had married so soon after his mother died. Then his father was assassinated eleven years ago outside Calais. Poor, grieving Antoinette had died a short time later when taking an interval of rest at the Louvre at Catherine's invitation. Afterward, Fabien had become Sebastien's ward until his Bourbon kinsman contested the decision. King Henry relented and Fabien was made a ward of Prince Louis de Condé. Thereafter Fabien had grown up making the rounds of the royal chateaus between visiting his blood kinsmen in Moulins, Vendôme, Châtillon, and Chantilly. Fabien had recently come of independent age and now inherited his own marquisat of Vendôme.

Fabien's kinsmen were many, some were enemies; others, like Maurice, were constant competitors. Maurice was a goad to be endured with friendly irritation. Fabien had not yet decided whether Maurice would emerge an enemy or a reluctant ami.

Maurice wore a ruby encircled with diamonds in his earlobe, and his lean fingers sparkled with various rings. At other times he adorned himself with exquisite pins, pendants, and bracelets. He always dressed in colorful satins, brocades, and feathers, and was not above using rouge on cheeks and lips. Today he wore a pretty velvet maroon cap with a pink flower in the rim ribbon.

Fabien had a mischievous urge to pluck the flower, knowing it would so enrage Maurice that he might forget anything he had noticed about Rachelle.

"You forget yourself, Maurice," he said with affected gravity.

Maurice's brows shot up as if he did not understand. Fabien knew he did, but out of pride wished to avoid proper protocol. Because Fabien was a marquis, next below a duc and a prince, and because he was of the blood royal, Maurice was obligated to offer his deference. Fabien enjoyed making the proud popinjay sip his cup of humility. Maurice had always envied his title and future marquisat by right of birth through Jean-Louis. When a boy, Maurice often insisted on playing the role of a duc. If he did not get his way, he ran to Françoise, his maman. After being coddled, Maurice would tell Fabien, "If I had your Bourbon blood, I would become king. Why would you turn away from Marguerite when it gives you the chance to marry a Valois?"

"Margo is an amie. But knowing you, you would marry an enfant or an old woman to become a duc. And if you had royal blood as I have, you would poison your Grandmère to snatch the throne, I assure you."

Maurice had kicked his shin and Fabien had pushed him into a muddy patch.

As Fabien locked gazes with Maurice near the stairway, no longer children but young men, Maurice's melting gray eyes measured Fabien, but at last he straightened from the wall where he had been leaning and bowed gracefully.

"Monsieur de Vendôme," he acknowledged silkily, then straightened again.

Fabien smiled lazily. "Bonjour, mon cousin, mon ami. Now, tell me. Why do you tiptoe about the stairs? Spying again, are you ... for the House of Guise, perhaps?"

The accusation would put him on defense at once.

"Ha, very shrewd, Marquis Fabien, I swear it. But you will not throw me off course with your deliberate accusations. I have observed a sight most interesting—you cozying up to the belle mademoiselle Macquinet."

"Ah, but you need not concern yourself since Françoise Beauvilliers is plotting your advancement at court by trying to arrange your marriage to Duchesse Belangée, a woman who turns seventy this year."

Maurice's face became ruddy. His shoulders stiffened beneath his velvet. "Did not His Majesty King Henry II love Diane de Poitiers?"

"I would not venture to guess what fires burned in His Majesty's bosom."

Maurice straightened the lace hanging at his satin cuff. A haughty sniff sounded from his nose. "When Duchesse Belangée dies—and as you say, she is aging—and should Maman arrange my marriage to her, all Belangée's wealth and lands become *mine*." Maurice's lips turned with satisfaction.

"Ah yes, and the fat ruby from Charles V. I remember it well . . . from afar. I would be surprised if you did not now possess it. It was easily bartered for."

Maurice narrowed his long eyes. "You insult me." His hand dropped to his rapier, but Fabien lifted a brow.

"Come, come. Away with offensive airs. We know one another well, do we not?" He said then, in a serious voice: "Draw your rapier, and you will have made a foolish error."

Above them on the stair landing, firm footsteps interrupted, and they glanced up.

Two of the royal Swiss guardsmen, carrying halberds and wearing black velvet doublets with slashed sleeves and feathered hats, looked down suspiciously. The captain, one of the guards, recognized Fabien and bowed.

"It is you, Monsieur de Vendôme. I did not mean to interrupt. This section is secured as Her Majesty orders, and we heard voices."

Fabien saw his chance to be rid of Maurice. Afterward he would return and enter the secret listening booth.

"It is of no matter, Capitaine. My cousine and I are on our way back to our chambers. Is the order still on to journey to Amboise?"

"It is, Monsieur. We leave in the morning."

"Do you know why His young Majesty gave this order?"

"No, Marquis, it was not King Francis but le Duc de Guise who ordered the departure. The Queen Mother then authorized it."

Le Duc de Guise. Fabien was convinced now that he was plotting vice. He saw Maurice eyeing the Swiss guardsmen suspiciously.

"Is mon oncle, Comte Sebastien Dangeau, in the council chamber, Capitaine?" Maurice asked.

"Non, Comte, there is no one here yet."

So Rachelle was correct when she had mentioned that Maurice too was trying to locate Sebastien.

The news that neither the Guises nor Avenelle had as yet been received by Catherine heartened Fabien. There may yet be time to ensconce himself inside the listening closet. He had to dispose of Maurice.

Fabien took the lead and departed the gallery. He reached the first floor salle and glanced over his shoulder with impatience. Maurice followed down the stairs in lazy fashion. When he reached the bottom stair, Fabien grasped his arm and led him aside by one of the oriel windows.

"We must talk about our oncle."

Maurice wore a moody face, brushing his satin sleeve as though Fabien had smudged it.

"What is happening with Sebastien?" Fabien asked.

"How should I know? I have been looking for him. One of the guards thought he might attend the council meeting. That is why I waited on the gallery."

Fabien frowned. "Then no one has seen Sebastien since early this morning. It is not like him."

"No. His absence at court is troubling. He was worried."

"What made you believe so?"

Maurice shrugged. "He used his lace handkerchief too much, always blotting his forehead. Most unbecoming at the feast table."

"That is very telling, mon cousine. Did he speak of his concerns, any hints at all?"

Maurice looked out the window at the forest, then glanced around them. "Non."

"Do you know something more?" Fabien demanded. "For Sebastien's sake, this is no time to withhold anything. Who knows whether our oncle may be in disfavor?"

All sparring between them vanished.

"I have wondered if there might not be some calamity waiting in the wings," Maurice admitted in a hushed tone.

"What do you know?"

"It is not that I know anything, but there is to be a meeting between Her Majesty and the Guises. And did not le Duc de Guise bring a stranger with his face concealed to court but a few hours ago? I have learned this stranger's name: Avenelle, a Huguenot."

But of course Maurice would have discovered this. He had his own ring of spies and made it his ambition to learn everything he could, hoping it would aid him in whatever purposes he involved himself in at court. He had learned the art of intrigue from his mother.

"A Huguenot? Pray tell, why has our galant Duc brought such a miserable heretic here to court?" Fabien pretended scorn.

"I swear I do not know, but have you heard how this Huguenot has renounced his Calvinist beliefs?"

Then Madame Macquinet was right. Avenelle had been a spy among the Huguenots and now was their betrayer. Unless, at the fear of being turned over to le cardinal's inquisitors, his courage broke.

"And pray, what business is of such importance that the court would move to Amboise to fulfill it?" Fabien said.

"One wonders."

"Perhaps one of our other cousines has seen Sebastien. You go to see Andelot."

Maurice's mouth curled with disdain. "Andelot? A *cousine?* By all the devils, what are you hinting? I pray, reconsider. He is socially inferior."

"A cousine, nonetheless." Fabien was attached to Andelot as one might be attached to a younger brother.

"Why do you befriend him?" Maurice scorned. "His harlot mother gave him birth in a ditch behind the battlefield. He was born while the cannons were being fired at those cursed British."

"So that explains his disposition," Fabien said lightly, disliking, but accustomed to the pride of the nobility.

"It is no amusing matter. But for the concern of Oncle Louis Dangeau he would have died an enfant, his remains left for the carrion."

"You are a heartless wretch. Sainte Denis! You task him with his ill birth, but was it not your blood oncle, this Louis Dangeau of whom you boast, who impregnated her?"

"I swear, but you are an odd one, Marquis. If I were in your boots, I would have him wiping them clean and rubbing down my horse. But you? You permit him to take advantage of your protective comraderie."

"Andelot is without guile. I find him a refreshing change from all the ambitious noblemen at court. But take heed; it may be that Andelot will one day surprise you. The footprints of ancestry may lead to unlikely places."

Maurice's eyes flickered uneasily. "What is meant by this?"

"You will live to see it for yourself, I am certain."

"What do you know? Why was he brought here? Ah, there is more you are not telling me, mon cousine Marquis. Even so, if I were a marquis such as you, I would gain a following and plan how I should take the throne—"

"And find your head lolling in the Seine ere long. I have my own plans." He thought of the Dutch corsairs again. "For your tongue alone, mon cousine, Catherine would have you carved on her table. The walls have ears, mon ami, so be careful of your words when you speak of seizing the Valois throne. Else I may need to use my men-at-arms just to free you from her dungeon."

Maurice smirked. "Would you? Ho! Now there's a wonder."

"But do not count on my grace," Fabien added heartlessly. "I may instead choose a choice seat at the carving table."

Maurice appeared to take the warning of listening ears seriously. He cast a glance about. He took out his gold snuffbox, took a pinch, and inhaled it delicately at each nostril.

"And what do you plan? About Oncle Sebastien I mean? I doubt our peasant cousine knows what is afoot."

"Nor do I. So we must find out. If you will not honor Andelot with your awesome presence, then do at least inquire from your other cousine, the soldier ... Julot Cazalet, is it not?"

"You know his name," Maurice smirked. "He is loyal to you, as is the master swordsman Nappier."

Fabien waved his remark aside. "Is Julot not at the armory?"

"Julot Cazalet—another peasant—yes, at the armory. Doubtless he knows little of these intrigues. Julot is slow-witted, a barbarian, a soldier, an archer."

"Do not count on his thick mind. Soldiers and guards are well-informed." Fabien's amusement was sardonic. "This barbarian Julot, I saw him at sword practice with Nappier this morning at the armory. He is *par exemple* in wielding the blade. If he is a barbarian, then I desire such barbarians on my side."

Fabien knew Maurice prided himself on use of the rapier and looked offended.

"Thunder. I could best Julot."

"By your life, may you never try, mon ami. Now, for Sebastien's sake, waste no more time. Go to the armory, talk to Julot."

Maurice regarded him, then gave a nod of grudging assent. He sauntered off, the flower on his cap bobbing.

Fabien shook his head ruefully, and when Maurice was out of view, turned to look toward the stairway. Fabien dashed up the stairs and back along the gallery from which he had come.

He neared the wall where the tapestry of King Francis I concealed the small, secret door.

At last! But was he in time?

Chapter Eight

Marquis Fabien stood on the second floor gallery in Chambord Palais. The two Swiss guardsmen had returned to their salle de garde which connected with the state council chamber on the floor above. He centered his gaze onto the heavy gold fringed wall tapestry of Francis I, with his aquiline nose and small, sharp eyes, his dashing figure in full regalia. This was the place Rachelle Macquinet had indicated to him earlier that morning. If she was correct, and he had no reason to doubt her, the priceless tapestry concealed a small door to a secret stairway and a listening closet outside the council chamber.

Fabien glanced along the gallery to make certain he was not being observed. The moment was clear.

He went straight to the tapestry and, satisfied no one was near at hand, lifted it aside. *Yes, a small oval door.* He used the key Rachelle had removed from Catherine de Medici's secretary of drawers in her royal chamber.

The door unlocked; he ducked under its rim and entered a dark void, allowing the heavy tapestry to settle smoothly into position. He closed the door behind him.

Fabien stood cloistered in darkness, breathing the stale air of ancient construction. His sight adjusted to a dim beam of light above and ahead, reached by a steep, narrow set of steps which he assumed would bring him near the council chamber.

He felt his way cautiously. After a minute he reached a square platform no more than two feet wide, railed on either side, known as a secret step. In the darkness he saw a bright spot—the peephole. Looking through it, he was greeted with a grand scene—the interior of the state council chamber with its long square table and chairs. A large window with brocade draperies looked onto a spring garden. The hole was located somewhere high in the council chamber wall, and it commanded a view of most of the chamber.

Someone had recently installed a listening tube, no doubt on orders from Catherine de Medici to one of the loyal Italian lackeys, or dwarves, she kept. Fabien suspected she might occasionally choose not to attend certain council meetings in order to spy on the king's counselors to hear what they said on certain matters in her absence. She took perverse enjoyment in such activities. He was reminded again how much he distrusted Madame le Serpent.

Fabien centered his eye on the peephole and saw Catherine, garbed in black, pacing. *Where were the Guises and Avenelle?*

The Queen Mother ceased her pacing, became very still, and stared straight toward him. The hair bristled at the back of his neck, as he almost credited her with knowing he was watching. He could imagine himself standing on a trapdoor with controls at her fingertips that would drop him into a pit of poisonous snakes.

She looked away, staring elsewhere, as though deep in thought. Fabien rebuked his reaction. The hole would be undetectable from inside the chamber except to those who knew it was there. She did know, of course, but would have no reason to believe anyone was watching her, as *she* had watched countless others while hatching evil designs against them.

The Queen Mother continued to stand perfectly still. Then, abruptly, she lifted her head. Fabien saw the stern face, the unblinking eyes, as though a decision had been reached in her cunning. She strode to the long council table in the midst of the chamber, surrounded by chairs, picked up a mallet, and struck a gong.

The door to the connecting guard chamber opened. Fabien could see two of the royal Swiss guards inside. A dainty page boy hurried in and bowed to her.

She commanded boldly: "Call for Maître Avenelle to come to me at once."

Her voice came plainly to Fabien even without the listening tube.

With his eye to the hole he wondered that the Guises were not present, unless they were seated in a corner of the chamber out of his view — though he had not heard them, and it seemed unlikely they would remain mute.

A short time later the door opened and a guard hauled in a nervous man with sallow skin and a thin, wasted figure.

Yes, this is Avenelle. I recognize him. Fabien felt pity and scorn. *Le misérable! What has happened to him? He is like death housed in skin!* But do I need wonder what has befallen him?

Catherine de Medici was seated opposite him at a writing table, a pen in her hand and parchment before her. Avenelle stood facing her, and Fabien had a good view of the side of his face as well as of Catherine's.

"Your M-Majesty," came his tremulous voice.

Fabien narrowed his gaze. *No matter who a man may be, none should cringe and fawn before such an unrighteous ruler.*

He realized that his thoughts were treasonous and had emerged quite unexpectedly. In questioning the Queen Mother's right to rule, he questioned the authority of the throne of France.

"Maître Avenelle," Catherine demanded, "Le Duc de Guise and his brother, le Cardinal de Lorraine, have spoken to me of grave information you claim to be true. Tell me! When did you speak to the duc?"

Pale, he intertwined his fingers, pulling on them.

He bowed again, too humbly. "I spoke to the duc this very day. Monsieur Marmagne, his secretary, first brought me here to Blois from Paris so that I may speak to your sacred person."

"I see. So you are a barrister, Maître Avenelle?"

"Oui, I am that, Your Majesty."

"I see. A friend of Seigneur Barri de la Renaudie from the Bourbon region of Moulins and Berry?"

At the mention of the Bourbon region Fabien became convinced Prince Condé was in danger.

"I *was* his friend, Madame," he hastened.

Catherine's twisted mouth was visible. "Ah," she said with dripping scorn. "But no longer his ami. I see. This *leader* of the vile Huguenot plot of which le Duc de Guise has been warned by the Catholics of England — you are willing to betray Renaudie to me?"

Avenelle's face turned ruddy. His nervous fingers traveled up and down the front of his surcoat.

"I — I do not wish Your Majesty or that of our cher King Francis to be injured by these zealot heretics, Madame."

"How kind of you, Maître Avenelle," came her sarcastic voice. "You are most generous. Now tell me. Have you been paid well by the duc's secretary, Marmagne, to tell all you know of this plot?"

Again, he fumbled, turning an ugly color. "Yes, Madame." He swallowed. "I have come at the duc's will to inform you of what I know of a grave Huguenot conspiracy ... and le Duc de Guise has rewarded me."

Fabien tensed. *A plot?* If Prince Condé were in any way involved, and Sebastien with them, it would mean their deaths. But how could there be such a plot? Would he himself not be aware? But knowing Louis Condé, he might not have wanted to involve him in such a risk. Fabien recalled several Bourbon-Huguenot alliance meetings he had not been told about until afterward, as though Louis did not want him there.

"And you have confessed to the duc all you know of this wickedness?" Catherine almost shouted.

Avenelle cringed. "Oui, Madame, I — I have confessed all."

She bounced from her high-back gilded chair, pointing a finger at him. "You had best hope so, Maître Avenelle. Oh, you had best hope so, I swear it."

He bowed low, both hands pressed against his heart.

Cringing coward, Fabien thought with disgust. *Betrayer.*

"This plot is hatched by Calvinists, is that so?" she inquired.

"Yes, Madame, entirely."

Fabien gritted his teeth.

"How many Huguenots are involved?"

"Over two thousand, Madame."

Two thousand! Fabien stared.

Catherine sank back in her high-backed chair as though receiving a blow. Her face hardened with surprise, then fury. She pushed herself to her feet again and strode toward him. Avenelle sank to his knees.

"It is why I have come, to warn Your Majesty — "

"Silence, worm! Who — *who* is at the head of these rebels? I demand the truth! Speak! If you hold back their names, I shall have you delivered to the torturers to be flayed alive."

Avenelle was shaking so violently now that Fabien wondered if he would become sick to his stomach. Could the poor creature even speak without his teeth biting his tongue?

The vicious tone of Catherine's voice and her autocratic manner had him paralyzed. Watching such a foul, despicable scene, Fabien clenched his fist. *Diabolical woman.*

"Speak!" she cried. "Or I swear I shall have you put to the screw!"

Avenelle wiped his dripping forehead on the back of his sleeve. "I-I am unable to f-find my voice — "

Catherine walked around the table and looked down at him, waving her hand with an impatient gesture.

"Fool! You will answer me, Maître Avenelle. The torture chamber is at hand; the way of wisdom will loosen your tongue or you will have none with which to speak either truth or lies."

"Oh Madame, oh Madame . . . I am come to tell you all."

"Who, then, is at the head of this plot? Their names. I want their names."

"That heretic Prince Condé, Madame."

"So."

Fabien's fingers tightened convulsively on his sword hilt.

"And Admiral Coligny?"

"Non. Though the admiral knows of the plot, perhaps . . . I cannot swear for certain, Madame, but his brother Monsieur Odet, le Cardinal de Châtillon knows, but — but they are not involved as deeply. They will not draw swords."

"Hah," Catherine said. "Go on, Maître Avenelle."

"The military leader of the plot is Barri de la Renaudie; but, Madame, he is a subordinate acting under Prince Louis de Condé's orders. Heretics all, Your Majesty."

"Heretics you call them?" she mocked. "You yourself are a Huguenot, is that not so?"

"Oh, Madame, I am no longer a Calvinist, I assure you."

"No?" she continued with scorn. "Why so?"

"Le Duc de Guise has — has helped me to see that I was wrong, Madame, and to recant."

A crisp, mocking laugh came boldly from her lips. "Indeed, Maître Avenelle! How tender the shepherding heart of our great le Balafré and his brother the cardinal. I swear their concern for your soul and the souls of all the Huguenots in France is wondrous to behold. Has the pope yet struck a medal celebrating their love for their enemies, Maître Avenelle, as he has before?"

"I do not know, Madame," came the shaking voice.

"This Renaudie, this Huguenot retainer under Prince Louis de Condé, is he not the commander, your bon ami? Did he not lodge with you as a brother in Paris?"

Avenelle was staring at the chamber floor. He spoke, but Catherine interrupted: "I cannot understand you, Maître Avenelle. Speak up."

"Yes, Madame. He did stay with me in Paris for a short time, but no longer. You see, I will have no bon ami who is not loyal to your sacred person and to the sacred person of King Francis Valois."

"And the Guises? Do not forget to mention the House of Guise," she said with stinging mockery. "One would think, Maître Avenelle, that the Guises were as much a part of the royal Valois family as my own sons!"

Avenelle cringed and kept silent.

The Queen Mother stalked about the chamber, her stiff skirts swaying, reminding Fabien of a giant dark bird ready to swoop down and eat the flesh of her enemy.

"Maître Avenelle, tell me the purpose of this Huguenot plot."

She walked to her chair of state, ornamented with the arms of France, and placed on a dais covered with thick carpet. She sat down, her eyes on Avenelle.

"Your Majesty, the Huguenots all say you are the power that governs France, not your son, His Majesty Francis II, and that under your rule freedom of worship and justice will never be granted Frenchmen of the Protestant belief; they say, Madame, that you seek the counsel of le Duc de Guise and le Cardinal de Lorraine, who are even more bitterly opposed than you are to Protestant interests. Therefore they have addressed themselves to Prince de Condé who is believed to share their opinions, both political and religious, for present redress. The conspirators propose, Madame, to place His Highness Prince de Condé on the throne as regent, in your place, until—until such measures are taken as will confirm their independence from burnings."

Fabien stifled a groan. This would mean the end of Condé—unless he formed an army. A religious civil war in France would rip the nation in two.

"The Bourbon-Huguenot alliance think to put Your Majesty under palais confinement; send the young king and queen to some unfortified place—such as here at Chambord or Chenonceau—and then banish the Guise brothers from France."

Better to kill them, Fabien thought, his emotions like ice. *And I, for one, would gladly put the sword to the duc.* Fabien's heart thudded evenly in his chest. But what of Sebastien? Thus far Avenelle had not mentioned him.

I must alert Louis that Avenelle has betrayed them, and the plot is known.

Avenelle had finished speaking. Catherine's face was tight with rage. Then her voice shattered the silence, a sudden clear and unemotional command, showing Fabien she was once more in control.

"Proceed, Maître Avenelle."

"U-under Renaudie, two thousand Huguenots expect to come here to Chambord from various points of Nantes to attack on the fifteenth of this month of March."

Saintes! Fabien thought. *It was almost the fifteenth now.*

Catherine stood looking unexpectedly calm and cold. Her face was still, and her eyes took on a steady, almost hypnotic stare.

"So le Duc de Guise spoke the truth to me when he ordered the royal court to the fortress castle of Amboise."

Now matters were slowly unfolding to Fabien. The unexpected call to journey to Amboise came from Guise as a military tactic to thwart the attack of Renaudie's army.

"Have you told me everything, Maître Avenelle?"

"Oui, all. I swear it. Have mercy and remember, I beg of you, that it was I, Avenelle, your humble, devoted servant who has saved Your Majesty and the young King Francis from their evil schemes."

Catherine swung toward him, lifting a hand and pointing. Avenelle flinched as though she had hurled a whip.

"You will be kept a prisoner until His Majesty's council tests the truth of your information. If you have told me the truth, I will spare your life.

Even so, when this is over, you will leave France forever, is that understood? If I find you have lied, you will surely die, Avenelle. I swear it. Now go from my presence." She turned her back to him and strode to the window.

Her words echoed through the lofty chamber. She struck the metal gong. Two guards entered, grabbed Avenelle's thin arms, and took him away.

Fabien leaned against the wall, staring in the darkness, frowning, calming his fervid brain. Avenelle had not mentioned Sebastien as one of the plotters. This bode better for his head staying in place than Fabien would have dared to hope only an hour ago. But where was he? Did le Duc de Guise and le Cardinal de Lorraine have him under bolt somewhere in the palais chateau questioning him even now to gain new information and names of Huguenots?

Fabien must find a way to warn Louis Condé, who in turn could warn Renaudie that their plot was known. Or was it already too late? Perhaps even now Renaudie's troops were gathering in the forest for the march to Blois?

Neither the duc nor the cardinal had arrived to discuss Catherine's meeting with Avenelle. Fabien watched her throw back her shoulders. With a bold step she walked toward the door, her black skirts rustling. She threw open the large, heavy door and barked a command, then she passed through into what he knew to be the salle de garde.

Fabien scowled. She was leaving. Why hadn't the Guises been present? Where had they gone after he saw them climb the stairs? Were they badgering Sebastien in some dank chamber?

Fabien fought against the wash of helpless rage that pounded his mind. Rushing about with haste and thunder would gain him nothing. He must plan his every step with clear thought. If the enemy suspected he was aware, they would move against him in a moment's notice.

Fabien had no time to linger; he needed to escape the listening closet now while the moment was in his grasp. He dare not meet Catherine de Medici a second time today loitering near the state council chamber.

RACHELLE WAS STUNNED when word arrived that all work on Reinette Mary and Princesse Marguerite's wardrobe was to be postponed until further notice from the Queen Mother. The Macquinets were to pack their grand arsenal of precious materials and return to the Chateau de Silk in Lyon. The news came as a complete surprise.

"What of Her young Majesty's accessories?" Idelette asked the royal page in blue and gold satin.

"The royal retinue will be leaving for Amboise. The accessories must wait for another time, Mademoiselle Macquinet."

Rachelle was pleased that she had at least completed Marguerite's burgundy and cloth of gold. But what would the princesse think of the stoppage? She had wanted other gowns for the summer. Knowing Marguerite, she would not at all be satisfied.

The page departed, and Grandmère clasped her hands together and took a turn about the chamber. "I am worried about your sister. What will Madeleine do when she hears Sebastien is missing? And the enfant due within weeks! Ah, ça non! If I could join her at Paris — but the Queen Mother will assuredly desire us to work on the royal wardrobe at Lyon." Grandmère sighed and took Rachelle's arm. She drew her aside and spoke in a low voice.

"You heard the page. I am called away to oversee the packing and storage of the bolts of silk. The marquis should come soon with the key. Let us anticipate that all went well. Wait for him and explain what has happened. The key, bien sûr, will need to be returned."

Rachelle and Grandmère exchanged worried glances as Idelette came toward them.

"I will go with you, Grandmère. I can be of assistance as overseer," Idelette said.

Rachelle and Nenette were left to fold and wind the various bolts of cloth and lace remaining in the chamber on the shelves.

Rachelle found it difficult to concentrate. Bolts of cloth remained on the long cutting table waiting to be stored in trunks, when growing restive, she sent Nenette to keep watch at the outer chamber door for a sign of Marquis Fabien. Had matters gone well?

Nenette opened the door a crack and peered out for some minutes before she hissed: "He comes, he is in a hurry — la, la — how beau he is, I shall swoon!"

Rachelle snapped her fingers. "Shh, Nenette. Show yourself dignified, I pray you. Show him in at once — and remember his station with a curtsy."

"Oui, Mademoiselle. I know, I know."

Rachelle drew in a deep breath, arranging herself near the bolts of silk in a languid stance that she had seen Princesse Marguerite use. She checked her wealth of hair to make certain it showed to its optimum beauty. The arrangement that she and Nenette had labored on so long after déjeuner was of courtly fashion, a bundle of braided sections mingled with petite curls into a waterfall, which then cascaded down her back and across her left shoulder.

Nenette stepped into the outer corridor to welcome the marquis inside. Rachelle waited, aware that her heart fluttered with strange excitement and fear. What had he discovered from the listening closet?

The marquis entered the chamber. He must be the most handsome man at court. His glance told her of his approval, making the work she had done on her hair worth the effort.

"Mademoiselle," he said smoothly. He then looked toward Nenette with what Rachelle took as a suggestion for her dismissal.

"That will be all for now, Nenette, you may go," Rachelle told her.

When the girl had left them, Fabien stepped closer to Rachelle and took hold of her hand. Her heart leaped at his touch.

"Where is Madame Henriette?"

"She and Idelette are packing. We have been ordered back to Lyon. I will return the key to the Queen Mother's chamber. Whatever the news, do not fear to report it to me. I will inform Grandmère with my utmost caution."

He remained solemn, convincing her he had discovered reasons for travail. She was suddenly ashamed of her actions. Here she was trying to capture his interest when Sebastien and her fellow Huguenots might be in danger.

"The stranger with Guise was indeed Maître Avenelle, who has betrayed the leaders of the Bourbon-Huguenot alliance. The Queen Mother knows everything."

A queasy wave rolled over Rachelle's stomach. She listened in dismay as he went on to give a brief, hurried account of how Avenelle uncovered a Huguenot plot to overthrow the House of Guise and secure an end to Huguenot persecution throughout France.

"And Sebastien?"

"I can only assure Madame Henriette that Avenelle did not mention Sebastien's name to Catherine, but that in no way clears him for the future. The Queen Mother's ways are often strange and Machiavellian."

"Then Maître Avenelle would not know Sebastien is a Huguenot?"

"Do not rely on that. Catherine may already know it to be true and merely be waiting.

She could see his thoughts racing, trying to make sense of the details he had heard. The twists and turns of the events also confused her.

"These are the days of danger, ma cherie," he said gently.

He had called her that endearing name before, though they had only recently met. That he did so brought unusual happiness, yet the emotions it evoked also made her wary. It would be a long time before she was likely to forget that fiery embrace on the gallery, but her Grandmère was right to consider where her interest in le marquis would end.

He walked to the window and looked into the courtyard. "The plot to rid France of the Guises was to have occurred here at Blois. Now with the court to depart for the fortress of Amboise in the morning, why do I feel that there is something amiss in all of this?"

He turned from the window, scowling, and looked as if he would speak, but then glanced at the table where several dazzling bolts of silk were awaiting transport back to Lyon.

"You are readying to return to Lyon, I see. Do you have men-at-arms to see to your safe traveling?"

"We have servants from the Chateau de Silk. Perhaps five are able to use a sword."

He walked to the long table where a bolt of pale green silk had caught his attention and touched the cloth. He moved to the burgundy silk gown over the cloth of gold belonging to Marguerite.

"Were you thinking of bandits, Monsieur Fabien?"

"Yes, bandits," he said absently. "Five men are hardly enough with such rich booty to be taken as a prize." But his sweeping glance of her intimated a wider meaning. "I will send a dozen of my men and two swordsmen with your Grandmère for the journey. You will tell her for me? I may not see her again by morning. I have some matters to attend this night."

"Monsieur is most kind."

He looked at her with a brief, wry smile. "It is not kindness. This burgundy silk, it pleases me. Is there enough to make another gown of the manner of this one?" He gestured to Marguerite's gown.

She joined him at the table. "By all means." She released several folds of the burgundy onto the table and held it so that light from the chamber window caused it to shimmer. "The silk, it is always in the process of being replenished through our silkworms. We have *mûreraies* groves to feed them, you see. If we did not, we would soon have no silk business in Lyon."

"Silkworms," he said thoughtfully, as though his mind were on anything but that.

Rachelle tucked her lips into a small amused smile and carried on with gravity. "Yes, thousands upon thousands of petite worms, Marquis Fabien. We Macquinets have the finest silk filaments in France ... and Italy, I promise you. Grandmère knows of but one family in all Italy who is able to match the silk we produce. Ours is of a finer grade than anything made even in Assam, India, or the East."

He smiled lazily, but his violet blue eyes were anything but casual as they looked at her. "I do not doubt it at all. I have long heard of Macquinet silk, but when Duchesse Louise-Marie, my mother, had gowns made, the chateau was called Dushane-Macquinet."

She shrugged gracefully. "Oh, it remains so. You see, Grandmère is a Dushane, and of course, Maman. We merged with my père's family, the Macquinets. The two families were competitors at one time, but amour has brought us all together."

His smile lost its grace. "If only amour could bring Catholics and Huguenots together."

"It is not we Huguenots, Marquis Fabien, who are lighting the faggots and burning women and children."

She saw the lazy gleam in his eyes harden into iron.

"You task us all with brutish severity, Mademoiselle. I assure you, having come from generations of Catholics, we are not all anxious to light the flames below heretics or to stand and gape at another's sufferings."

She felt her temper rise, a sign that religious zeal was not always born of the sweetness of the Spirit. Heretic. He had used that word deliberately, she was sure of it. The beau Marquis Fabien de Vendôme could be cynical as well as elegante.

His gaze held hers, watching her, then he smiled unexpectedly and offered a light bow. "I have angered you."

"We have, it appears, angered one another."

"Then let us not discuss religion, Mademoiselle Macquinet. Let us discuss more pleasant things."

"Some would find discussion of religion most pleasant, Marquis."

"They would?"

"Very much, it brings to our minds the precious promises of the One who cannot lie." She looked down at the bolt of burgundy silk again and busied herself.

"I must come one day to the chateau," he said. "You must show me the little silkworms."

She smoothed the creamy Alençon lace on the table. "You will always be welcome, Marquis."

He straightened from the table. "I want a dress made of this silk, with a quantity of gold tissue."

"I should warn you, Monsieur, of the price, for it is most expensive."

"But of course!" He smiled.

"When will you wish this gown to be finished?"

"By June."

She gave him a quick glance, playing with the lace. "We, that is, Grandmère, will need to take precise measurements of the mademoiselle who will wear this gown, you understand, Marquis?"

"You would know best of that. The gown is for you. A gift. I wish to see you wearing it when next we meet in Orléans."

She fumbled with the bolt of silk, nearly dropping it. "Oh, I could not ... but—"

"But yes, ma belle, you *can*, and will," he said softly. "It is what I wish, you see. And I do not wish to be disappointed."

"What ... you wish ...?"

And again he smiled at her discomfiture, as though he enjoyed surprising her. "I shall assure your Grandmère all is well and upright. She is a reasonable woman, is she not?"

She straightened. "Yes, but ..."

Fabien laughed. "Then I am sure she will listen to me."

"And you are a reasonable man?" Rachelle laughed. "I think, Marquis, you expect to always have your way. But in this situation, perhaps—"

"Not always, ma cherie Rachelle; only sometimes. The payment will be made in full before we leave Chambord. Now it is settled." He picked up his wide-brimmed hat from the cherry table by the chamber wall. "I must depart."

He went to the door and she followed. He turned and bowed, and taking her hand once again, this time pressed the secret key against her palm. His touch would have sent her heart tripping, except for the sobriety in his eyes. She felt naught but the burdensome key, as though it weighed as much as the chains in the Bastille.

"I would not risk your going back into her royal chambers," the marquis said. "I shall find some other way to return the key."

"That would be most difficult, would it not? I assure you I can replace it without her notice. Marguerite's gowns, which I brought there for her perusal, will need to be collected so the demoiselles can pack them for the trip to Amboise."

"I rebuke myself for having encouraged you to take the key the first time. If she suspects at all, ma cherie, she will forever be your enemy. And I, I could do little to save you if Catherine moved suddenly. I have little authority outside Vendôme, while Paris bows at the feet of Guise."

"To their shame, Monsieur. The duc does not measure up to your wisdom or fairness."

He smiled faintly and placed a finger beneath her chin lifting her face. His touch, his intriguing gaze, caught hold of her senses. For a breathtaking moment she expected to find his lips on hers and the thought frightened her. The strong emotions she felt recently were new and dangerous. She did not wish to show them so soon.

Rachelle turned away with a movement of her hand as if to push her hair from her throat.

"You, Monsieur Fabien, must not worry about me. You would be one of the first to say that life is full of risks. *Ma foi* itself, which I have embraced in such a time as this, guarantees a walk shadowed with risks. I must do this for the good of my fellow Huguenots."

There came a moment of silence. Then his voice lowered with a serious note. "You enchant me, Mademoiselle. I meet few women of your inner qualities. If it is your faith, then I commend its mastery of you — or should I say His mastery? It is most memorable, I promise you."

"That you would think so pleases me more than I dare say, Marquis."

"Then au revoir. I will have my men-at-arms waiting by your calèche in the morning."

"Merci, au revoir, Monsieur Fabien."

He lingered a moment, looked at her, a brief smile on his lips. "And to think only a week ago I was seeking an excuse not to heed the call to come to Chambord. And if I had not come, would we have met elsewhere? I wonder."

As he left, Rachelle looked after him, her heart aflame.

Chapter Nine

After Fabien departed, Rachelle stood for a long moment until her heart calmed again. *Oh, Rachelle, how foolish you are behaving in this matter. He has merely taken a romantic fancy to you, but a lasting one? It is impossible. Do not permit yourself to fall in amoureux with the marquis. Amour and marriage? It is not to be. So what can come of this le coup de foudre?*

I will not think about it now. I will merely enjoy for a short time his exciting attention. After Orléans I will forget Monsieur Fabien.

She thought of the gown he wanted made for her. She wondered what to do about it. Grandmère was not likely to approve, and what of Maman when she returned to Lyon from Geneva?

Ah, but what delight in having such a gown made from the same burgundy silk and gold cloth as Princesse Marguerite's. The marquis was rich, there was no doubt of that, and if he wished to honor her with a gift for helping him get the key ...? How wondrous to wear such a gown at the palais in June, if she managed to attend with Comtesse Claudine.

Rachelle became aware of the key in her hand. She must return it soon. Despite her brave words she knew a chill along her back. *I must show courage. Surely the Lord's grace is with me. The Queen Mother will merely think I have come to reclaim Marguerite's gowns, thinking they were now approved. And it is already late afternoon and the gowns need to be packed carefully for the journey to Amboise.*

The key —

A light click as of a door closing quietly snapped her alert. She turned her head toward one of the doors leading off to other chambers and antechambers; she saw no one.

She tensed. Had someone been listening to the discourse between her and Monsieur Fabien?

Nenette, of course. Rachelle smiled to herself. She was quite fond of her la petite Nenette. Rachelle did not worry about her for she too was a devout Calvinist, and loyal. Nenette already knew of the Macquinet fears over Avenelle and the Huguenots.

Grandmère and Idelette would return soon. How could she tell Grandmère about the belle gown in burgundy silk and gold?

DRESSED IN A PLAIN BLACK GOWN and covered from head to foot in a veil, Catherine de Medici moved quietly about her chamber that was aglow with tapered candles. The crowned *C* above her bed glittered in the candlelight. She walked from her main chamber and entered her closet, locking herself in. She cast her attention to her poison chest. Her gaze fixed upon it. A sense of power pulsated through her heart.

Men are generally so simple and weak that one who wishes to deceive can easily find dupes.

The Guises ... She despised them. The sly, hypocritical cardinal; the proud military bearing of the duc! She must placate them now, but she was planning their ruin. Did they think she was a fool? But yes, she knew they had told the reinette Mary to spy on her.

That foolish Francis had been warned not to marry the Scottish girl—the spy! Catherine curled her lip. Ah, but Henry, her husband, had insisted. And why? Because of his mistress, Diane de Poitiers. She had insisted Francis wed Mary of Scotland.

"Henry was a fool," she murmured bitterly. "But not Diane. She had wanted the marriage because the nasty petite spy, Mary, always did what her oncles, the Guises, told her."

She stared at her poison chest and reached a hand toward it. Then she drew back, her chin lowered, her hand dropped to her side. Though she might wish to remove the Guises, she had to bide her time until she could plot against them. She must move with care. The Guises were watching her closely; one careless move on her part could be disastrous. She was confident that the Guises told their niece to report to them everything she did. Well, she had her own spies, including Madalenna.

Catherine laughed boldly. "Oh yes, I know just what they are all saying and planning behind my back. But in their presence I will pretend innocence. I will remain the humble Italian woman who submitted meekly to Diane de Poitiers, when the hag stole *my* husband from me."

Catherine's wide mouth spread into a frank, contemptuous smile. She had her revenge on the old beauty. She had taken away all the royal jewels Henry gave her and the chateau at Chenonceau that meant so much to her.

Her smile vanished. She would also have her revenge on the Guises — and Mary.

Catherine turned from her poison chest. Patience. For the present she would practice her fine art, which she had been gradually mastering, upon those less significant, who threatened her power.

She left the closet and shut the door, then strode back into her main chamber. She rang the gong. Little Madalenna, whom she had brought with her from Florence, came like a shadowy wraith into the chamber and bowed.

Ah, it is good that you are frightened of me, Catherine thought. *Fear makes for obedient servants.*

Catherine, after having come upon Rachelle Macquinet and Marquis de Vendôme in the gallery, had been suspicious of what the two lovebirds were about. Returning to her chamber, she had ordered Madalenna to watch Rachelle and to glean whatever she could.

"Were you able to enter the Macquinet chamber as I told you, Madalenna?"

"Yes, Madame."

"And did you hide without being noticed?"

"Yes, Madame."

"And now you must tell me everything."

"Yes, Madame. I heard Mademoiselle Rachelle discussing with Madame Henriette Macquinet how she would take the key from your chest."

"What? From my chest! Madalenna, which key?"

"I listened, Madame, but they did not say which key it was."

"And how did she know where to find it?"

"Mademoiselle Rachelle knew of it through Comtesse Claudine Boisseau." Catherine stared at her. *Claudine ... another untrustworthy spy. It was well that I disposed myself from her when I did.*

"Then after some time, a page came and I heard him say that the Queen Mother had left her chamber. Then—"

"Whose page?" Catherine demanded.

"Marquis de Vendôme's page, Gallaudet, Madame. Then Mademoiselle Rachelle brought many gowns to your chamber for Princesse Marguerite."

"And did Mademoiselle Rachelle retrieve the key from my sleeping chamber?"

"Yes, Madame. Later the marquis came and told Mademoiselle Rachelle many things, and that she must take care when she returns the key to the Queen Mother's chamber."

Catherine was turning cold with fury. "And what things did the Marquis tell Mademoiselle Rachelle?"

"I heard him say that the stranger with le Duc de Guise was Maître Avenelle. That he betrayed the leaders of the Bourbon-Huguenots. He said there was a plot that was to have occurred here at Chambord."

"And did the marquis say anything else?"

"He said that the Queen Mother knows everything."

Catherine narrowed her eyes and her fingers formed into fists. *The key to the council chamber listening closet!* That contemptuous fox! A dangerous young man, another Bourbon, a kinsman to Prince Condé and Condé's oncle, Admiral Coligny.

Catherine walked over to the candle on the table and watched the steady, burning glow ... If Fabien had heard her discussion with Avenelle, then he would warn Condé that she knew of the plot. She smiled and her loud, gurgling laughter echoed through the chamber. Little did they know that she was not alarmed over their planned attack on Chambord. She and the Guises were prepared. She looked at Madalenna. The girl stood somberly in the candlelight, unresponsive to the laugher. Ah, Madalenna knew her moods so well.

What to do with Marquis Fabien de Vendôme?

The young marquis was a Bourbon, and as such, was important in the intrigues at court. He was still young, and she had not concerned herself with him. She now realized that the marquis would become a threat in the future as he came into his own. He was much like Jean-Louis, his father. That Fabien had been audacious enough to *dare* eavesdrop on her meeting with Avenelle showed potential. Though enraged, it also amused her. She could wish such a brazen young man was on her side. She could use him, just as she used her escadron volant, for the marquis turned the eyes of the women at court, as Catherine had noticed.

Catherine paced slowly, thoughtfully, her skirts moving. The candle flames flickered upon the priceless tapestries displayed on the walls.

Trickery could work. Her father Lorenzo de Medici had been a protégé of Machiavelli.

"Do you know what Machiavelli wrote, Madalenna?" she turned to look down at the girl.

"No, Madame."

"No?" Catherine mocked, stepping back, hand at heart. "After you have been so long with me? Then I will tell you: 'A prudent Prince cannot and ought not to keep his word, except when he can do it without injury to himself; or when the circumstances under which he contracted the engagement still exist. It is necessary, however, to disguise the appearance of craft and to thoroughly understand the art of feigning or dissembling; for men are generally so simple and weak that he who wishes to deceive, easily finds dupes.'"

Catherine smirked. She walked to the window and drew aside the heavy brocade drapery to look out. A light rain was pummeling the pane.

She had already devised her trickery, using the duc and the cardinal. They too loved deceit. In this matter of the Renaudie plot, she was working side by side with the Guises. After she had met with Avenelle, she and the Guises had met together in another chamber where they had devised a plan to summon the Bourbon-Huguenot princes and nobles to Amboise. She would offer the Huguenots an edict of toleration for freedom of worship signed by her son King Francis. This act of speaking peace while devising death would confuse Prince Condé into thinking their plot, revealed by Avenelle, had frightened her into cooperating. Emboldened by her accommodation, she would lure the unwary Huguenot army under Renaudie to the forest around Amboise —

"And when they come they will be slaughtered, all of them. I tell you, Madalenna, I will hang their headless bodies on the ramparts and fill the Loire River with their rebel heads!"

She would show them what it meant to turn against Catherine de Medici!

She nodded to herself. She widened her smile. She looked over at Madalenna and laughed loudly.

"We will teach them a lesson, ma petite Madelenna," she whispered. "It is good, non?"

"Oui, Madame. It is good."

She paced again. Yes, deception would be her tool of survival. She would fool her enemy into thinking she offered peace. And then—then she would strike.

She stood without moving. That would defang Prince Condé and the handsome Fabien, but there remained Rachelle ...

Catherine's rage remained unabated. She allowed the drapery to fall into place, turned on her heel, and moved restlessly about her chamber.

"I underestimated Rachelle."

Not fearing the Queen Mother's wrath will cost her dearly. She dared take the key from my private chambers? The Macquinet and her family had made an unforgivable error. What else does the spy from Lyon know? And what does Madame Henriette know? And the other grisette—Idelette, was it?

Ah, Rachelle Macquinet knew too much. The three Daughters of Silk knew things that were better kept secret. Did they also know of her poison closet? Of Cosmo, her astrologer? Of the Italian brothers, Ruggiero and Rene, both expert poisoners?

"Thief," she said to the walls of the chamber. "The three of them will pay for their treachery against me."

Catherine turned back to Madalenna, her skirts swishing. The girl stood stiffly, fear written across her face. One eyelid twitched.

"Tell me again what you heard la petite Macquinet and the marquis say to one another in her chambers."

Madalenna licked her lips and repeated the conversation, concluding in a hushed voice: "Madame Dushane wishes she could be at the Louvre Palais when Madame Madeleine Dangeau gives birth."

Catherine smiled at what she had achieved with petite Madalenna. Her fear of being sent back to Florence to Alessandro the abuser had kept her loyal these years.

"And now, Madalenna, see that my petit Italians are sent to me at once."

"Yes, Madame." Madalenna bowed very low, then fled to do her bidding.

CATHERINE WAITED PATIENTLY. So Madame Henriette worried about her eldest granddaughter, Madeleine, did she? Henriette wished to go to Paris to be with Sebastien's wife when she gave birth?

"Well, then, she will go. Far be it from me to keep them apart."

Catherine's mouth turned into a contemptuous smile.

The Ruggiero brothers entered her chamber by the back stairs, wearing dark capes. They bowed, and she came straight to her business.

"Where are the gloves I ordered?"

"They are here, Madame. We have brought several pairs already made for you, Your Majesty."

"You are certain that when drawn onto a lady's slender hands, the poison produces death?"

The two Ruggiero brothers from Italy looked dolefully at one another and spoke in hushed Italian.

"There is no doubt, Madame."

"Bien! Leave them on the table."

They bowed and departed, again by the back stairs.

RACHELLE HEARD THE TIMID KNOCK on the Macquinet chamber door. She sent Nenette to answer. The demoiselle hurried back, her eyes wide with concern.

"It is the Queen Mother's confidential attendant, the Italian girl, Madalenna."

"Enter!" Rachelle called. She touched her sleeve to give herself confidence that the key was snugly in its secret stitching.

A moment later Madalenna padded silently into the chamber. Rachelle pitied the demoiselle, whom she had heard Marguerite's ladies-in-waiting whispering was an utter slave of the Queen Mother. She had no life of her own and slept in a gilded box like a pet cat, near the foot of the Queen Mother's bed, her most nimble spy. Duchesse Xenia Dushane had also told Grandmère she had once seen the demoiselle slinking out of le Duc de Guise's chamber, deceiving even the great duc. Madalenna had been horrified at being seen by the duchesse and so upset by her failure to slip away unseen that she admitted that the Queen Mother had sent her to hide in the duc's cupboard. Madalenna was to report back on his meeting with his young son Henry. The Queen Mother had wanted to know if the duc was telling young Henry de Guise that he should try to marry Marguerite.

Now Madalenna stood in the doorway of the Macquinet chamber watching her with a sad, sallow countenance.

Rachelle smiled gently. "Hello, Madalenna. I have not seen you in some days."

"No, Mademoiselle."

"Are you well?" Rachelle had hoped to win the demoiselle's confidence but so far, to no avail.

"I am well, Mademoiselle."

The Queen Mother could not possibly know about the key, Rachelle solaced herself, sensing danger from the behavior of Madalenna. *No one saw me remove it from the drawer.*

Rachelle noticed how Madalenna shivered. She too might allow her fears to weaken her if she permitted them to reign. She often thought that entering the chambers of Catherine de Medici was like entering a nest of poisonous spiders. How easy to get caught in the sticky web. One must be constantly alert.

"What is it, Madalenna?"

"Her Majesty, the Queen Mother, desires your immediate presence, Mademoiselle. She has approved the gowns for the Princesse Marguerite and wishes you to come for them now."

Rachelle searched the demoiselle's face.

"It is because Her Majesty will depart in the morning for Amboise," Madalenna said meekly, her eyes dropping.

The opportunity I was hoping for, but how will I get the key back in the drawer if the Queen Mother is in the chamber?

"I will come tout de suite," Rachelle said, surprised at the calm in her voice.

Madalenna curtsied and left the chamber on stealthy footsteps.

Perhaps a way will open once I am in her presence. If she would leave the chamber for a moment ...

A SHORT TIME LATER Rachelle entered Catherine de Medici's royal chambers. She knelt before the Queen Mother until at last Catherine decided to lift a hand, biding her to rise. Rachelle noticed her carmined lips turning into a smile, but the reptilian eyes watched her. Rachelle's heart quickened. *Caution.* Take one faux pas and death will surely await you. The key hidden underneath the lace on her wrist cuff weighed like a rock. She could almost fear Catherine's gaze sliding to her wrist.

"You may sit, Mademoiselle Macquinet."

"Yes, Madame, merci."

Rachelle sensed the temptation to swerve her gaze to the dim corner, to the drawer where she must return the key.

"So," Catherine said amiably, "the gowns are c'est magnifique. Marguerite is most pleased, as am I. Your talent is most telling, Mademoiselle Macquinet. You will surely ascend to the skills of the Grand Dame Henriette, your Grandmère."

"Your Majesty is most kind to say so. Speaking for Grandmère and Mademoiselle Idelette, my sister, we are honored to have served the royal Valois family once more, Madame."

"Ah? Then perhaps the day shall come again. We shall send for the Macquinets when my daughter, Marguerite, shall marry. Marguerite will wish a large wedding trousseau, I assure you."

Rachelle remembered Marguerite's dismay over the rumor that the Queen Mother wished her to marry Prince Henry of Navarre, the son of King Antoine de Bourbon and Queen Jeanne d'Albret. A marriage between the Catholic princesse and Huguenot prince would suit the mind and cause of the Queen Mother.

"Madame, it will be an honor to design and sew the princesse's wedding garments."

Catherine smiled, but Rachelle found in the expression no genuine warmth.

"Ah, you are most charmante, Rachelle Macquinet. Marguerite has taken a special fondness for you. She wishes you to go with the royal party to Amboise."

Rachelle's heart tripped. *Amboise.*

"Ah yes." Catherine gave a brisk nod, still smiling, her prominent eyes watching Rachelle's every response.

"Princesse Marguerite also wishes for you to design and sew a few more items in a certain color of silk. So you will be with us for several months. You will arrange for this with your Grandmère, Madame Dushane?"

Rachelle's mouth was dry and she could not speak. *She would be left alone at court. Was this some sort of scheme?* She saw her eyes upon her burning with inner mirth.

"We — I deem it a grave honor to serve my king and the royal family, Madame, but — "

"But, Mademoiselle Macquinet?" came the needling tone. "Are you not a cousine to Comtesse Claudine Boisseau who was my mignon maid-of-honor until her unexpected frailty? And are you not related through your Grandmère to Duchesse Xenia Dushane?"

"Yes, Madame — "

"Then who better for me to choose to become a lady-in-waiting to ma cherie Marguerite?" Her smile broadened.

"But — "

"But?" Her eyes flashed with sudden anger. She leaned forward in her elevated chair.

Rachelle hastened a bow. "I am at your service, Madame."

"Ah." Her voice became soothed.

"Your Majesty knows that I am so young, that — "

"Au contraire. Ladies-in-waiting come to us much younger. Our ducs and duchesses do all in their power to gain the privilege of sending a daughter or a son to court. Most are not belle enough for this honor, but you, Mademoiselle Macquinet, have shown yourself acceptable."

Rachelle saw the mockery in her smile and knew she was laughing at her, reminding her of the romantic scene near the gallery with the marquis. Rachelle prayed fervently that Catherine would change the subject and not force her into committing herself to a life at court with so much debauchery. *Oh Father God, help me, protect me. My life belongs to you.*

Catherine's square jaw set. Her eyes gazed down at her evenly. A thought flashed into Rachelle's mind of Joseph in the court of Pharaoh. Could God not keep his own wherever they were?

Catherine waited as though she took malicious amusement in her struggle.

She is evil, this woman, Rachelle thought. She cast her eyes down in submission to Catherine's demanding stare.

"Yes, Your Majesty, I am honored to serve Princesse Marguerite at Amboise."

Catherine nodded. "Ah, well then, we shall arrange these matters at once, for we journey in the morning."

"Your Majesty," Rachelle rushed boldly, "perhaps the princesse would also find it helpful if Grandmère and Idelette accompanied the court to Amboise? If the princesse has other items she wishes made — "

Catherine lifted her hand. She looked scornful. "Surely, Mademoiselle, you do not wish such a thing."

"Madame?" Rachelle inquired, bewildered.

"Comtesse Madeleine Dangeau, your sister, is in need of their attendance." She lifted a message from beside her and held it up. "I received this plea from Madeleine this very morning. She has begged me to arrange for Madame Henriette to travel to Paris to be with her until the enfant is born."

Rachelle kept stunned silence. *Was this true or a ploy? Was the letter in her hand genuine?*

Mention of her eldest sister, which reminded her of Sebastien, frightened Rachelle. Could the Queen Mother be hinting of anything, and if so, what? Dare she mention Sebastien's absence? Or was this also a way in which the Queen Mother could discover how much they knew about Sebastien? Perhaps it was wiser not to admit they knew he was missing.

"Yes, Madame, Madeleine Dangeau will give birth soon."

Catherine laughed. "I understand why our petite Comtesse Madeleine should wish to have her Grandmère's company at such a time. I shall give orders to set her up in a chamber near at hand. She will need Madame Henriette very soon now."

Rachelle attempted to understand this affected friendliness, yet the unmistakable curl of lip, the flash of something like malice in her eyes, baffled her. *I feel like a caged mouse on its way to a hungry snake. Or are we all in the Queen Mother's cage?*

"Madame Henriette will leave for Paris in the morning. I shall have one of the servants arrange for a traveling calèche with more comfortable seating. We, too, leave early for Amboise."

"And my sister, Idelette? Should she not also journey with our Grandmère to Paris?"

"Non." Catherine leaned back into her chair, placing the letter on her lap. "Idelette must return to Lyon with all of your Macquinet silk and grand equipage. She must be there to explain the change in the Macquinet family when your maman and père return from Geneva."

Catherine knew her parents were in Reformational Geneva! Again, Rachelle hastened a cry for God's protection for them all.

The sighing of the wind as it swept along the surface of the Seine was broken by the steps of the guards in the antechamber.

"Comtesse Madeleine Dangeau has been much on my mind of late," Catherine stated, looking at her own white hands with rings of jewels. "It is fitting that one as *loyal* as mon Sebastien, her husband, should be *rewarded*, and this reward is to be given to his wife, Madeleine, as well as to him. And to their *un amour de bébé*. And what manner of ruler of France would I be, Mademoiselle Rachelle, if I also did not *reward* all of their loyal family?"

Rachelle sat in silence unable to move. *Sebastien's reward ... given to his wife, Madeleine, and her little baby ... to all of the loyal family.* Catherine could not be speaking seriously? Did she not suspect Sebastien of loyalty to the Huguenots? But then, Avenelle did not speak of Sebastien as a Huguenot traitor. Or was her promise of reward a two-edged sword?

Catherine was smiling down at her from her elevated chair. "I have a gift for Sebastien's belle Madeleine. I trust you to see that your Grandmère has this gift at the birth of Sebastien's healthy enfant son, for it must be a boy." And Catherine laughed. "Your Grandmère will bring this present with her, for I will not return to Paris until the weather is more fair and le bébé already born."

Rachelle bowed her head. "Your Majesty is — most gracious." *A gift from the Queen Mother!*

Catherine stood and Rachelle arose and curtsied. There was no time to return the key —

But Catherine smiled. "Wait, Mademoiselle Macquinet, while I go and retrieve the gifts." She turned and left the room with her stiff black skirt tearing the silence.

Rachelle's heart sprang to her throat. The wind was scraping the vine against the outside window. She cast a desperate glance around her. There was no one else in the chamber, not even Madalenna —

CATHERINE DE MEDICI shut the door behind her in the antechamber, then swiftly removed the plug in the wall that faced her front chamber. Her breath quickened. Her heart thudded. She fixed her eye to the peephole.

The Macquinet mademoiselle was casting an anxious glance about the chamber to see if she was being observed. *The thief. Look at her flee like a rat to my chest of drawers.*

Catherine watched Rachelle pull open the drawer and open the petite box of filigree gold. Though Rachelle's back was toward the peephole, Catherine had seen enough. The Huguenot mademoiselle had replaced the key that she had taken that morning. She shut the drawer again and rushed back to the window.

Catherine narrowed her eyes. *You too will be rewarded.*

RACHELLE was standing by the window when she heard the antechamber door open. The Queen Mother returned, a placid smile on her white face, her lips appeared a deeper carmine. In her hands she carried three boxes painted red with gold fleur de lys engravings.

"One is for you, my favorite couturière, to be opened on the birth of your sister Madeleine's and Sebastien's enfant. The other two, for Madeleine and Madame Henriette."

"Your Majesty, you have been most kind. We shall treasure your gifts endlessly and hand them down to our children."

Catherine laughed aloud. "I am glad you are pleased. That is all. You may go, Rachelle Macquinet. I will see you at Amboise, I promise you."

Rachelle bowed low, and with the gowns being packed by her ladies, she departed the royal chambers.

Once free of the Queen Mother's chambers, she thought her knees would go out from under her. For a moment she leaned her shoulder against the salle wall near a diamonded window, calming herself and praying the Lord's Prayer, then walked slowly, tiredly toward the stairway and climbed to the second floor.

GRANDMÈRE AND IDELETTE had returned for the evening, and while waiting for her were busily gathering possessions to pack into their personal trunks. Grandmère looked up when Rachelle entered. Her silver brows nipped together. She walked quickly toward Rachelle.

"Ma petite Rachelle, have you seen a *diable*?"

"I returned the key," she whispered. "I shall explain everything, but first, I must sit down ..."

Idelette also came to her side. "Did she catch you?"

"Non."

Grandmère closed her eyes. "Then I praise God."

Rachelle remained uneasy. She sat down with her skirts spread and placed the gifts from the Queen Mother on her lap.

"Tell us of Avenelle. What did Monsieur Fabien learn?" Grandmère asked. "Were our fears justified?"

Grandmère and Idelette listened to Rachelle's whispered report, their faces losing any earlier relief as worry again returned.

"The traitor," Grandmère scoffed. "But to God more than to his fellows."

"Was he ever a true believer?" Idelette asked doubtfully.

"One thinks not," Grandmère said sadly, "but who can know except the Lord? And still there is no Sebastien ..."

Rachelle drew in a breath and explained the Queen Mother's unexpected demands. Grandmère frowned over the news of Madeleine's health and her urgent request to Catherine to send Grandmère to Paris.

"I wish I were going to be with Madeleine," Idelette said. "I can be of help to you both. Grandmère, is there any way I could?"

Grandmère, while appearing to understand her desire, was insistent. "You will see Madeleine another time, after the child is born. You must return to the chateau, since Rachelle will not be returning to Lyon yet. The Queen Mother is right about our need to see the Macquinet silk equipage home to Lyon. Someone with calm reason will need to explain all of these crucial changes, especially about Rachelle, to Clair and Arnaut when they return from Geneva."

"She knew about Geneva," Rachelle said.

Grandmère and Idelette exchanged concerned glances.

"But she could not be wrathful if she has granted such gifts," Idelette said. "But where is mine?"

"How odd that you did not get one," Rachelle said thoughtfully.

"Perhaps because I worked on reinette Mary's gowns."

"Yes, ma cherie," Grandmère said, patting Idelette's arm. "I am sure Mary will also reward you."

"What could they be? Open them now," Idelette urged. "Perhaps there is a jewel inside."

Although Rachelle too wondered, she shook her head. "Ah, ça non! We cannot. Her Majesty made me promise we would wait until the birth of Madeleine and Sebastien's enfant."

"I do not like this," Grandmère said unexpectedly. "Why would the Queen Mother do this for us? And with Avenelle betraying the Huguenots and Sebastien missing. She cares for no one. A comfortable calèche for me to journey in as well?" she tapped her temple. "Something is not right, but what? I must think ..."

Rachelle felt emotionally exhausted after confronting Catherine, but what could she do? She must go to Amboise, and Grandmère must go on to Paris. And Idelette —

"We three Daughters of Silk will be separated in our work for the first time," Rachelle said sadly.

"Yes, I do not like this at all," Idelette said. "But what choice have we?"

"I fear we have none," Rachelle sank back against the velvet chair.

"We must trust the will and purpose of God in this royal decision," Grandmère said. "There is naught else we can do to oppose Catherine de Medici."

Idelette nodded briefly, but her face was pale and her mouth tight.

Rachelle collected herself for their sakes. She stood and put her arms around Grandmère. "Do not fear. I shall be safe. And I am sure that after Amboise I shall be sent back to Lyon."

Grandmère looked into her face. "I wonder, Rachelle, will you?"

Rachelle considered, then lifted her chin with dignity and resolve despite events that were determined to tear down her faith. She had seen so much of this same resolve in her mother, and she knew that deep within her grandmère's heart there also was a reserve of strength and godly trust that would rise to the need of the hour. Rachelle, too, now reached out for that same strength to be found in Christ alone.

"I will pray for you, ma amour," Grandmère said.

"And I you, Grandmère. Always." She kissed the pale wrinkled cheek. She turned to her sister. They embraced but Idelette looked less tranquil than Rachelle had ever seen her.

Somehow ... after the Queen Mother saw me with Marquis in the gallery, I suspected something like this might happen. The question is, why? Why does Catherine want me with Princesse Marguerite; why at Amboise? Why does she want Grandmère in Paris with Madeleine?

Rachelle looked at the gilded red boxes.

Chapter Ten

THE QUEEN MOTHER DISMISSED MADALENNA FROM HER SMALL BED AT THE foot of her own, then proceeded to dress herself in her usual black dress with lace ruff collar that opened like a tulip. Her head *coif* was in place, forming a *V* shape over her broad forehead. Her round chin was set, and her eyes, appearing light and obscure in her Venetian mirror, gazed back, revealing nothing. She must mask her true plans.

She had agreed to meet with le Duc de Guise and le Cardinal de Lorraine just after dawn this morning to discuss further plans. The cardinal preferred to keep her son, her petit King Francis, totally uninformed.

Catherine despised the Guise brothers . . . Little did they know how she wished to drop poison into their wine goblets or send gloves —

But no. Gloves must not be used again at court for a length of time. Her enemies were already whispering that she had sent her Italian cupbearer with water to her husband's older brother, the dauphin, when he was sick. The dauphin died soon afterward, and Catherine's husband, Henry, had become king in place of his brother.

Catherine shuddered. Even Henry had once all but suggested she had eliminated his brother so they two might rule France.

She poured herself tea. She was a hearty eater and usually enjoyed her large meals, but not this morning. There was too much to do, to plan, and to seal those plans in her mind for the future. As long as she knew her humiliation under the Guises would not endure forever, she could accept their arrogance. Their combined power over her could not last long because her petit Francis was sickly; everyone knew he suffered from poison of the blood.

She stared at the two wax tapers as if hypnotized by the weaving flames.

As long as Francis is king, the Guises will hold the key to power in France through Mary. Mary!

She both loathed and feared the Guises, for they were as shrewd and sly as she. Had she not tried to placate them, to assure them she was loyal to Philip of Spain and the pope in Rome?

But they accuse me of secretly reaching out to the Huguenot Coligny and Bourbon princes.

She did not agree with the Huguenots anymore than she agreed with the Catholics; she used one against the other to maintain her own control. But when the Guises learned of her secret meetings with Coligny and Condé to thwart their power, the duc had confronted her.

As if I do not know that the authority of the duc and cardinal will grow as Francis matures and draws further from my influence. And Mary, already clever, will mature in her ability to exercise authority as Queen of France. All the while, her oncles would grow bolder as the months pass, until —

Catherine banged her fist down on the table.

Her son Charles was still a boy and would be for many more years. *My hold over his mind is almost complete. Charles will do everything I tell him, though there are times when he shows his independence and rebels.* When that happened she had to frighten him into submission by telling him details of the Inquisitors.

"Ah, you do not want to be sent to the Bastille do you, mon petit? The Huguenots will have their revenge on you. They will pour molten lead down your throat. You must trust me, you must do as I say, for only I, your maman, can protect you from them."

Catherine stood tall and straight. She walked to her window and drew aside the heavy drapery to look into the garden below.

The early dawn sky was beginning to show pink. As she scanned the garden she noticed two people creeping back toward the palais. She clamped her mouth. It was Marguerite, looking disheveled. Her black hair was partly loose and she was clinging to Monsieur Henry de Guise's arm and looking up into his comely face with those sick, adoring dark eyes of hers. "Ah, the harlot. I must marry her to a prince soon or none will have her."

Catherine could not think about Marguerite now. She would handle her wanton daughter at Amboise.

Catherine laughed coarsely. *Petite Margo will be dismayed when she learns of the plans I have to marry her to another Henry — Prince Henry of Navarre.*

Catherine sobered. But first she would need to convince Jeanne d'Albret, Queen of Navarre, that her Huguenot son should marry the Catholic princesse. The clever Jeanne was a delicate problem. Catherine did not feel comfortable around her and had not since the first time they met when both were in their teens. Jeanne, the Protestant, was too much like Princesse Eleonore, the pious Huguenot wife of Prince Condé. Clever women, both. But not as clever as she.

Catherine rang her gong. Madalenna appeared silently and bowed.

"Send for Charlotte de Presney."

"Oui, Madame."

CHARLOTTE DE PRESNEY knelt before the Queen Mother. She had been rushed out of her bedchamber, hurriedly gowned, and her hair arranged. Charlotte was always nervous when Catherine called for her. As a member of the escadron volant, she was, for all practical purposes, owned body and soul by the Queen Mother. In return, she received a pampered life and jewels, and moved among the courtiers freely. She was not liked by the women, but that did not trouble her; there were few of them that she wished to be friendly with.

"Ah, Charlotte, you are looking winsome this morning."

"Merci, Madame."

"How are you coming on your wooing of the most beau young man at court?" She smiled slyly.

Charlotte was still kneeling for the Queen Mother had not yet lifted her hand to allow her to rise.

Charlotte tried to shield her surprise and her shiver at the mention of Marquis Fabien. It was one thing for the Queen Mother to order Charlotte to spy on others, but that Catherine also was watching her was ominous.

"Oh, come, come, it is no trifling matter to me whom you seek for your newest lover. So you are attracted to Marquis Fabien de Vendôme? That is well. He is just the man I want you to turn your charms upon. You are to find out from the marquis just what his plans are toward someone most important, le Duc de Guise.

"Ah, you are surprised, as I expected. You need not be. You should understand what constrains the man you wish to influence your way, Madame de Presney. Marquis Fabien believes the duc is responsible for having his father, Duc Jean-Louis de Vendôme, assassinated at Calais in the last war with Spain. I see by your shock you did not know this. Marquis de Vendôme has been suspicious of the duc for years, since but a boy. What could he do about his loathing but set aside his plans until manhood? Ah, but now he has arrived, as you have surely noted," her lip curled, "and I want to know of his plans for revenge."

"But—what can I possibly do, Madame?"

"It is most simple. You will plant little seeds in his mind. You need merely make suggestions that you have the evidence he is seeking."

Charlotte saw how this might work to gain his attention. And once she had that . . .

Catherine smiled broadly. "He will be most indebted to you, I assure you."

Charlotte smiled in return. "Yes, Madame, merci. But how can I convince him of such things when I know nothing?"

"Do not be a fool. I intend to give you the proof you need at the proper time. But only when I say it is time. Understood?"

"May I ask, Madame, why you wish to help Marquis de Vendôme in his suspicion of le Duc de Guise?"

"I would think that would have dawned upon such a sly mind as yours." She motioned for her to rise. "First, sow your seeds. I need not tell you how. You have your ways. He will take the bait, I assure you. He has no liking or trust for the Guises. Then learn his plans for revenge on

Guise. When you have them, come to me. We will proceed one step at a time."

"Madame, if I may ask a favor of Your Majesty?"

Catherine looked at her impatiently. "Be quick, I soon have a meeting."

"Yes, Madame, that—you would have your Florence perfumer, Monsieur Rene, make me a vial of *amoureux* potion? I believe it will help me convince Marquis de Vendôme of his desire for me."

Catherine did not laugh, and Charlotte had not expected her to do so. Rene and Cosmo were the Queen Mother's chief parfumer and poisoner.

Catherine stood abruptly. "Be in the garden, waiting. I will send Rene's assistant to bring you a small vial before the king rides out of the gate this morning."

"Merci, Madame." Charlotte could hardly contain her excitement.

Catherine looked at her coldly. "And remember, Madame de Presney, if even one word of what I mentioned about the duc is made known to anyone, you will curse the day of your birth."

"Yes, Madame, I will not disappoint your confidence in my loyalty."

"You may go now."

Charlotte bowed and left, now sure of her future success, yet ever afraid of Madame le Serpent. She doubted not that failure would bring her disfavor, and that she would be sent away from court.

THE SUN WAS CLIMBING over the Touraine hills when Andelot Dangeau swung himself into the saddle of his horse. He reminded himself the fine beast belonged to his cousine by marriage, Marquis Fabien. He rode slowly from the armory and barracks toward the front of the palais chateau for the journey to Amboise.

"This malevolence is deliberate! The fates must be amused to frustrate me, to bring me to woe," he spoke aloud to the horse. He straightened his handsome cloak and hat, also borrowed from the marquis, and sidled into his lowly place in the long line of soldiers gathered outside the gate at Chambord. The royal retinue was soon to begin a twenty-odd mile journey to the fortress castle of Amboise, which he had learned about only this morning.

He glanced about and saw the scurrying members of the nobility dutifully making preparations for the unexpected journey without yet knowing its purpose.

Andelot struggled with disappointment. His one reason for coming to Chambord, for which Oncle Sebastien had called him, and for which Marquis Fabien, at his own expense, had brought him here, was for Andelot to meet some recently identified kinsmen. Kinsmen so important that the news coming from Sebastien had left Andelot dazed.

"I am related by blood to le Duc de Guise and le Cardinal de Lorraine."

Andelot thought of little else. He was to meet the two most feared and powerful men in France, the Guise brothers; the beloved duc was Marshal of France and the cardinal was so powerful in the state church of France the pope had once called him the Transmonte Pope.

"And if the cardinal approves of me after my interview, then he will grant me the high privilege to enter training as a court page, perhaps even to le Cardinal de Lorraine himself."

Failing that position, Andelot thought he could at least become an important courtier at the Louvre in Paris, perhaps to his Oncle Sebastien.

Andelot shook his head. "I can still but scarcely believe it," he murmured to the horse. The horse lifted its ruddy head and pawed the ground restlessly, as though unsure about his new master.

Andelot straightened his forest green hat with plume. He squinted, frustrated. "And now my important meeting is delayed until Amboise. No one even knows why we go there. And where is mon Oncle Sebastien? My life is but full of thornbush and stumbling stones, on paths that wander uphill and down dale and lead to stagnant pools of green slime."

He jerked his hat still lower.

He had thought to surprise Mademoiselle Rachelle at the revelation of his connection to the Guises while they were both here at Chambord and win her admiration. "And now, before I even get the chance to impress her with my grand prospects, she has met Marquis Fabien and I am still without notice or regard by Cardinal Charles Guise de Lorraine."

Andelot entertained some noble ambitions — of one day attending the university in Paris. All now surely seemed possible. Becoming a page to the cardinal should lead to gaining special privileges and further opportunities, but then perhaps — now Andelot felt as though a thorn stuck in his throat — perhaps to dark infamy. He was aware of the reputation of the House of Guise for terror against heretics.

Andelot shivered. He was a Catholic; he had nothing to fear; he disagreed with the Huguenots, with Calvin, and with that diable Monsieur Luther and his Reformation, but his heart pitied his fellow Frenchmen. He agreed with Duchesse Anne d'Este, wife of le Duc de Guise, when she implored him, "Please, at least spare the children and the women."

Andelot could no more stomach a burning than he could imagine going to Calvin's Geneva and becoming a Protestant scholar.

The pale sky showed blue in places between drifting white puffs. In the distance rain clouds loitered, threatening to drench the auspicious royal caravan soon to be on the road to Amboise. The breeze told a different story, of a fine spring full of gala events and amour. Andelot noticed that the lovely demoiselles of the nobles believed so anyway; they laughed behind bejeweled fans and paraded about in startling frocks with all manner of jewels. At first Andelot stared at the sight. "Fie. It is a miracle they are not robbed," he had said, and Marquis Fabien had found the remark so amusing he had laughed aloud, whereupon, the marquis had given him lessons in savoir faire.

Andelot shaded his eyes with his hand and peered toward the courtyard where the gates now stood open for the royal retinue to come riding through.

He saw that the king's attendants were waiting for the signal to emerge. Andelot marveled at such splendor. The nobles were well-fed, no skinny peasants, these. They wore sight-dazzling garments and were adorned with diamonds and rubies. They gathered either on horseback or in horse-drawn calèches, bearing armorial flags. All had peasant lackeys following on foot with the hunting dogs and house dogs, and wagons overflowing with royal provisions.

It yet remains a wonder to me we are not robbed by highwaymen. But then Marquis Fabien's laughter may be realistic after all. I have seen what happens to a peasant who dares to hunt in the king's forest for a coney. How much worse to hunt for jewels and furs?

Andelot's position on horseback was near the queue of common soldiers, far behind the royal grenadiers in their blue and white uniforms, or the grand red, white, and blue of the House of Bourbon, of which Marquis Fabien's retinue was a part.

I might at least have been invited to ride in Fabien's guard.

Andelot waited with the archers on horseback. To his left, astride a fine specimen of a horse, was another of his blood cousines, but of humble birth like himself—that is, before he had learned he was part Guise. The chevalier, Julot Cazalet, was a skilled archer and an excellent swordsman—and in secret a Huguenot, though Andelot was not supposed to know. As if he would betray his own cousine! Andelot told himself he would not tell the Guises this for any amount of silver.

Chevalier Julot Cazalet, also befriended by the generous Marquis Fabien, who was seeking to lure him into his own men-at-arms, so far without success, was old—fully twenty-eight. He had steely eyes, an angular chin, broad cheekbones, and hair a burnt ruddy color. It seemed to Andelot that Cousine Julot was always angry. He had been so ever since his brother was pulled apart limb from limb for carrying a heretic book in his saddlebag. The warning to Julot not to follow his brother's ways included being tied to a post to watch his brother's ordeal. It was whispered later that Julot had fainted before his brother, who had quoted words from the Psalter before he had gone into shock and died.

Julot had a right to be angry. But Andelot was uneasy of that steely rage. Even so, Julot continued to serve the royal House of Valois. Why? Andelot cast a side glance toward the man with broad muscled shoulders and lean hips. The swell of muscle in his arms assured Andelot that Julot could send the king's arrows far and with strategic power. His sword arm might lop off an arm or a hand. Andelot shuddered. He did not like the sword. He liked manuscripts and quiet chambers of learning.

Andelot's leather saddle creaked as he swiveled to crane his neck once again toward the gate searching for a hint of Marquis Fabien. Where was he?

In the courtyard, Marquis Fabien walked up to where his golden bay waited with the groom. Fabien was about to swing into the saddle when Gallaudet came trotting toward him. Fabien paused. He had sent Gallaudet with his men-at-arms to safeguard the Macquinet calèche and wagons back to Lyon.

"Monseigneur, I have news you will wish to hear now."

"Say on."

"Mademoiselle Rachelle will not be returning to the Chateau de Silk in Lyon. I have learned this but minutes ago from Mademoiselle Idelette Macquinet. She is the only one returning to the Chateau de Silk."

"The only one returning? Saintes! What is this?"

Gallaudet explained how he had arrived at the Macquinet calèche with the marquis's swordsmen when Madame Dushane told him of her journey to Paris with the Queen Mother's blessing. "Mademoiselle Rachelle is now a lady-in-waiting to Princesse Marguerite Valois."

Fabien's immediate anger flared. "Lady-in-waiting!"

"And your wish, Monsieur? Does it remain the same for your swordsmen to ride with the Macquinet *coterie* to Lyon?"

"Yes, but you, Gallaudet, do not journey onward to Lyon as first intended. I have other plans. I may need you. Meet me at the road."

Lady-in-waiting to Margo — this displeased him, for Amboise would prove most dangerous. Fabien left his horse with his groom and entered the inner courtyard where the queue of calèches had gathered, waiting for the king to ride out. Princesse Marguerite and her ladies-in-waiting stood outside the two royal calèches awarded her for comfortable travel.

The vivacious and attractively plump Margo, dark eyes snapping with fervency for young Henry de Guise, huddled with him on one side of the calèche. Her ladies and pages were shielding her as she bade au revoir to Henry, though he was also going on to Amboise. In reality, Margo and Henry's amour for one another was known to any who bothered to notice. Fabien, for one, had small interest in their goings-on.

Fabien waited, bored. Henry, upon seeing him, unwrapped himself from Margo's clinging embrace. He scanned Fabien, his jaw hardening. Though unsought by Fabien, there seemed a veiled competition between them at court for first place in the ladies' admiration. Another foolish frivolity as far as Fabien considered. He wished to avoid the belles dames.

Henry, however, with his golden looks, his proud and arrogant idolization of his father, expected to be adored because he was the duc's son.

"A Guise, a Guise for a king," the Parisians would shout when father and son with their men-at-arms rode from Lorraine into Paris.

Henry now approached Fabien. A stern look overtook his comely face, and his hair, a golden red, glinted in the sun. As soon as he was out of earshot of Margo and her attendants, he said, "A Bourbon."

Fabien's temper, a problem since childhood and now worn thin by recent events, flared, for he believed it was Henry's father who had plotted the demise of his own father, Jean-Louis. Yet this young Henry spread his proud feathers as though he, and not Fabien, was of the blood royal. The House of Guise was already in the place of authority that rightfully belonged to the princes of the blood, Antoine and Louis de Bourbon, only because the Guises were favored by powerful Spain and meddling Rome who believed in their political rule over kings.

Fabien stepped closer, keeping his voice low, for there were ladies present, and the animosity between them was theirs alone, developing since childhood.

"Your haughty address offends me, Henry. A Bourbon, yes, and where France is concerned, of higher rank than you or any in the House of Guise. If I were an arrogant Guise, I would draw my blade now before the ladies and demand your humble obeisance."

"After Avenelle? After my father has discovered a plot hatched by Bourbons to overthrow the king?" Henry de Guise snarled.

"Avenelle," the marquis said with contempt, "is a traitor, a small rat. A rat bribed by the duc to lie, and for whose rise to power? The duc's own. Your oncle, the cardinal, scorns the king as well."

"You speak thus of my father and oncle!"

"Your father deigns to overthrow the rightful rule of the house of Bourbon to usurp it for the House of Guise. He fills the king's youthful mind with lies. There is no plot to overthrow a Valois king but to remove those around him who usurp a position not rightfully theirs. Men who are more loyal to Spain than to France."

Henry stared at him open-mouthed. "Marquis! I demand apology or I shall call for an *affaire d'honneur* with the sword."

"Then call for it. You will die here and now before Marguerite. Do so and be counted a fool, Henry. I shall best you. You will have nothing but infamy. Is that what you wish to portray before the royal princesse and courtiers?"

Henry de Guise drew in his chin. A look of confusion and then surprise crossed his face, and his faltering gaze said his rash call for a duel of honor had been a mistake.

Fabien wondered if Henry had ever been informed that the Guises of Lorraine ranked below Jean-Louis de Vendôme and the deceased princesse, Marie-Louise de Bourbon, Fabien's blood mother.

"No one has heard our exchange. I shall be generous and spare your reputation before Margo. But know you have foolishly accosted mine. It is I who has the right to call you out for lightly esteeming my rank. But I am not so insecure. Do ask your father, the duc, if he thinks it is wise for you to have done so. He will not be pleased by your rash action, I promise you. Also ask him why he would not be pleased, if you so choose."

Henry stood stiffly. The look of uncertainty remained in his light blue eyes. "What do you mean to imply?"

"That is for you, your father, and your oncle the cardinal to decide. Ask them about the death of Jean-Louis de Vendôme in the last war with Spain. Tell them you *also* accused a Bourbon of treason. Tell them I told you to ask about my father, a prince of the blood who was so accused."

Henry de Guise studied him with growing unease. "Your father was a prince of the blood?"

"He was."

Doubt over his haste now showed in Henry's eyes. "It is the first I have heard of it."

"Pray consider why. Some wish to not talk of it, but to tout their own honors."

Henry looked at him a long moment. "It seems I was hasty. I was under the impression . . ." He stopped.

"That you admit it is satisfaction enough. We will forget this happened if you wish."

Henry de Guise hesitated, then gave a grudging bow of his head to Fabien, showing deference. He walked away, his attendants following.

Fabien was also turning away when Comte Maurice Beauvilliers, who was lounging in the background near one of the calèches, watching the confrontation, left his pages some feet away and sauntered toward Fabien.

"I have important news, mon cousine Fabien. Do you wish to hear it? Where can we talk that none else hears?"

Chapter Eleven

Marquis Fabien walked away from the royal retinue of calèches and attendants with Maurice Beauvilliers. They paused beneath the shade of an arbor.

Maurice sniffed a crimson rose he had pinned on his emerald green surcoat. His almond-shaped gray eyes were as languid as ever.

"Did you discover news of Sebastien from Julot at the armoury last night?" Fabien asked.

"Non. But I have other news. Did you hear that Rachelle Macquinet, la belle des belles, is among Marguerite's ladies? She will go to Amboise. The winds of bonne fortune blow my way." He smiled to himself and breathed deeply of the fragrance of the red rose.

"Is that your news? I know it already," Fabien said, irritated to be reminded of Rachelle going to Amboise and of Maurice's interest. "What other news have you?"

The glimmer of sobriety in Maurice's eyes surprised him, and he paused.

"I was passing Duchesse Dushane's calèche and she called to me."

Mention of the duchesse sharpened Fabien's interest.

Maurice sniffed his rose again. "She believed it was safe to speak to me of important matters, as who would suspect Maurice of favoring the Bourbons, eh? She gave me profound news, mon cousine. Oncle Sebastien is away on proper business for the throne."

After what he had heard in the state council chamber?

"You are surely mad. The duchesse told you so?"

"She did. Sebastien departed Chambord soon after le Duc de Guise rode into the courtyard with Avenelle. Oncle Sebastien is on his way to Moulins with a royal summons for Prince Condé, Admiral Coligny, and his brother le Cardinal de Châtillon. There is to be an edict of pacification signed at Amboise, and your Bourbon kinsmen, the Huguenot leaders, are summoned there."

Fabien's impulse was to hotly deny every word of this revelation. This must be a ruse after what he had just heard from the mouth of Catherine herself. Peace? There would be no peace.

"Milles diables, but this must be trickery of the darkest sort."

Maurice shrugged languidly, as though he had now lost all interest since hearing Sebastien was safe and still in favor with Catherine.

"Then speak to Prince Condé yourself. I have more pressing matters to attend, Cousine Marquis. But I will tell you this one thing more, learned not from the duchesse, but a belle dame at court who knows. It was none other than le Cardinal de Lorraine who sent Sebastien with the royal summons to Amboise."

"The cardinal!" Fabien could scarcely take it in. "Treachery. What else can it be? Ask yourself why it is the Bourbon princes and Calvinist nobles have been requested to come to an important council meeting at Amboise after Avenelle betrays a Huguenot plot. How many edicts have there been in our lifetime?"

"Several at least," Maurice said.

"All of them repudiated by the Guises before the ink dried on the page," Fabien murmured thoughtfully. "So why another? And why now does the cardinal call for the Bourbon princes and nobles to Amboise for the kiss of peace?"

"Strange to fathom, is it not?" Maurice agreed.

"Or is it?" Fabien did not like it at all. "This smells of a trap."

"If you ride to Moulins, take caution. Adieu, mon cousin." He strutted away.

Fabien returned to the line of calèches and baggage wagons. His mind was busy.

So Sebastien was sent to Prince Condé with a royal summons, but assuredly that summons came not from Francis but the Guises and Catherine. *Could this proposed edict of pacification be genuine?* Surely

Sebastien would be wise enough to see through le Cardinal de Lorraine's sending him to Prince Condé. The question now was, did Sebastien know of Avenelle's betrayal of the Huguenot plot before he rode off to Moulins? If not, he was at a disadvantage.

As Fabien neared Marguerite's calèche, he saw Maurice again, this time flirting with one of the charmante ladies-in-waiting. As Fabien passed by he reached over and plucked the ripe rose from Maurice's surcoat.

"Merci, mon cousine."

He walked to Princesse Marguerite Valois who stood outside her royal calèche under a silken, gold-fringed canopy sipping some refreshment. Coming before her, Fabien bowed deeply and handed her the rose with *fanfaronade*.

"For you, most fragrant of all flowers, my undying fealty."

Margo laughed, and though he knew she had taken note of the earlier meeting he had had with Henry de Guise, he was sure she had not overheard. Nor did he want her to guess they had nearly come to swords at Henry's challenge. Presently, her one bel ami was Henry de Guise. Fabien thought she might have called Henry foolish for his rash challenge, for though his father the duc was a masterful soldier and the younger Henry was fair with a sword, Henry was not capable of mounting an adequate defense in a match against him. Fabien was kindly disposed toward Margo, who perhaps was the least cruel of the Valois children, and their bantering friendship had endured for years.

He glanced about for Rachelle and located her, but she had not seen him yet. She stood in the courtyard nearest the garden with the rest of the ladies-in-waiting, talking to Louise de Fontaine. Charlotte de Presney walked up to the group of ladies, and as she took in Rachelle's rich brown-auburn hair, her face was easy to read from even this distance.

"There will be jealousy between those two," Marguerite said, watching Rachelle and Charlotte. "If there is, I know who I shall blame. Charlotte is the worst of cats."

Fabien leaned into the shade beside Marguerite, taking the goblet of refreshment she offered him.

"Now why, cherie princesse, did you need to call Rachelle Macquinet to Amboise?" Fabien asked in a wearied voice. "Have you not enough belles gathered about you that you need this one as well? And with rumors of trouble brewing."

Margo smiled, her eyes flirting as always, and she extended her white hand to be kissed.

"La, la, Fabien, mon ami, but how beau you are this day. Madame Charlotte de Presney is most unhappy. She claims you have been breaking her heart. Ah, how cruel of you." And she laughed, her eyes twinkling.

He smiled. "Cherie princesse, do not grieve. If her heart is broken, I assure you, it is only because it is so tender. But we may take solace in her quick recovery, for she need but set her heart upon another and it will be quickly healed."

Margo gave him a delighted look from beneath long lashes. "But of course, my beau Bourbon, you are taken with my new mademoiselle. Is it not so? Oh yes, I know, it is the talk already among the ladies at court. She has made them all so jealous. And Charlotte has been trying to get your attention and has thus far failed. Charlotte does not often fail."

His voice was dry. "So I have noticed, Princesse."

"Oh, do not be so *sotte* and formal. You have been calling me Margo for years. So you find my Rachelle of much interest, do you, mon amour?"

He followed her gaze to the courtyard where Rachelle stood with the ladies-in-waiting. As if sensing his scrutiny, Rachelle turned her head. The distance between them was too great for speech, but he bowed toward her and she curtsied. Charlotte de Presney appeared to take note of this exchange and the displeasure on her face was evident.

"I requested Rachelle Macquinet to attend me at Amboise," Marguerite said.

"Can you not find another? Ladies are easy to come by, are they not? Look how many courtiers wish their daughters to serve you. Why not return her to the Chateau de Silk where her skills and interests lie?"

Marguerite grimaced. "*Nenni*. She behaves well. You are wrong. Loyal ladies are not easily found, and Rachelle pleases me well. Madame de Presney has cast her eyes on Henry. I cannot trust her. If I see her do so again, I shall have her punished. I mean it. Do not look at me like that. She is a spy for my mother. As if I did not know this. I may put Rachelle in her place as my maid-of-honor."

"Margo, la belle, do me a favor?"

"But yes, what is it?"

"Do not make her your maid-of-honor. See that she is protected from your ways — and do not make her the object of Charlotte's wrath."

Margo arched her dark brows, then laughed good-naturedly. She reached beckoning bejeweled fingers toward his chin, but he caught her wrist.

"Fabien, I should be insulted at such wanton words. But from you? I will take my reproofs. So you have special interests in Rachelle Macquinet, do you? Ah, this will not please your cousine. Maurice too is interested in the Daughter of Silk."

"My interest will displease many of the strutting cocks. But she is young and innocent. Keep her so, *ma fleur*, or you shall hear from me." He smiled winsomely.

She pursed her lips and made a kissing sound. "La, la."

"Do as I ask, ma cherie?" he requested seriously.

"I shall keep her under my sisterly wing, I promise you."

Fabien winced and Margo laughed, then she beckoned for one of her pages to assist her into the calèche.

"Au revoir, Fabien, unless you care to ride with us?"

"I have other business."

Marguerite took her chief place in the lush velvet seat of the calèche, her principal ladies coming forward, one by one, to be assisted in beside her.

Rachelle was about to enter the second calèche with attendants of lesser position when Marguerite sent word through a page, instructing her to come forward and ride with her, no doubt for Fabien's sake.

When Rachelle neared Marguerite's calèche, Fabien took her arm and turned toward the princesse. "Five minutes, Princesse." And he walked with Rachelle to the edge of a nearby garden where bougainvillea rambled along a stone fence.

"Monsieur Fabien, you have made me the point of every woman's jealous attention."

"You imagine it, I assure you," he said too lightly. He did not wish to acknowledge he was sought after, for it seemed to him the utmost of foppery. "This decision for you to journey to Amboise is most unfortunate, Mademoiselle."

She did seem troubled, but he also noticed the excitement flickering just below the surface of her eyes.

He grinned. "I vow you are enjoying this unexpected change in your future."

She lifted her chin with dignity. "Should I not, Marquis? Is it not an honor to serve Princesse Marguerite?"

He glanced the short distance to where Maurice and his lackeys were watching them. Maurice stood lounging against the courtyard wall, arms folded.

"That depends," Fabien said ruefully. "You know, do you not, that you are as a lamb among wolves? One bite, ma belle, and you are gone, I promise you."

Her dimples showed. "How graphic you are. You are not, are you, among those hungry wolves?"

He regarded her, arching a brow. She suddenly flushed and looked toward Marguerite's calèche. "I must not keep the princesse waiting ..."

"You are not. We will not depart until the royal entourage of Francis goes before us. Know that I have tried to change Margo's mind on making you one of her ladies-in-waiting, but she is insistent."

"Monsieur, I believe my days are planned by One far greater than the princesse. There is a divine purpose in my being called to her side. Perhaps I shall be used of God in some way, either to help the princesse personally or my fellow Huguenots."

Her simplicity was part of what attracted her to him, but it was also annoying.

"I cannot imagine a lamb walking boldly into an arena of wolves to reason with them of their need to discipline their ravenous appetites."

She refused to yield under his gaze. His eyes narrowed. He had expected her to be afraid, overwhelmed by such company, but instead, she was committed to the notion that she had been called of God.

"You would not listen if I told you the Bastille is full of men and women who also had the same noble belief? Yet they will undoubtedly die."

"Death is not the end. They look beyond the fiery stake to enter the Lord's pleasure."

For a moment he became frustrated with her calm confidence.

"Actually, what I am called to Amboise to do is rather simple."

"Is it?" He did not believe her for a moment.

"Yes. I shall be adding to Marguerite's wardrobe, and there is some talk of a wedding, though distant, of which I shall have the great honneur of assisting."

"Who told you of Margo's wedding?" He saw the hesitation in her eyes. Then she did understand the risk in going to Amboise, though she affected bonne cheer.

"The Queen Mother mentioned a future wedding."

"Then it was not Margo's idea to make you an attendant lady."

He saw the look of alarm break through her affected calm. "It was the Queen Mother," she said. "You have also heard of Grandmère being sent to Paris?"

"Yes. Curious, but there is more to trouble us. Duchesse Dushane, your kinswoman, has learned the king is calling for a council at Amboise to discuss and sign an edict of pacification. The king is to permit Huguenots the right to worship in peace. The Queen Mother has sent Sebastien to Moulins with a summons for my kinsmen to appear there."

"But this is bonne news, Marquis, is it not? I confess I am relieved by this turn of events, yet bewildered as well. An edict! Then Sebastien is safe?"

"Safe? Perhaps none of us are safe. No, not as long as the House of Guise holds sway over the king through their niece. Mary is obliging to her oncles. She is very young, as is Francis. I know them, and aside from being wholly taken with each other in amour, they hardly understand what is happening in France. The ruling authority lies somewhere between Catherine and her enemies, the Guises."

"She fears and despises them. Yes, so I have heard."

"She understands she is not popular enough with the people to stand against them should they come against her. The name of Guise is more esteemed in Paris than is the name of Valois. Catherine walks a balancing act between the House of Guise and the House of Bourbon, and the Huguenots are caught in the midst. She is loyal to none. She uses one against the other and so maintains her power. What disturbs me is they appear to be working hand in glove in this royal summons of the Bourbon-Huguenot leaders to Amboise."

"Your kinsman, Marquis, and the Bourbons, what of them? You say Sebastien was sent to bring them a summons to come to Amboise. Yet Maître Avenelle betrayed them to the Queen Mother as plotting against her."

"That is what worries me. Avenelle has laid the plot at the feet of Prince Condé, and one of his retainers, Renaudie. Yet now they are called to sign an edict of pacification. Catherine will not lightly forgive an enemy. So what is behind this summons?"

"Then they will not heed the royal summons to appear at Amboise, surely?" came Rachelle's hopeful question.

"I am afraid, Mademoiselle, you are somewhat misinformed about how little liberty we possess. We, that is, the Bourbon princes, are not in a position to ignore a summons from the king. Not unless we are willing to be declared in rebellion against the throne. If it comes to that, there is a death sentence."

"But your kinsman Louis Condé is a *royal* prince. How would they dare move against him?"

"Princes of the blood are murdered for much less than refusing a king's call, but Louis is no fool. He does not trust Catherine. He will look upon the summons with the eye of a fox. He will obey the call, but he will come with men-at-arms, enough to make Guise think hard before he tries to arrest him, I assure you. I will ride to Moulins myself to make certain they know of Avenelle's betrayal."

He walked her along the wall where roses meandered in untroubled beauty. "Now that you will go to Amboise, do listen to my advice, for I know these people well. Marguerite is reckless, but she will pose no deliberate danger to your life. Beware of Henry de Guise; he is dedicated to his father, the duc. Avoid the Queen Mother when possible. And say nothing of your being a Huguenot."

"Your concern for my safety is much admired, and may it please the marquis to think well of both me and my calling."

Fabien looked into her eyes until warm color came to her cheeks. He remembered that passionate embrace on the gallery and promised himself it would not be the last.

"I will think of you, you may be sure."

Fabien heard a rustling sound on the other side of the trees and garden wall. Rachelle, too, turned her head toward the sound, but no one appeared.

BEHIND THE GARDEN WALL, crouching beneath the overhanging clusters of bougainvillea, Charlotte de Presney cursed Rachelle under her breath. Charlotte had not intended to spy on them, though the Queen Mother ordered it. Her reluctance was not due to conscience or reticence, but because she was here to meet someone she must *not* be seen with.

Charlotte scarcely dared to breathe. If Fabien hoisted himself up onto the wide wall and looked down she would be called into account.

Any moment now she expected to see those sensuous violet eyes gazing down at her. She imagined his surprise slowly turning to chilling displeasure.

How a galante could be so dismissing of a woman who wanted him, she could not fathom. He bewildered her. She could have most any man at court, but Marquis de Vendôme turned her down! It was humiliating, especially when she had seen the haste with which he *could* pursue when he became interested in someone.

That young woman is proving to be a prickly rosebud among the ladies at court. Well, she now has the serpentine attention of the Queen Mother.

But Fabien had not hoisted himself up to the wall. Their voices grew muffled and faded. Charlotte breathed easier, and conscious now of her rendezvous, hurried alongside the wall to where the lime trees grew. She was late. She would also be missed at Marguerite's calèche. But the king would not yet leave, of that much she knew. So Marguerite would not depart without her. She could make up some excuse of where she had been, for she had done so many times before when she needed to protect herself.

She neared the lime trees and waited a moment. She picked up some pebbles and tossed them against the trunk of one of the trees. A man stepped out, wearing a dark cape and wide-brimmed hat. He bowed and came to meet her.

"Did you bring it, Monsieur Rene?"

"I have it with me, Madame. Do you have the gold pieces?"

She produced a tied handkerchief with the quantity inside. She watched with cool impatience while he counted the pieces.

She held her palm toward him. Satisfied she had brought the exact amount, he laid the vial in her hand.

Charlotte looked upon the tiny, glittering vial. She had tried other potions in the past, including the ashes of animals, but had no success.

"You are most certain it will do its work?"

His dark baleful eyes gazed back from beneath heavy lids. Even Charlotte, who was accustomed to the Queen Mother's expressionless serpentine look, felt a momentary chill blow through her. She had deliberately decided not to wear a fur-lined cape this morning because she had wished to show her figure. Now, with the chilling wind against her, she barely restrained the shudder that threatened to travel down her spine.

"Madame, the list of important women who do business with Monsieur Rene speaks for itself."

She knew the Queen Mother held confidence in Rene. He made up her parfumes and potions, just as the Ruggerio brothers arranged for her poisons. Charlotte knew of Catherine's poison closet, but would have been a fool to ever discuss it.

Charlotte left him and hurried alongside the pathway beside the vine-covered wall. She came upon a patch of sweet smelling flowers: stock, tuberoses, and jasmine. Now was the opportunity to put to test the famous potion. She turned her lips into a satisfied smile. She plucked several of the small roses, sprinkled them with the potion, and tucked them onto the lace at her bodice.

Soon she came to the small unlatched gate through which she had first entered the garden area.

In the courtyard again she wasted no time in removing herself from the area lest the marquis see her about and guess she had been behind the wall. She knew many side paths and shortcuts around the grounds of Chambord, and she took one of these now.

Ah, Fabien had told Rachelle not to reveal she was a Huguenot.

Charlotte stored away the priceless information, all but certain it would do her well one day.

PRINCESSE MARGUERITE VALOIS leaned forward and called through the open door of her calèche: "Enough, Fabien, ma beau petit, you give us all reason for jealousy of Rachelle. Come, Rachelle, you will ride beside me to Amboise. Do not trust the marquis too much. He is more dangerous than he permits you to realize, I promise you."

Margo blew him a kiss. "Au revoir, Fabien. Remember the masquerade to be held at Amboise next week. I will see Rachelle is there."

Fabien walked Rachelle to the calèche.

"Will I see you at Amboise?" Rachelle asked.

"Yes, but I may be gone for two days. I intend to ride to Moulins, but do not mention this to any of the others lest it get to the Guises."

"I will say nothing, Marquis, you may be sure."

He helped Rachelle into the calèche where Marguerite made room for her. There was another empty seat beside Louise de Fontaine who remarked, "What is delaying Madame de Presney?"

"She is always late, that one," Marguerite said. "I will one day have her thrown to the king's bears, I swear it."

Charlotte de Presney came hurriedly beside the calèche. "Pardon! But I am not late." There was a look of smug excitement in her blue eyes as she looked at Fabien.

"Marquis," she murmured, casting her eyes downward as she dipped a low bow, dropping the tuberoses from her bodice as she did.

Fabien reached down and retrieved them. Their eyes met. A cloying fragrance clung to his fingers as he bowed, handing her the cluster and as he did, her fingers deliberately caressed his hand.

"Merci," she murmured and waited to see if he would assist her. He took firm hold of her arm and helped her inside.

"Au revoir," Marguerite called again cheerfully as the attendant closed the door.

Fabien was still looking at Charlotte as the door shut between them.

GALLAUDET waited with Fabien's horse as he came up. He handed Fabien the reins. Fabien took them and swung into his ornate saddle.

"Monsieur," Gallaudet said after Fabien turned his horse to ride. "Andelot is with the common soldiers and his cousine Julot, the archer. Shall I send for Andelot to ride with us?"

"No, I will ride with him and Julot."

Gallaudet's eyes widened with surprise, for he held more strictly to title and rank than did even Fabien.

"I have a purpose in mind," Fabien said. "Once the royal party comes to the fork in the road that turns toward Amboise, I will slip away. I wish no one to see me. You do the same. We will meet on the road to Moulins."

Gallaudet lifted his brows. "Moulins, Monsieur?"

"I have a trusty word that Comte Sebastien has gone there to see Prince Condé. It may be that the Bourbon princes are gathered there as well, including Admiral Coligny. We ride to intercept Condé before he leaves for the royal summons at Amboise."

Gallaudet's brows shot up. "As you say, Monsieur. And Andelot? Is he to come with me?"

Fabien turned his bay to ride on toward the line of soldiers in the outer courtyard. "No, let him ride on to Amboise. It may be we shall meet up with him again on the way to Amboise castle. The king is in ailing health. They will journey slowly with his royal retinue in train." Fabien rode away toward the outer gate to find his favorite of cousines, Andelot Dangeau.

Once in the saddle he felt free again, the fresh wind on his face and throat was cooling and clean. He thought of Charlotte de Presney and frowned. Why was he thinking of her?

Then he suddenly lifted his hand and sniffed. The fragrance was strong. He wiped his hand on his velvet hosing but it did no good. He was sure now that the fragrance had not come from the flower he had retrieved for her. He lifted the lace on his sleeve and smelled. She had managed to place a potion on him when her fingers had caressed him. Where had the potion come from? Rene, the parfumer of Catherine de Medici used for her intrigues? And what was this potion supposed to do? Lure him to her bed?

His anger sizzled. What a comely and determined little witch she was, but a witch just the same. And one he would need to battle with in the future, of that he was becoming certain.

Chapter Twelve

ANDELOT DANGEAU WATCHED THE MARQUIS RIDE THROUGH THE GATE on his magnificent golden bay. *What a horse!*

Andelot removed his borrowed hat and lifted it high to get the marquis's attention. Fabien turned his reins and proceeded along the line of archers and soldiers, riding in a sprightly fashion toward him and Julot. He drew up in front of Julot, leaned across, and spoke in a low voice. Julot showed no expression, but Andelot, knowing him well, guessed the reason for the hardening of his jaw.

The marquis took a place beside Andelot in the line of horsemen. The soldiers nearby glanced his way, pleasure showing on their rugged faces that he chose to ride in their company instead of with the nobility.

"I spoke with Maurice alone for a few minutes this morning, and he confirms a royal meeting with the Bourbon princes at Amboise. King Francis will sign an edict of pacification allowing for freedom of worship in certain areas of France."

Andelot could hardly fathom the good news.

"Bien! Then the danger of a plot is past. But then, Monsieur Fabien, you look as though you do not believe it."

"I assure you, though the king himself wishes for the good of all his subjects, Catholic and Huguenot alike, I vow, mon cousine, this smells of Guise's treachery."

Andelot's enthusiasm wavered. "Treachery, Monsieur Fabien! Oh, but surely no."

"The Queen Mother is not called Madame le Serpent for want of reason. I learned she held a secret counsel exceedingly early this morning with the duc and the cardinal, and the king was not privy to it."

Andelot stoutly resisted. The marquis's suspicions were misguided. He suggested such with caution.

"But, Monsieur knows well, does he not, that the king is ailing? Is it not good for the Queen Mother and the duc and the cardinal to permit him rest until shortly before we depart?"

Fabien appeared to ignore the idea and went on in a low voice, musing, as if to himself. "Why would the House of Guise favor an edict of pacification? There have been other edicts, always broken by Guise's war campaigns. What has changed now? If anything, matters for the Huguenots grow more troubling throughout France. There are more arrests, more burnings."

"I pray you consider, it may be the Queen Mother did not favor the edict, Monsieur Fabien, and that is why she held council this morning, to convince them that such a pacification was not necessary for the good of all France. Even so, the Guises prevailed ..."

Andelot felt a bit sheepish when the marquis turned slowly toward him and gave him a level stare, which spoke plainly that he considered the explanation naive.

"You may choose to think well of them for your own reasons, mon ami. But do not imagine the Guise brothers are of a mind for compromise. The duc is very bold, and the cardinal is a man of sneering cruelty. I have little reason to trust them."

Andelot plucked at his reins. It perturbed him that Fabien regarded the House of Guise no better than his archery target pads in the armory. Why did he distrust them so?

"I am most sure, Monsieur —"

"The cardinal knows both King Philip and the pope sanction their actions here in France, so they are as bold as gamecocks."

Andelot felt his face turning hot with resentment. "Pray consider you may be errant in your conclusions, Marquis."

"It is the cardinal who brings Catherine orders from both men, and I promise you, the throne of France yields to them for fear of invasion from Spain's minions."

Andelot stirred in his saddle. He felt it unfair to his religious loyalties to even listen to this, though he did not think it wise to say so. He held the marquis's opinion in high regard, knowing him a man of his word. But Andelot also cherished the cardinal's office, even if he could not always cherish the character of the man in crimson. He wondered at times if the marquis, a Catholic who faithfully attended Mass, might not have secret penchants toward heretical Geneva?

He looked at Fabien out of the corner of his eye. No, it could not be. Why, Fabien was even wearing a silver Latin cross around his neck as he always did. There was a Huguenot cross as well, but if Fabien was one of the Calvinists, then he certainly would not wear the Latin emblem.

Andelot felt ashamed he had even thought such of the marquis, since he owed Fabien his unwavering loyalty. He admired him more than Fabien knew. Fabien had befriended him some years ago while they were boys. Andelot had gone to Paris to stay a month with his Oncle Sebastien. While Maurice shunned him and the other sons of the nobles looked upon him as a mere serf, Fabien, of higher rank than any of them, had cloaked him with dignity. And now, at Chambord, Fabien had brought him to his own chambers and called him cousine instead of sending him to sleep on the floor in the soldier's barracks. He had even given him fine clothes, put loose coins in his pocket, and told him to ignore Comte Maurice's arrogance.

And so, it had been a severe disappointment when the Marquis manifested but token enthusiasm for Andelot's proud announcement that he was related by blood to the House of Guise. He had thought surely the marquis would be impressed, just as he himself had been. But instead, he had cautioned him concerning any plans the duc and the cardinal might have for him.

The marquis was now saying, "It is of singular interest to me that this very morning the Queen Mother elevated Guise to become the new Marshal of France, the most powerful of positions. And the cardinal *made* himself treasurer. Do you not find these actions telling?"

Andelot was uncertain what to conclude. The internecine feuds and intrigues of inner court life, so prevalent and so understood by the marquis, were confusing to him. He preferred to say nothing.

"Does it not sound as if Catherine and the Guises are preparing for war and not for a time of peace?" Fabien insisted, turning his gaze upon him.

Andelot plucked at the leather reins. *Why did Fabien expect him to agree?*

Andelot straightened his shoulders. "Yet, Monsieur Fabien, is there not the promise from King Francis? You say you trust his benefice toward all his subjects."

"Saintes! You seem disposed toward bestowing benign favor upon the House of Guise no matter which way the wind blows, and all because of sharing an unexpected connection in their bloodline."

Andelot twisted in his saddle and refused to meet his scowl.

Fabien said no more, evidently thinking it useless to continue, while Andelot felt guilty as though he had shown disloyalty. He pondered in disturbed silence all the marquis had suggested and liked none of it.

Crimson and blue flags flurried in wind gusts. Silver trumpets sounded forth, commanding the attention of all.

Andelot was alert to everything going on around him, the tinkle of bells, the snapping of flags, the restless snorts from the horses, the smells that came to his nostrils now and then on the breeze. Were events foreshadowing trouble being born before his very eyes? Was Marquis Fabien merely being perceptive? Could it be that something important was happening? Something smelling, as Fabien had said, of treachery?

Fabien had once mentioned he did not believe the death of Jean-Louis de Vendôme was brought about by an ill-fated turn in a battle against Spain during the reign of King Henry II, Catherine's husband. He had hinted that he thought his père's death was an assassination, and that le Duc de Guise was involved.

So his mistrust must surely be due in part to his suspicions.

Andelot felt somewhat relieved by his thoughts.

As trumpets blared announcing the young king and queen were preparing to ride through into the courtyard, Andelot sat up straighter, his eyes were busy, and his skin tingled.

Another loud trumpet blast announced King Francis II.

Andelot snatched his hat from his head and held it to his heart. A shout rang out from the king's men and another blare of trumpets came with a quick beating of drums. The hooves of many horses clattered proudly across the cobbles.

"The king comes!"

"Vive le Roi!"

The royal horses and the glittering procession neared, attended by the pages of the royal household wearing red velvet embroidered in gold, followed by the king's musketeers in red and blue uniforms, and the Swiss guards with halberds and plumed helmets, their doublets with slashed sleeves showing black velvet.

Sixteen-year-old King Francis rode in the midst, a slight but elegant figure astride his horse. Mary Stuart, eighteen, Queen of Scotland and now Queen of France, rode prettily beside him. The royal couple looked to be much taken with one another. She was dressed in a robe with gold embroidery and trimmed with ermine.

"His Majesty does not appear in fine fettle today," Andelot whispered with worry, again drawing Fabien's attention as to why he may not have been called to the meeting this early morning with the Queen Mother and the Guises.

"He has been ill since birth," Fabien told him. "He has a sickness of the blood. It is unfortunate, for he is the most likable of the royal sons. He enjoys music, art, and listening to the reinette play her flute just for him. He is unlike his younger brother Charles. Charles is mad."

Andelot cast Fabien a shocked look, at first thinking that he poorly jested; however, the grave look on his handsome face convinced Andelot otherwise.

"Mad?" Andelot whispered. "Marquis, why do you say such a thing?"

"Why? Because it is so, I assure you. You will find out for yourself," came his low, warning voice, "when you meet him at Amboise. Beware of him, for he is shrewd. It is wiser that I am with you, mon ami, when you meet the prince."

Andelot mulled the information over in his mind. *Mad?* Prince Charles Valois?

Just behind Francis and Mary rode the queen regent, Catherine de Medici, dressed in black as usual. Beside her rode le Cardinal de Lorraine himself, almost as regal in his crimson vestment as the king.

Andelot watched the cardinal, who also bore the name of Charles, and the duc, who bore the same name as Francis. But this Charles was sane. Was he also as shrewd and cruel as Fabien thought? As Andelot stared at Cardinal Charles de Guise from Lorraine, he felt a tingle of pride. *My* kinsman. A powerful man, he! He was comely too. His neat beard was short and blond with a hint of red. His crimson vestment was lined with white fur, and he wore a wide-brimmed crimson hat of Spanish style, the same wide-brimmed hat worn by all higher churchmen.

Fabien leaned toward Andelot. "The cardinal keeps several mistresses."

Andelot flushed. "Marquis, one can never think so about the cardinal! Ah, ça non!"

"Ah, but you are gullible. You think these men of lofty rank are honorable, whether they are holy or not. What if they are whited sepulchers — full of dead men's bones, mon ami Andelot?"

Andelot refused to be baited. "Lofty of rank, yes. Therefore of honor."

"Non! Why do you think Luther and Calvin strive for reform in the Church?"

"Heretics!"

"That description, of our own Calvin, comes from a Church that has become a comfortable nest for rats."

"Marquis de Vendôme, you make me tremble. Do you not speak blaspheme?"

The marquis turned his mouth with impatience. His violet blue eyes burned with frustration. "You have a wrong conception of blasphemy. In speaking of wayward men, I do not impugn God."

"You do. For these men speak for God."

"Then all the greater their responsibility to present God's truth rather than replace it with their own exalted pronouncements, then persecute those who turn elsewhere to worship."

"You *are* a Huguenot. I swear it!"

"Non, non, Andelot. But what will you do? Run to your boasted kinsman, le Cardinal, with my heresy?"

Andelot sucked in his breath, leaning back away from him. "*Sûrement pas!* How can you think so, Monsieur Cousine? But when you speak of — of wrongs in Christ's Church you give the infidels reasons to mock and reject."

"Did not Jesus make a cord of whips and clean the temple of those who polluted it? Did he cover the sins of the religious rulers to hide their hypocrisy? Why do you think the religious rulers plotted his death? Was it not because he showed their need for repentance?"

Andelot stared straight ahead. He tightened his mouth.

Fabien smiled and whispered, "Should we turn like snarling wolves on Calvin and Luther when they shine their candles upon the Scriptures, revealing corners of the Church where cobwebs of uncleanness breed? What are you and the others afraid of? Is your faith so fragile that only that which cannot be shaken remains?"

"Monsieur!" Andelot gripped his hat, holding it flat against his chest, his teeth gritting. "Shh!" He looked about in fear of being overheard, but Fabien's voice had been low, and all eyes were on royalty. "Where have you learned this, Monsieur? I beg of you — someone may hear — ah, the faggots, the faggots they burn hot, they scorch, they smoke — "

Andelot's heartbeat doubled. "Surely you are a Huguenot, Marquis, like the rest of your Bourbon kinsmen, and have kept it from me."

"No," Fabien said calmly, "I am not. If I were, I would not be ashamed to say so. I am a Catholic, mon ami. But I am no blind zealot either, believing everything and anything these men tell me. We should search the Scriptures ourselves and see whether these things be so. I see no insult done to God by calmly hearing what Calvin and Beza say, as they are learned and righteous men. I would even read the *Institutes*."

This idea brought Andelot further alarm. A feeling of dejection smothered him. *How could the marquis have come up with such a wild tale as this? Jesus making a whip and driving people and animals from the temple? Such a thought! This could not be in the "real" Bible, but only in the heretic Bible, the one written in French. Did the marquis have one?*

Andelot wanted to ask him, but feared the answer.

John Calvin, who had fled France, was now in Geneva leading the Reformed Church and governing the city. His *Institutes* were banned in France, just as they were elsewhere in Western Europe. If one possessed these books, one would quickly be condemned a heretic.

"Ah, Marquis, do you know what happened to a shopkeeper in Paris who printed Calvin's works?"

"I can well imagine."

"He would not divulge the names of the Huguenots he had sold the books to."

"A man whom Jesus will commend one day, I am sure. That is why you must honor these martyrs, Andelot, because the Lord will honor them. Do not think lightly of your brothers and of their past sufferings. They put us and our loyalty to the great Christ to shame."

Andelot hung his head. He could not bring himself to say "heretics."

But they are heretics. They "must" be. Rome said so.

On occasion Andelot, too, admitted to his heart that he wondered what Calvin had written in those books that made him so hated and feared, but he would not risk finding out. If he were caught speaking as the Marquis had just spoken ... Andelot groaned within. He glanced toward Fabien who did not appear intimidated and merely saluted the king and queen with savoir-faire as they rode past toward the road. It amazed Andelot to see the King and Queen of France smile and acknowledge Fabien.

Andelot sighed. He took courage in remembering that Fabien went daily to Mass. He told himself that Fabien was merely of a curious nature, always wanting to know more than was considered safe to know. He enjoyed learning, and even books meant for burning interested him. And, for the sake of disputation, Fabien would even debate issues from a side he did not fully agree with. Surely that was what he was doing now. Oui, bien!

"Come, mon ami, it is time to ride," the Marquis told him and smiled. "I see I have vexed you to your bones."

Andelot twisted his mouth into a wry smile. Yes, he had certainly made him sweat. He wiped his brow and turned his reins to ride out with the soldiers and the marquis.

THE RETINUE OF ROYAL CALÈCHES was moving toward the gate and the road to Amboise. Rachelle sat in Princesse Marguerite's calèche, looking round at such bountiful luxury. Her excitement rose. The well-padded interior of Marguerite's calèche was upholstered in green velvet; the gold velvet cushions and matching footstools were corded in blue with gold tassels. Compared to the Macquinet calèches in which she and her family had ridden all the way from Lyon, this was luxury in the extreme.

Hardly had the royal calèche left the grounds of Chambord when Rachelle glanced across at Charlotte de Presney and noticed mud on one of her fancy slippers and a smudge on the edge of her hem, as though she had trailed it through wet soil. Rachelle's eyes lifted to Charlotte who was looking out the window. Her blonde hair was slightly windblown, and she was still breathing as though she had run to get to the calèche. *Had it been Charlotte behind the garden wall, eavesdropping?*

Just as most women sensed romantic tension between a man and a woman when emotion was meant to be hidden, Rachelle had noticed the prickly tension between Marquis Fabien and Charlotte de Presney. Well, it was no secret where Charlotte's aims were concerned. Rachelle had seen her hand caress Fabien's. *She deliberately dropped that flower.* With that thought came a sickening dart of pain, and yes, even fear, as she remembered the look in the marquis's eyes when his gaze locked with Charlotte's. Not that she could blame him for reacting to a woman who was belle of face and figure and who flaunted her bosom in a shockingly low décolletage.

Rachelle struggled not to glare at Charlotte. It was positively shameful the way she had not worn a cloak to cover herself! But then, her behavior was intentional.

Rachelle scanned her once again, uneasily. She had few scruples, and it was plain to see she was determined to snare the marquis as a lover.

Charlotte turned her head and caught Rachelle's stare. Rachelle attempted to keep her feelings hidden and quickly relaxed her expression. The smug turn of Charlotte's carmined lips told her she had not succeeded. Rachelle was relieved when Princesse Marguerite began to talk incessantly as she was prone to do, her ladies agreeing with her and assuring her that all her self-depicted woes were justified.

Andelot, as he rode alongside Fabien, was comforted to see that fierce emotion had left his eyes. Fabien frightened him, confronting him with ideas that must be avoided if one were to live life and see good days.

For some time they rode in silence, the long royal train of King Francis II slowly winding its way along the road. The winds cooled him, and he began to enjoy the ride.

After they had ridden for a time, Fabien gestured that Andelot should let the soldiers behind ride on ahead of them. After a time, with the yardage between them and the other horsemen widening, Fabien drew rein and Andelot came beside.

"Adieu, Andelot. I ride on from here toward Moulins. Tell no one where I have gone. I will see you in two days at Amboise castle."

Andelot knew at once why Fabien would venture to ride to Moulins. He saw his men-at-arms waiting at the side of the road; young, stalwart men wearing the Bourbon colors and the family lineage of Vendôme. Andelot felt a sudden longing to be one of them. To turn his back on any prospects with the House of Guise and follow the marquis. Dare he ask?

"Monsieur? I—"

Just then a horseman galloped up, and Andelot turned to see Gallaudet, the marquis's loyal page.

"Monsieur," Gallaudet said, "there are horsemen riding this way with the flag of the House of Guise. They are likely to join the duc at Amboise. Should we not leave at once before they know we have seen them?"

"How many soldiers?"

"Monsieur, at least five hundred, maybe more."

Andelot looked quickly at Fabien and saw what he was thinking. This was more evidence that made him think the Guises were up to harm. He could not think they were merely going to Amboise to safeguard the king and royal family.

"Adieu, Andelot. We ride." Fabien saluted him in a friendly way and rode off with Gallaudet. His men-at-arms followed in behind and galloped after them. Andelot watched until the great golden bay had raced across a green meadow toward the distant forest to the chateau of Moulins.

Chapter Thirteen

THE PALAIS CHATEAU OF MOULINS WAS LESS THAN A TWO-HOUR JOURNEY from Blois. The sun was high in the pale aqua sky with puffy clouds over the Val d'Oise. Fabien and his retinue galloped swiftly across the plain toward the Forez and took the much-used route along the river where it followed the green embankment. Water tumbled over gray rocks where the spray caught the rays of the sun in a rainbow mist. Birdsong refreshed and assured the listener's heart, if not the mind, that all was well in the world.

Fabien turned his golden bay and began the final ascent into the forest around Berry. Moulins was not far now. The redolent smell of the dark soil, damp and rich, and the scent of pine warmed by the sun, canvassed the region around them.

In the early afternoon the vast chateau came into view. It was embraced on three sides by the gleaming lake and on the fourth side with the tall pine trees that framed the sky.

Fabien and Gallaudet rode the edge of the lake, followed by a dozen men-at-arms and as many lackeys, and then up to the gate. The *portier* came hurrying from his lodge nearby, and recognizing the armorial bearing of Vendôme, bowed, saluted, and went to draw back the gate.

They rode through, horse hooves clattering over the cobbled road that ascended toward the grand chateau where the Bourbon Prince Louis de Condé and his wife, Princesse Eleonore, were gathered with other Bourbon nobles.

At the entrance the hostlers came forward to take his horse. Most of his men-at-arms went off to refresh themselves at the barracks and stables with the grooms and lackeys.

Fabien entered the palais and was shown along the great corridors with their gold lacquer and silk-paneled walls to a large salon overlooking the *Cour d'Honneur*. A meeting was now underway, and Prince Louis de Condé was present, a man of middle height, with dark hair and eyes, of elegant fashion and bearing that announced he had not forgotten he was a royal prince.

Fabien did not see Admiral Coligny, but his elder brother, Odet, le Cardinal de Châtillon, was there and in deep conversation with Sebastien.

The women were gathered in an adjoining chamber. Fabien recognized Prince Condé's wife, Princesse Eleonore, a blood niece of Cardinal Odet. She was leading a discussion on the plight of fellow Huguenots who had been deprived by the state church of their houses, shops, and estates for holding the outlawed Protestant faith.

Fabien had great respect for the older Princesse Eleonore who was most earnest and devout in her worship of Christ. He had heard how she was involved in aiding the persecuted and needy and setting up safe houses to care for them.

Prince Louis de Condé looked up from across the room and Fabien bowed lightly. "Monsieur le Prince."

Condé's charming face creased into a smile and his dark eyes sparkled. He strode forward to meet him.

"Marquis Fabien, mon cousine, our gathering here is now complete with your arrival. Tell me, have you just come from Vendôme?"

"Non, mon cousine, but from Chambord. The king has left for Amboise this morning. I broke away and rode straight here to Moulins." He looked toward the others and said in a louder voice to gain their attention: "Messieurs and Prince, I bring you news that has developed since Comte Sebastien brought the royal summons to you here at the Bourbon Palais."

A sober silence fell across the room. The nobles of the Huguenot-Bourbon alliance ceased their discussion and gave him their full attention.

Sebastien moved forward, concern showing on his face. "Is it as I fear concerning the masked gentleman that rode in with Guise?"

Fabien looked at him. "It is, Oncle. The hooded stranger is a monsieur all of you know well from your times in Paris; he was one of you, a Huguenot, but now he has shown himself your betrayer. Maître Avenelle arrived at Chambord yesterday, brought by le Duc de Guise to confess to the Queen Mother all he knows of the Blois plot to abduct Francis, to remove the Guises from power in France, and to set up our Prince Condé as regent of France."

A dazed look crossed their faces. Sebastien turned pale, convincing Fabien he indeed had been involved, although Avenelle had not named him. A low murmur circulated among the nobles. Louis showed himself grim, but determined.

"Then I was named before the Queen Mother?"

Fabien looked at him. "With scorched words you were named and denounced as a traitor, Monsieur Louis."

Fabien told them of the listening closet and of all that Avenelle betrayed, how he had set the crown of treason on Prince Condé's head and accused him of fully backing and helping to supply his retainer, Barri de la Renaudie, a nominal leader of Huguenots.

A groan circled the room.

"Heaven save us!" Cardinal Odet said.

"Avenelle, the betrayer. Who would have thought so of him?" Louis said in a shocked tone.

"A man of such pious prayers," another said.

Fabien said, "Messieurs, though I am not a Huguenot as you know, I am a loyal Bourbon and am as enraged as you over this hypocrite Avenelle who was willing to turn you all over to the Bastille inquisitors to save his neck. I see that la Renaudie is not here. He must be warned at once. If he tries to carry out his attack against the House of Guise, then I fear for the life of our Bourbon Prince Louis."

"Avenelle," Sebastien lamented. "I feared it was him from the moment I looked below into the courtyard and saw the masked rider with Guise. But I could not bring myself to fully accept his fall from our ranks."

"Whose names were mentioned, Marquis Fabien? Tell us again," Cardinal Odet said gravely.

Fabien did so, and Sebastien shook his head. "The half has not been told. It is you, my prince, who has taken the heavy blow for us."

But Louis showed his courage by an elegant lift of his hand. "Mon ami, do not overly concern yourself for me. We will battle le Duc de Guise and his hired soldiers, and if necessary, we will arm the Huguenots and take to the fields. I am willing to take whatever blow our good God permits. I have no regrets, except that our plan to save France from the grip of Spain's legates, the duc and the cardinal, is known."

"Monsieur, this call to Amboise for the signing of an edict of pacification is naught but another of the Queen Mother's gambits," Sebastien warned. "I have said so to all of you from the moment I arrived. There will be no peace. Not as long as Spain and Rome demand the removal of all heretics from France. And so say I again, beware of le Cardinal de Lorraine. He is as cunning as the Queen Mother."

Fabien agreed. And if any understood Catherine and her Machiavellian wiles, it was Sebastien who served on her privy council.

Fabien turned to Louis. "Sebastien speaks well. Even now we should disperse. Guise may have sent men to watch this chateau. My page has warned of messieurs following."

"Let us end this gathering as quickly as possible, I beg of you, mon Prince," Sebastien said. "For your sake, let us separate."

"There are loyal men-at-arms on guard around this chateau, and be assured none can come upon us in surprise." Condé walked to the middle of the room again, commanding their attention. "Messieurs, I say we must go to Amboise as summoned by the king. If we do not, Guise will have reason enough to gather an army and come against us for rebellion. You have heard what Marquis Fabien has told us, that le Duc de Guise has been made Marshal of France. He now has unlimited power to wage his fight against our Huguenot towns and hamlets."

"The Queen Mother will live to regret the added power she has so unwisely put in her enemies' hands."

"She may have regrets even now," Fabien said. "Already she has learned her compromise with Guise has benefited his move for the throne."

"We need time to gather our troops," Louis said. "We must sign with the king and put this edict to the test."

Princesse Eleonore stood listening with the other women. Fabien admired their calm, their dignity, their confidence in God. *What noble women are these!* She approached Louis now, and showing her great deference, he lifted her hand to his lips.

"Louis, I fear every step you take toward Amboise will bring you closer to your own destruction. Is it not wiser to confront the danger head on? To bring the facts into the light? Let the Queen Mother and the House of Guise know you are aware Maître Avenelle has spoken to her. So much intrigue only permits deception to grow among confusion and darkness."

"I agree," Fabien said. "Do not go to Amboise. Send a letter in which the intrigues of Avenelle and Guise are shown to be beneficial to Guise's rise to power. Appeal to Francis and Catherine only. I will deliver your letter and also seek to convince her."

Louis took a turn around the room, one hand on his scabbard. "We must pay heed to the summons of the king," Louis said again. "They have no evidence of my wrongdoing. It is all Avenelle's tale to save himself. I will send a rider this night to warn la Renaudie not to leave his chateau."

"Then if you will go to Amboise, my husband, attend with a strong show of force," Eleonore advised. "Let them know you will do battle before you allow them to arrest you. You are a prince of the blood royal and you must remind the Guises of this."

Louis laid a hand on her arm. "We have several days before the council is to be held, time enough to prepare." He then turned to Admiral Coligny's brother, Odet. "Cardinal, you will see to it that your brother is told of Maître Avenelle?"

Fabien admired the young cardinal for his warmth and humility. *How he contrasts with Cardinal Guise.*

"I will send a message to Gaspard, Monsieur. As you know, he remains at his chateau in Châtillon. He was not involved in Renaudie's plot, though he fully sympathizes. He will obey the summons, and knowing Gaspard as I do, he will bear the truth to the king concerning the reasons for dissatisfaction among his Huguenot subjects."

"I have no doubt. A greater ami we have not found for our just cause, nor a greater Calvinist." He took a sharp turn looking at each of the Bourbon nobles. "Messieurs, we will of a truth go with a show of arms. We will ride to Amboise, but we will send a message ahead through Monsieur

Fabien—" he gestured toward him with a nod of his head—"assuring King Francis of our loyalty to the House of Valois. Therefore they cannot, and will not, move against princes of the blood."

Fabien was not as certain, but Louis had made his decision.

Sebastien, who had spoken little, looked pale and tense. Perhaps he thought he had more to lose with Madeleine so soon to give birth to their first child. Fabien's sympathy was with him.

Fabien grew restless. "What of Renaudie? We must act now to contact him, Monsieur Louis."

"Yes, there is no time for delay," Louis said.

"I have my men-at-arms with me," Fabien said. "I can easily raise more from Vendôme. My page can ride there in but a few hours."

"You are not part of the plot," Sebastien said, looking anxious. "Do not join us, Fabien. You must keep your reputation with the throne for a future day."

A ripple of firm agreement went around the room.

"If it had not been that the Queen Mother betrayed Coligny at Reims, there would be no plot now," Louis said.

Fabien looked at him, wondering. This was the first he had heard of a betrayal of Admiral Coligny.

"How so, Prince?" Fabien asked curiously.

Louis scowled, as if remembering.

"It concerned the Huguenot minister, Anne du Bourg. Admiral Coligny and others at court pleaded with Catherine to spare him after Henry II died from a joust at Tournelles. It was her husband, the king, who allowed the cardinal to have Anne du Bourg arrested and placed in the Bastille. With Henry dead, the Huguenot leaders hoped Catherine would show favor toward them and release Anne. Catherine met secretly with the admiral and hinted she would. She even promised to attend a meeting of Huguenot ministers to discuss peace with them at Reims. She was journeying to Reims for the crowning of Francis. Coligny brought all the Huguenot leaders to Reims, even Calvin considered coming. But—" Louis shrugged elegantly—"Catherine failed to show up. Then Anne du Bourg was burned. It so angered the Huguenots that we felt we must do something. The plot Avenelle betrayed to le Duc de Guise was our answer to the House of Guise and the Queen Mother for their falseness to us, and for the murder of Anne."

Fabien considered in silence.

"I shall send two of my pages," Louis said. "La Renaudie has four thousand Huguenots armed and ready. If Guise already knows this then Renaudie's chateau will surely be under watch."

Fabien was uneasy when he recalled the men-at-arms Gallaudet had witnessed riding west. Surely they had been sent by Guise to watch la Renaudie.

"It will be difficult to get through without being noticed," Fabien warned. "If one of your men is taken captive, they will torture the facts from him. If he were my man, I would safeguard him, and us, by telling him as little as possible except a few words that Renaudie will understand. And the fewer men sent, the better chance of slipping through."

"If it is not already too late." Sebastien paced, plucking at his sleeve. He was frowning and looked more doubtful by the moment.

Montmorency, who had been replaced as Constable of France by le Duc de Guise and in bitterness went over to the Bourbons, also showed growing alarm and doubt. "Ah, Monsieur Prince, I know of the battlefield and armies. It may not be possible in so short a time to inform so many men."

"We will not fail," Louis said. "I will ask Capitaine d'Empernon to get through to Nantes. He can leave as soon as it is dark."

Fabien thought they should send a man dressed as a peasant, not a known captain in Louis's army, but he hesitated to again suggest amending the prince's decision.

Louis smiled affectionately as he turned to Fabien. "You have done well by coming to warn us, Cousine Fabien. But now there is no cause to further risk yourself in association with us at Amboise. Far wiser for you to ride to your chateau at Vendôme."

"Yes," Sebastien urged. "Avoid getting caught in whatever intrigues may be planned by Catherine and the Guises."

Fabien was standing near the terrace. The breeze blowing in had turned colder. The sun was beginning to set with a sullen yellow stain spreading behind the trees and mountains. Thunderheads were beginning to gather, threatening to veil the last of the sun's rays. Darkness would soon settle.

Fabien had no intention of withdrawing to Vendôme. Andelot Dangeau would be at Amboise to meet the cardinal. Fabien did not know why, but he had always held a sense of responsibility and concern for him, though Andelot was but a few years younger than himself. And now, the Macquinets of Lyon were involved. If there was trouble, he could not imagine himself riding away from it and leaving Rachelle and Andelot in its midst while he sought refuge at his chateau.

Louis grinned, his dark eyes adventurous. "I see you are offended at the thought. You are a true Bourbon, mon cousine. The courageous blood of Jean-Louis is also yours."

Fabien bowed. "But with your leave, mon prince, I would not wait here with you and the others for the admiral's arrival from Châtillon. I will leave for Amboise as soon as our men and horses have rested and eaten. It may be we can overtake the king's retinue, as they are journeying slowly."

Montmorency came to him, throwing an arm around his shoulders. "Will you at least stay for the afternoon feasting?"

"May our good God agree our plans are just in his sight and sanction our lives in this matter," Cardinal Odet said.

"We daughters of God will be on our knees for each of you, messieurs," Princesse Eleonore said, "and God be with you, Marquis Fabien." She had come up to him with a reassuring smile. He bent over her hand.

"Merci, Mademoiselle Princesse."

Louis took her hand and laid it against his heart, his dark eyes speaking deepest respect for her earnest faith. The look between them went deeper than physical amour, and again Fabien took note. He bid them adieu and left to find Gallaudet and his men.

Chapter Fourteen

THE ROYAL PROCESSION, MAKING ITS SLOW JOURNEY TOWARD THE fortress of Amboise, had stopped for the midday meal, and to permit the ailing young king to rest and walk among the trees with Mary.

Rachelle knew that Andelot Dangeau, who had spent his first fourteen years in Lyon at the Chateau de Silk and was an ami to both her and Idelette, rode among the king's soldiers. She had on occasion seen him around Chambord and had wished to visit with him, but her demanding agenda had left her days filled.

She walked as near to where the soldiers were resting under the trees as was fitting for proper conduct and hoped that Andelot would notice and recognize her. It was not long until she heard the sound of horse hooves and he rode up, smiling. She thought him comely with his brown wavy hair and eyes.

"Mademoiselle Rachelle!" He swung down from his horse. "Bonjour, but what bonne chance to meet you on the journey."

She laughed. "It was not by chance, I assure you, Andelot. I was hoping you would notice I was here and have some time to spare. I have wanted to visit with you since you arrived at Chambord with the marquis. I thought we could visit during our déjeuner."

"How fair it is to see you again, Mademoiselle. I too had wished to see you at Chambord but your time belonged to the princesse. I hear your work with the silk has so pleased royalty that you have become one of her court ladies. You are pleased?"

"I am honored, yes, but it is all so new and strange. There are so many in the nobility to meet and whose names I should remember. But tell me of yourself! The last I saw you, Sebastien placed you at a monastery school in Paris."

"That was three years ago. New changes have befallen me and you will hardly believe my good fortune."

They sat together on an old log beneath an alder tree lunching on the food that Rachelle had brought along and pouring tea from a jug into two cups, as Andelot stunned her with news of his kinsman relationship to the House of Guise.

When he concluded his tale of how his oncle had visited him at the Paris school with the information that had emerged from the cardinal, she hardly knew how to fathom the change it would make in Andelot's future.

"Sebastien must have been profoundly shocked by this, as well as yourself. How is it you are related to the House of Guise without his knowing? And why did it take so long for the matter to be discovered? So many questions! You *are* a blood nephew of Sebastien, are you not?"

"Yes, one wonders, to be sure, and I am not at all pleased, because in truth, few answers have been given to me. I yet await my first introduction and interview with the cardinal. I only know what mon Oncle Sebastien told me recently, that mon père, Louis Dangeau, was not his blood brother as we always thought, but only related. When Louis's parents died, he was brought into the Dangeau family, and as it were, adopted."

The explanation was unsatisfactory to Rachelle, and she could see by the thoughtfulness in his eyes that it was to him as well, but it was not her place to cast doubt upon Sebastien's explanation. Perhaps even Sebastien did not know the true facts.

"So your père was related to the House of Lorraine?"

Andelot's brows tucked together beneath the lock of brown hair that fell across his tanned forehead. He stared at his roast venison and bread loaf. "One wonders," he repeated. "I believe Marquis Fabien may know something, but he changes the subject when I bring it up." He shook his bread with deliberation. "Oui, I suppose that is how it happened. Sebastien has told me that it is the duchesse who would not receive Louis."

Rachelle frowned. "The duchesse?"

He looked at her. "Le Duc de Guise's maman, the unsmiling dowager of Catholic orthodoxy — did not accept Louis because my mother was ... a woman of ill repute." He took a big bite of meat, avoiding her eyes.

"That is no shame to you. Do you know who your maman is?"

"Non."

"Perhaps the shame is equally the House of Guise who refused to accept you until most recently.

"I am told le cardinal only recently discovered who I was. It was then he sent Sebastien to take me from the monastery school. You remember when I left Lyon?"

"Idelette had sulked for weeks afterward," she confessed casually.

"She did?" came his surprised voice. "Ho! Who would ever have guessed?"

"What will you do now? Have they told you what they are planning for your future?"

He frowned. "I suppose I shall discover it when I meet the cardinal at Amboise. Sebastien believes I shall be chosen for the privilege of entering the *corps des pages*."

She could see that he watched her eagerly for her response. She was, indeed, proud for him, but dare not give him any suggestion that she was pleased romantically. Though they were near the same age, Andelot seemed yet a boy to her after meeting the marquis.

"Doubtless that would be an honor for you." She added gentle meaning: "Would you then be serving the cardinal?" The idea made her uncomfortable, but even so, she did not wish to foil any sense of pride he might have over his recent status.

"I will not know that until I meet with him." He then frowned. "I am unsure what becoming his page would mean. That is, I am aware of my duties, but ..."

He did not finish, and Rachelle politely kept silent. They were both thinking along the same paths, she was sure. Would the time come in the future when Andelot was expected to carry out the cardinal's policy of persecution against heretics?

They finished their meal. He helped her gather a bowl and a few dishes together into a bag for one of the lackeys to carry away, then he offered to walk her back to where the royal coaches were gathered in the shade of the trees, the flags of Valois rippling in the breeze.

"I suppose I shall see you again at Amboise," he said, his tone hopeful.

Rachelle smiled absently, for her attention was focused back along the road. "Look, there are riders coming. They are halting beneath those alder trees near the stream." Was the main rider who she anticipated? The golden horse had a jeweled harness and the rider wore a cloak and hat that even from where she stood showed par excellence.

"It is Marquis Fabien and Gallaudet. They will join the king's caravan once we are back on the road to Amboise."

"He arrived only in time. It appears as though the king is ready to ride on again."

"I was uncertain if Marquis Fabien would return from—"

He shot her a glance, as if he had misspoken.

She hastened to put him at ease, to let him know that she was aware of Fabien's secret journey to his Bourbon kinsmen.

"It is a mercy of God that Marquis Fabien has returned safely from meeting with Prince Condé. I wonder if the Bourbon chieftains will decide not to heed the king's summons to come to Amboise?"

"Then he told you? The marquis has shown confidence in your trust, but who would not?"

"Merci. But what do you think, Andelot? Will Prince Condé and the others come?"

"How can they not? It is the king's demand."

"Yes, but not a light thing when you are uncertain of your reception, though the Queen Mother speaks of an edict of peace." Remembering her foray into Catherine's bedchamber and the sinister interview following, Rachelle again felt her nerves curl.

Andelot looked off toward the royal caravan preparing for its journey. "If only there could be peace between Catholics and Huguenots."

Not as long as the House of Guise are legates of Philip II of Spain and control the throne.

She became aware of Andelot's scrutiny and busied herself by taking notice of the clouds drifting in from the hills.

"It looks as if it will soon rain. Au revoir, Andelot, I must make haste to la Valois before she misses me."

"Au revoir, Rachelle." He bowed.

Rachelle tossed him a smile of affection, then walked back toward the royal calèche where she noticed a flurry of activity. When would she again talk with Marquis Fabien?

As she neared, Charlotte de Presney approached her from the trees.

"Where have you been?" she asked crossly. "The princesse has been inquiring." Charlotte turned her head and looked off toward the soldier's camp. "You must not wander off. Your reputation will soon be questioned, I assure you." She turned and walked in the direction of the coach.

The minx!

Rachelle hurried up to the royal coach, expecting a sharp rebuke from Princesse Marguerite, and instead found her *bon vivant*, her dark eyes feisty. *Now what has she planned?*

"I shall ride horseback the rest of the journey to Amboise, and you shall come with me. You and Madame de Presney."

Rachelle was certain the Queen Mother would not approve of Marguerite riding off without her guard. She was equally certain that Marguerite had some plan to meet Henry de Guise along the way in the woods.

Rachelle was relieved when Charlotte saved her from the necessity of trying to reign in the princesse's enthusiasm for indulging her whims.

"Princesse, it will rain soon, and you know you are of weak disposition in the cold, wet months. May it please you to remain dry in the comfortable coach."

Marguerite was surely in no mood for hindrance. "It is you who fear a trifle of rain. We will ride."

As Marguerite turned gaily to the rest of her ladies, Louise de Fontaine leaned toward Rachelle and whispered, "There is only one thing that could be so feverishly upon Marguerite's mind: Monsieur Henry. He is no longer among the courtiers invited to Amboise."

"Why so?"

"The Queen Mother has most sternly forbidden her to be alone with Monsieur Guise. Marguerite will meet the King of Portugal at Amboise and it is hoped by the Queen Mother that a marriage could be in the future."

"With the King of Portugal? But what of Prince Henry of Navarre, the Huguenot?" Rachelle whispered.

Louise held her fan near her lips, glancing about as she spoke to make certain they were not being watched.

"I have heard it said the Queen Mother has several important princes in mind for marriage to her youngest daughter, and that she is wooing all of them to gain but one. The one monseigneur she truly wishes for Marguerite is the son of King Philip of Spain, but the king is displeased with Catherine."

"Displeased, but why?"

"Spain insists that the king destroy all heretics in France. There is some discussion that the Queen Mother may even go to Spain with Marguerite in a year or two to convince him of the marriage with his son. If they do visit Spain, Marguerite's chief ladies will travel with her."

Louise looked at her thoughtfully. "I am sure Philip will have a message for the Queen Mother as well. If she wishes peace with Philip, and for Marguerite to marry his son Don Carlos, then Catherine will need to cooperate with the Guises in destroying the Huguenots."

A dart of both fear and excitement tingled Rachelle's skin. Spain! Would she be among the ladies-in-waiting for such a grand excursion? But what of Spain's demands upon the Queen Mother to rid her land of Huguenots?

"The rest of you will proceed by coach," Marguerite was saying to her ladies.

It was very like Marguerite to behave with abandon and do something of this daring nature by sneaking off into the woods for a rendezvous with Henry de Guise. Why it was that Marguerite had decided to trust her and Charlotte with her plans was anyone's guess. Rachelle was uncomfortable with any situation that might bring her to Catherine's attention. That unblinking gaze had already fixed upon her, reminding her that she walked and moved in slippery places.

A brief meeting with Henry in the Amboise woods was troublesome enough, but there would be challenges for Rachelle in the future that could be far more demanding. What would she do if Marguerite insisted she attend Mass with her each morning? Neither Madame Clair nor Grandmère had spoken to her about her duties as a Huguenot. With her fellow brothers and sisters being burned at the stake for their refusal to attend Mass, how could she shrug her shoulders and say it mattered not? The thousands of Christian martyrs in the early centuries in Rome had died in the arena for refusing to put a pinch of incense before the image of Nero. She supposed arguments could have been made at that time for dismissing the act of obeisance as unimportant. With a chill she remembered the words: *In those days wherein Antipas was my faithful martyr, who was slain among you, where Satan dwells.* She must not treat lightly that which was hallowed by the blood of hundreds of thousands of Jesus' martyrs.

Marguerite snapped her fingers impatiently, frowning. *"Peste!* Wake up, Rachelle! You are to attend me. Get my cloak from the coach, quick! *Dépêchez-vous!"*

Rachelle did so, and Marguerite ordered her page to bring up her favorite horse, a little brown jennet, along with two mild tempered riding horses for Charlotte and Rachelle.

Rachelle had learned to handle a horse at the Chateau de Silk with her sisters when she and Idelette rode down to the bungalows near the mûreraies where the weavers were at work at the looms. Little had she known back then that her riding would one day qualify her to ride with the princesse.

Charlotte de Presney had a perceptive look in her eyes. Rachelle guessed the woman knew what Marguerite had on her mind, and for reasons of her own was pleased.

They rode around a bend in the road, and drew up short. Rachelle's breath caught.

The Queen Mother herself waited for them, a formidable figure in black astride her strong horse. Catherine was known for being a horsewoman par excellence and had ridden on hunting trips with King Francis I.

Waiting behind the Queen Mother, King Francis, and Reinette Mary, were Mary's oncles—le Duc de Guise and le Cardinal de Lorraine, looking equally formidable. With them rode several courtiers and the bodyguard.

Rachelle's stomach flipped. She glanced toward Marguerite and saw the color drain from her cheeks. Her own tension continued to heighten.

Rachelle and Charlotte de Presney bowed low in their saddles, as custom demanded, first toward Catherine as the regent of France, then toward the young king and queen.

Marguerite was no match for her Machiavellian mother, Catherine de Medici.

IT WAS LATE AFTERNOON and the low angle of the sunlight through the forest fir trees reminded Andelot that there would be little chance to reach the castle of Amboise before sunset. He stood leaning against a tree trunk waiting for Fabien to finish talking with a galante seated on a muscled black horse opposite him. Andelot had no idea who the other monsieur might be, for he was covered closely in a heavy black cloak and his broad-rimmed Spanish hat concealed his face. Andelot was convinced he must be of noble rank. Marquis Fabien remained astride his golden bay facing him, in close discussion.

IN THE DEEPENING PURPLE SHADE of fragrant pine boughs forming a forest canopy around Amboise, Fabien listened to the complaints of Henry de Guise over his frustrated plans to marry Marguerite Valois. Henry had ridden his black horse skillfully through the woods unseen by the royal retinue to keep a rendezvous with Marguerite and foil the Queen Mother's plans to have Marguerite meet the King of Portugal.

Henry's handsome features were scowling with outrage over not being invited to the divertissement at the castle, where the King of Portugal would be entertained.

"The talk of Marguerite marrying Henry of Navarre is laughable, for what can Navarre bring to France? Just as this possible union with Portugal is an error," he stated loftily. "My père's house is as powerful and important as the House of Valois, except that Francis is now on the throne, and he will not last long."

Henry must have realized his omission, especially after their angry confrontation earlier over the insult to the Bourbon name. Henry added: "And the House of Bourbon, bien entendu! Tell me, Marquis Fabien, why should Marguerite be forced to marry the poor and weak-eyed king of such a country?"

Fabien could easily have told him, but he doubted that Henry would accept it. Catherine was no fool. For Marguerite to marry Henry would place the throne within grasp of the Guise family. They were already saturated with ambition, and too powerful. Catherine was not about to make Henry her son-in-law and place her sons at risk.

Fabien had not intended to meet up with Henry de Guise, but he had been riding through the woods from Moulins on his way to Amboise when he came across Henry racing to keep another forbidden meeting with Marguerite.

Fabien remained patient though he cared little about Henry's frustrations. He hoped to uncover some hint about the edict of pacification to be signed. Henry was close to his father and likely to know something of his plans with Catherine. But for all of Fabien's casually garbed questions, he had learned little that was new.

"Then the King of Portugal will also be at Amboise when the Bourbon princes and nobles arrive for the signing," Fabien suggested.

Henry showed neither suspicion nor interest. He merely shrugged. "They should not honor him with their presence."

Fabien was becoming convinced that Henry, at least, was not privy to whatever the duc and cardinal had in mind.

He lost interest in Henry's troubles with Marguerite.

"I will ride with you to meet Princesse Marguerite," he said, and when Henry's gaze swerved suspiciously, Fabien explained: "She has a new lady-in-waiting, Mademoiselle Macquinet, the silk grisette. I find her of particular interest."

Henry relaxed, and even smiled, looking amused. "Ah yes, I have seen her. You have worthy tastes. Then let us be on our way—but wait—" He turned in his saddle and motioned for his page. "There is a spare mask for you."

Fabien took the mask. The two laughed and turned their horses to ride swiftly for Amboise.

ANDELOT DANGEAU thought that reaching Amboise would be his crowning moment, where he at last was to be favored by le Cardinal de Lorraine. Strange, however, that Rachelle had not appeared so impressed, as much as she had seemed shocked, that he was related to the Guise family.

He frowned and paced to and fro under the alder tree, mostly thinking, but sometimes reading from his Latin prayer book and fingering his rosary. He looked up. Horse hooves came barreling down the road. At last! Marquis and the galante with him had left the trees to ride on to Amboise. Andelot ran to put his religious objects back inside his saddlebag and mounted, riding to the side of the road to join them. He bowed as the two young nobles of princely blood rode in his direction, their retinues coming swiftly behind. As the galante neared, Andelot recognized him. Monsieur Henry de Guise.

"Ho!" Andelot cried. "Wait for me—"

Henry de Guise galloped by without so much as a glance his way, though Andelot believed he knew of his blood relationship from his father. *He could at least nod to me,* he thought, offended.

Fabien drew up, smiling, and his men-at-arms and his page, Gallaudet, also halted. They rode on together toward the Amboise castle, Guise and his retinue keeping some distance ahead but in view.

A short time later they neared a gray rock fortress that dominated the view. Storm clouds boiled over the Loire, and the few drops of warning rain had become a drizzling shower that began to drench the misty forest. A streak of light plunged through the eastern sky and snarled viciously.

Andelot could almost believe he sensed pending doom and imagined evil as real as a fiery steed riding upon dank winds and gaining on them. He started to look over his shoulder, except the marquis was there. Andelot grimaced at his imagination. He slowed his gallop until Fabien rode past and then maneuvered behind him. They rode over the wooden planks of the bridge with water flowing below.

"There is a sense of doom in the thunder and lighting," Andelot called out, "like an evil omen. Do you not feel it, Marquis?"

Fabien glanced at him over his shoulder, the breeze tossing a lock of golden-brown hair across his forehead. His dark cape, lined with fur, whipped in a gust of wind. He laughed mockingly.

"I vow, but your imagination does run wild, mon ami. Let thunder be thunder, naught else."

After a few minutes, Fabien added: "I prefer to think of the king's hunting party, of stags and boars. I will snare one or the other on this venture. We are to make merry at Amboise."

It was almost an order. Andelot cast him a glance. Why did he think the marquis was affecting indifference? Andelot merely felt relieved he was not expected to ride with the king's hunting party.

"I should rather see the poor creatures of God roaming freely through the king's forest than shed their blood, except for meat on the banquet table."

"Saint Denis! But you have a 'mothering' heart, Andelot. How it is I find your company well chosen, I cannot say." He shook his head and lowered his hat with its plume.

"Be cheerful, Marquis. The custom of the hunt will not cease because I find no pleasure in it, I assure you."

"By all that is fair, I hope not. I shall favor you with the knowledge so your conscience may rest. All the animals taken in the king's hunt will find their way to the banqueting table to keep the King of Portugal content. There is to be celebration, a masque. There will be no wasted game where I am concerned, I promise you."

"Bonne!"

"You have to learn our ways. Be warned, mon cousine; if the cardinal takes serious his new guardianship of you, he will please his own interests by turning you from his page into a priest. Is that what you want?"

Fabien was looking at him now with serious intent. Andelot shrugged. "I do not wish to become a priest. But—"

"No? But you will have no say in the matter." Fabien's eyes sparkled mischievously. "Then what will you do about the mademoiselle with the brown-auburn hair? What was her name? I must have forgotten ..."

Andelot knew he had not. He then remained silent, refusing to say what her name was. Fabien laughed and spurred his golden bay ahead.

They raced on toward Amboise, pausing only to allow the horses to drink. Andelot began to whistle, which brought a glance from Fabien who had lapsed into a quiet and more thoughtful mood. Andelot thought it had something to do with his secret visit to Moulins, but though he had inquired about what happened, Fabien had not seen fit to tell him much except that his Bourbon kinsmen were coming to Amboise as summoned by King Francis.

Now as they raced along with the wind throwing rain against them, Andelot unexpectedly grinned at him.

"What do you think about, mon ami, that makes you suddenly happy?"

Andelot laughed, for he was thinking of Rachelle and how his change of fortune extended his chances to win her hand. "A secret, mon cousine."

A SHORT TIME LATER, Andelot rode in Marquis Fabien's retinue through the gate at Amboise. Monsieur Henry de Guise had been smuggled in among Fabien's pages so as not to be noticed. They passed stone walls and reinforced battlements and entered the cobbled courtyard where flags flurried. Here, Henry de Guise cut away toward the woods skirting the broad avenue to the castle, and Andelot dismounted. Rain ran down his neck and made him shiver. Fabien remained in the saddle and looked around and up toward the tall windows of the castle.

"Let us hope the rain ebbs and does not ruin the hunting party," Fabien said, but Andelot noted the indifference of his tone, as though the hunt were the last thing on his mind.

Andelot scowled. "What awaits us, Marquis Fabien? Do you yet doubt royalty's good intentions in issuing the summons to Prince Condé and Admiral Coligny?"

Fabien was making a casual summary of the soldiers on the ramparts.

"Do not imagine for a moment that I trust the House of Guise," he said in a low voice, and he looked off toward the forested hills once more, thick with verdant green.

He turned in his saddle. "Gallaudet, settle our ami Andelot into my chambers."

"Are you not coming up, Marquis?" Andelot asked, surprised and curious.

An unexpected gleam of amusement showed in Fabien's eyes, which made Andelot wonder what he and Henry de Guise might be planning.

"Soon, mon ami, I will join you. Henry and I have something to attend first, if we are not too late." And he looked toward the trees.

"You and he are not too late, Monsieur Marquis," Gallaudet said, riding up from the direction of the trees. "We have made far better speed than the royal party, which moved as slowly as a March hare. The king is but now arriving."

Andelot, curious, watched Fabien turn and ride off to where he had seen Monsieur Henry ride but minutes ago.

For Andelot, the unsettling premonition of some insidiousness in the making awakened once again in his mind. Madame le Serpent. That was the name the marquis had used when speaking of the Queen Mother and her insidious plans.

Andelot wished he had never heard of Catherine de Medici, even if it meant he would not meet the cardinal.

Will I ever meet him, or le Duc de Guise?

THERE HAD BEEN NO CONFRONTATION between the Queen Mother and her daughter on the bend of the road when they had started again on the journey after the midday meal. Catherine, Francis, and Mary, along with the Guises and the royal guard, had ridden down the winding road toward Amboise castle, while Marguerite meekly followed with Charlotte de Presney and Rachelle on either side of her.

"Saintes preserve me," Marguerite whispered, still pale and trembling.

The forest soon thickened around them as Rachelle rode toward Amboise. They galloped into a clearing where a grassy meadow crept to the river's bank, and here they drew up. There came a flurry of wind sending a few drops of cool rain spattering against her tired face and dampening the horse's brown mane. Ebony crows soaring high above cawed their laughter down upon her.

Rachelle's first glimpse of the castle intrigued her. Even from a distance the formidable fortress, built upon a bleak pile of rock, loomed above the landscape with its grim, stone walls casting shadows across the dove gray waters of the Loire.

The wooded silence ended as the royal trumpeters announcing the king rang out. The ostrich plume in the Queen Mother's black velvet *toque* fluttered as the procession rode from the forest road to the banks of the Loire. Here, the river widened into a lake that was divided by an island and crossed by two wooden bridges.

The main gate to the castle of Amboise opened, followed by a flourish of more trumpets and flags flying. A large number of royal men-at-arms rode out to greet the boy-king and his young queen.

"Vive le Roi!" they shouted. "Vive la Reine!"

The procession of King Francis crossed the first bridge with the thunder of many hooves, the royal musketeers in blue and white in the lead.

Rachelle rode near Princesse Marguerite and Charlotte de Presney as the procession followed across the bridge.

Catherine rode ahead along the wide avenue toward the castle and Marguerite rode to her right, her brown jennet prancing. Behind her came le Duc de Guise. Rachelle, uncomfortable in his presence, glanced his way, but he seemed deep in thought and unaware of her. She was grateful his keen judging eyes were not weighing her in his scales of religious justice. Was Marquis Fabien right? Did he want to take the throne from the Valois sons?

There were also two cardinals mounted on donkeys. Le Cardinal de Lorraine, whom Rachelle found one of the most haughty men she had ever seen. He was younger than his brother, le Duc de Guise, handsome, and he had already cast an appreciative eye in her direction. Fabien said he was unscrupulous and more of a religious politician than a devotee of God and Church. The other churchman was Cardinal d'Este, newly arrived from Ferrara, Italy, and related to le Duc de Guise's wife, Anne d'Este. The cardinal was artistic and treacherous. Rachelle knew there must be many goodly cardinals who sought to honor God and serve his Church, but not these two.

Cardinal d'Este had brought, with his great entourage from Florence, the magnificent poet Tasso. Rachelle learned that the poet followed his cardinal wherever he took him to perform for royalty, princes, and nobles. She assumed he was here now to entertain the King of Portugal when he arrived to see Marguerite.

The Florence poet wore rich gabardine and a cap of dark satin sprinkled with deep, glimmering rubies. Now and then his dark eyes would stray toward Marguerite who shamelessly flirted with all, when out of sight of the Queen Mother.

Rachelle was impressed with Ronsard, a poet also, but Ronsard served the Valois court and accompanied them wherever they journeyed among their palais chateaus. Next to Ronsard rode Chatelard who was obviously enamored with the queen, Mary Stuart-Valois of Scotland. *He looks devoted enough to die of love!*

All of these individuals and many more, intrigued her and made for never a dull moment. If one was not flirting, one was scheming. *This is not a safe place to be,* she thought, wryly amused. But her smile faded when she thought of her godly Calvinist père. *What will darling père say when he learns I am here among what he once called a "court full of wolves and jackals"?*

Rachelle turned her attention on the green acreage that formed part of the outlying region of the castle lands. As they rode at a brisk trot down the broad way, from the corner of her eye she saw two riders, mounted on powerful horses, keeping pace with their entourage, neither fully concealing themselves, nor cutting across the lawn to join their procession. Had she imagined these phantom riders? But no, there they were again — two of them.

As they rode, weaving easily in and out of the trees and shrubs edging the thick forest, Marguerite slowed her jennet until Rachelle and Charlotte were on either side of her. Rachelle saw the flush of excited pleasure on the princesse's face, who gave a low husky laugh for their ears alone.

"It is my amour, Henry. Is he not brave and daring, my Guise?"

"What if the Queen Mother recognizes him?" Rachelle whispered.

Catherine, however, rode ahead with stately rigidness as though unaware.

"I did not ask Henry de Guise here. But his father, the duc, is here, is he not?" Her dark eyes portrayed amused innocence. "Since the duc must have called for his son Henry, how then shall I be reprimanded?"

It was plain to Rachelle that Marguerite had indeed expected Henry de Guise, perhaps much sooner in the woods along the road than he had managed. His secret arrival was no doubt the reason for the princesse having wished to ride the remainder of the way to the castle.

"There is someone with him," Charlotte said. It was clear to Rachelle her interest was fixed on the second rider. "It is Marquis de Vendôme, I can promise you. I recognize his golden bay."

"Be ready to ride after me," Marguerite ordered them.

"But Princesse—" Rachelle protested, for it appeared impossible to her to ride away into the skirting woods without being seen by the royal party.

Marguerite hushed her. "There is no royal law that says I cannot ride through the trees to reach the front of the castle. I have often broken away and done so. Just follow me." Her sharp glance at Rachelle corrected her audacity to protest. When Henry was near, it seemed her fear of her mother faded.

"As you wish, Princesse."

The Queen Mother turned in her saddle and spoke to le Duc de Guise, whom she had beckoned to ride up beside her. At the very moment she was speaking earnestly, Marguerite rode away, laughing and making her horse leap over some ditches in the grass as though frolicking with her two ladies. For a time she rode in open view of the Queen Mother as though she had nothing else on her mind.

Charlotte followed, and a moment later a reluctant Rachelle, mustering her courage, also cut away and rode after them, leaping her horse over the ditch. A dart of fear zigged down her spine for she fully expected the royal guards to ride them down, but no one followed. Marguerite had more freedom than Rachelle would have thought, but then she must, to carry on with her lovers. Rachelle wondered if she ever bribed the guards to look the other way.

A moment later Marguerite, laughing boldly, turned from the edge of the woods and rode deeper into the trees as though intent on a frolicsome race with her ladies.

Rachelle turned her horse away from the outer rim of the trees along the park lawn, and followed. She found herself riding a length behind Charlotte. Marguerite was several horse lengths ahead of them, cutting into the trees. Just then a rider wearing a wide sombrero and a heavy cloak on a strong black horse raced alongside the princesse. A swift exchange took place as he handed her something and she snatched it.

Rachelle saw Marguerite raise her hand, kiss it, and blow it toward him. He bowed, then leaped his horse over some bushes into the thicket, and was gone.

Then the second rider, on a golden bay, came alongside Rachelle. He slowed the animal's eager pace from too easily overtaking her smaller horse. Rachelle could not possibly mistake those violet blue eyes in the slits of the mask. He tossed her a crimson rosebud that was beginning to open.

"Tonight." And he galloped into the woods.

Rachelle clutched the soft velvet-petaled rose and realized he had cut away the thorns with a knife. She smiled and raced ahead to catch up with Princesse Marguerite.

Earlier she had lost sight of Charlotte, but when Rachelle came back out of the trees onto the broad avenue leading up to the castle, Charlotte was there with Marguerite. The two rode sedately once more, trailing a little behind the royal entourage. Rachelle caught up and took her place behind the princesse.

Charlotte de Presney's face was impassive and hard as she took notice of the rose in Rachelle's hand.

Chapter Fifteen

KING FRANCIS I HAD TRANSFORMED A HUNTING CHATEAU NEAR THE ROYAL forest and the open area of champaign into a castle within large walls of defense, enclosing green lawns, overhanging bowers, and formal lime alleys and flowering groves. Here, in the shadows of its fortified bastions, stately terraced gardens overlooked the Loire which flowed inside its walls. The castle boasted sculptured windows and architectural facades and noble halls with broad galleries. Rachelle's sense of color and design was at its height as she rode with the king's troupe across a drawbridge and down an avenue between a double line of attendants garbed in satins and velvets. Retainers with titles and pages serving the various houses in the nobility, all proudly bore their lord's colors intermingled with gold, silver, and a display of peacock jewels. The armorial flags fluttered. Even the mizzling rain had ceased.

Rachelle's gaze sought the red, white, and blue of the House of Bourbon. It was prominently displayed with Marquis de Vendôme standing to offer his bow to royalty. She noticed a magnificent fresh cloak of violet, embroidered with gold and pearls, draped over his shoulders. She imagined with some amusement how one of his retainers must have been anxiously awaiting Fabien's late arrival as the king's procession drew ever nearer. She suspected the cloak had been readied and tossed over him hurriedly as Fabien came just in time for Catherine and the king and queen to pass by and look in his direction. Fabien gave an elegant bow, as though he were not out of breath from running and dashing over hedges.

Her eyes met his as she went past and saw his faint smile as he bowed in her direction, sending a thrill down her spine.

CATHERINE dismounted from her horse at the arched entrance into the castle, as did Francis and Mary. The other Valois princes—Charles, Anjou, and Hercule, the youngest—walked away in the care of the chamberlains with their white wands, who conducted each one to their various appartements.

Catherine coolly gestured for Marguerite to follow. Rachelle saw a quick look of alarm cross Marguerite's face.

"You too Madame de Presney and Mademoiselle Macquinet. Come," Catherine said.

They passed into a long stone passage that brought them to a large gallery, a staircase, and to the various appartements and chambers.

Rachelle walked beside Charlotte who was just behind Princesse Marguerite with the Queen Mother's black-clad figure in the lead.

"Did the Queen Mother recognize Monsieur Henry de Guise?" Rachelle whispered to Charlotte.

There was cool indifference on Charlotte de Presney's face. "The princesse is aware, I assure you, of the dangers she flaunts so recklessly each time she meets with the future Duc de Guise."

Rachelle realized, perhaps fully for the first time, that Charlotte had small concern for Marguerite. Why did the princesse even keep Charlotte as her maid-of-honor?

I would have women about me who were loyal, who had some affection for me, and I for them.

Louise de Fontaine had told Rachelle it had not been Marguerite, but Catherine, who had chosen Charlotte de Presney as maid-of-honor. Charlotte was one of Catherine's favorite women in her escadron volant.

Rachelle's sympathy for Marguerite grew, even though the young woman was shameless when it came to her immorality.

Catherine turned to the left and they trailed her, Rachelle nervously wondering what might be in store for her as well. Would she be sent home to Lyon?

Rachelle almost hoped she would be!

Almost, but not quite ... soon there would be a great masque and banquet in honor of the King of Portugal. Or had that been canceled after Maître Avenelle's disclosures?

But if the Bourbon princes were called here to sign a peace treaty with the king, would it not end the threat?

Logically, yes. But Rachelle was learning that royal plans were not all devised with understanding and honesty. A smile, a word of flattery, could not be taken at face value. They were often meant to deceive.

Rachelle glanced about the lofty guard chamber as they passed through, their steps echoing up to the high, raftered ceiling. The stone walls were hung with tapestries showing royal hunts and kingly battles of triumph. Elsewhere, gleaming *cuirasses*, swords, lances, *casques*, shields, and banners, were suspended in boastful display.

Rachelle suspected these weapons might have belonged to the past kings of France, or to their noble retainers who had fought victoriously.

Next, she followed into a comfortable salle, large and spacious, that opened into a suite of chambers Catherine long ago had chosen for herself.

The Queen Mother turned imperiously, her round jawline as firmly in place as the marble from Florence displayed here and there in Italian splendor. Her unblinking eyes swept past Charlotte with comfortable indifference, then settled upon Rachelle. For a moment Rachelle wished she could shrink and dart up to the vaulted ceiling for refuge.

Catherine continued to watch her, making Rachelle wonder if she did not have some devious plan for her future. She imagined schemes forming in the deep pools of her eyes.

Suddenly, Catherine gave a short, bold laugh. "Well, Mademoiselle Rachelle, it appears that you are the one young belle at my court who has caught Marquis de Vendôme in her net. You are to be congratulated. Many have tried — " her eyes fixed coldly on Charlotte — "and failed."

Catherine's features hardened into stone as she pronounced the word *failed*. Rachelle looked away to avoid Catherine's gaze and kept silent. She sensed enmity coming her way from Charlotte as well, who accepted her humiliation in silence.

Why was Catherine bringing this up? What did it matter to her who Marquis Fabien found to his personal liking? Did Catherine want Charlotte to snare Fabien? If so, why?

Catherine turned and entered her appartements, shutting the door behind her. Rachelle slowly released her breath. *She loathes me. I must be on guard.*

The salle, used by Catherine as a sleeping room, with a high vaulted ceiling of dark oak, heavily carved, the walls paneled with rare marble statues brought at her command from her native Florence. There were busts on sculptured pedestals — some of which were ivory — ponderous chairs, inlaid cabinets, and carved tables. In one corner stood a large bedstead of polished walnut, with heavy hangings of royal purple. The material was gathered into a diadem with the gold embossed initials *C. M.*

Very clever, Rachelle thought. She would like to have looked and touched to see how exactly the couturières had done this splendid work, but of course, this was out of the question. She was favored to even be inside the Queen Mother's private chambers, especially where she slept.

The antique silver toilet table was also *merveilleux* with a mirror in Venetian glass set in a frame of Alençon lace, which greatly interested Rachelle.

She walked across the glossy, polished floor to the long windows. Looking south she could see the Loire and the forest. She turned and glanced at Charlotte, who refused to acknowledge her. The marquis had become the wedge between them, earning Rachelle the woman's dislike.

Mademoiselle — who was in actuality *Madame,* since she had taken lovers like a married woman — Princesse Marguerite now flung herself into a chair and raised her eyes toward the ceiling with hopeless despair. She put a palm to her forehead. "I swear she has eyes in the back of her head like a forest ghoul."

"Princesse," Charlotte warned, aghast, and her blue eyes moved cautiously about the walls.

Marguerite arched a brow and clamped a hand over her mouth. Rachelle felt a chill. Charlotte was hinting there might be a listening device.

Rachelle at last sat down on a ruby velvet settee, and Marguerite waved a careless hand.

"We are in trouble, ma belles," Marguerite whispered.

"I warned you," Charlotte said in a cool whisper. "I told you not to meet him in the woods — "

"Peste! Silence! Have I not had agonies enough without your prim and hypocritical lectures?" Marguerite's dark eyes flashed. "We must decide on one story." Marguerite's whisper was barely audible. "We did not know it was Monsieur de Guise, c'est bien compris? We went into the woods so that Marquis Fabien could speak alone with his bel ami."

Rachelle opened her mouth to protest, but Marguerite snapped her fingers. "It is so. And you will agree, or else I shall make it difficult for you, I promise you." Her eyes spat fire.

Charlotte de Presney stared without visible emotion in the direction of the door into Catherine's other chambers. "Use the rose. It offers proof."

"Ah!" Marguerite leaned forward with a smile and nodded to Rachelle. "Oui. Bien sûr! I should have thought of it. The rose will work, ma Rachelle."

Any moment now, Rachelle thought, the door will open. The woman in black would call them in. One at a time?

Her shaking fingers tightened around the rose stem. Thankfully Fabien had taken away those thorns! *But I feel my path is strewn with thorns and not fragrant petals.* She hastened her prayer for deliverance to the Lord and waited.

CATHERINE stood alone inside of her appartements. There was a narrow door in one corner of the chamber, and she passed through it into a turret that was turned into a small writing closet. A secret stairway led from here to the chamber of her stargazing observatory. Cosmo Ruggerio had arrived before the royal party and was upstairs making a star chart on Francis, though he had not yet finished. And now she must send him back to Blois to her poison closet to bring her a vial . . .

She needed some minutes to be alone with her thoughts and settle them into a plan. Henry de Guise, that clever handsome son of the duc was here. Le Duc de Guise denied knowing anything about his son's presence, but Catherine trusted him no more than she trusted that wily, fanatic, Philip of Spain. *My son-in-law,* and she gave a spurt of ridiculous laughter. Her smile vanished as quickly as it came. Philip wanted a Guise on the throne of France. And a Guise—any Guise—was only too pleased to çooperate. Something needed to be done to thwart their plans. The House of Valois would reign! And if Francis continued to submit to the cardinal's every wish through Mary ...

She sat beside the window casement. The current of the Loire flowed near the castle to where it followed a bend and disappeared into the thickets. The graceful willow trailed its lacy greenery along the banks, and the alder trees grew tall. Farther away, the woods thickened into forest.

She pressed her lips into a tight line. She took no pleasure in what she must do for the House of Valois. She must act for herself, for her little Anjou to one day reign. Ah, her favorite child, the beautiful little Anjou who looked so much like her husband, Henry—Henry, who had spread his banner of love not over his queen, but Diane de Poitiers. Anjou, the one son who was conceived on a night when it appeared Henry was *truly* her own and not Diane's.

Her hand formed a fist. Little Henry Valois, Duc of Anjou, would be king one day after Charles ... after that fawning Francis with his sotte attentions poured upon Mary. *And petite Mary spying on me for her oncles.*

Catherine ground her teeth, seething. *How dare she spy on me?*

The matter she was planning must be altered. She could no longer depend on Charlotte to ensnare Fabien. It must be the belle Macquinet mademoiselle. Somehow she would lure Rachelle into her escadron volant to be used to capture the handsome marquis.

She turned her mouth into a smile. She would use Fabien to eliminate le Duc de Guise in an assassination plot. All she needed was a few more pieces of the puzzle. When she had them, she would be able to plan better. Until then, she would humor the petite silk girl and the marquis. She would treat them very well indeed to throw them off guard.

But now. Her fingers drummed. She must deal with her foolish wanton daughter and her disgusting passion for little Henry de Guise.

Catherine stood, her mind settled. She calmed herself. A minute or two later she summoned her chief chamberlain. Holding his white wand of office, he bowed.

"Are all things in readiness should the King of Portugal arrive?"

"Oui, Madame. I have prepared for a gala masque, an evening of music, colored waterfalls, boats on the Loire, and a grand feast for the ball in which gifts will be given away."

Catherine nodded satisfaction. She dismissed him.

THE DOOR OPENED. Rachelle rose swiftly and made her obeisance as did Charlotte and the princesse. Catherine beckoned Rachelle into her writing closet.

Lord, be with me, I pray.

The door shut. The silence was astute in the stone chamber, shutting out even the sound of the river, for the windows were all closed.

Rachelle saw a desk covered with dispatches and papers. The Queen Mother sat herself behind the table and left Rachelle bowing.

"Arise, Rachelle."

She did so, trying to relax her face muscles, meeting the limpid eyes with the notion she had done nothing deserving of punishment.

Catherine's gaze lowered to the crimson rose. After a moment a smile came to her mouth.

"Marquis de Vendôme has the blood of a romantic after all. You are pleased with his awareness of your charms, Mademoiselle?"

Rachelle resented her intrusion but could do nothing to avoid her.

"Marquis is a galante from whom any woman would be pleased to receive attentions, Your Majesty."

"No doubt. You are aware that Madame de Presney is also aware of the marquis?"

"I have not made Madame de Presney's notions my affair, Madame. As yet, I hardly know her. But I have heard that she has a husband." The meaning was clear. Catherine laughed her bold, almost lewd, laugh.

"You will find her a worthy opponent."

Rachelle kept silent.

"Did you meet the marquis in the woods just now?"

"Yes, Madame."

"He gave you the rose?"

"Yes, he did."

"And said what?"

Rachelle bit her tongue. She felt the heat in her face. "He asked that we might meet at the upcoming masque."

Catherine smiled broadly. "I am sure two young people will find the divertissement most pleasurable." Then her smile faded. "Who was the galante with the marquis? The one in the Spanish hat?"

Rachelle felt her throat go dry. She could not lie to the Queen Mother, yet she agonized over causing Marguerite punishment, and so soon after becoming one of her ladies.

"I did not see his face, Madame, for I rode two horse lengths behind."

"A clever response, Mademoiselle Macquinet."

"I speak the truth, Your Majesty."

"I do not doubt it. You did not recognize him then?"

"No, Madame."

"Very well. You are new among us. I shall not make matters more difficult than necessary. I would not wish to rile the marquis against me," she said in a teasing vein. "I will need, perhaps, his services in the future. Yours as well."

Rachelle saw a gleam in Catherine's eyes and wondered.

"You are amenable, are you not, Mademoiselle, to the idea of serving your king for *la gloire de la France?*"

Rachelle bowed. "Oh, Madame, there is no answer I would give but yes."

"Then a day will come when we will discuss such important matters. Now call the princesse to me, then take a seat by the window."

Rachelle did not expect to be told to stay for Catherine's interview with Marguerite and found the demand she do so embarrassing.

Rachelle opened the door and stepped into the salon, where Marguerite waited, looking anxious.

"Are you safe?" Marguerite whispered.

Rachelle gave a small nod. "Her Majesty calls you, Princesse."

Marguerite rolled her eyes toward the vaulted ceiling, gave a sigh, but then stood with resolve. Rachelle stepped away to let her pass through into the Queen Mother's writing closet.

Marguerite entered and bowed, kissing her mother's hand, and stood before her, waiting.

"My daughter," Catherine said, "you look pale. Are you ill?"

"No, Madame, I am well."

"That will suit you I am sure, since I have commanded a masque on the river and a banquet in the water gallery to celebrate the company of the King of Portugal on his arrival. You will attend him, bien sûr, and be most wise not to leave him or behave untoward in any way, my child."

Marguerite remained silent a moment too long. Catherine squinted at her and stood from behind the desk.

Marguerite curtsied quickly. "But yes, yes, I will do all you say, Madame Maman."

"Strangers were seen in the forest nearby. With the dangers of a Huguenot plot freely discussed, it is most unwise to be darting off in the woods as you did this day."

Rachelle tensed. She glanced at Marguerite.

Catherine gave a stern, level look. "Was the galante riding with Marquis de Vendôme a friend of his?"

"An ami of Marquis Fabien's? Oh, but yes, that is, I think so."

"You think so?"

Again, Catherine turned her hypnotic gaze upon Marguerite, who flushed.

"My daughter, the weather has overcome you — be seated."

Marguerite lowered herself into a chair near at hand.

Had Catherine recognized the son of le Duc de Guise, even with his costume and mask? It appeared to Rachelle as though Marguerite believed so.

Neither Catherine nor Marguerite exchanged a word for some tense moments. Rachelle still gripped her rose, now growing limp.

Catherine came out from behind her writing desk and appeared to be gauging the effect of her words on her daughter. "You are a disappointment to me, Margo. Would the saints had given me another daughter as meek and obedient as Claude or Elisabeth. How well they did their duties as daughters of France. Elisabeth the Queen of Spain and Claude—"

"I have done all Madame requires of me," Marguerite said.

"Lies! That was Henry de Guise you rode out to meet secretly in the woods, was it not? Speak!"

"I did not ask him here, I promise you."

"You need not. He knows all he must do to have you chase after him. And you! You spent much of your time before you left the Louvre with Comte la Molle. Does young Henry know the comte's company also amuses you?"

Marguerite lifted her chin. "Madame, it was you who bid me converse with those young nobles whom you and my brother the king have called to the court."

"Ah yes. And you have done so, to a far greater degree than one would have dared to imagine," Catherine said with sarcasm. "You have, doubtless, served our purposes too well. But far better you saved your attentions for the King of Portugal than Guise!"

"I do not want to marry the King of Portugal—"

"My daughter, you will marry whomever the king and I decide is best for France. And Guise is an enemy of your Valois brothers."

"Ah, Maman." She suddenly dropped to her knees, hands clasped, using the voice of a little girl pleading for affection. "He is not your enemy, I swear it."

Rachelle dropped her head, both troubled and even ashamed that she must be privy to such intimacy between the Queen Mother and Princesse. Why had she told her to stay?

"Our cousine, the young duc, Henry, is an enemy," Catherine said, speaking very slowly. She turned her eyes full on Marguerite, who for an instant returned her gaze boldly. "I warn you, Marguerite, that neither the king, my son, nor I, will tolerate more alliances with the ambitious House of Lorraine. They stand too near the throne already."

Marguerite dropped her dark head, hands still clasped, as if not daring to look up to meet the steadfast glance of the queen.

"Your Majesty has been disposed against the duc by jealous enemies of Henry."

"You will support the Valois throne by a royal marriage."

"Oh, Madame!" Marguerite looked imploringly at her mother.

"Avoid Monsieur Henry de Guise, Marguerite. I warn you. I have already spoken with his father about his uninvited presence here, of which he professes entire ignorance. The King of Portugal is soon to arrive. He is the nephew of Philip of Spain. You will not destroy what is good for France over a foolish affaire d'amour with Henry. Avoid the duc, I say, and let me see you please the King of Portugal. Your hand must ultimately seal a treaty, important to the Valois."

Marguerite was speechless before the Queen Mother. At this last sentence, her lips parted as if to speak, but she restrained herself and was silent.

"The daughters of France," Catherine continued, "do not consider personal feelings in marriage, but the good of the kingdom. We will discuss this no more. Very shortly I hope to arrange a marriage for you with the King of Portugal. Au revoir, Princesse."

Marguerite curtsied low before her mother, kissed her hand, and turned toward the door. As she did, Rachelle saw the pained and angry look on her white face. Rachelle curtsied and was about to follow when Catherine stopped her: "One moment, Mademoiselle Macquinet."

Rachelle paused. "Yes, Madame?" Her voice was taut.

"You have heard all I have told the princesse. I have permitted you to hear for one purpose, for the good of Marguerite. Charlotte de Presney has failed me in that she has allowed my daughter to meet Monsieur de Guise in the woods. You will now see to it that the princesse does not make a fool of herself while the King of Portugal is here. If Marguerite plans to meet Henry again, it will be your obligation to inform me at once."

The blood seemed to drain from Rachelle. The burden of such a task fell like bricks upon her shoulders.

"You may go, Mademoiselle Macquinet."

Dazed, Rachelle fumbled a curtsy that her own maman, Madame Clair, would have groaned over had she the misfortune to see it, and left the presence of the Queen Mother.

Chapter Sixteen

CHARLOTTE DE PRESNEY SPOKE TO HER SERVING GIRL. "WERE THE VIOLETS that arrived secretly brought to Mademoiselle Macquinet?"

"Oui, Madame, I put them as near her nightstand as was possible, just as you told me."

Charlotte smiled to herself. The flowers gave off a certain substance that brought on a severe headache — *poor petite Rachelle.*

When evening came and the moon rose over the Loire with silvery gleams, Louise de Fontaine, lady-in-waiting to Marguerite, commented to Charlotte, "You are looking most fine this evening, Charlotte, after so long a ride from Blois."

"Merci. Where is Mademoiselle Macquinet? Will she not stroll with us tonight?"

"Rachelle is indisposed with a most dreadful headache."

"Oh? But what a pity. And so lovely an evening too."

"Rachelle blames it on some violets that were in her chamber."

"But how odd ... Oh, surely not! They must have come from one of her admirers."

Louise looked at her thoughtfully. "One wonders."

Later, Charlotte slipped from the castle and came into the garden.

After a few minutes she saw Marquis Fabien near the lattice arbor where crimson roses were lavished in bloom. She pulled the corners of her carmined lips into a smile.

Charlotte had gone to great care to prepare herself for this moonlight meeting with the marquis. She had washed and scented her golden tresses, curled and arranged them into a complicated crown of intertwined ribbons of gold with braided locks. The ribbon matched the gold cloth of her gown, and seed pearls adorned the puffed sleeves and bodice. She carried a gold lace fan with flecks of sapphires that matched her eyes, the jewels sparkling in the starlight. She had used her pots of creams and rouges and powders from Rene, and she had added some of the potion of amour to her throat and temples.

She came quietly into the garden and watched the marquis for a moment with unconcealed desire. He was dressed most handsomely in a coat of black velvet embroidered with his armorial bearings in rubies. His cap matched and there was an *aigrette* of rubies on it, with a golden *B* for Bourbon, signifying his princely lineage.

Tonight she would have him. She would feel his lips on hers, his arms enclosing her.

Fabien turned at her footsteps. She saw that he wore a scabbard housed with a jeweled sword. He looked momentarily surprised to see her, but the way he also noticed her body gave her confidence. He had expected Rachelle, but she was here now.

She dipped a low curtsy, then raised her eyes to his.

"Monsieur de Vendôme."

He bowed. "Madame de Presney."

She walked closer, choosing a spot where the garden lamp shone to declare her beauty. She tried to form an expression of concern and even sadness.

"Monsieur Fabien, I fear I bring you trying news."

She saw his gaze take her in and enjoyed the flicker of wariness that showed in his violet blue eyes. It made him more attractive. She wanted to break down his resistance.

"Madame," he said politely, "I wonder what news can be as trying as your tempting presence?"

She smiled sweetly, knowing there came at such a moment a dimpling about her mouth. "That you find me so, Monsieur, pleases me, but that you do not trust me brings grief to my heart."

"Tell me, Madame," he said dryly, "what does your husband think of his wife at court luring men to her bed for the Queen Mother's political ambitions?"

"Ah, I confess, Monsieur, I have not always lived the dutiful life of virtue, but I assure you, my devotion to you is not to please the Queen Mother but to satisfy my own lonely heart. You see, Her Majesty *forced* me to betray my husband. If not, she would send him to the Bastille. Although I fear he thinks I have done him injury, it was in loyalty and amour that I sacrificed my virtue."

"Ah yes, I see. A great saga, Madame. But you need not confess your lost virtue to me. I have been familiar with the ways of court since a small boy. Naught surprises me where an exchange of virtue is bartered for mere trifles. But I am even less surprised when it is sought with little more than deception. And with your leave, Madame, I choose not to be deceived by your charms, which I confess are many."

Charlotte heard only what she wanted to hear, which had been enough. He had confessed to her charms, which strengthened her resolve to crack through his veneer. She walked slowly toward him, humbly and sweetly, innocently in need of his masculine protection.

"Oh, Monsieur Fabien, you are right, I am a woman to be scorned and pitied — "

"I did not say so, Madame."

"But it is true! I am unworthy of you, but my heart is smitten and wishes only for your friendship, your galant consideration of my growing feelings for you. Would you be so hard on a woman who loves you so?"

"If you were my wife, you would not be here at court walking in the garden in the spring moonlight. I would go to the Bastille if necessary to keep you from the bed of knaves."

"Oh Monsieur, if I were but yours, and yours alone, I would run away just to be with you wherever you were, to be in your arms in such moonlight, and even rain."

He laughed, and she was surprised he did not appear overwhelmed by her amorous words.

"If your words, so fair, were but spoken by another ..."

She tightened her mouth. *Rachelle.* Charlotte almost lost her facade and spat out her venom for Rachelle Macquinet, but she caught herself in time, for it would have cost her the advantage she believed she was now gaining.

Her spoken words sought to bind him in a silken net so that she might draw him to her. That he made no effort to escape alerted her. *The potion of Rene, it is working!*

"What is this trying news you brought me?"

"I confess now that I am with you where she would have been, and that though I am pleased she is indisposed, even so, I assure you that I am most sympathetic of her unfortunate headache. She has asked me to inform you and to keep you company."

"How thoughtful of Mademoiselle."

"I am sure her sickness was brought on because she is in the Queen Mother's displeasure over the incident in the woods this afternoon. Her Majesty guessed at once that it was Monsieur Henry de Guise who rode to meet the princesse. Mademoiselle Macquinet, so young, so inexperienced at court, went into hysterics. It was dreadful to watch."

She had thought the implication of Rachelle's weakness under the frown of Catherine would diminish her in Fabien's estimation. She was surprised to see concern. It stung as her jealousy came to the forefront. If only he would show such depth of gravity for her troubles and dangers at court.

"Are you saying Mademoiselle Macquinet was called in alone before Catherine this afternoon?"

"She was called into the Queen Mother's private appartements and questioned about Henry de Guise, and you also, Monsieur, were mentioned."

"I should have understood our antics might have put her at risk with the queen. What happened? Is Catherine then displeased with her enough to send her back to Lyon?"

Charlotte lifted her brows. "You sound as if you wish her to go."

"But yes, bien sûr. I had hoped she would return to the Chateau de Silk with her family this morning."

His reasons could only be because he wished to protect Rachelle. Well, it would also suit Charlotte quite well if the Macquinet grisette-couturière were sent back to Lyon.

"It may be that she will so displease the Queen Mother she will be sent away. She is a novice and knows little of how to behave among royalty and nobles such as you, Monsieur de Vendôme."

"Is she? I had not the faintest inclination of that. Tell me, and what of your Princesse? How has she fared with the Queen Mother over Henry de Guise?"

"The queen is exceedingly displeased, I assure you. Marguerite will marry the King of Portugal. Her Majesty has made that clear, but the princesse is stubborn, as you yourself know, Monsieur Fabien. She is bent by the winds of her declared amour for Monsieur Guise, even as I am for you." And not waiting a moment longer for fear he would take his leave, she threw her arms around him.

"Kiss me, Monsieur Fabien ..."

He removed her arms from around his neck, but she threw herself against him, reaching out again. She pulled his face toward her lips and kissed with abandon, trying to break down his resistance, her own desires leaping out of control.

LOUISE DE FONTAINE, upon hearing voices in the garden, crept up to the rose lattice on tiptoe and looked over into the garden where the lamp was lit. *I knew it. That wanton Jezebel!*

Louise saw enough to narrow her eyes. She must warn Rachelle that Marquis de Vendôme had succumbed most easily to Charlotte's womanly charms.

RACHELLE was resting on her bed with pillows behind her. She had never experienced such a headache, so much pressure inside of her pounding temples, daggerlike stabs that plundered her strength with each thump of her heart sounding loudly in her ears. She turned her head to the side and the pain seemed to flow. She stifled a groan. If only Maman or Grandmère were here ... a cup of special tea and cold cloths on her forehead would make her *think* she was gaining some minor relief. She moaned, for her stomach turned nauseous. Any moment she feared she would be sick.

She was aware that her chamber door opened, and she slowly turned to see if it was Louise, who had promised to look in on her before bed.

Louise tiptoed over to the side of the bed and peered down.

"I hate Charlotte de Presney," Louise said forthrightly. "I found her in the garden with Marquis Fabien."

Something in Louise's voice caused Rachelle to focus on her face. *With Fabien.* Rachelle moistened her dry lips and tried to swallow.

"I knew she would not give up until she had worn down his resistance. They were together. Locked in one another's embrace — and he seemed most obliging. I left quickly enough, for it appeared to me as though ... well, she was trying to unloosen his shirt."

Rachelle's heart thudded, causing the pounding in her head to swell to a groan that escaped her lips.

"M'amie, oh, I should not have told you now. Do forgive me," Louise cried, "but I hate her, and now she has stolen your beau galante."

CHARLOTTE GASPED, STARTLED. Had she tripped or had he pushed her aside? Dazed, she sat staring at him. He was straightening his jacket and tucking in his shirt that was awry.

"Saint Denis! If I did not know the truth, I would not believe it," he said. "I have heard of lusty musketeers attacking belles dames, but rare is the occasion when it is the other way around. You have actually ripped the lace on my shirt." He looked down at her with a malicious grin.

"Because I love you!"

He laughed.

Charlotte, humiliated, cried tearfully, "Fabien, no, I beg of you — my leg, I hurt it when I fell ..."

There was no smile on his face now, and his eyes were like hard jewels gazing down at her. "You lied. Rachelle is not ill."

"Non, she is, I swear it. Oh — ouch — my leg — oh!"

He looked down at her in his indomitable way. She shrank away. She had gone too far and now he was disgusted with her boldness. She tried tears. She buried her face in her palms and cried softly. "Oh, Monsieur, what have I done? Oh, forgive me, I was such a fool. But my love for you is so great, I do not mind being a fool if only you would care for me a little ..."

He hesitated, bent down, and lifted her up. She clung to him.

"I do not suppose you can walk on your own?"

"Non, my leg hurts too much."

"As I expected you to say."

"You will need to take me to my chamber."

"And then to your bed? You little witch."

"Whatever you say, Monsieur Fabien."

"I say the men you hunt with your gilded net, Charlotte, are to be most pitied, for I suspect few, if any, have escaped."

She smiled, her arms reaching. "Forget that child Rachelle, Monsieur. It is a woman you need to make you happy."

He removed her arms again. "You will not make a man happy for long, Madame, I assure you. You may give your husband my condolences. I bid you adieu." He snatched his hat from the lawn where it had fallen, turned, and walked away.

"But how shall I get to my chamber?" she cried. "My leg is hurt, I promise you."

"I shall send one of my pages. *À bientôt*, Madame."

Desperate, she hissed: "But I can help you prove that le Duc de Guise assassinated Jean-Louis de Vendôme."

He stopped. He turned slowly. His stare was even.

"Repeat that, Madame."

She let out a breath of relief. Charlotte pretended to hobble to a bench where she sat down and smoothed her hair into place. "We cannot talk here. I was already unwise to speak of it as loudly as I did."

Fabien walked up to where she sat, gazing down at her.

"If you are lying to me again — "

"Non. It is so."

"Proceed," he said. "You were saying?"

"Ah, surely, a man as wise as yourself knows we *cannot* discuss such matters openly. It is very dangerous."

"We *will* discuss it here, if you please, Madame."

"But we may be overheard by someone spying on us from the bushes."

"Then they would have already raised their brows. However, I shall have one of my pages bring a calèche. We will ride, and you will explain your words."

She smiled. "I shall wait here for the calèche, Monsieur Fabien."

She watched him stride off to locate one of his pages and arrange for a calèche to take them out. She rubbed her ankle and calf. Actually, she had twisted it a little, but her success tonight was worth the mild discomfort. Never had it been this difficult to capture her prey for the Queen Mother, and even now she had not yet won over the marquis — but the night remained young.

THE NEXT DAYS FOR RACHELLE were miserable in their passing, so she buried herself with her work as a couturière. Now that she knew Charlotte had been with the marquis, Rachelle was furious with herself for having fallen for him so easily. She had played the fool with her heart. Grandmère had been right when she warned her at Chambord. Idelette, too, had tried to warn her in her sisterly way, but she had thought she knew more than they. How wrong she was. She would not speak to Fabien de Vendôme again. No, not ever. And as soon as she could leave court and return to Lyon, she would be only too pleased to pack her trunk and depart. She would also write Maman at the Louvre to see if Madeleine could have Sebastien do something, *anything*, to see that the Queen Mother would send her home. Rachelle even thought of playing the coward by pretending to be sick. If she were sick in her *coucher* for days on end, the queen would soon see she was of no use and send her away.

Though she considered all these possibilities for escape, she would use none of them, for she would not dishonor herself with lies and weakness. She would be grateful to God for showing her in time what manner of man Fabien was before she had allowed her heart to go even further with him. And yet, all of her pleasant thoughts had been tossed by the wind and she was left with disappointment and a strange heartache that seemed to gnaw at her day and night.

Rachelle worked tirelessly on her designing efforts to please Marguerite to keep her mind off of her painful disillusionment over the marquis. She also tried to avoid Charlotte. Charlotte was more smug than ever, and now and then dropped hints to Louise or one of the other ladies of her midnight meetings with her new bel ami.

"Princesse, should we not begin discussing your wedding trousseau?" Rachelle broached Marguerite cautiously, hoping to bury her emotions in her skills and beloved silk and lace. She was more than anxious to sketch some designs for the trousseau and return to Lyon for Grandmère's help.

"The only monsieur I will marry is Henry," Marguerite said stubbornly. "I will run away with him to Lorraine, and we will rule there, I promise you."

"Will Monsieur de Guise be content with ruling Lorraine?" Charlotte looked up from her own sewing.

"Monsieur Guise would rule all France and Navarre if it were mine to give him," Marguerite said.

"Such words will not endear you to the king, your brother, Princesse," Charlotte said.

Marguerite, eyes snapping, walked over to where Charlotte sat and took hold of her earlobe.

Rachelle winced as Marguerite pinched hard and said between her teeth, "Watch your tongue, Charlotte, or you will pay for its flippancy, I assure you."

She released Charlotte and walked to the window, while Charlotte massaged her ear.

"I only meant to protect you, Princesse," she said calmly.

"The protection I need is from the King of Portugal." Marguerite moaned, for her ladies watched her with momentary disfavor for her treatment of Charlotte. Now she had their sympathy again, and Louise de Fontaine said soothingly, "I hear the king is handsome and very rich. He may inherit Spain from his oncle, King Philip."

"There are none as handsome as my golden Henry. Ah, Rachelle, that design is most charmant." Marguerite came up beside her desk where she sat with her stack of drawings and patches of cloth and lace.

But would the Queen Mother approve? Marguerite insisted on redoing Rachelle's designs by either altering the décolletage or using colors that did not go well with her coloring. She was fond of blue, but it made her look sallow.

Marguerite could not make up her mind. One day she approved a drawing that the next day she would dismiss. Whatever promised her the most male attention was what she consistently insisted on.

"I shall wear blue to the banquet," she said.

"But was not the burgundy and cloth of gold meant to wear when you meet the King of Portugal?"

"I will save that for when I meet Henry de Guise, at the masque."

Rachelle felt alarm when she recalled the words of the Queen Mother.

"It matters what I want," Marguerite said.

But they all knew it mattered what Catherine wanted. Marguerite could pretend with her ladies, she could throw her emotional tantrums, but once in her mother's overpowering presence, Marguerite changed into a frightened young woman.

"And what do you plan to wear to the masque, Rachelle?" Louise asked.

Rachelle had no desire for the celebrations, but would not say so in front of Charlotte. She told Louise of several of her gowns she and Grandmère had designed and sewn for her while in Lyon. One was a green silk with gold trim and gathered sleeves, a matching cap and feather. Another was blue silk, for blue was one of her colors, and the third gown was a rose velvet with rosettes of cream Brugesse lace. It was with bitterness Rachelle remembered the burgundy and gold gown that Fabien had made a point of in her chambers at Chambord, a dress he had wanted her to have made and wear to Orléans. Doubtless, she would not be seeing him at Orléans now. Her entire life had unexpectedly taken a different path. The burgundy gown he had wanted was no longer possible, not after his tryst with Charlotte. She thought longingly of the Chateau de Silk. What could she do to influence Catherine's decision to send her back home to Lyon?

Chapter Seventeen

Andelot Dangeau wished he had never left Paris. Several days had passed and still there was no summons to meet le Cardinal de Lorraine. They had forgotten him, and even his cousine, Marquis Fabien, was seldom in their appartement. He left early and returned late, leaving questions unanswered. He behaved so suspiciously Andelot began to think he may have a secret amour within the castle with whom he was spending his time. He rather hoped he had, for that meant Rachelle would be left alone. Nor had he seen her. He had caught glimpses of her, but always in the company of Princesse Marguerite Valois, attending to couturière business, so that he could not speak with her.

Once she had looked at him and smiled, and he could have sworn she wished for his company, as though homesick or at least troubled to be at court. Perhaps she had been concerned about something, he knew not what, but not even Fabien sought out her company as he had at the first. This was curious. Fabien was seen more in the company of Madame de Presney. They would go off together in a calèche.

On day five of their arrival from Blois, Andelot began to worry. His Oncle Sebastien had not yet returned from Moulins with the Bourbon princes and retainers, one of which was the Huguenot Admiral of Picardy and Normandy, Gaspard de Coligny, and his brothers. This, however, did not seem to trouble Fabien.

"They will not come until the Admiral Coligny joins them from Châtillon later in the month."

But for Andelot, all things began to be cast with dark suspicions.

Andelot was deciding how to slip out of the castle and locate Julot in the soldiers' barracks, when an unexpected invitation was delivered to him by a royal page.

The boy-prince, Charles Valois, brother of King Francis, sent word ordering Andelot Dangeau the peasant to come to his chambers for tea, sweetbreads, and an afternoon of games. Andelot was duly surprised by this. Perhaps Prince Charles could tell him why the cardinal had not yet summoned him, though it was not likely a boy younger than himself would know, or care to know, about what befell one of his lesser subjects. He recalled the odd warning from the marquis concerning young Charles.

FROM THE MOMENT ANDELOT met Prince Charles Valois, he became uneasy. There was something about the royal prince's personality that went beyond the typical haughty manner of royalty. His troubled mind showed on his young face with aquiline nose and small, tight mouth that sneered, but seldom smiled. His eyes were prominent, like his mother's, Catherine de Medici. And like her, he had a cruel streak that lingered beneath his boyish veneer that could unexpectedly spring forth, like a tiger lying low in the bushes, and demand satiation.

Andelot had been escorted into the princeling's chamber and was there but a short time when Charles, slim and sullen and tall for his age, looked Andelot over keenly and boasted: "I hunt everything. Stags, bears, even dogs. Watch!"

To Andelot's horror, Charles grabbed one of his own pet royal dogs, one of the numerous pets, including caged falcons, he kept in his chambers. He drew a dagger from his secret sheath.

Andelot was certain the prince was trying to frighten him, to somehow impress him with his savagery, but when an ugly, dazed look crossed the otherwise boyish face, and he began to foam at the mouth, Andelot knew a dart of fear. He was convinced he would wound, if not kill, the dog. The small, trembling animal appeared to be aware of such horrors from the past. The dog yelped and quivered. Its terror stricken whine infuriated Andelot, who could not endure to see the innocent suffering.

Without a moment's hesitation, Andelot threw himself against the prince and wrestled him down to the gilded rug, forcing the jewel-handled dagger to drop from Charles's hand.

Andelot stared down, scowling; Charles stared up red-faced, astonished, blinking.

Andelot realized at once what he had done in laying his hands on the heir apparent to the throne of France. He had actually attacked a royal prince. He could be sent to the Bastille, even quartered! He had spared the dog, but could he spare himself?

Andelot, startled by his own action, jerked back, releasing the prince and scrambling to his feet. The dog had escaped under the bed where it hid, unseen. Andelot wished he might crawl in after it. Trying to cover his anxiety, he pretended that his action was of no great consequence. He pushed his brown hair from his damp forehead; realizing his mouth was dry, he tried to smile. He was sure it was quite inadequate. When the prince remained on his back, Andelot, now shy, stepped forward, bowed stiffly, took his hand, and lifted Charles onto his red satin slippered feet.

"Pardon, Monsieur le Prince." He bowed a second time, this one more graceful than the first.

Charles breathed heavily, his eyes bulging with incredulity.

"You see, Monsieur, I cannot bear the sight of innocent things being tormented. The little dog ... it did nothing wrong. Nothing worthy of your dagger. I—I better go now. Adieu, Monsieur Prince." He bowed a third time, wishing Marquis Fabien would suddenly materialize in the royal chamber. He backed slowly toward the door leading to the outer corridor, hoping to placate Charles.

Charles gave a piercing yell that froze Andelot in his tracks.

Andelot, frightened, expected the prince's nurse to come rushing in with guards to see whether the prince's guest might have attempted an assassination. But to Andelot's amazement no one came to check, and the door into the nurse's chamber remained shut. He decided she must have chosen a fortunate moment to take a brief respite.

Charles needed no assistance from his nurse. He leaped past Andelot like a wiry, lean cat and scrambled toward the door on all fours, he leaned against it, arms folded, his mouth in a tight pucker.

"You will not leave until I say so, peasant!"

Andelot wondered at the tormented expression of rage and became afraid for the boy when his body trembled as though he had been in the icy water. His teeth chattered. His slim, white hands bedecked with heavy jewels, clasped together and unclasped, then he pressed them hard against his chest as though his heart were in pain. Little bubbles began to froth at his lips.

Andelot was stricken with fear, more for the mental state of the boy than for his own safety, though he would not be surprised should Charles rage at him with dagger in hand.

"Your Highness," he whispered. "I beg your pardon! Please, do calm your soul. Are you well? Shall I call for your nurse? Oh please, be calm, be calm!"

"*You!*" came the high-pitched squeak like a hoarse old woman. "I shall have you w-whipped! You d-dare touch me, heir to the t-throne of France? I will send you to the dungeons below! I will have you torn limb from limb. I will have you disemboweled. I will have one tooth pulled at a time until you faint!"

Andelot stared, dumbfounded. He began to worry that his imprudent actions might also reflect upon the Marquis Fabien, or would evoking the name of Vendôme grant him protection? Rank, here, meant everything as he well knew. Or perhaps he should go down on his knees and beg the prince's forgiveness. Yet, he saw not a prince, but a cruel and unreasonable boy that Fabien had warned him to be cautious of. Even so, Andelot took heart. Charles was still a child and not a fiend, a mere boy who had sent for him to entertain him.

But Andelot could not bring himself to fall on his knees and beg. He sensed Charles would take sadistic glee from his begging and prolong the agony.

Andelot took another approach. He said calmly: "There are no dungeons at Amboise. And I am not afraid to be whipped if it will make Your Highness happier." He bowed.

Charles's eyes narrowed. His lips tightened into a line, his chin quivered.

"Oh yes, there are dungeons," Charles protested. "This is a fortress. The dungeons, they are not merely packed full of hungry little rats, but many nasty Huguenot heretics are there now waiting for their just due."

Huguenots in the dungeons below? Was he telling the truth? Did he know this? Where had they come from?

"The cells, they are as dark as a hellish night when bats fly." Charles grinned and poked a finger toward Andelot's left eye. "I shall have you placed there, peasant!"

Something moved from under the bed. Andelot saw from the corner of his eye that one of the little dogs was still trembling. Charles saw it too for he started toward the bed angrier than before.

"Monsieur le Prince," Andelot said softly, "why do you even have dogs about your chamber if you hate them enough to kill them at a moment's notice? Why not give them away? I shall take the one beneath your bed."

Almost at once, the erratic mood of the prince leaped to the other end of the pendulum. He began to tremble and tears filled his eyes. Then, just as though Andelot were not a subject beneath him but his mentor, he sank helplessly to the rug and wept, crawling on his hands and knees toward his bed and calling his dog.

"Come, mon amour! I will not hurt you. Come!"

Andelot watched the unnatural change in Charles, wondering if he should call the nurse. The older woman had seemed a gentle person who was genuinely attached to the prince.

He must get away from Charles as quickly as he could. The excitement he had felt earlier at being invited into the prince's chambers had vanished. Nor was he hungry for the promised tea and sweetbreads. He looked around for a way of escape. If he could get past him and dart out the door ...

Charles caught the small quivering dog and held it to his chest, smothering the animal with kisses of penitential remorse. "Mon petit cher, mon amour. Oh forgive, forgive, I did not mean it."

Andelot now pitied him. *Oui, Fabien was right about Charles.*

"I—I do not *want* to hurt my dogs," Charles confessed.

"Non?" Andelot questioned dully. "Then why do you do it? I should rather die than wound something I loved. My stallion, for instance."

Charles jerked his head toward him. Andelot expected another outburst of rage. Instead, a cunning look darkened his eyes.

"You have a horse?"

At once Andelot was sorry he had mentioned it. He kept silent thinking of some way to turn the prince's mind.

"I will trade you this dog for your horse," Charles said, standing with the dog in his arms. "What say you, peasant? And — and this dagger. Look how many diamonds and rubies are encrusted in the handle. C'est magnifique, oui?"

"Oui," Andelot said softly, "magnifique, but you are a prince, Monsieur. You could have a hundred horses."

Charles's mouth turned hard. "Then I shall ask Maman to order you to give me your horse, and I will give you nothing in return. If I do not get the horse, peasant, then I shall take to bed with illness until my wishes are satisfied."

Andelot refused to show fear at the thought of turning his horse over to Charles. "The horse, Your Highness, it is not mine to give. The horse truly belongs to Marquis Fabien de Vendôme — *your friend*," he added, hoping to salve matters over.

Charles hugged the dog. "Fabien. Sometimes he is my friend. Sometimes he is not."

Andelot scrutinized him. He wondered what action Fabien may have taken with the prince to make him say that.

"S-sometimes I cannot help myself ... the dogs, I mean. Something happens inside. Only my nurse helps me. She soothes me, she prays for me. When I feel these moods coming, I send the dogs away until I am better." He looked up toward the gilded cages. "And my falcons ..."

He gave a tormented sob. There was a moment of awkward silence as Andelot glanced apprehensively toward the nurse's door.

Charles saw the direction of his glance. Oddly, his expression became tender. "My beloved nurse, she asks me to pray with her."

"You should, Monsieur Prince. The Lord is merciful. I am certain he can aid you."

"I have not prayed ... not yet."

Andelot felt the eyes of the young prince studying him.

"You are a Huguenot?"

"Non, Monsieur."

"My nurse is a Huguenot."

"His Majesty, your brother Francis, he has many Huguenots in his service, oui? Ah, but yes! Monsieur le Prince, many loyal and faithful Huguenots. All serve the throne of France."

Charles turned red in the face. "Traitors. Le Duc de Guise and the cardinal say so."

Andelot gave a bow. "Then pardon, but you have heard in error." He moved again toward the door and his coveted escape. "I must go now, Prince."

Charles interrupted petulantly: "Non!" He loosed his dog, which slunk away to hide again. Charles now behaved all prince and heir to the throne of France. He strutted about in his velvet finery.

"Non. Have I not asked you here? And I have not said you could take your leave of me, peasant. Then be seated. I sent for you to play games. What games do you play with Fabien?"

Andelot could hardly say they had outgrown playing games years ago, or for that matter they had never done so. He recalled their times together. "Archery."

"Such a dull game."

"Archery? Dull, mon prince?"

"If I say it is dull, so be it. Dull, unless you play for *real*." He smiled maliciously. "Dull unless you dip the arrow into poison. I know about poison. My maman — " He stopped. He paled slightly. "Non, we shall do something else." Then he appeared to change his mind again. He was animated now. He turned in a circle, struck his white hands together, and looked about his gaudy chambers as if trying to decide. He looked at Andelot with a wicked little gleam.

"I shall take you to a forbidden place."

"I would rather not, mon prince."

Andelot's heart thumped. Caution.

"Monsieur, if it is forbidden — "

"Aha! If it is forbidden, mon ami, it is all the more exciting, is it not?"

Non, not always, Andelot thought wryly. Aloud he asked, "Where is this forbidden territory, mon prince?"

"In the fortress of Amboise, where else? Come, I shall take you on a secret exploration of forbidden territory."

Andelot remained wary, but his interest was also enticed, just as Charles had meant it to be.

Amboise would be exciting to explore at any time, but more so now with the inactivity of the last four days due to the king's delicate lapse in health, or so the excuse went. Andelot hesitated, however. He cast a glance toward the door.

"You, mon prince, can do most anything you wish, but I will know displeasure if caught where I am not wanted."

Charles waved a careless hand. "Not if you are with me. It may be I will decide to keep you as my cher ami."

Andelot kept silent. He could not say what he truly thought of that idea.

"Monsieur, should we not send for Marquis Fabien to join us first?"

"Non. He is Francis's ami more than he is mine. We will go now."

"Your nurse, she will be very upset, I promise you." Andelot worried that Charles might find it amusing to lock him up somewhere.

"Here now, peasant, do all I command, and it may be that when I grow up and become king after my brother Francis, I will make you an important man in my court. You and Fabien. I shall grant to Fabien his father's duchy once more, then he will rule more than Vendôme. Perhaps I shall have him marry my sister Margo. Maman says she is very wicked. My maman, she chases Margo around the chamber and then ties her up, then whips her and whips her and whips her."

Andelot was revolted. Was the Queen Mother mad also?

"Become King of France, Monsieur Prince, and I will serve you with a loyal heart," Andelot said dutifully. "So will the marquis, but do thou let me depart, lest I anger the Queen Mother by going afar into chambers where I am not invited. And think, mon prince. Ah! What will the Queen Mother do to *you* if you wander into forbidden places?"

Fear rampantly scrawled itself across Charles's white face, until he set his little mouth. "Maman is too busy telling Francis how to rule France to concern herself with me. She hates me."

"Perish the thought, mon prince, that could not be, I assure you."

"Maman! Fie! It is Anjou she loves. Her petit Henry, her amour. He is a year younger than I, yet it is *he* whom she wishes to be king, not me, not Francis." He whispered, "I know secrets about the Queen Mother."

A twisted gleam came to his prominent eyes. "The stars, peasant. Do you believe in the stars the way she believes? She calls upon Monsieur Nostradamus to read the stars for all of us. Sometimes Cosmo and Lorenzo Ruggiero also read the stars and make plans."

"I have heard of Nostradamus, but not messieurs Ruggiero. In what way should I believe in the stars, mon prince? They give light on a dark winter's night and beauty in summer. You could see them tonight if it were not raining. Bright, like broken pieces of ice. I have been taught a verse in the Psalter. 'The heavens declare the glory of God; and the firmament sheweth his handiwork. Day unto day uttereth speech, and night unto night sheweth knowledge.'"

"Maman keeps a man who studies the stars and planets in a cubicle next to her chambers wherever she travels—he is here at Amboise, but he left the castle this afternoon to go on a mission back to Blois. I do not know what the mission was, but it is important to Maman. He tells her what to expect from the kingly rule of her sons." He leaned toward Andelot. "The stars told her my father King Henry II would die in the joust at Tournelles. And he died. The Black Knight rode into the arena from nowhere and fought the king, and the king died—by accident; the stars say Francis will die soon." A wicked little smile turned his mouth. "Then I will be king of France."

Andelot stepped away, disturbed. He shook his head and said quickly, "None know what tomorrow may bring but God. There is a certain man who once said a word to me that I always remember; he said that there is but one source of unchangeable truth, which is the Scriptures. The present king may live many years, mon prince. The stars could not know his death. Who told you this ill omen?"

Charles's lips tightened, and his hand dropped from Andelot's arm. "It matters not who told me. Maybe I overheard. The Ruggiero brothers are from Florence. They make potions." He smiled again, smugly. "You are upset. Ta ta."

Poison? Did the Queen Mother ever help the stars fulfill those predictions of death?

Charles must have tired of sharing his family secrets, for he walked swiftly across the chamber floor to another door. He put a jeweled finger to his mouth. His eyes reflected that he knew too much darkness for a boy his age. His hands shook as they did when he was about to lapse into what was called a ranting delirium.

"Let us go," he hissed.

Andelot found himself close behind Charles in a central gallery and followed him through a chamber door. Charles shut it silently behind them. Then he moved a small stool in front of the door. Once on the stool, he slid the bolt solidly into the socket. He smiled at Andelot.

"We are safe now. They cannot follow!"

"Wait, mon Prince, how … will we get back inside your chambers?"

"Ta ta, peasant. Leave such matters to your new master."

Andelot turned hot. "You are not my master, Monsieur Prince. You are not yet the king. And even if you were — "

"And even if I were?" Charles repeated ominously.

Andelot looked at him.

"Treason?" Charles leaned toward him. "Are you saying that *I*, Prince Charles, son of Henry II, heir to the throne of France, would not be *your* master? Will you dare to speak treason?"

Andelot felt a surge of helplessness, but also anger. *He is unfair.* He drew in a breath, and looked at Charles. "Not treason, my prince. I *will* serve you. But only God is my Master. Do not ask me to choose."

"Very well," Charles said haughtily. "I can see only too well that your devotion to the religion places *me*, your liege, at risk."

Andelot felt his temper rising and knew that he dare not show it. "I have told you, mon prince, I am not a Huguenot. I speak with the same loyal tongue as do all the king's subjects."

Charles scowled. "Not the Huguenots, not according to Guise."

"Le Duc de Guise is — "

Andelot caught himself and stopped. He had been about to say was *too zealous for the Holy League.*

Aware that Prince Charles watched him as they walked along, Andelot quickened his steps down the corridor, hoping to end the subject, but Charles was perceptive.

"You do not trust Guise?"

Andelot smiled. "I am related to the House of Guise."

"You do not look like the Guises."

Andelot wanted to turn back but could not. *I am in for much woe,* he thought helplessly.

"If I am to know something, pray tell what it is, Monsieur."

But Charles took on a mysterious face, the corners of his mouth turning upward. He looked over his shoulder. He caught Andelot's arm. "Quick, peasant! Footsteps! This way!"

He rushed to another door, listened, opened it a crack, then beckoned for Andelot to follow.

Somewhat awed, Andelot discovered yet another passage, another door — many doors, all with intricate carvings and the fleur de lys.

Charles hurried on and Andelot stayed at his heels.

He would never find his way back to the chamber he shared with Fabien. They had taken too many turns, entered too many rooms, walked too many passages. He was fully disoriented.

"Where are we going, Prince?"

"Ta ta."

"The Marquis Fabien will be wondering where I have disappeared."

"Ta ta."

They stopped at last before an imposing door. Charles listened before he opened it. His eyes were excited, his face flushed, as he turned to Andelot.

"There is no one here."

"Wait, mon prince —"

But Charles did not wait and passed through into a large chamber bringing Andelot with him.

Andelot found himself inside a stately suite of rooms with large mullioned windows that reached from floor to ceiling and overlooked the garden, terrace, and Loire River.

Charles quietly inched the heavy door shut.

"Come, this way," Charles whispered.

Folding doors opened into a gallery wainscoted with richly gilded oak, the high vaulted ceiling was emblazoned with coats of arms. The walls were covered with crimson brocade set in heavy frames of carved gold; chandeliers of glittering pendants hung from open rafters formed of various colored woods arranged in mosaic patterns.

He looked upon marble statues and busts displayed on sculptured ivory pedestals, inlaid cabinets, and carved tables. In one corner there was a large bed of polished walnut with heavy hangings of royal purple. The material was gathered into a diadem with the gold embossed initials *C.M.* —

Andelot turned on his heel to face Charles.

"But this is the royal chambers of the Queen Mother!"

"Oui!"

"Thunder, Monseigneur! Do you wish to have me quartered? You have deceived me."

"Silence, peasant. She will not be here until tonight. She is in a meeting now with the Guises. I brought you here in good faith — come!"

Andelot followed with uneasy steps. Marquis Fabien had conveyed chilling tales of the Queen Mother's reliance on "soothsayers," as Fabien had called them. Wherever she chose to reside, either in Paris or in Touraine, an observatory for the stars was always at hand, and Cosmo Ruggiero, who had attended her from Florence, never left her except for short periods of time. Cosmo was an astrologer, alchemist, and philosopher. He fed the glowing furnaces with gold and silver, sometimes with dead men's bones; concocted essences, powders, and perfumes; drew horoscopes; and modeled wax figures in the likeness of those who had incurred the queen's enmity. These were supposed to suffer pangs from each stab inflicted on their images and to waste away as their wax similitudes melted into the flames. Cosmo was also a purveyor of poisons to her majesty and dealt largely in herbs and roots fatal to life. His appartements and the observatory were always near those of the queen and connected to them by a secret stair.

Charles led him into a small writing closet built into a turret.

"Behold a secret stairway," Charles told him boastfully. He opened a small, narrow door built into the stone and pointed upward.

Andelot peered past him and saw a flight of narrow steps going up to some secretive portion of the upper story. Charles lit the lamp on the tall table and gestured.

"Quickly, peasant! We have work to do while there is time."

Andelot was both repelled and intrigued. He followed the prince up the steps. The sighing of the wind as it swept along the corners of the castle roof was broken by their footsteps and heavy breathing. The lamplight wavered in the windowless stairwell. Andelot looked over his shoulder expecting to see trailing ghosts.

Charles stopped before a door at the top. He removed a golden key and entered, Andelot behind him. He found himself in a narrow laboratory under the roof. The small room contained a bed, a desk, and some chairs, thick rugs on the stone floor, several antechambers, and one small window.

Charles went to the desk, set his lamp down, and lit the larger lamp on the crowded desk. Andelot came up beside him and saw an ancient manuscript. Always interested in old writings, he all but itched to read it. He looked at the writing and saw that it was Latin and had something to do with astrology.

"Star charts," Charles said.

"Horoscopes, mon prince."

"What say the stars, peasant? Can you read them?" He drew a bundle of papers over to Andelot. Look, here are the celestial signs within the House of Valois, all my brothers, myself, even Margo ... Look, Cosmo traced them with the magic pen from the dates Maman gave him."

"Monseigneur, do not believe this. There is no magic pen, only his interpretations, and I assure you he cannot know your future."

"Nenni, peasant, do not be a dull dog. Oui, here is our future, mine and Francis's. Look! Can you read what Cosmo has written?"

"I will not read it, Monsieur."

"You will read it to me or I will have you beaten!"

"You would listen to lies, to chance guesses, to half-truths?"

Charles snatched the chart to himself. "A cloud now rests on the star of Francis—What could it mean? And look—he says Margo's marriage to Henry de Guise is glowing and favorable. Ha! What will the King of Portugal think of that?"

But Andelot was looking at something else that set his heartbeat drumming in his ears. A cabinet stood against the wall and it was open. He saw many vials and sealed packets, dried herbs and powders, and on one of the sealed packets was written: *For Her Majesty. White powder. Very strong. Sprinkle on flowers, book pages, and inside gloves. Death within days.*

"Look over here," Charles said. Andelot joined him. There were ashes in a small hearth and what looked like small bones.

"I have seen enough," Andelot whispered. "We must leave at once, Monsieur, before we are caught."

And if we are, he thought grimly, *we will not live to tell of it.*

"I shall soon be king," Charles told him proudly. "The star chart casts a shadow on the king, my brother."

"Too convenient, Prince, is it not? Almost as if … as if it allows for decisions to be made that are already planned?"

Charles looked at him long and hard, then his eyes widened. "Someone is coming. Downstairs, I heard footsteps."

Andelot froze. "Is there another way out of here?"

Charles gestured across the chamber to a door. They bolted for it and darted down the outer steps that wound around the side of the castle to the second-story terrace. The wind blew against them and splashes of rain whipped into their faces. There followed a streak of dazzling lightning over the gray rushing waters of the Loire beneath them. The forest trees swayed in a wind that howled like wolves around the outer crevices and crannies of the gray stone castle.

CATHERINE DE MEDICI stood still, listening to the wind and the rain striking against the panes in her writing closet. The sudden spread of clouds made the day appear as twilight. She went into her closet and lit the lamp. She was turning away to her desk when she noticed the secret door was slightly ajar. She narrowed her eyes.

She pushed it aside and entered, holding her lamp high toward the narrow steps. Had Cosmo returned sooner than expected? She climbed the steps and found the door to his laboratory also ajar. She set her teeth and stood without moving. Cosmo was not fool enough to leave secret doors ajar.

Catherine entered the astrologer's chamber and her dark eyes surveyed the cloister. Her gaze halted at the desk. A lamp was lit, the lamp was familiar. She recognized it as the one kept below at the bottom of the steps. Had Madalenna been lax?

No, Madalenna would not dare be lax in her service; this was not the intrusion of Madalenna or Cosmo, but of a clumsy fool. Even the door across the laboratory to the outside steps stood open, creaking in the wind. She went there and pushed it open, stepping out into the wind and rain.

She stood there, staring, her eyes seeking a glimpse of whoever had dared intrude into her observatory.

ANDELOT DID NOT MOVE. He was below crouching with Charles behind some bushes. The rain soaked through their clothing, and he heard Charles's teeth chatter.

"Do not move, Monsieur Prince, only moments more and she will go inside."

Catherine stood above them shrouded in black, the wind blowing her skirts and veil. Andelot knew a sickening feeling in his chest. *This is a woman who will stop at nothing to secure her rule, not even murder.*

Chapter Eighteen

On the day of the masque the weather was clear, sunny, and pleasant. Rachelle rushed to finish Marguerite's mask while the other ladies at court added flourishing touches to their own.

"Ah, tonight I shall see Henry," Marguerite said boldly. She stood and did a twirling pirouette on the floor, causing her ladies to smile and share in her happiness.

"The King of Portugal arrived this morning," Rachelle told her quietly. "Is not Mademoiselle Princesse expected to entertain him at the banquet in the water gallery?"

They all knew this, but the delicate reminder from Rachelle went unheeded by Marguerite.

"I shall marry no one except Monsieur Henry de Guise," Marguerite repeated with firm resolve.

Charlotte spoke up from the other side of the room as she worked on her own mask. "If you are not at the banquet, Your Highness, the Queen Mother will take notice of your absence."

Marguerite leaned over and whispered in Rachelle's ear: "You will help me keep the rendezvous with Monsieur Guise."

Rachelle, sewing a burgundy band of ribbon onto Marguerite's golden mask, looked up with dismay. How could the Queen Mother expect her to keep the princesse away from Guise? How unfair royalty was! In one breath they give impossible orders, in the next, they accuse of insubordination. The task of thwarting Marguerite from seeing Henry de Guise was quickly becoming impossible.

Rachelle saw the smug smile on Charlotte's mouth. Until days ago it had been Charlotte de Presney's responsibility to answer to the Queen Mother for Marguerite's willful antics. Charlotte's placid pale face appeared content at being relieved of the task. However, it was clear she was not pleased over her demotion from maid-of-honor to lady-in-waiting. The bitterness that brooded in her eyes whenever Rachelle looked at her was apparent even to Marguerite. Marguerite, too, appeared to notice the sullen change in Charlotte.

"It was my maman who removed you, not I. Need I remind you, Madame, that neither did I first choose you as my maid-of-honor? I am pleased with Mademoiselle Macquinet whom I can trust to keep her hands off Monsieur Guise."

Louise spoke up. "Madame de Presney has newer interests. Is that not true, Charlotte?"

Charlotte kept her blue eyes on her mask as she sewed the ribbons into place, but a petite smile turned the corners of her lips upward, as though she enjoyed a delightful secret. Rachelle felt her muscles tensing. She did not wish to hear any further chatter about Charlotte and Marquis de Vendôme. Rachelle was certain she saw Charlotte laugh over the impossible task now assigned her by the Queen Mother: keeping Marguerite from her bel ami.

Might as well try to shepherd the wind.

"Princesse," Charlotte said, "I have not lifted a finger to complain over my removal as maid-of-honor, though I may wish to return to Tours, to my father's estate, for the other ladies at court are whispering of my humiliation. It is hard to bear, I promise you."

"You may go home sooner than you had planned," Marguerite said with sarcasm. "I am sure I and my ladies will not object."

Louise and Madame de Pomperant sniggered, but when Charlotte looked over at them, they went back to completing their masks.

None of this benefited Rachelle, who wondered how she could avoid answering to the Queen Mother should she learn Marguerite had slipped away.

"Your Highness, the King of Portugal will wish to spend every moment with the belle princesse, since he is hoped to sign a contract with the Queen Mother to marry you one day. To meet Monsieur Guise at such a moment will surely enrage the queen. She will have spies watching us, I am sure."

"Non. I will not hear of it. My heart tells me to fly to Henry and so I shall. The queen will be busy with the King of Portugal and his retinue. She has already warned me, as you know. She will not assume I shall be so bold as to slip away while the king is here."

Rachelle, exasperated, fell into silence. Louise brought over the burgundy silk and cloth of gold gown and held it to the light so that it shimmered. Each time Rachelle looked at the gown her painful thoughts rushed back to the meeting with Fabien at Chambord, when he had wanted such a gown for her.

Do not think of him. You were stupide to ever think you could claim and hold such a man true to you only. Every belle woman has cast her net for him. Few men in such a situation would be true except one like Joseph of ancient days—How can I do this and sin against God? Unless the marquis had deeper reasons for shunning the banquet of sin, he would have little conviction but to feast to the full. She pricked her finger and winced.

Charlotte said, "Where is your thimble, Rachelle?"

"My weakness, Charlotte. I seem to misplace them. I have lost so many since I was eight and first began my training."

"Ah, such a dress," Louise was saying. "I am happy you decided to wear it tonight after all, Princesse."

At first Marguerite insisted she would wear the blue satin. "My burgundy is too exquisite for the King of Portugal," she had said. So Rachelle had worked twelve hours a day to finish the blue satin. Then came the secret message from Henry de Guise, delivered to Marguerite by Charlotte, in which he begged her to meet him on the south bank of the river the night of the masque. Marguerite changed her mind again, and announced with fanfare that oui, she *would* wear the burgundy silk.

"I will wear it only for Henry," Marguerite now repeated to Louise. "Did I not promise such that day at Chambord? Ah, Monsieur Guise and I shall both wear royal purple. It is all planned. Henry will come as a Babylonian prince wearing a purple mask and turban. I must see him. I must hold him in my arms again and smother him with my kisses. If not, I shall pine away."

Marguerite showed herself to her ladies so gay and excited by the romantic prospects before her that they all laughed at Rachelle's dismay and bade her to accept the intrigues of court life. Danger, they claimed, was all a part of its elaborate charm, and that there were at least a thousand women in France who would change places with her to become the princesse's maid-of-honor, if only they could.

Rachelle agreed it was undoubtedly so, but she hoped to return soon to Lyon with the many drawings of Marguerite's wedding trousseau to discuss them with Grandmère at Chateau de Silk.

"I will think about your leave of absence from court," Marguerite said. "But it is not common that a maid-of honor should be granted such leave so soon after becoming one."

"True, my princesse, but it is rare that a maid-of-honor also has the privilege of being the couturière for Her Highness's wedding trousseau. Such a grand trousseau as this must have the Macquinet family assisting me."

"There is time," Marguerite said. "The marriage contract with the king will not be signed tomorrow, I promise you. And my marriage to Monsieur Guise will not take place for several years at least."

Rachelle was uneasy. What gave Marguerite confidence the contract would not be signed when Catherine was equally determined it would be so?

Rachelle finished Marguerite's charming mask of gold with burgundy ribbons, then as Charlotte was called to fix Marguerite's hair, Rachelle rushed to finish her own mask. It was green velvet with gold ties, matching the gold trim on her gown. Her heart was heavy and whether her dress was exquisite no longer mattered, for who would be there to appreciate it? She thought of Andelot Dangeau, one galante, at least, who was a safe harbor for her ailing heart.

AS THE PURPLE AND GOLD TWILIGHT deepened over the river, the torches sprang into flame up and down the waterway and in the emerald forest adjacent to the castle. Rachelle found the gala affair most stunning. All the courtiers and ladies were at the banquet to pay homage to the visiting King of Portugal.

Although the festive ceremonial meeting between Marguerite and the nephew of Philip of Spain proceeded with appropriate decorum on Marguerite's part, Rachelle knew Marguerite was only feigning meekness.

The king, too, played his part well. As to whether he was deceived by the princesse, or was made by his Oncle Philip to understand Marguerite was an untamable wanton, Rachelle could but wonder. It all seemed to her a theatrical play, all of them fit for the masque later that evening. The glittering candles shining on the gold and bejeweled goblets of wine, the gowns, the rings, the smiles — all were cut of the worst kind of ruse.

Therefore it came as no surprise when the king declared openly that there was no one more lovely than the Valois princesse, nor was there a more fascinating woman at court. Marguerite let it be known by her charm that such a marriage match was most suitable to her.

Rachelle was fascinated watching the Queen Mother. Catherine, for a change, did not wear black but rather a most extraordinaire dress of rose lace. But her eyes were fixed upon her daughter, and to those who did not know her, Catherine appeared emotionless. But the unblinking gaze of Madame le Serpent spoke its secret warning to Marguerite: one faux pas and it would be dealt with when the goblets were empty and the servants were sweeping the floor.

RACHELLE knew she too was one of the most beautiful ladies in attendance in her emerald green velvet. And as an attendant to the princesse, she had caught the interested eyes of several titled men, including Comte Maurice Beauvilliers, Sebastien's nephew. She did not see Fabien at the banquet. Then he had opted not to come — why? Andelot Dangeau was also there. He would undoubtedly know why the marquis was keeping himself away.

During the dancing, with the many courtiers on the great floor in two opposite lines, Rachelle was able to nod to Andelot that she would meet him near the open gallery on the other side.

The air was cool coming in from the river, which was lined with colored lamps. Andelot was waiting, looking vulnerably handsome as he approached her in his less flamboyant clothing.

"There is le Cardinal de Lorraine," she said in a low voice.

Charles de Guise wore crimson and white, his gold cross gleaming. There was a somewhat haughty smile loitering around his mouth, and his gray eyes were watchful. He had turned those eyes now toward Andelot and Rachelle. Rachelle felt an odd sensation as he looked at her, and she pretended she did not notice his gaze.

"He is coming," Andelot whispered, consternation and excitement mingling in his voice.

Rachelle shivered. She dipped a curtsy as the powerful man walked up. She could smell the fragrance from his rustling garments, saw the white hand with its rubies and sapphires being extended toward her for the perfunctory kiss of obedience.

Andelot grasped his hand and kissed it.

"Monseigneur Cardinal, I am your dutiful servant. I have longed to meet you since I arrived at Blois."

She knew Andelot had risked looking brutish by his action, and that it had cost him, for he wanted more than anything to appear worthy of his kinsman's attention and betterment.

The cardinal turned his attention away from Rachelle and looked at Andelot with a lean smile and observant eyes.

Rachelle thought he looked amused.

"Monsieur Andelot, I trust our meeting will go forward tomorrow without further interruption. We have much to discuss, including your future in Paris. We must wait for your oncle, Sebastien, to return from Moulins." His mouth showed cynicism. "He is taking a long time to return to the queen regent, is he not? But then, perhaps he has more in common with the Bourbons."

How much does he know? Rachelle wondered. *Does that subdued mockery mean he knows Sebastien is a Huguenot?*

"Did I hear the honored title of Bourbon, Monsieur le Cardinal?"

They turned. Marquis Fabien stood garbed in rich Genoan velvet of black and scarlet, holding a broad-rimmed hat turned up with a scarlet plume and fastened to an aigrette of rubies, with the armorial device of a *B* in gold.

He bowed. "Mademoiselle, Monseigneur le Cardinal, mon cousine Andelot. What is this you say, Cardinal ... Sebastien has not returned from Moulins? Ah, but he has!" And he gestured with his golden brown head toward the salle.

They all turned. Sebastien stood with the cardinal's brother, le Duc de Guise, their heads bent, talking soberly.

Fabien smiled lazily. "He rode in last night, Monseigneur."

Cardinal de Lorraine's gray eyes swept him. "At last, this is good news, Marquis. We have been waiting ... And will your kinsman, Prince Condé, show himself?"

There was a moment of silence, in which Rachelle, sensitive to the interplay between them, tensed over the cardinal's seemingly innocent remark.

"You will be pleased to know that the members of the House of Bourbon will be here within two days to meet with King Francis. Louis has much to worry him, with Spain meddling in how Bourbon serfs decide to conduct their private worship."

Rachelle scarcely breathed. Beside her, she felt Andelot stiffen. Was he nervous because he feared that Marquis Fabien would undermine his opportunities with his kinsman the cardinal, or was he concerned that Fabien was removing his mask of cooperation with the cardinal?

Le Cardinal de Lorraine's handsome face was chiseled with lines of contempt. His power and authority over France intoxicated him.

"If the Prince Condé would rid his duchy of heretics and so solace the King of Spain, then he would not need concern himself with a possible bull issued by Rome for his arrest and trial in sponsoring heresy, Marquis."

Rachelle glanced sharply at Fabien. The muscles in his jaw tensed and the blue-violet of his eyes burned like hyacinth. Prince Condé was a true protector of the Huguenots, and Princesse Eleonore charitably sponsored safe houses for fleeing Protestants from elsewhere in France.

Why were the Bourbons risking so much to come here to Amboise?

"Do Philip and Rome perceive that a movement against Prince Condé could provoke a war? William the Silent of the Netherlands is prepared to bring his Protestant soldiers to Bourbonaise, and if necessary, to fight alongside Louis."

"Does the Marquis mean to imply that he too would join Prince Condé to raise swords against the king of Catholic France?"

Fabien bowed. "Monseigneur knows that I am a most loyal Catholic — as was my father before me, Duc Jean-Louis de Bourbon."

Rachelle picked up the subtle interplay. Her heart was beating quickly. Fabien was hinting that his father's loyalty to the cardinal in the last war with Spain had not served to protect him from the Guises' arranged assassination.

The cardinal's cynical mouth tipped at one corner and froze there. "Rome may choose to reconsider your allegiance and wonder if it is genuine."

"May it never be. For surely, Monseigneur, I do not measure up to your good witness of the faith."

Andelot choked on his wine, bending over and holding his throat with one hand, clutching his goblet with the other.

Rachelle seized the moment he provided. She grabbed his arm and cried: "Andelot! Oh, Marquis de Vendôme, aid me in getting him to a chair, *s'il vous plaît!*"

The cardinal gave a brief nod of his head and looked at Andelot. "Come to my chambers in the morning, cousine — if you survive choking on your wine. We will meet with Sebastien over *petit noir*. The day will be long and we have much to decide about your future."

Cousine? Rachelle thought.

Andelot ceased his coughing at once. A look of shock spread over his face. The cardinal then turned to Fabien who also showed alert interest.

"Marquis, do you not think it most interesting that I have discovered the parentage of Andelot?"

He turned to Rachelle. "Mademoiselle Macquinet, I trust we will meet in Paris at a more convenient time. Adieu." He walked away toward le Duc de Guise and Sebastien, his crimson vestment rustling, leaving a fragrance of musk.

"Ah, Marquis Fabien," Andelot whispered with dismay. "You have done yourself grave injury. Why did you do so? You made him angry. He will not forget."

"A *fait accompli*, mon ami. Do not concern yourself unduly. I know the cardinal's ways as a stag knows his watering holes. I was never secure. Nor will you be now."

"What?" Andelot blinked.

"Listen, mon ami, do not go to his *petit déjeuner* in the morning. You will not find Sebastien there."

"What! Mon cousine—not go? When I am here for this very purpose? And such a purpose. Why, I might end up the page of the cardinal himself."

"That is what I fear. We must talk tonight after the masque."

Fabien's violet blue eyes hardened like jewels as he looked after the cardinal. "He believes he is very clever, that one. A pity a holier man than he is not in his position."

"You made that clear," Andelot grumbled. "I do not understand you, Marquis. You have deliberately made yourself abhorrent."

Fabien smiled. "You but think so. And now, Mademoiselle, it is you and I who have much to discuss. Will you accompany me on a boat ride to the south side of the Loire? S'il vous plaît." He bowed.

Rachelle's mind was still floundering in a turbulent sea of its own. She looked from Andelot, who was scowling in obvious bewilderment, to Fabien, whose smile caused her guard to snap into place.

"Monsieur, merci, but I cannot leave the princesse. I am under orders from the Queen Mother."

"Yes, you better not go," Andelot agreed hastily.

Fabien looked at him with a brief, wry smile. "Au contraire, cousine. Mademoiselle Rachelle *must* come with me." He reached over, smiled, and took her arm. He bowed lightly to Andelot. "Adieu. I will talk to you later tonight."

Rachelle found herself being guided with a firm but gentle hand along the gallery to the downward stairway.

The night breeze was comfortable and bore the lovely strains of a symphony from the royal musicians, who played from the center of the river on an anchored barge, with the raised platform covered with purple velvet embroidered in gold.

"I have a boat ready, Mademoiselle. Your company is most charmante."

"Monsieur!"

"Fabien."

"Marquis Fabien," she said, "you have a certain finesse for taking command even when it is uncalled for. I cannot go with you on a boat, although a moonlight cruise would also be most charmante in the plans of Madame Charlotte de Presney."

She took her arm away and stopped on the stair, looking at him with what she hoped was a cool stare, though his presence made her feel anything but that. She could not resist the jealous anger growing in her heart.

"I am sure that Madame de Presney is more preferable to my company as it *was* in the garden when I was to meet you ... You do remember, Marquis."

"Yes, I remember well, Mademoiselle. You decided to have a headache and leave me helpless and hopeless to combat her bewitching wiles. She ruined the lace on my shirt, because of *you*. But as you are such a fine grisette, I am sure you can sew it for me? I will pay you, assuredly."

She made an unearthly sound, gritting her teeth, then turning sharply she started back up the steps to Andelot, but Fabien took her arm again and laughed.

"Mademoiselle, do you take me for a fool? A boy when it comes to such matters as you speak of? Do you think I am so naive that I cannot see through Madame de Presney's wiles from the beginning? Or that I shall melt at her slippers for the opportunity of her bed?"

"Monsieur!"

"Come, come, let us be honest. That is what you are hinting about, is it not? I see I must remind you. I was raised at court. Nothing surprises me; little shocks me. I have seen it all and heard it all. I have already decided on what I wish from life. There are many Charlottes, I assure you, both young and aging, and beautiful and powerful enough to do injury to anyone who snubs them. But I will also remind you again that none of them interest me. Did I not tell you so at Blois?"

Yes, he had told her, and she believed him until Louise informed her otherwise. That he had mentioned his shirt, however lightly, proved Louise had spoken the truth of what she saw in the garden.

"Believe me, I care not what the gossips report. None of this disturbs me, Mademoiselle. It is your thoughts toward me that are of concern.

I would have seen you before this to deny it, except I had some very important business which took me away for two days. We cannot talk here with courtiers coming and going. Come with me to the boat." He drew her down the stairs and lowered his voice. "Margo is there waiting now."

"The boat? How did she escape the banquet?"

"By walking in the garden with the King of Portugal. She made an excuse and ran off."

"What excuse?"

"Mademoiselle, I did not ask her," he said wearily. "She will meet Guise on the south side. He is there now, pacing impatiently, I imagine."

She looked away quickly to break the spell of his gaze. "Then, if the princesse is aboard the boat, I shall need to go with you, Marquis," she said stiffly. "Otherwise —"

"Merci," he interrupted suavely. "Otherwise you would deny me. I am well aware. I have much to explain to you. From your coldness toward me I see I am not a minute too early in doing so."

"You owe me no explanations, Monsieur."

"I wish to give you such an explanation. I have already told you how you interest me. I know you are a Huguenot ... that you keep your virtue intact until marriage. I expect nothing from you, Mademoiselle, if that is what you think my attention is hoping for. Court gossip has drifted to you about Charlotte and myself. I want you to understand that I turned her down."

She had never heard such plainly spoken words before on a subject that made her face hot.

"You must not say these things."

"Saint Denis! Did I not warn you at Blois what it would be like for you at court? You are accustomed to your quiet ways at the Chateau de Silk, to the morality of the Macquinets and your neighbors. Believe me, it is not so here; the natural ways of the flesh abound."

"Are you now suggesting the manner of your excuses?"

"Is that what you heard from me when I spoke to the cardinal? Excuses? I will now warn you about the cardinal. You had best understand and give him no cause. Non, not even a smile."

When she was silent he said wryly, "So then, I have shocked you."

"Non," she said quietly. "I am not that naive. I had guessed about the cardinal. But I thought you and Charlotte de Presney ... that is, I was told ... I see I was too hasty."

He stopped and looked down at her, his gaze warming her. The soft music sighed in the distance, mingling with the breezes in the forest trees.

"Believe me, I would not throw away so easily what has recently been shared between us. Charlotte's appearance is enough to tempt any man with eyes to see, but—"

"As she intends, I assure you."

"It is you, Mademoiselle, who stirs my passions."

She sucked in her breath at the word *passions*. Such a word should not be spoken, but the marquis evidently did not share the same mind.

He stepped toward her, scooping up her hand into his, and at his touch her heart yearned for him. He brought her fingers to his lips and held them there for a moment.

"I will not exchange a possible future with you, non, not for ten women such as Charlotte de Presney. I think you will be worth my patience."

Rachelle could not speak. Her heart beat quickly with the sheer thought of his words. He had deliberately emphasized the word *future*. He would wait to have her.

"The Bourbon men, Mademoiselle, are not always wise in their behavior, but the ladies they have chosen to marry are the most honorable in France. Antoine and Jeanne of Navarre. Prince Louis and Eleonore, a niece of Coligny. These are the manner of women I will seek for a wife at Vendôme. Except I intend to be worthy of such a woman. Antoine is a moral weakling, and Louis hardly better, though I believe he sincerely loves Eleonore. He is also loyal to the Huguenots."

She turned away, overwhelmed. "But why do you say these words to me? Surely you do not mean that—"

"Surely you know the answer. I see we are being observed. Come, let us go to the boat to seek Margo. If I do not bring her to the south side of the Loire to be with Guise, she will never forgive me. Despite her exasperating ways, I am as fond of her as a sister. I saw her grow up with Francis, Mary, and Charles."

"I, too, grow more fond of her with the days. But I wish she had not made me her maid-of-honor. I prefer, as you said, the quiet life at the Chateau de Silk."

"I could wish she had not as well! It appears as though we have been foiled on that, does it not? Let us hope Catherine does not ever consider you for her bevy of spies."

"I would never accept, Marquis Fabien."

"Catherine has her ploys, and they are always devious, believe me."

She shuddered. "Let us not discuss her now. Let us look at the boats plying up and down the river. For that one entertainment, at least, let there be no dark clouds to hide the moon."

Chapter Nineteen

UPON THE RIVER, THE RED AND GOLD LANTERNS ON PAINTED BARGES floated past the bridge with its arches trimmed with colored lamps. The water swells reflected the flickering lanterns with bright glimmering patches of color.

Rachelle looked back toward the castle and saw its windows all aglow, while the turrets had become beacons against the dark sky. Surely this beauty could offer no danger? This castle of Amboise would never become a dank and treacherous place, and the dungeons, even on this night, surely must be empty, swept, and varnished?

Her soft emerald velvet gown sparkled with seed pearls in the lantern light, confirming her thoughts. They walked along the winding path toward the Loire.

"There is Gallaudet," Fabien said.

He drew her under the shadow of the *parterre* to wait for him. The page came walking up carrying something dark and furry under his arm. *A dead cat?*

Fabien pointed. "Dare I inquire what it is?"

Gallaudet produced a dark wavy wig and a silver eye mask.

"For your sport, Monsieur."

"You chose well." Fabien plucked the long wig from Gallaudet's hand and sniffed it.

Rachelle laughed.

Fabien threw a red cloak over his shoulders and bowed. "Your servant, Madame."

"Oh, dear," she said with a laugh, "the marquis is a toad. I fear I have nothing to wear but my mask." She slipped her emerald velvet eye mask over her face.

"It will take more than that to hide such beauty. Your hair gives you away, as does the dimple at the corner of your most delightful lips."

Gallaudet cleared his throat. Rachelle managed to keep her poise. "Does your Monsieur often have such a way with words, Gallaudet?"

"Rarely, Mademoiselle. And upon first awakening he merely grumbles."

"Silence, you traitor. That reminds me, awaken me at dawn. We have important business to attend to. And keep an eye on Andelot and the cardinal. Find Sebastien also. Ask him of the handful of Huguenots I noticed in the woods this afternoon. See what he may know of them. It will be a grave mistake if Monsieur de la Renaudie was not fully warned as planned at Moulins."

"At once. I have brought these for Mademoiselle." Gallaudet lifted from a satchel a Spanish hat, gold fringed with jewels, and a black cloak.

"Where did you get them?"

"From your trunk, Marquis. The hat you wore once at Fountainbleau."

"Did I? No wonder I never wore it again ... At least the jewels are handsome."

"Oui, I was thinking of cutting them off and bartering for a new horse—"

"You asked too late. They, and the hat, are now the petite grisette's."

Gallaudet shrugged and handed them over.

"Oh, I could not," she said as the sapphires gleamed blue. But she placed the hat over her hair and tucked as much as she could under its rim.

"That will do well," Fabien said cheerfully. "Come, our boat is long ready." He turned to Gallaudet, who bowed.

"Oui, Marquis, it is ready. Capitaine Nappier himself will steer it."

"Nappier?" Fabien laughed. "From a twenty-gun corsair ship to a butterfly boat. He must be in profound spirits this night."

Rachelle did not know what to expect, but she felt suddenly bold and daring in her Spanish hat with its shimmering gold fringe, her emerald eye mask, and a dashing black cloak that belonged to the marquis — and she had the marquis himself.

She bowed. "I am ready, Monsieur."

THE SILVERY MOON and the fragrant spring flowers wove their enchantments.

The quay where the barges and boats were boarded was not far from the king's musicians, so that the lilting sound of a lute playing a haunting refrain of a love song carried toward them.

The painted barge was waiting for them ... and what a barge! It was constructed in the shape of a butterfly with gossamer wings reflecting the moon's beams.

"May I present my master swordsman, Capitaine Nappier," Fabien told her with a grin. "Tonight Nappier is an elf, as you can see. So Nappier! Do you expect to harry Spain's galleons with your magic wand?"

The tall Frenchman Nappier, rippling with muscle, displayed his green hose and a tunic. He bowed very low, his green cap bobbing with a rose. In his hand was a white wand that appeared to have been borrowed from a friendly chamberlain. He straightened, his teeth gleaming against his rugged, scarred features.

"Ah, Marquis de Vendôme. Maybe one day you will sponsor your humble servant with a twenty-gun buccaneering ship, eh?"

"And for the effort, see myself dangling from one of Philip's yardarms."

"You will not dangle Marquis, not with Nappier by your side, I assure you."

"That, at least, is comforting. I must think about such a venture, Nappier. Tonight you remain an elf."

Rachelle stepped into the gently rocking boat under Fabien's guiding hand. As they left the riverbank, Princesse Marguerite came from beneath a dark cover where she had been concealed. She laughed, fanning herself, and tossed back her hooded black cloak. She came to Fabien and kissed him. "Merci, mon amour Fabien." Then she turned happily to Rachelle and clapped her hands in delight at her dashing hat with its saucy gold fringe dancing in the starlight.

"Oh, this is gleeful, to be free, *free!* I shall run away with cher Henry. We shall become corsairs on the wild surging sea with Nappier! And we will drink in our amour, amour, amour!"

Fabien arched a brow at Rachelle, and she laughed. It was amusing to see Margo so free and happy—far from court and its political demands, away from the molding power of Catherine and her iron ambitions and the ruthless shackles of corrupted religion.

"But the King of Portugal," Rachelle asked, "where did you leave him?"

The question somehow struck Marguerite's fancy. She threw back her head and laughed. She began to dance about the little boat, clapping her hands. "Where is the King of Portugal?" she cried to the moon. "Why—the good King of Portugal is with the wicked King of Spain. And the King of Spain? With the King of France—and the pope." And she laughed again as though this were most hilarious.

Fabien leaned toward Rachelle. "I assure you, the little hoyden has had one sip of wine too much. Come, ma cherie, let us look at the shore and listen to the orchestra."

The forest on both sides of the Loire was ablaze with festoons of lanterns looped from tree to tree. There were other boats as well, shaped like swans and peacocks, filled with masked courtiers.

Nappier laughed. "Now there is a capitaine for you, Monsieur Fabien." He gestured to where a boat crew was caught in a thick tangle of water lilies on the banks beneath willow trees.

Laughter filled the night. The other boats slipped past the water lilies and hooted at the entangled boat with its courtiers wading ashore, the women squealing as they hoisted their skirts above their knees.

Marguerite grew more animated as they neared the southern bank. It was here she would meet Monsieur Henry de Guise.

Nappier drew the boat to the bank, and they disembarked and mounted broad marble steps of the parterre with white balustrades and marble statues now appearing red in the colored lamps. Fountains were splashing rainbow colors.

"There is Monsieur Henry now," Marguerite said, and Rachelle turned her head to catch sight of a figure garbed as the King of Babylon in purple and yellow with a jeweled turban and purple mask.

Marguerite threw back her hood and displayed her burgundy silk and cloth of gold gown.

The Babylonian king advanced toward them.

Marguerite met him with a playful bow. They clasped hands and rushed aside beneath the shadow of a portico.

Rachelle quickened her steps in their direction, but Fabien held her back.

"Ma Rachelle cherie, they are running into the forest. We will not see her again until morning. For Marguerite it is always *toute la nuit*."

"But the king—"

"Word will reach him by spies, believe me; no matter how careful we are, the news will be known. Come tomorrow this nephew of Philip's and his retinue will be journeying from Amboise with injurious disdain. This is what Margo wants. She is now free again to try to marry Henry."

He drew her onto a path that wound into the lighted trees where music played.

"She courts the wrath of the Queen Mother," she protested. "We should not have brought her here."

"Cherie, she would have managed, even if she had to swim. If Catherine cannot clip her wings, do you suppose your honorable efforts would curtail her? Non. I have known Margo since she was five. She was attached to Henry even then. They use to hide in the closet together."

"But the rage she will face. I fear for her."

"You do well, for Catherine will be livid when this hoped-for marriage contract fails despite her best intrigue. Margo understands this. She has chosen the path her footsteps take her."

They wandered onto where plots of smooth grass grew lush beneath well-pruned trees. Along the parterre there were tents of satin and velvet, fringed with gold, offering the passing masquers refreshments and places to linger and listen to the music.

They strolled the borders of the white marble terraces into the woods, where masked courtiers danced under decorative hangings spread among the branches of the trees, and others reclined on soft cushions arranged on carpets. Tables were filled with displays of wines, fruits, cheeses, and confectioneries, constantly replenished by busy servants under the watchful eyes of the chamberlains.

They came to a pavilion lighted with colored lanterns, and he turned her aside.

"I prefer this spot. You can see the bend in the river, and there are fewer courtiers."

He led her up the steps to a terrace. Below, the lighted court was filled with distant dancers and diners, but it was the sound of flutes and flageolets that filled the woods around them.

He removed his wig and mask, and she did the same so that the breeze was refreshingly cool. They leaned against the rail, listening to the music. He bent over the rail and caught the attention of one of the lackeys, who brought up a platter of refreshments.

Rachelle was anxious to ask him about some of the bewildering things he had said earlier at the banquet and again later to Gallaudet.

She glanced toward him and said suddenly, "What did you mean when you told Gallaudet there were Huguenots in the woods? Do you mean now, here?" She lifted a hand toward the miles of trees receding toward the hills.

She saw his sobriety. She was right, then. What he had told his page was important.

"When I was at Moulins, Louis decided messengers should be sent to warn de la Renaudie that Avenelle disclosed the plot to Catherine and the Guises. The Huguenots I have noticed here in the woods have given me reason to fear that the messengers were thwarted, that Renaudie did not receive the warning to remain at Nantes."

"How horrible. Then there are Huguenots here in the woods? Sent by Monsieur Renaudie? But they are in danger! They must be warned."

"That is what concerns me. And I have sent a message, you can be sure, but I wanted Sebastien alerted."

"Perhaps Monsieur Renaudie did not send these particular Huguenots?"

"That too is a possibility. Let us hope so. Julot, a cousin of Andelot's, is trying to make contact now in the woods to see where they came from.

With so many courtiers roaming about, there is less chance of Julot being noticed. I only wish Louis would have accepted my offer to go to Renaudie. With Gallaudet, and perhaps Julot, we would have gotten through, I am sure."

"Then if Monsieur Renaudie is being watched," she said cautiously, "who would do so except the Queen Mother?"

"None but le Duc de Guise, though she and the cardinal would know about it. The duc was appointed head of all military forces in France before we left Blois ... a curious and troubling fact when the Bourbon nobles are called to come here to sign an edict of pacification. Why is Guise suddenly made marshal?"

"You think they continue to suspect Renaudie will attack?"

"Or worse, Mademoiselle."

"What could be worse?"

"A trap," he said savagely. "That is what I fear — a trap. But I cannot convince Louis to listen. He comes to save face, fearing he will be thought a coward if he does not come. And Coligny, honorable man that he is, is too trusting of royalty. He often declares he would rather trust the Queen Mother than live in fear of constant intrigue, but in that I do not believe he is being wise. I know the Guises and Catherine. They are devilishly shrewd."

Rachelle stared off at the woods. Huguenots ... were they out there? Would they attack? And if they did, what manner of trap did le Duc de Guise have in mind?

"My retainers and men-at-arms were chosen because they are witty and cautious. Nor do I make apology for their wariness. These are times to doubt the proffered cup of peace. Catherine is not above dipping her finger in poisons."

Rachelle gripped the terrace banister. The colored lanterns, the masks of the courtiers, all took on a sinister new form.

He nodded below toward some trees. "Over there ... even now, my loyals are near at hand. Gallaudet would be nearby if I had not sent him to Sebastien. We are always on watch, Mademoiselle. For my father, Jean-Louis — you may have heard me talk of him — was assassinated. Bourbons are rife for death, for they are closer to the throne than the Guises."

"Then you suspect the House of Guise is to blame for his murder?"

"Yes, but I have no proof. One reason I have spent time recently with Charlotte de Presney is because she promises me evidence."

Her head turned sharply. "Where would she discover such proof?"

"Need you ask?" His voice was wry.

"The Queen Mother?"

"Among other lucrative sources. I can tell you the men Charlotte knows are often in high positions. A word from them would soon garner some facts."

So Charlotte was promising him benefits for an association with her.

"What does she expect in return, Marquis Fabien?" she asked in a chilly voice.

He regarded her. She looked away. She should not have disclosed her concern since he had already made known his thoughts on such matters, especially about Charlotte.

He gently removed the dark cloak he had provided her and admired her emerald green silk dress. She had not intended for it to happen — or did she? Perhaps he did not plan it either, but the music, the silvery moonlight; all worked their enchantment. He drew her and she came to him.

"How is it possible," he breathed, "that I feel so strongly about you so soon?"

"I confess my heart yearns for you also. You told me at Chambord it was love at first sight."

"I meant it. But I am not so young as to believe such love as this can be rushed into a marriage. Love needs time to be tested, Rachelle, ma petite. We must make certain it is an enduring love and not only passion."

"I hardly know you, but I do not want to say adieu."

"I would grieve if I were never to see you again."

Their lips met — and like a blazing torch toppled accidentally into a dry haystack, what was intended as a light demonstration of promises to come burst into a consuming desire.

Rachelle trembled inside at his tightening embrace, while the heat of his lips melted the safeguards put in place by a young and tender will. *Lord Jesus,* her soul cried out in a plea for strength and wisdom in the gale of a storm newly experienced.

Fabien abruptly held her away from him and took her face between his hands. She shut her eyes against the burning blue of his gaze.

"Rachelle, my cherie," he spoke in a low, husky voice. "I must be cautious — for your sake and mine. I promise to pursue our love, to see where it brings us in the future, but it is too soon to swear our hearts to eternal love when the passion is so strong."

It took her a moment to find her voice again and calm her heart. She moved further away, allowing the cool breeze to blow against her, to bring sanity. "Yes, it is soon, too soon . . ."

"We would be unwise not to discuss some differences between us."

A soft uneasy murmur awakened in her heart. "You speak of my faith, a Huguenot, and you — a Catholic."

"There is that . . . and, some things I must do that I feel strongly about."

She looked at him, questioning.

He frowned. "I shall doubtless make you wonder, for this is hardly the moment to show you on one hand how I feel strongly about you, and on the other to tell you that I am leaving France, but such is the situation now. So I must explain."

Her heart sank. A dullness crept over her.

"Going away?"

"Admiral Coligny has begun a colony in America. It is in a place they call Florida. I have already told the admiral I will help sponsor the journey, to bring new colonizers to replace those who have died of sickness. I will be gone a year, maybe more."

She was silent a long troubling minute.

"Rachelle," he said very softly.

Her heart hit bottom. "I see."

"Non. I do not think so. This has been long planned. Before I ever saw you at Chambord. I must see it through. Nappier has been trying to convince me to buy a ship. We would sail together to the region around St. Augustine."

One moment it had seemed the love of a lifetime was at her fingertips. Within mere moments happiness was wrenched from her grasp and a door was closing. A year! Maybe two. It was impossible. The flame kindled between them in the mere weeks they had known one another could hardly be expected to burn for so long. But how could she tell him? He was so sure it would last. And she had no right after only weeks to demand, or even to plead, for him to stay. She could see in his eyes he could not stay.

He walked over to her and lifted her face as though he read her mind.

"I could not forget you, ever. Not even if I tried to forget."

"It is not fair," she whispered vehemently.

"Cherie, I will return. Even if I stayed, it is too soon for us to marry. We are both young. There is much to do and learn that we will share with each other when I come back to you. And you, ma belle, you will have your wondrous silk and your Grandmère to make you into the renowned couturière you desire."

"Yes, my silk. I will have the silk," she said with consolation. "I will go home. They cannot keep me here. I will not stay."

"Ma amour, you will have your way, I promise you."

"Oh, Fabien, you will make Marguerite let me go home?"

"I will do something."

"*C'est bien promis?*"

"Yes, I promise you, ma Rachelle cherie."

For a timeless moment he took both of her hands in his and held them to his lips as the beauty of the starlight shone like silver on the river.

Chapter Twenty

Princesse Marguerite Valois did not hear as much as a whisper as she crept down the various corridors on her surreptitious route to reach her appartements before the sun was up. It was dawn and the castle was quiet except for guards moving here and there, sleepy, and waiting to be relieved by the next watch. She knew these night guards well, and they were rewarded at various times for looking the other way when she snuck back to her chamber from some rendezvous.

This dawn was different. There were more guards than usual, and some were strangers to her. This worried her, but not enough to change her plans.

She neared her appartements. There came a rush of footsteps and a loud command, lamps flared with firelight, stinging her eyes, and she threw up an arm against the glare.

"How dare you accost the Princesse of France this way," she cried.

Her breath stopped at the reply: "How dare a princesse of France behave the harlot! Bring her to my chamber immediately!"

Catherine.

Marguerite broke into a dazed tremor, her body soon wet with sweat.

Charlotte de Presney, standing unseen in the shadow of a chamber door, tucked her mouth into a satisfied smile. Her betrayal of Marguerite's activity to the Queen Mother would also bring Rachelle into grave trouble. Rachelle had returned before midnight with the marquis and was asleep in her chamber but would soon be called to account.

Charlotte slipped away silently.

CATHERINE crossed her chamber to the door and turned the key in the lock. She moved slowly and regally toward Margo.

"You fool. It is not shame enough you behave the Jezebel of France? And with whom but the House of Guise? Our enemy. And of all times — during the King of Portugal's visit to the palais!"

Margo stood, hands clasped together, head bowed, trembling.

Catherine walked toward her, her eyes slits of rage.

"Harlot! I was on the verge of arranging your marriage with a nephew of Philip, uniting a bond between France and Spain. And you, wanton daughter, turn us into fools as you run off into the woods to beg favors of Henry de Guise like some prostitute on the street. "Oh Henry, mon amour," she mocked her daughter's voice, "I want you so. I am yours, Henry. Lie with me, Henry, lie with me in the weeds and bushes." Catherine sneered and backhanded her across the face, her rings bruising her daughter's cheek.

Catherine took another step toward her as Margo stepped back. "Ah! Our cunning Monsieur de Guise has found the Princesse of France as wanton as the lowest of peasants. Princesse? Harlot! You have ruined everything I worked for!" She slapped her again on the other side of the face. Margo reeled, catching herself on the couch.

"Within an hour, talk of your rendezvous with Guise will sweep the palais, and the King of Portugal will hear of your wanton ways. Marriage! Bah! Should he marry a whore? And with the House of Philip zealous fanatics for Rome? Nay, I tell you there will be no contract now. King Philip will not allow it even if he were to overlook your whoredoms."

And with these scornful words, Catherine flung Margo from her with all her strength.

Margo lay stunned on the floor, more dazed with fear than pain. Whenever her mother was in a cold, ruthless rage, Margo became paralyzed.

Catherine went to the door of her closet and gestured to someone inside. A moment later an attendant came out wearing a black-hooded cloak with eyeholes. The jeweled whipping cane in Catherine's chamber was taken from its place and handed with fanfare to the mock executioner. Catherine lifted her hand for the phantom to proceed.

"Beat some sense into this Jezebel who dares to call herself a princesse of France! Do not touch her face. No one will see any marks but Henry de Guise."

She had been beaten many times since a child, but never like this. She begged for mercy, to no avail.

"Do you think Monsieur de Guise loves you?" Catherine demanded. "But non. Le Cardinal de Lorraine told him to seduce you so it would be impossible for you to marry the King of Portugal!"

The cane whacked again and again, bruising and cutting.

"Henry, mon amour," Catherine mocked. "'Do you love me too, mon petit Henry?' ... 'Ah, I cannot do without you, Margo. And especially do I love all you bring me — the possibility of the throne of France!'"

"You lie," Margo whispered through her parched throat. "Henry does love me."

"You little fool."

The cane came down again and again. Margo was coming in and out of consciousness.

Catherine took her by the shoulder sleeves of her gown and dragged her to a couch. The burgundy silk and cloth of gold ripped, stained with blood.

"You dare to throw yourself at the feet of a Guise who threatens to take the throne from the Valois family?"

In a sudden rush of fury, she grabbed the cane from the mock executioner and struck her until Margo fainted.

The black-hooded figure came up and kicked Margo several times.

"Enough!" Catherine breathed. "She would not be the first disobedient child to die from a royal beating, but I have not given her up yet. There is still a chance I can arrange a marriage."

Catherine unlocked her door and beckoned to Madalenna. "Have the princesse taken to her chamber. If word of any of this becomes gossip, I shall have every last one of you thrown into the dungeons. Tell them I said so."

"Y-yes, Madame."

"Be quick about it."

"Oui, Madame!" Madalenna scampered to fulfill the Queen Mother's wishes.

RACHELLE came awake to find Louise de Fontaine bending over her with a contorted face and fearful eyes.

"Wake up, Rachelle, it is Marguerite. The princesse was beaten by the Queen Mother. She is yet unconscious, and her wounds are most dreadful to see."

Rachelle heard the pity in Louise's whisper but knew it came not for love of Marguerite, but for fear of Catherine de Medici. Rachelle sprang from bed and put on her chemise, following Louise from her closet into the princesse's main appartements. As they passed an antechamber they saw Charlotte was up and yawning, ordering the serving girls to make tea. Her blonde hair looked too neat to have just awakened.

Louise whispered, "It was Charlotte de Presney, the Queen Mother's spy, who betrayed Marguerite and Monsieur de Guise."

Rachelle suspected Charlotte, but was uncertain. "Have you proof, Louise?"

"Non. But who else among us? We all love the princesse, though her ways are often immoral."

Rachelle knew Charlotte had been privy to all of Marguerite's plans to meet Henry de Guise on the south bank.

Louise took hold of Rachelle's arm, her eyes alarmed. "Charlotte despises you even more than she does the princesse. Surely she has betrayed you and the marquis taking Marguerite on the butterfly boat. Oh, Rachelle, what can you do to protect yourself?"

"My protection, Louise, is the will and mercy of my Savior, Christ. If God allows me to be punished, then I will but continue to trust him."

Louise shook her head in amazed doubt. "You Huguenots are besotted with foolishness. Run away. Go back to Lyon. The Queen Mother may decide to forget hunting you down."

"When I go home to the Chateau de Silk, I will go with royalty's leave. I have a future to think of. But how did you know I was a Huguenot?"

"Petite sotte," she said affectionately. "Every one of us knows you are of the forbidden religion. The princesse knows too. I think even the Queen Mother knows."

"And Charlotte de Presney?"

Louise glanced back over her shoulder. Charlotte was pouring tea and now and then glancing in their direction. Louise's eyes hardened. "That one knows everything. You can be sure she knows you are a Huguenot."

Rachelle could do nothing except add that to her other list of worries to pray about. She entered Marguerite's chamber where the older nurse, Madame de Vigne, was bathing her wounds.

At first sight of Princesse Marguerite Valois, Rachelle's heart twisted with shock, then anger. She moved quickly to the side of her bed and knelt, taking her hand and bringing it against her cheek. She closed her eyes against the tears and prayed ardently for Margo. Margo the sinner, Margo the wanton, as so many called her.

Poor Margo, though a princesse, was a slave. Enslaved to her infatuations, undisciplined and seeking love through immoral excursions, she would not find the true love she craved. First, it was one galante. When he proved imperfect, she sought another to make her happy, to ease her boredom. She was now totally consumed with Monsieur Henry de Guise. Even if Guise actually did love her, Rachelle believed it was the love of Christ that Marguerite needed to give meaning to her shallow life. Only he could forgive her, embrace her, accept her, clothe her nakedness in his righteous robes, and make her holy and presentable to his Father God. Only Jesus Christ, who was wounded for their transgressions, could bathe her corrupt wounds and make her a true princesse.

"Oh, Margo," she whispered, forgetting for a moment that she spoke not to a friend but to royal rank.

Marguerite's eyelids opened. She took her hand away from Rachelle and laid it on her shoulder.

"M'amie, I—I was caught. Caught, and the mock executioner beat me with the royal cane ... B-but Henry, mon amour, does love me, even if my mother denies it."

"Yes, Princesse, do not talk now, I beg of you. You must rest and get well again."

"The burgundy silk gown is ... ruined. She ripped it off me—it is stained with my blood."

"Oh, Princesse—"

"You may be called to her," she warned in a hoarse whisper. "Do not try to protect me. Blame me for everything, understand? I forced you to go with me on the boat."

"But—"

"Non, listen, I know what I am doing, though all of you think I am a fool. There is little more they can do to me except kill me, and my mother will not do that, for she now will want me to marry Henry of Navarre, that Huguenot. They think I do not know. I too have spies. So blame me for what happened. I am to blame, truly. Spare yourself her rebuke. When I can, I will try to send you home to Lyon where you will be safe. That is what Fabien wants me to do."

Rachelle nodded. "I understand, Princesse. Do not worry about me."

"I will do my best on your account, but I can promise nothing. It is Catherine who rules—and le Cardinal de Lorraine."

Rachelle thought of her interaction with the cardinal and concealed a repulsive shudder. She nodded. She understood.

"Then go and prepare yourself. She may call you soon."

But, surprisingly, the Queen Mother did not call Rachelle to her state chambers. It seemed that concern over Marguerite's wayward excursion of the night before was set aside as heralds brought news to the castle that Bourbon princes of the blood were even now at Blois and riding to Amboise for the state council meeting.

THE MEETING was much on the mind of Andelot Dangeau. He wondered what had happened to Marquis Fabien. After telling him they would speak of important news, Fabien had not returned to the chamber last night even though Andelot had heard from Gallaudet that he had escorted Rachelle back to the castle. Andelot tried to get Gallaudet to talk, but the fair young man from Normandy refused to impart any other information except—"Marquis Fabien de Vendôme has ridden toward Blois to intercept his kinsmen, Prince Louis de Condé and others."

"Intercept them? Why so? Is there trouble I know nothing about?"

"There is always trouble, Monsieur Andelot. My monseigneur will surely explain to you when he comes back."

"And when will that be?" Andelot asked, feeling frustrated. He was always bewildered, kept in shadows. Besides, he had some things he had intended to tell Marquis Fabien. The journey into the soothsayer's laboratory with Prince Charles, for one thing. And the vials of poison—what else could they be?—was another important matter he wished to tell him. The poison worried Andelot. He could not sleep at night wondering why the Queen Mother wanted the poison, and who it was that troubled Catherine de Medici the most. He hoped it was not himself, Rachelle, or Marquis Fabien!

As for Andelot's important meeting with le Cardinal de Lorraine, which Fabien had warned him last night not to attend, Andelot felt relieved his decision was not needed. One of the cardinal's attendants came to Fabien's appartements while it was yet dark and told him the meeting was once again to be delayed.

Sleepy eyed and discouraged, Andelot murmured to himself after he closed the door upon the black-clad churchman. "It is just as well it is delayed again. For now I know not what is happening. For a toss of coin I would pack my satchel and return to Paris for school, even if it means leaving mon cousine's fancy horse here at Amboise and walking."

But Andelot would not walk to Paris. He would see the cardinal after all, and the king, for another summons arrived within the hour.

KING FRANCIS II sat in a chair when Andelot entered and bowed before him. "Your Majesty."

The Guises were there, moving boldly about the royal chamber as though they and not Francis were king. Andelot was surprised by the indifference showed to the seventeen-year-old boy-king. The duc gave orders; the cardinal had a certain sneer about his mouth and speech that made unkind jests at Francis's expense because he stammered. Andelot was shocked.

Andelot acknowledged his kinsmen, le Duc de Guise and the cardinal. The duc seemed preoccupied. He paced the floor between the window overlooking the courtyard and the open balustrade where the breeze blew in and moved the gold fringe on the edge of the royal chair where Francis sat, or rather, slumped. He was pale and the line around his small mouth was drawn tight. He suffered from the sickness called poison of the blood, as Andelot had learned from Marquis Fabien. Whatever poison of the blood was, the English called it a French sickness; the French called it an English sickness. Andelot suspected it was handed down through intermarriage of so many of the royal families. The present king's grandfather Francis I had suffered from it, though not as grievously perhaps, and so had his Medici grandfather in Florence.

Andelot wondered why he was privileged to be here in the presence of the king and the two Guises. He was not long in finding out. The cardinal walked over to him with that smile of his. A smile Andelot was beginning to know, and the more he knew it, the less he liked it. There was something most lecherous about a man who was unholy portraying holiness. The crimson and white, the beautiful gold cross, the bright ruby and emerald rings laid in thick gold ...

"Well, Andelot. Last night I called you a cousine. Today I affirm that it is so. You are the son of a Guise."

Andelot looked from the cardinal to the duc who did not look pleased.

"I was told by Comte Sebastien that I was the son of his younger brother Louis Dangeau."

"So you are," le Duc de Guise stated crisply. "Louis was a Guise, a cousine, rejected by the family."

Andelot hesitated. "Then my maman? Who was she, Monsieur le Duc?"

"Your mother was a foolish and stupide belle dame who ruined Louis. She died of fever at Flanders during the last war with Spain. I was there. I tried to help her once she sent word to me she was about to give birth to Louis's child. She was at a medical tent on the field. When I arrived you were already born, but she had died. We, the cardinal and

I, agreed it was best to turn you over to the care of a nurse. Sebastien worked through his wife, Madame Madeleine, to arrange for this at Lyon where his family is located." He turned his back.

Andelot's throat was parched. Matters were not much different than what he had already been told except that Louis had been a Guise — and out of favor with the Lorraine family.

"My père was out of favor because he married my maman, Monsieur le Duc?"

The cardinal was examining his long, slim white fingers flashing with jewels. The duc looked impatient.

"She was a hoyden, perhaps much like — " he bowed toward King Francis — "Marguerite Valois. Your pardon, sire, but it is so. Just as it was not my son Henry who is to blame for her abandoning the King of Portugal at the masque, but your sister."

Francis looked down at his lap in total submission to his oncles.

Andelot did not press for more information. The more he learned, the more unpleasant the circumstances of his birth grew. It was enough, presently, that he was alive, here, and a *Guise* — of sorts.

"And now we have some news for you," the cardinal said. "You qualify for training in the *Corps des Pages*. After your training, if you excel, you may be elevated to serving as my page. Are you pleased, Andelot?"

Andelot bowed. "Very pleased, Monseigneur." He had a suspicion he would *never* be permitted to call these two powerful men cousines. The truth was, he doubted if he could bring himself to do so. The more he saw of them, the more uneasy he became.

The cardinal patted him on the shoulder with another smile. "Now, we must not detain the king with family affairs. You are here in his presence, Andelot, because you are needed to serve King Francis on a certain matter. I am sure you will be honored to serve His Majesty?"

Andelot glanced from the cardinal's wily smile to the sober-faced duc, then to King Francis. He liked Francis ... Andelot bowed toward him.

"I will do whatever His Majesty requires of me."

The young king nodded and smiled faintly, but he looked nervous and kept fidgeting. The scene was most unflattering, and Andelot was disappointed. Francis was more of a boy than he himself.

"Tell the king what your cousine by marriage, Marquis Fabien de Vendôme, has been doing recently?" le Cardinal de Lorraine said.

Andelot came wide alert now. He saw the sharp, interested eyes of the duc, the smile of the cardinal encouraging him, and the uncomfortable, almost nervous glance of King Francis. It was a time for caution.

"What Marquis has been doing, my lords? I have not seen him today, Monseigneur le Cardinal," Andelot said.

"What of yesterday, then?"

Andelot delayed for time. Why such interest in Fabien? "The masque . . . he was most attentive to Mademoiselle Macquinet."

"Yes, yes, Andelot, we are aware, but what are the marquis's interests beyond Mademoiselle Macquinet? He has ambitions, surely, that he discusses with you?"

"I must confess the marquis does not talk much with me, Monseigneur le Cardinal. I have been alone most of the time I have been here at Amboise, and at Chambord before that."

"Oh, come, come. You need not be afraid to share the little secrets that Fabien *must* share with his mon ami?"

"He shares nothing, I assure you. Except, perhaps . . ."

"Yes?" The cardinal's eyes latched hold of him.

Andelot rubbed his chin and tried to look as innocent and boyish as he could. "He has mentioned taking me on a visit to his père's lands and estate at Vendôme that we might ride and hunt together, Monseigneur le Cardinal. That is all."

Le Duc de Guise looked impatient and began pacing. He was a man of strong military bearing, and the scar on his face taken in battle made him appear more so. The glittering eyes were also restless as they seemed to give up on Andelot.

"Desist," he told the cardinal. "He knows nothing." He paced and then turned to the king. "Sire, men seek your life and that of the young queen."

"Mary?" Francis turned toward him, showing concern for the first time. "Why would the Huguenots wish to harm the queen?"

"Huguenots are sworn enemies of the throne, Sire," the duc said impatiently as if speaking to a child. "You do not think in abducting you for ransom they would spare our niece, do you?"

"Your niece, Duc, but my wife and the Queen of France," the king said, showing strength for the first time.

"It is no secret they wish to see you dead so they can put Prince de Condé on the throne. We must protect you, Sire, and the rest of the royal family."

Andelot decided they had forgotten him, for even the cardinal turned his attention to Francis. Andelot wondered if the council meeting with the Bourbons had been called off. But had not Gallaudet told him early this morning that Fabien had ridden toward Blois to meet the Bourbon entourage coming from Moulins to attend the meeting? Andelot decided he was either confused, or that events were skewed for some purpose favoring the Guises and the Queen Mother. And why was the Queen Mother not here for this important meeting with the king?

Andelot stood very still, hoping they would forget his presence and continue their discussion. The cardinal walked over to a crimson velvet curtain and pulled it aside, peering about inside. Andelot saw a couch and two chairs, a table and some candles on gold urns.

"We can listen from here," he told his brother the duc. Then the cardinal smiled at Francis, who moved uneasily. "That way, Sire, if you know your oncles are behind this drape, you will not be uneasy in the presence of the spies."

Francis looked at him and then reached for his goblet and sipped.

Why, the cardinal is cunningly threatening the king! Andelot was shocked. *What spies? Did they think Marquis Fabien was a spy? Or was there something else going on that was more insidious?*

"Andelot, my boy," the cardinal said, smiling again. "You are a friend of the Huguenots, are you not?"

He lifted his head high. "I am a Catholic, Monseigneur le Cardinal. A *good* Catholic—"

"Yes, yes, no one is accusing you otherwise. Only we may need your help. Are you willing to assist your king?"

Andelot looked over at Francis who still looked uneasy and ill. He was feeling more sympathy for him by the moment.

"I will do whatever the king wishes of me." He bowed.

"Yes, I thought we could trust you to aid us in a certain matter. You are friendly with certain of the Huguenots from Lyon. Mademoiselle

Macquinet, for instance. Non, do not look alarmed — this has nothing to do with the belle with the auburn hair ... but other Huguenots, who are friendly with the pestilent Bourbons, enemies of our good king. These spies, we fear, are loyal to the Lyon nobles, including one Comte Arnaut Macquinet."

Andelot's stomach flopped.

"We have reason to believe this Macquinet makes forbidden trips into Geneva for heretic Bibles and brings them back into France for distribution to the Huguenots. These writings, as you know — " he smiled — "as a *good* Catholic, are forbidden. Those who possess such writing or distribute them receive a death sentence. For the good of all the Church, the leaven must be purged out. This, to protect the whole lump of God's dough. So you have been chosen to help your king in this matter."

Andelot's heart jumped to his throat. His lips would not move.

"Ah, then." The cardinal looked across at le Duc de Guise. "Andelot will prove useful to us. He learns well."

Useful? Andelot looked from the cardinal to the duc. The two men exchanged questioning glances. At last the duc gave a brief reluctant nod, then continued his pacing.

"There are enemies in the woods," le Duc de Guise told Francis Valois. "They must be destroyed, Sire."

"We caught several of them," the cardinal joined in. "Spies. They will talk to no one, Sire, but you."

Andelot's mind hastened to keep one step ahead. This must be part of the plot Maître Avenelle told the Queen Mother about at Chambord.

"Mary and I feel like prisoners here," Francis complained. "She wishes to go for rides in the woods."

"Everything has changed since the masque, Sire," the duc said. "These spies behave most suspiciously. Your life and Mary's are heavily on my mind as your Marshal of France. Remember, the queen regent, your mother, also agrees with what we are doing."

"Yes, Oncle. I am grateful for your loyal commitment to keeping us all safe from the rebels."

"It is important to find out their plans, but as the cardinal has said, they will not talk to anyone but you."

"We want you to receive these heretics, Sire," the cardinal added. "We will tell you just what to say, so it should not be difficult ... We know you are not feeling strong today."

The door opened and the Queen Mother walked in. There was a cool look in her prominent eyes. Andelot marveled at her composure, at how she kept her face seemingly devoid of thought. It was an art he wished he had at the moment. They expected something from him, but what? They needed him, else he would not be permitted to witness such inner intrigue as was now in play.

She walked over to Francis.

"My son, you do not look well today. Did the banquet and masque wear you out? Let us hope you are strong enough to receive these spies."

"Yes, Mother. I am able, but is it necessary to deceive them?"

The awkward silence that followed was soon broken by Catherine's smile.

"Ah, my clever son, sometimes it is most necessary to keep hidden certain matters so as to learn the truth of your enemies. I assure you, the knife they would gladly plunge into your heart is concealed. You cannot trust anyone but those of us nearest you, who love and protect you and Mary."

Andelot watched Francis. Did he believe her honey-coated lies? Maybe not, for a glimmer showed in his eyes, but there was a look of fear in his tense face. Andelot felt a surge of disgust toward those who bullied him.

"If—if they wish to see me and swear their fealty, then they wish me no harm, so why should I lie to them?"

"Ah, Francis, my poor sick boy. You have a fever, yes, your forehead is burning ... Where is the quinine water I ordered for him?" She turned to an attendant hovering in the background. "Go and find it," she commanded. The guard hastened away.

Andelot knew a moment of alarm. His mind flashed back to Prince Charles and the laboratory of the Queen Mother's astrologer and poisoner, Cosmo. Non, not Francis. Not her *own* son. Not even Catherine de Medici would go that far.

Their diatribe continued as they rehearsed with Francis what he was expected to say and do. The young king was to give each one of them a crown apiece and pretend to be pleased they had come to rescue him from enemies near his throne. This was to convince them he was on their side. Whereupon he would ask veiled questions of them to discover who it was who had sent them to Amboise.

"If the Bourbons are on their way here now," the duc said, "it seems conceivable that it was Prince Condé. We have the word of Maître Avenelle that Condé and his retainer de la Renaudie were behind the plot."

Andelot soon found himself the focus of attention. His neck grew hot under the studious dissection of the Queen Mother.

"Andelot is now in my service," the cardinal told her. "He will enter the Corps des Pages in Paris when we return. He knows the leaders of the Huguenots in Lyon. He will identify these men. I thought it wise if he stayed with the king during his interview with them. He may help put them at ease. And if they are from Lyon we will soon know it, Your Majesty."

Catherine did not comment on whether this pleased or displeased her. She turned to Francis.

"Remember, my son, I will be attentive to every word spoken by way of a listening tube in the wall. Your oncles, the duc and the cardinal, will be located behind that curtain should you need them."

Andelot began to sweat. What if these spies were friends of the Macquinets? What if the cardinal already knew who they were and was testing his loyalty? He surmised this was a warning to him as well, for her eyes swerved to his before she walked from the chamber. The Guise brothers slipped behind the velvet drape. Andelot looked at the king, now pale with small beads of sweat on his forehead.

I should never want to be a king.

Francis nodded that he was ready. Andelot went to the door and gestured to the Swiss guards in their bright red plumes and gilded armor to bring in the prisoners.

A short time later the Huguenot messires were brought into the king's chamber. They were humble Frenchmen, strong of face and wearing peasant clothing. Andelot felt a sickening dread. He recognized the older man from the village near the Chateau de Silk. He remembered that he sold duck eggs on a corner near some rustling mulberry trees. He was loyal to Comte Arnaut Macquinet and no doubt helped smuggle Bibles in the French language to other areas of Lyon in his egg cart.

The man looked at Andelot now and blinked as if trying to remember where he had seen him before. He must have recalled, for a smile started to split his weathered cheeks. When Andelot quickly looked away, the man did not proceed. Now and then he glanced at him, but Andelot avoided his eyes.

The king smiled at them. "Fear not, messires," he told them in a weak voice.

Be afraid! Andelot wanted to shout.

The boy-king held out his hand, and they bent over it dutifully.

"The Lord bless thee, O King."

"The Lord grant you peace," said the other.

"The Lord is your Defender," said the third.

Francis looked pained. He glanced toward the door, the curtain—

He fumbled, handing them each a crown. He asked stiff questions that sounded as rehearsed as they indeed were.

"Did you come into the king's forest to glean a glimpse of the divertissement on yester's eve?" he asked hopefully.

"Non, Sire, we do not agree with the carnal display of the flesh that leads to corruption."

Andelot gritted his teeth. *Non, mon ami, you waste your opportunity to confess to only lesser offenses. This was your excuse!*

Francis cleared his throat as if embarrassed. "Then what were you doing in the forest, messieurs? Hunting perhaps?"

"Oh non, Sire. We would not hunt the king's meat. It is against the law. God's Word tells us to obey our magistrates."

"Do you also obey and seek my right to rule as your king?"

"We do, Sire." They placed fists to their hearts. "Vive le Roi!"

Andelot was feeling better. He smiled and looked confidently at King Francis. See? They are not your enemies, Your Majesty, he wanted to say. But from the corner of his eye he saw the curtain move a little. Francis must have noticed too. For he said sternly: "Why were you in my forest, messieurs? You are spies."

Andelot was dumbfounded when the men smiled, and trusting the young king at face value they began to tell him everything the Guises wanted to know.

Andelot's head ached from the pounding of his heart. Quiet! Quiet! You are too trusting!

Yes, they had come from Geneva. Soon now, their leaders would join them in the forest.

"Sire, we are your servants and your loyal subjects. You have naught to fear from us or our leaders. Au contraire, Your Majesty, but we have come to rescue you from the domination of the House of Guise, of Spain, and of Rome. There are over forty thousand of us on the way to save you — and France."

Andelot's spirit groaned. He longed to tell them that the Queen Mother, le Duc de Guise, and le Cardinal de Lorraine had just heard every word.

Francis was pale and his hands were shaking as he bid them adieu. The men bowed, again promised their allegiance, and departed under the watchful eyes, and swords, of the guards.

The curtain opened and the Guise brothers stepped out.

Andelot turned and faced the tall, handsome Cardinal de Guise.

"Did you recognize them, Andelot?"

Andelot bowed. "Non, Monseigneur. I have never seen these men before."

There was a moment of silence.

"Are they not allies of Comte Arnaut Macquinet who is even now in Geneva?"

"I do not think so, non."

Another moment of silence.

"You are certain?"

"Oui, Monseigneur le Cardinal."

"Then you may go for now, Andelot."

Andelot bowed, kissed the ring, and made haste to leave the king's chamber. Guards stood in the corridor.

Andelot was thinking, *If I can escape, I can warn Fabien. If not him, then Sebastien, or even Comte Maurice Beauvilliers to ride to Fabien, or Chevalier Julot Cazalet.* Andelot looked up, startled. He had hardly taken a step when three guards stood shoulder to shoulder blocking his way.

"Monsieur, we are under orders to take you to your new chamber."

He studied their immobile faces. Their eyes were unreadable.

"New chamber? Ah, honored sirs, it is not necessary, I promise you. I like my bed in the chamber of Marquis Fabien de Vendôme!"

"Come with us, Monsieur. Orders from le Cardinal de Lorraine. You are to be locked in a chamber for safekeeping for a few days."

Andelot let out a long breath. Foiled. He walked away surrounded by the guards.

Chapter Twenty-One

Marquis Fabien and Comte Sebastien went into the Amboise council chamber with the Bourbon princes and nobles, all representing the Huguenots and their cause before the King and Queen of France. The chamber itself set a somber mood, Comte Sebastien thought. There were no windows, and lamps glimmered on the dark oak-paneled walls with rafters crossing the high ceiling. It was a chamber with much history, remaining untouched by decoration since the early years of Louis XI.

Would history be made here today? Sebastien wondered. His troubled mind jumped to Paris, to the Louvre, where Grandmère Dushane was staying with Madeleine. Soon now his child would be born ... Was all well?

A long council table stood in the center of the chamber surrounded by leather chairs with heavy wooden arms and backs carved by craftsmen. Fabien had not taken a seat at the table for he was not yet a member of the council, but Louis had suggested before the Guises that he remain. The Guises had made no objection, but the duc measured Fabien.

Fabien stood across the chamber near a guard, looking as unreadable as did Louis de Condé. Both had, with debonair elegance, refused to surrender their swords. Comte Sebastien was pleased with Fabien. There was an air of authority about him that showed itself in every glance he cast around the chamber at those gathered. *He is a man born to command.*

Comte Sebastien, because he was a member of Catherine's privy council, sat at the table on the side of royalty. He fought his fatigue, his anxiety that matters could go awry, or worse, had already done so. The news from Gallaudet on the night of the masque continued to nag him. What if those in the woods were Huguenot spies? Would that not mean the message Louis had sent to Renaudie had not gotten through in time? Fabien also thought so. They had discussed it between them on the ride here from Blois.

Sebastien studied the men in assembly across the table.

Prince Louis de Condé sat at the highest place on the Huguenot-Bourbon side of the table, since he was a prince of the blood. His comely face and dark eyes appeared anything but deceived, even if he had chosen to come here. The news Fabien had brought to him on the road had been accepted gravely, but still he had ridden on toward Amboise with Admiral Gaspard Coligny, who had arrived from Chatillon with his entourage.

As Fabien once commented about Coligny, "I fear such a pious and decent man to open his mouth in speech. For without guile, he is taken in by the Valois and Guise treachery." Coligny was older than Prince Louis, a sturdier man. He sat in his chair with shoulders straight and a certain humility about him. His hair was gray, rather long, and he was dressed in dark woolen Huguenot clothes, absent from all fanfare. His rough complexion showed a soldier who had lived a life of exposure and need, of courage and honor.

The admiral's brother, le Cardinal de Châtillon, of Calvinist persuasion, had seated himself beside le Cardinal de Lorraine. Each Frenchman wore the same scarlet robe of a cardinal, over which fell a deep edging of open guipure lace. Their broad red hats with tasseled silken cords were in front of them on the table.

Sebastien saw le Cardinal de Lorraine's face, haughty, superior, and deliberately affronting his fellow cardinal of Protestant persuasion.

But le Cardinal de Châtillon looked unworried about his affront. He was bland, but astute. A smile was upon his lips as his eyes wandered around the table.

The door opened revealing a carved platform on which was a dais raised one step from the floor of the council chamber. The boy-king Francis and Mary stood there fully garbed in royal attire.

Sebastien stood with those at the council table and bowed in their honor. Francis and Mary then sat down under a purple velvet canopy, embroidered in gold with fleurs de lys and the *Oriflamme*.

Next came Catherine as regent and le Duc de Guise, a sight that Sebastien knew angered Fabien, for Monsieur de Guise had less right to be at her side than did Louis and his brother, Antoine of Navarre.

Sebastien, who was not watched as closely as were the Bourbons, noticed how le Duc de Guise's sharp eyes gravitated to Louis, then to Fabien, which troubled Sebastien. *He knows Fabien is a future leader, the man to contend with one day. Does he suspect Fabien of discovering that he had arranged the death of his father, Duc Jean-Louis de Bourbon?*

Sebastien had never told Fabien that he knew the facts of his father's death, for he had feared that Fabien would seek revenge at his own ruin. Sebastien had recently heard disturbing news that there were spies at court who were contacting Fabien about having certain facts of proof against le Duc de Guise. This talk was, of course, dangerous to Fabien. If either of the Guise brothers believed Fabien posed them a threat, they would try to have him killed. Sebastien did not doubt that possibility. Le Duc de Guise, bold and unscrupulous, was ardently on a path of his own glory.

When le Duc de Guise had first seen Louis, Coligny, and le Cardinal de Châtillon, his eyes had chilled with a sinister expression that spread over his features. Sebastien knew that he took pity on none whom he judged to be heretic. He could murder in the name of God without a twinge of conscience.

The young king and queen sat motionless, reminding Sebastien of two young people bewildered by sober adult ceremony. They looked confused and concerned, as if neither truly understood what was happening. Sebastien believed the facts were kept from them.

Francis was ill, too taxed to probe too deeply into his mother and oncles' schemes. Nor could he have stood up to them if he had so desired. And Mary, quietly astute, had received few answers to her many questions of her oncles.

Catherine received the Bourbon princes and nobles of the Huguenot faith with cool reserve, with the same manner she received the Guises, Nemours, and the other Catholic leaders.

All took their seats with tense silence. Naught was heard except the sound of chairs scraping on the hardwood floor. They now sat in a semi-circle facing King Francis and Queen Mary on the royal dais.

FABIEN'S MIND AGAIN WANDERED. Andelot had not been in the chamber when he returned this morning. Fabien had inquired of Gallaudet, who had also been surprised by Andelot's absence.

Catherine was speaking. Fabien did not believe a word she said. She spoke of danger to the crown from the Huguenot party, which to Fabien was nonsense. If there was danger, and there was, it came from two of the men in the chamber—the Guises.

The Queen Mother hinted of a "treasonable plot." There were some men near the Valois throne involved in this plot, she stated gravely. She called on the Huguenot princes and nobles who supported the Protestant cause to offer their support to King Francis and also to lend her their excellent advice.

Fabien marveled at her Machiavellian ruse. As if she wished for the advice of Louis, Cardinal Odet de Châtillon, or the admiral. She was trying to flatter them so as to drop a shroud over their unsuspecting minds!

"I have summoned here my son's wise and trusted counselors of the Calvinist religion to hear your decision on whether an edict of pacification, designed to guarantee all his faithful servants round his throne the rights to peace and worship, has been granted."

I can almost believe her, Fabien thought dryly. *If I did not know the perfidy of this woman.*

Fabien was more interested in King Francis's reaction. He appeared to listen and wonder at his mother's words. Perhaps he was asking himself why his mother was duping the Huguenot leaders with talk of pacification when she had been in a rage promising vengeance at Chambord after speaking to Avenelle.

This was Fabien's question as well. Why had she changed her mind? Where was the call for the death of every last man who had plotted to set her aside in favor of Louis?

Had she changed so much in a few weeks? Had she suddenly forgiven? Absurd!

When Catherine concluded, le Duc de Guise applauded with enthusiasm. That in itself convinced Fabien it was a ruse.

King Francis looked momentarily astonished. Why? Had he heard his oncle promise the very opposite? Undoubtedly.

It was a grave miscalculation to have come here, Fabien thought again and looked at his kinsmen.

Fabien saw Mary glance at her oncles.

She knows the truth, Fabien thought. He stared at her. Her eyes turned toward him, widened slightly as if unmasked, blushed, and looked quickly away.

Prince de Condé, crafty at times, was more suspicious. He had not come because he was duped, but because le Duc de Guise, now head Marshal of France, could have put out a missive to arrest him for the treason of disobeying a royal command to appear at court.

Had Louis taken note of Catherine's words, "Some men near the throne are involved in a plot"? He must know to whom she applied those words. Louis then stood and in a few choice phrases swore himself ready to defend the royal cause with his life. Royal cause, as Fabien understood it, was a kingdom free of the meddling House of Guise who served the interests of Spain and Rome.

The others followed suit, but Fabien noted their casual tone.

But Admiral Coligny, always a man with a true face, stood and answered forthrightly.

Fabien, encouraged by this, secretly cheered Coligny's denunciation of "a second group of certain men near the throne" whose only ambition was to usurp the government of France for Spain.

"There are two million Protestants in the kingdom, Your Majesty — " he looked carefully about the chamber for emphasis — "who look to us, the political representatives who share their faith, and look for relief from religious tyranny and injustice under which they have long languished. Two million," Coligny repeated slowly, looking firmly but gravely round the circle, "who seek to live at peace with Christ and their earthly king. Good Frenchmen who are industrious, who are tranquil, and who are loyal to this throne.

"But these two million demand that they shall enjoy equal privileges with the least of His Majesty's Catholic subjects. This is now refused them. They ask neither to be suspected of treason nor heresy. They are weary of being spied upon by churchmen loyal to Rome. Nor are they persecuted and slaughtered by the thousands for any wicked reason except that those who oppose the Bible are determined to silence the truth of the Reformation.

"If any conspiracy exists, Your Majesty, such as is now spoken of by the queen regent — and we accept her statement in part as being true, for it is with the deepest sorrow that a conspiracy is deemed necessary by the persecuted — it can only have arisen from the bitter feeling engendered by the disgrace toward the Calvinistic subjects of this realm. The same who are uniformly treated as aliens and repulsed with cruel persistency from such places of trust and honor as their services have entitled them to enjoy."

Coligny glanced about the chamber again. "Let these heavy grievances be removed; let His Majesty reign for himself *alone* — " Coligny's gaze moved from le Duc de Guise to le Cardinal de Lorraine, and finally to the Queen Mother — "with equal favor over both political-religious parties in our beloved France, Catholic as well as Protestant. Let the conciliatory edict now before the council be made public, and I, Gaspard de Coligny, bind myself upon my plighted word as a noble, and upon my conscience as a devout Calvinist, that the House of Valois will forever live in the hearts of our people, and receive from them an entire devotion ever subject to his sovereignty."

Ah! Bravo! Fabien thought.

A stern silence pervaded the chamber. The angry duc and cardinal exchanged glances of stifled indignation.

A royal parchment with gold seals of state was born to King Francis by the chancellor for his signature. But Francis simply stared at it, dumbfounded. He looked up and over at his mother as though he could not understand why he was being asked to sign a document granting peace to the very subjects that she and his oncles but only a day ago had sworn to him were his greatest enemies.

Catherine stood quickly from her chair. For once, her face showed her alarm. Was she afraid Francis would ask embarrassing questions? Fabien frowned. This was a ruse. He was sure of it now.

Catherine advanced toward her son. With an imperious gesture, she took the pen from the hand of the chancellor and handed it to Francis.

"Sign, my son. Why do you delay? This edict was drawn up by the unanimous advice of your council in favor of your loyal subjects."

"Truly, Madame. I call God to witness that I desire the good of all my subjects, Huguenot and Catholic."

He took the pen from her and signed the edict of pacification.

The council was adjourned, and Fabien watched the cold indifference with which the Guises brushed past the Bourbons and left the chamber.

"Peace, indeed," Sebastien murmured ruefully to Fabien, coming up beside him.

Fabien frowned. "I would say our young King Francis was as bewildered as any I have seen by this action today."

"Where are you going now?"

Fabien had started toward the door. "To make certain my kinsmen ride safely out of the courtyard," Fabien called dryly as he strode from the chamber after the Bourbon delegation.

Chapter Twenty-Two

ANDELOT PACED THE CHAMBER WHERE HE HAD BEEN BROUGHT TWO DAYS ago after Francis the king had finished the interview with the Huguenots captured in the woods.

Andelot had no idea in what section of the castle he was kept, or how long the cardinal would keep him there. He had been brought a plate of bread, cheese, venison, and a bottle of wine last night. He had tried to glean information from the guards without success. A priest had come who showed himself more friendly.

"Fear not, Andelot. You are being protected here, not punished."

"Monsieur Père, I do not understand."

"You shall later, my son. Eventually you and I will travel together to Paris where you will enter the Corps des Pages."

"But what is happening here at the castle? Did the House of Bourbon come as planned? Did His Majesty sign the edict of pacification? Why do I hear the sound of soldiers and horses as though a battle has broken in the woods — "

"Rest, Andelot. Be thankful le Cardinal de Lorraine is protecting you. Do not ask so many questions. Here, I have brought you a writing to ponder. Not heretical writings as from those diables Calvin and Luther, but written by the great archbishop of Carpentras, Jacopo Sadoleto. My son, the archbishop was one of the ablest of our theologians. His encounter with Calvin by public letters addressed to the civil leaders of Geneva was a notable challenge to heterodoxy."

When the priest left, Andelot heard a key turn in the lock.

Andelot paced with a copy of the writings of Sadoleto in hand.

Marquis Fabien would surely seek him after enough time had passed, as would his Oncle Sebastien, who was also somewhere in the castle.

It was some time in the afternoon when the door unlocked and Prince Charles Valois, gloating, stood garbed in satin and gold. His pointed nose and small mouth fit his haughty nature well, and he shut the door behind him and held up a gold key.

"So, peasant, they brought you here. They could have put you in the dungeons with the heretic spies, but the Huguenots are no longer in the dungeons below. Remember how I told you of the dungeons? Now they are not only packed with hungry rats, but also many Huguenot heretics. The spies were put there when they left the castle meeting with the king, my brother, but they are not there now."

Andelot expected the worst. "They are not there now, mon prince?"

"Their heads decorate the ramparts. I will show them to you."

"Non, Your Highness ... but can you lead me out of here to find Marquis Fabien?"

"Fabien has returned. There was a meeting with the Bourbon princes this morning, but they have ridden away toward Moulins." Charles looked at him slyly. "There are more Huguenots in the dungeons below, now awaiting their just due."

More Huguenots in the dungeons? More? Was he telling the truth? Where had they come from?

"They are in the dark cells, dark as night."

But then a wicked little gleam came to his eyes.

"So you do not wish to see the spies' heads?"

"I wish, mon prince, to be brought to Marquis de Vendôme. Can you help me?"

Charles considered, folding his arms across his chest. "Remember the soothsayer's laboratory?"

"How could I forget, Monsieur Prince?"

"Now I will show you something even more shocking."

"Monsieur—"

Charles shook his head. He closed his lips tightly. "Do you wish to be taken to Fabien or non?"

"Merci, Monsieur Prince. I shall be most grateful."

Charles opened the door and glanced down the corridor. He lowered his voice. "Come, then, I shall even show you how it works."

It?

"There is a garden. You can see the river and the trees. The steps on the terrace will take us down into the garden."

Andelot took heart. If he could get into the garden, he could escape to the barracks to Cousine Julot.

"Our walk will be worthy of the effort. Wait until you see it."

"It," again. What was it?

Charles took him down a little used passage at the back of the castle and out through a door onto a terrace that overlooked both sides of a garden. Here, the Loire River ran alongside the castle and into the wider reservoir.

Andelot felt better now that the fresh wind blew against him and he tasted freedom. *But surely the cardinal had meant him no harm shutting him up in the chamber two days ago? Not if he would send him to Paris to attend the Corps des Pages? What then had been the reason for it? Would harm have otherwise come to him?*

"Ah! Look, peasant!"

Andelot jerked toward Charles whose flushed face was impudent, his eyes bulged.

"Behold!" Charles cried out and ran to the terrace rail, looking deliriously excited. "Did I not tell you I would reveal something magnifique? Look, mon ami, have you ever seen such a sight?"

Andelot joined Charles at the terrace rail. An involuntary gasp escaped from Andelot. "Saints preserve us!"

"Non, ami, they will not." Charles boasted.

Andelot curled his fingers around the terrace railing. So this was what had been going on since yesterday while he was closed up in a chamber.

Troops, troops, everywhere! Every gate was watched, every entrance into the castle, the gardens, the walled plateau, the galleries. His gaze shifted to a tuft of trees inside one of the bastions. There, on the pinnacles of the fretted roof belonging to a little votive chapel were more of the king's archers. The walls of the castle bristled with guns and archers. But that was not all. The heads of the Huguenot men from Geneva were posted on sticks on the ramparts. Already the vultures were greedily at work. Andelot, sickened, turned away.

"THERE WERE EVEN MORE SOLDIERS yesterday after the Bourbon princes and nobles rode from Amboise," Charles said, folding his arms. "I heard le Duc de Guise and le cardinal talking to the Queen Mother. They told her the open country toward Loches was full of soldiers. Guards now watch the double bridge across the Loire."

He looked at Andelot to see his response, as though he recalled Andelot's comments of a week ago that le Duc de Guise was unjust toward the Huguenots.

"Le Duc de Guise has absolute power these days," Charles said. "There was a battle in the woods that lasted all night and most of this morning."

A battle? Was that why he had been closeted away out of sight and perhaps trouble? Or had they guessed he had been on his way to warn Marquis Fabien?

"Then the council meeting with the Bourbon princes is over?"

"Oui. An edict of pacification was signed by my brother, the king."

"Then what is all this?" Andelot cried, spreading his hand toward the soldiers and battlements. "And what of the fighting last night in the woods?"

"It was le Duc de Guise who discovered the Huguenots moving in a great army in the woods. They were taken by surprise. Even Renaudie was captured," Prince Charles boasted.

"Monsieur Renaudie taken prisoner?" Andelot felt sudden pity and regret. If only he could have been more clever and escaped before the guards took him to the chamber —

"It is not easy to deceive the Queen Mother." Charles drew in his chin and gave a triumphant nod of his princely head. "We came to Amboise only because it is a fortress and easily defended from attack."

And the edict was a deception. To throw them off guard while le Duc de Guise put his army into order.

Andelot turned his gaze back to the archers and guns.

"But — " Charles shrugged his small shoulders with boredom — "the fighting, it is all over now. Le Balafré's army killed many heretics, and they carried Renaudie back here and cut him into four pieces. His head is on the wall by the Loire River, where the water runs into the great lake."

Andelot thought back to last night. He had not slept well. He had awakened several times in the night to hear voices and horses on the cobbles below his window, but when he had gone to look out he could see nothing but torchlight.

Andelot remembered with a rush about his Oncle Sebastien, about Cousine Julot, and the marquis. Oh, but they would not move against Fabien, would they?

Is this why he had not heard from them? He became aware that his palms were sweaty. *But they could not have been involved in treason against King Francis.*

"There are many prisoners." Charles's smile was smug.

Andelot looked away from his taunting eyes. His own heart thudded. Not his oncle, not Cousine Julot — *I beg of you, mon cher God, please, non.* Andelot was now afraid to look Charles in the eye. Was this the evil reason he had brought him here? To boast that Sebastien and Julot were in the dungeons of torture?

"They were Huguenots, all pestilent rabble."

Andelot's fear burst into righteous indignation. He turned abruptly to Charles, hand at heart.

"Not so, Monsieur Prince. I do not believe the Huguenots tried to harm the king, your brother. They are loyal. Monsieur Prince, is it not so that the past commander of the French army served your grandfather King Francis I during the Italian Wars? And Admiral Coligny, the Huguenot leader, is he not the nephew of that commander?"

Charles shrugged, looking moody now, as though he might not be as sure as he had thought. "But, come! You still have not seen what I brought you here for!"

"Have I not seen too much already? Let us go back at once, I beg of you — "

"You have seen nothing yet, peasant."

Charles smiled in triumph. "Now all the Huguenots are caught. Like little mice they will have their heads chopped off. Look here, peasant!" He ran along the terrace and beckoned for Andelot to follow.

Andelot glanced about for the steps leading to the garden so he could escape and find the barracks, but there were none in sight. He went after Charles.

"Behold, this is *it*! This is what I brought you to see."

Andelot sucked in his breath. He stepped backward at the sight, bumping into Charles who had come up behind. Andelot felt the prince's body trembling beneath his velvet and fur collar as they both stood huddled together, staring.

A scaffold stood like a giant warrior draped in black, scowling down upon them. A large chopping block and a massive hatchet waited ominously. The sharpened ax blade caught the rays of the sun that momentarily came out from behind the clouds and glistened. Andelot's heart trembled and his stomach turned.

The prince tugged at his arm, beckoning him to follow him along the terrace. There was a madness about Charles, like a glutton facing a banquet table.

The rain stopped earlier that morning. The sky was a gray-blue; some birds, oblivious to the scene of horrors, continued to sing in the branches of the forest and in a giant tree nearby, which had been growing since before the early reign of the king's grandfather, Francis I.

The promise of the French summer with flowers and sunshine leered in mockery at Andelot. There, in the courtyard, a gallery had been recently constructed with seats under a royal canopy of crimson trimmed with a golden tassel border. Royal flags from the *architraves* snapped stiffly in the windy gusts. The terrace, here in this spot, had been prepared, hung with a scarlet velvet canopy for more chairs.

Andelot whirled toward Charles who was flushed with excitement.

"To watch for the Huguenot prisoners?"

"Oui, but of course, mon ami." Charles ran down the terrace steps into the courtyard and Andelot darted after him.

Andelot looked up at the tall scaffold with dread.

Prince Charles, animated now, climbed the steps with difficulty. At the plank he struggled to lift the ax, which must have weighed over half as much as he.

"Stop, mon prince—"

Charles lifted the great ax as high as he could, then let it come down to the cutting block with a heavy, sickening thud. "Die, heretic!" Losing his balance, Charles took a quick step backward, falling to his knees.

Andelot raced up the steps, breathing hard.

"Come down."

"Go ahead, peasant, try it."

"I have no wish to touch it! Come down," Andelot said again.

Surprisingly, Charles did come down, Andelot close behind him.

At the bottom of the platform they looked at one another, the wind tossing their hair. Andelot could not refrain; tears filled his eyes. He thought the sight of his tears would bring malicious amusement to Charles, but instead Charles's face became naught more than a boy's. His features contorted, he whipped a shoulder toward him.

Andelot blinked hard.

Charles looked sullen, a pout on his lips. He seemed prepared to say something when there were footsteps up on the terrace walking in their direction ... and voices. Charles's eyes were wide and true horror showed on his face.

"It is the Queen Mother. I thought they would do nothing today."

Footsteps, many of them, sounded like marching soldiers along the upper terrace. Andelot froze, then glanced wildly about. An escape route—where! But the courtyard was surrounded by a huge stone wall, and he saw no gate, no exit. Footsteps and voices grew nearer.

"Peasant! Hide!" Charles was shaking, obviously in dread of his mother. Before Andelot could respond, Charles was fleeing across the garden courtyard toward some bushes.

Andelot was about to follow, heart thudding in his chest. But soldiers! They were coming now from every direction—marching across the courtyard—guards in black and crimson, toward the scaffold.

Andelot crouched in the courtyard, afraid to stand lest they should see him.

He noted the recently constructed gallery connected to the terrace. It was his only chance for concealment. *Hurry*, his mind told him. Andelot leaped his way like a hind on silent feet across the courtyard with all the agility of his youth. He slipped through rows of chairs over which a royal canopy hung.

Footsteps and voices were coming from the direction of the terrace now.

Andelot frantically searched for concealment.

A sturdy marble statue made in a wide circular adornment of cherubs with lofty faces stood on a large white pedestal. The cherubs held a thick trellis of green vine that swayed gently in the wind. Their faces seemed roused in sympathy over his dire predicament; their childlike marble eyes looked right at him; their pure hands invited him.

Footsteps from the guards and the voices of the entourage grew louder with each fleeting second, coming his way. Andelot crossed himself and dove for cover beneath the pedestal. He scooted under the vines and arranged the thick tentacles around him in a protective covering. He hunched his body tightly together, drawing his arms around his knees, saying his prayers over and over again.

When courage beckoned, he opened his eyes and peered through the vines. They were arriving. The guards, meticulous in their gaudy uniforms, had fanned out. Then Andelot saw *her*. Madame le Serpent, that Italian woman, Catherine de Medici. Clever, shrewd in her politics, the Queen Mother of palace intrigue. Her face was set. She was garbed in black, with a ring of stiff white frill about her neck. A long veil covered the back of her head, falling down toward her heels. Her Italian eyes were prominent, her jowls heavy and soft, her wide mouth was slightly open.

Andelot shut his eyes again, fortifying his courage. *Be strong in the Lord, and in the power of his might*, he thought in Latin.

The rustle of Catherine's garments came so close as she was escorted past the marble cherubs that Andelot could smell her *eau de parfume*. Revulsion overtook him as he recalled the laboratory of her astrologer and poisoner.

In a flash of self-pity he thought how unfair life was to place him here at this time. Even if he went undetected, which he doubted, how would he escape to find Fabien? Perhaps the marquis had already ridden out with Prince Louis and Admiral Coligny?

Charles might take pity upon his plight and return for him, but he doubted whether the boy-prince had that much conscience.

He ventured to open his eyes again. Why were they all here, what were they doing? Was this to be a bar of regal judgment?

Walking just behind the Queen Mother was le Cardinal de Lorraine, his expression one of haughty unconcern.

Andelot tore his gaze away to fix upon King Francis, walking beside his equally young wife, Mary of Scotland. She appeared as bewildered as he, and they seemed to draw strength one from another as they looped arms and walked slowly, somberly, forward onto the terrace. Mary wore a white robe with gold embroidery trimmed with ermine. Her dark hair was drawn back from her forehead to set off her fair face, and on her head she wore a small pointed cap, studded with jewels, to which was attached a thin veil that fluttered behind. Her cheeks were flushed, but she was in control of herself.

The king's pallid face and tight mouth confirmed his emotional duress. A lump formed in Andelot's throat, and he needed to swallow hard to control the emotions boiling up within his soul. He shivered and felt cold. *I must get out of here!*

The Queen Mother entered first. With an imperious gesture she signed to Mary to take her place under the royal canopy. Next came King Francis, followed by the Guises, and many others Andelot recognized but whose names he did not know.

But *Sebastien!* He was not among the king's cabinet!

Then to his horror he saw an executioner appear in the courtyard, striding slowly, somberly toward the scaffold and up the steps. Garbed in a black mask and a crimson robe, he picked up the ax.

Andelot clasped a palm over his mouth when he saw the long line of Huguenot prisoners already bloodied and bruised from torture. They were packed closely together as far as his eye could see, all the way past the outer walls of the chapel and beyond.

The sight shocked him. It could not be true. So many! Too many for one executioner to behead—there must be others waiting to take the executioner's place. The idea nauseated him. His throat ached as he tried to swallow. How many? Hundreds? No, a thousand—nay, even *two* thousand! The prisoners were like sheep for the slaughter, guarded by archers and musketeers who moved them along.

Andelot squinted as sweat from his forehead trickled into his eyes and stung. Still, he tried to catch a glimpse of Sebastien and Julot, terrified they might be in the line of death.

He tried to pray. *Help these, your sons, who will die this hour, O God. Give your children courage. Do not let them die without feeling your strength and comfort. Have mercy on us, Lord. Have mercy on France!*

He swallowed, his throat dry, his eyes following the horrific sight. Huguenot after Huguenot was led up beneath the royal gallery, up the steps to the scaffold, forced to kneel before the chopping block. They did not scream nor beg. He heard them singing psalms. And then—a heavy whack!

Andelot jerked with each blow, each whack.

He silenced the heave of emotion that welled up within him. A headless, quivering body was cast to one side to be thrown into the Loire River. Blood began to run ... a little at first, then in streams, then in pools.

Andelot plugged his ears. *Whack!* He squeezed his eyes shut tightly. Still unable to keep the whacking of the ax from invading his mind. Unable to control himself now, tears oozed hot and salty down his cheeks with his sweat, and he tasted both on his lips. *Children of God, followers of the Lamb. Andelot's brothers in the faith.*

Whack!

Andelot shook in silent sobs until he could hear his heart thudding in his ears, ready to explode.

Trumpets were blaring, fifes were screeching. The terror went on and on. The sun climbed higher in the French sky.

There was now a loud commotion in the royal gallery. Andelot opened his eyes and looked, feeling bleary-eyed. Young Mary of Scotland, Queen of France, had slumped in her seat. Francis bent over her, looking pale and sickened.

The Queen Mother Catherine turned with a frown toward her son, handing him something. King Francis fumbled and waved whatever it was before his wife's nose, and she revived. Mary sat up, looked about, cried out again, then standing to her feet she rushed forward, flinging herself before her oncle, le Cardinal de Lorraine.

Her voice came to Andelot with its pathos.

"Oncle, cher oncle, stay this awful massacre. Speak to the Queen Mother, or I shall die! Oh! Why was I brought here to behold such a sight?"

"My niece," the cardinal said solemnly, but his face was flushed with excitement. He raised her from the platform and tenderly kissed her on the cheek. "Have courage; these are but a few pestilent fellows; heretics who would have dethroned you and the king and set up a false religion in France. By their destruction we do the kingdom a favor. These deserve no pity. You ought to rejoice."

Andelot turned his gaze to Francis who had also stood. "Alas! My mother," the king cried. "I too am overcome by this horrible display. I would crave your permission to retire; the blood of even my enemies brings me no joy." He turned to his Mary as if to depart the bloody scene.

Catherine de Medici stood abruptly, and raising her hand to stop him, her voice was full of angry passion. "My son, I command you to stay! Duc de Guise," she called firmly, "support your niece, the Queen of France! Teach her the duty of a sovereign!"

As though intimidated by his mother's iron will, the king sat again, pale. Mary was brought to his side where she was once again seated.

The executioner was wearied and another took his place. Andelot had no notion of how many had gone before him. Once again the murderous display captured the attention of the royal audience as blood ran like a river.

The sunlight was waning as the disc sank lower in the sky.

Dazed, Andelot heard the cry and fainting of le Duc de Guise's wife, Anne d'Este. She was carried away. Andelot looked at Mary and saw that the reinette had also slumped in her chair again; again, she was recovered.

The Queen Mother sat erect and calm. Suddenly Francis stood to his feet. "My mother, you are periling the health of my wife. Govern my kingdom and slay my subjects, but let me judge what is seemly for my queen!"

Walking with Mary, his arm around her, Francis withdrew with her.

Huguenot bodies jammed the Loire River. They were piled in heaps as high as the walls about the castle. Headless corpses dangled from the battlements so that wherever one looked they saw dead Huguenots.

And still the butchery continued.

Chapter Twenty-Three

RACHELLE WAS STANDING ON THE BALUSTRADE OVERLOOKING THE courtyard when the gates were drawn aside, and with a flurry, the House of Bourbon rode through with a proud display of flags and emblems in the Bourbon colors of blue, white, and red. Men-at-arms with bronze and silver armaments, their *escutcheons*, on which the various coats of arms were depicted, glittered in the sunlight.

Her anxious gaze sought for Fabien and found him close to Prince Louis de Condé and Admiral Coligny. *Fabien, my future husband?* she wondered with excitement. *Could such honor and happiness await her? Or did death in the Bastille, or in some town square with faggots sizzling, licking up her feet, legs, and body —*

Louise de Fontaine walked up beside her. "Such sights as these make one wonder what will happen, do they not? But I must call you away. Princesse Marguerite asks for you to come to her chamber."

Rachelle tore herself away from the splendor of soldiers and princes and walked to the chambers of the princesse.

One of the maids opened the door and showed Rachelle inside. A heavy, dark wood-framed bed concealed by filmy crimson and cream draperies was looped around a deep alcove. Marguerite was propped beneath satin coverings, large red pillows with fringe of beaded gold lined the entire bedstead. Rachelle's compassion reached out to Marguerite when she saw her wan face, her thick black hair, which was tangled, for she sent her personal maid scrambling from the chamber.

"My head aches too much to be troubled by brushes and combs." Her dark eyes told Rachelle of boiling inner turmoil. "Close my door and bolt it," she whispered.

As Rachelle closed the door she glimpsed Charlotte de Presney watching from a window seat on the far side of the chamber. Charlotte held some embroidery work on the lap of her bright organdy pink skirts, but Rachelle doubted she was concentrating on anything as mild and pleasant as silken stitches. She too must have seen the Bourbon display below the window where she sat, and saw and coveted Fabien. Rachelle did not doubt for a moment that her nemesis had surrendered her hopes to become his maitresse.

"That spy," Marguerite hissed, glancing with dislike toward Charlotte. "If only I could be rid of her unwanted presence among my ladies-in-waiting, but the Queen Mother will not allow it. Come closer," she whispered, and Rachelle drew up the stool and sat beside her.

Haggard lines showed beneath Marguerite's eyes. She reached for Rachelle's wrist, her damp fingers clasping hold tightly. She shook for emphasis. "You must do as I tell you, Rachelle. I know of certain things that will happen ... may already be happening. Go to your closet and remain there out of sight for this day and tomorrow. Whatever you do, do not wander the castle or gardens."

"What is happening, Princesse? I have heard the noise of horses and soldiers in the courtyard."

"Do not ask. Do as you are commanded. I will call for you again in a few days."

Footsteps sounded just outside the drawn draperies of the alcove. Marguerite gritted her teeth. "Go now," she hissed. "She is watching us both."

Rachelle stood, and as she parted the curtains and stepped out into the chamber, Charlotte had left the window seat across the chamber and was straightening the bowl of white flowers on the tall gold-veined table. She walked back to the window and sat down again with her embroidery, without a glance or word in Rachelle's direction.

Rachelle watched her for a moment, then left the chamber.

Once inside her own chamber she tried to busy herself working on the book of her gown designs. One day soon she expected to bring the collection of drawings home to Maman and Grandmère. *Oh, for that day to be hastened.*

Sometime later she heard voices in the antechamber and footsteps. She stood quickly.

The door swung open and Marquis Fabien burst inside, banging the door shut.

"Monsieur Fabien!"

She searched his handsome features and was riveted by his compelling gaze as heated as molted violet blue fire. She understood well enough that he would never enter her personal domain like this unless he felt compelled to do so. The hardness of his jaw convinced her that he had reason enough. *So this was what Marguerite had meant. She too had known that trouble was ready to break forth like a flood to take them all away.*

Fabien was dressed for travel in dark woolen clothes, cloak, and hat. His scabbard was belted on and housed a deadly weapon. He was beside her in several strides, taking hold of her, and crushing her in his embrace, his lips taking hers with hungry desire. She struggled against the overwhelming need surging through her, trying to swim back from the passion conquering them.

"Fabien!" she gasped, turning her face away. "What are you doing?"

"Loving you, ma belle petite." And he propelled her over toward the window where he pushed the drape aside and peered out. Little could be seen, for the window looked out upon the distant forest. She wondered what he might have feared to see floating in the Loire.

"Do you have any idea what is happening?"

"Non," she said breathlessly, "except you come here to sweep me away —"

"I do not intend to lose you," he said, bringing her against him again.

"Fabien, bel ami, what is it? What is wrong? Marguerite demands I stay here in my closet. Something dreadful must be occurring, but what? Did your kinsmen escape safely?"

There was no smile, no apology for his bluntness. "They rode out yesterday morning. There is a slaughter going on at this very minute."

"A slaughter—!"

"Thousands of Huguenot prisoners are being dragged to the chopping block."

She gasped her horror. "Andelot and Sebastien."

"Andelot is not a Huguenot. Even so—" he frowned—"he is not in my chamber and no one knows where he has gone. Sebastien too is not in his chamber."

"Oh, Fabien we must find them."

"There is no time. It is you alone that concerns me now. We shall try to escape to my family castle at Vendôme. It is not far, some twenty miles. I have good horses."

She stared at him, numb, but his eyes persuaded her that he would not speak this way if there were not cause.

She looked around her chamber helplessly. *What to bring? So many priceless things that were part of her life from Lyon—*

He took her arm and drew her away toward her closet. "Bring a hooded cloak. It may rain. Nothing else."

"But Sebastien—"

"I have Gallaudet and Julot searching for both Sebastien and Andelot. They will do what they can. Come, Rachelle, make haste!"

She darted into her closet, looked about in despair at all her prized sewing things, then realizing he was at the closet doorway urging her on, she grabbed a hooded cloak and fled with him, pausing long enough to snatch her book of drawings from the table.

Moments later they were walking along the corridor, his hand holding to her arm as though he expected someone to challenge him and snatch her away. Her footsteps could hardly keep up with his strides. Frightened servants huddled, whispering, and slipped away as they neared.

Fabien pulled open a door and pushed her forward, following. She heard a bolt slide into its place. She saw they were inside an antechamber. He left her and crossed to a door. Opening it he stepped out, and she watched as he glanced about. He turned and gestured. She rushed to join him. With his hand once more on her arm, they stepped out together and walked swiftly along a balustrade that rimmed an entire section of the palais, until they came to a steep, stone stairwell that spiraled downward to a petite court.

Rachelle clasped her palms against her ears to stop the grotesque screeching of fifes and drums coming from somewhere on the other side of the castle. The fiendish glee of the musical noise curdled her blood. She looked at him in horror, but he refused to meet her questioning gaze.

Down, down they went, her feet flying over the stone steps so fast her mind spun, but his firm, steady hold left her with no fear of tripping.

She saw Gallaudet waiting in the small court with its high walls. She counted but two horses, the golden bay that Fabien rode, which she recognized at once, and another stallion that shook its head and sniffed the air uneasily, as though the smell of death troubled him.

"Everything is ready, Monsieur," Gallaudet was saying.

A different voice called down to them from a portico above their heads. Rachelle looked up. Comte Maurice Beauvilliers leaned over the rail. The wind tossed his dark hair and crimson cape. He held a rapier that caught the rays of the sun and gleamed.

"Ho, mon cousine Marquis, Julot tells me Oncle Sebastien has been arrested for treason!"

Rachelle silenced a gasp of despair.

"Do you know if this is so?" Maurice asked.

Rachelle caught Fabien's arm and looked at him imploringly. He frowned up at Maurice.

"I have heard nothing of this. I have not seen Sebastien since the council yesterday with the king. If he was arrested, then this treachery came while I was away with Monsieur Louis and Coligny. Where is Julot?"

"I left him near your chamber. He claims he cannot find the peasant, Andelot. Julot looks for you also."

Rachelle grasped hold of Fabien's arms. He looked down at her, his hand closing over hers, pressing it encouragingly.

"Ma cherie, what Maurice tells me changes my plans. I cannot leave, not with Sebastien possibly arrested."

"They will arrest you as well!"

"Why should they? I am a Catholic. Nor did I sponsor Renaudie. There is no reason to arrest me. I will be safe," he said gently. "It is you I worry about. This is no place now for a Huguenot. If I ride with you to the road to Vendôme, can you ride on from there with an attendant? I promise you, it is not so far that I cannot join you as soon as I am able."

She clutched him more tightly, pleading with her eyes. "I will not leave you. If you stay, then I too shall stay."

"Non, ma bel amie, I will not have you stay here. You must go." And he took her forearm and looked over toward Gallaudet, but Maurice called down with bravado: "Never fear, mon cousine Marquis, I shall attend the mademoiselle with my life if it must be." And he lifted himself over the balustrade and shimmied down the pillar with elaborate gracefulness. He dropped gently to his feet and gave an elegant bow, but his sparkling gray eyes and sensuous smile was for Rachelle alone. He swaggered up as though the day offered no terror, and lifting her hand, he bent over it.

"Mademoiselle, you can count on me to take you to Vendôme. I, Maurice, am your humble servant."

She drew herself up with dignity and looked at Fabien. He measured Maurice, his mouth tipping down at the corner, his violet blue eyes giving a sudden leap of fire.

Gallaudet spoke to him quietly. "Monsieur Fabien, if Andelot and Comte Sebastien are in peril, you will need my sword to back you up, and others' as well. May I suggest that I also remain at your side for whatever may await us and allow the comte to escort Mademoiselle Macquinet?"

"A helpful gesture, in truth, I assure you." Maurice smoothed the ruff at his throat, then he turned to one of his own men and snapped his jeweled fingers. "My horse."

Fabien drew Rachelle away and smiled briefly. "My cousine Maurice is an eager galante and a fop; he often irritates me, but he is no enemy such as we have in the House of Guise. At this moment, at least, I need him. He is worthy of his rapier, and he can be trusted to behave the gentlemen, as long as a mademoiselle gives him no cause to think otherwise. He knows you are a virtuous woman." He lifted a brow and glanced in Maurice's direction. "He also knows I will take off his head if he forgets himself even for a moment. Will you go with him?"

She glanced sideways at Maurice. "I would rather not, but if you insist I go with him, then I will."

"I shall come to you at Vendôme as soon as possible."

"Oh, Fabien, do be cautious."

He smiled with a tinge of wolfishness. "Permit me, bel ami, for I wish to give mon cousine Maurice something to be wary of. I want him to know he must not test me, or you."

He drew her against him and his arms wrapped around her possessively. Her head went back against his arm and his warm lips took hers, long and possessively, sending waves of hot and cold emotions stampeding through her every fiber.

Slowly he released her, and she held to him for support. His eyes sparked with fire. Her breath came rapidly. He brought her hand to his lips and kissed each finger, his gaze still caressing her.

Gallaudet brought her horse around to where she stood with Fabien. Fabien held her steady as she put her foot into the stirrup and swung into the Spanish saddle. She turned the reins on the sprightly animal. She glanced at Comte Maurice Beauvilliers. A smirk twisted his lips over Fabien's amoureux display. Anger tightened his dark brows.

"Adieu, Marquis, mon cousine. You have staked your ownership, but we shall see. This way, Mademoiselle Macquinet. Stay close to me."

In seconds she felt the muscled horse surging beneath her as if anxious to depart. She rode just behind and to the left of Maurice. They galloped down the broad avenue and toward the surrounding forest, leaving the castle of Amboise behind.

The wind blew behind her and seemed a friendly creation pushing her forward and away, away to freedom, to safety, leaving behind the screeching musical notes of Catherine's fifes and drums. How different the sounds from a few nights ago when she heard glorious symphonies, when the trees were aglow with colored lanterns, and the call of amour was in the air like fragrant blossoms.

Had the masque all been a dream, a fairy tale? How changed Amboise was now! Death was in the air, demonic glee shrieked as Christians by the thousands were tortured, then brought to the scaffold ...

The journey from Amboise to the safety of Vendôme was but twenty some miles as the crow flies. She rode with Maurice through land that was much the same as Blois and Amboise, full of verdant forest trees, grassy fields, and flowering hills, with high forest farther toward the mountains and streams.

They drew up to a stream to let the horses drink and rest.

It was the first time she could talk and her questions were many.

"I do not understand, Comte. Was not the edict of pacification signed by the Queen Mother and King Francis? Why then this terror at Amboise?"

"Le Duc de Guise knew the warning from Prince de Condé did not reach his retainer, Renaudie, at Nantes. I have heard from my own spies the two men the prince sent were captured and forced to tell all."

"Le Duc de Guise already knew this when the Bourbon princes and nobles met with the king yesterday?"

"But yes, he had his army hidden in the woods waiting for the heretics to come with Renaudie. Unwisely, Mademoiselle, the heretics came in small groups and were captured easily until Renaudie himself arrived. Le Duc de Guise overtook him while he rested in his camp."

Heretics. She disliked his easy use of the term.

"How despicable of le Duc de Guise!"

As Maurice used his snuff box it glittered in the sun. "So many despicable things in life, Mademoiselle. That is why I try to concentrate on more pleasant experiences ... The masque, it was most delightful, was it not?"

Rachelle was thinking of the betrayal and trap of the Queen Mother and the Guises. They had never intended the edict to be valid. But why had they not moved then and there against the Bourbons?

"Yes, it was most pleasant ... Why did they not arrest Prince de Condé?"

"They move more cautiously against the lions of the forest, Mademoiselle. If the lion should roar, then a very large army could rise to his defense. Ask the marquis if he would fight for his kinsmen and the answer is oui ... You were most belle at the masque, Mademoiselle Macquinet. The most belle of them all. I lamented the fact I was not able to dance with you or to spend time in your fair company. My cousine, the marquis, is a selfish man to keep you all to himself." He smiled and his gaze drifted over her. "I admit he has such wondrous taste."

Rachelle said stiffly: "How far to Vendôme now, Monsieur Beauvilliers?"

"Not far, Mademoiselle."

"Then please, let us be on our way, Monsieur."

He bowed and gestured her toward the waiting horse, a too-pleasant smile on his lips.

Rachelle had a notion that in the days to come she would be seeing more of Maurice than she would prefer.

They rode on and she saw the palais chateau toward late afternoon. Drawing up on a rise she looked across the grassy fields toward the gray stone palais. Refuge awaited her, but what of Sebastien and Andelot? What if the Queen Mother and the Guises discovered Fabien was using his men-at-arms to locate and deliver them? Again, her anxious heart reached in desperation to the Lord for protection and deliverance. A mighty fortress is our God, she thought of Martin Luther's hymn, a bulwark never failing.

A bulwark ... She turned her gaze again upon the Vendôme palais with its enclosed walls of defense; yes, here there was time for recovery, but for how long? They rode through the gate. She glimpsed terraced gardens and flowering groves, but her ragged emotions turned all to gray.

She was ushered inside by the chamberlain, to whom Maurice explained why she was there and how the marquis would arrive either late that night or the next day. The chamberlain was to have more rooms ready, for Marquis Fabien would be bringing others here for refuge until the madness at Amboise ran its course and matters quieted once more.

Rachelle wondered if matters would ever be the same. She had seen a change in Fabien, a great burning anger she believed would only push him forward to fulfill his quest with Nappier and Julot to strengthen the colony which Admiral Coligny wanted as a refuge outside France, a new beginning at the place named Florida.

Rachelle was escorted up a wide flight of stairs and to a spacious bedchamber furnished in various shades of blue and white brocade, with burgundy rugs and draperies. The windows opened onto a terrace promenade with a parterre of rounded greenery and shaped trees of petite size bursting with flowers, but in her mind's eye all she imagined was the bloodstained courtyard where thousands of Christ's faithful followers went like helpless sheep to their gruesome deaths. Had the Lord Jesus stood from his throne beside the Father as He had for the first martyr, Stephen, who had been stoned to death?

And I, she thought, a cramp catching her throat, *am safe here among flowers and pleasant gardens!*

Worn and emotionally exhausted she sank onto the soft bed. She closed her eyes, but the carnage paraded across her mind, giving no solace.

She stood again and paced. How soon until Fabien sailed? She recalled the things he had told her at Chambord when they had walked in the arcade of fragrant lime trees. How the gold and silver that paid for Spain's armies to wage the terror against Protestants in the Netherlands was taken from the Americas, and what was called the Main, or the Caribbean. Would Fabien be even more anxious now to strike back at those treasure galleons bringing gold to Philip of Spain? She was almost certain it would be so.

Yes, he would become more resolved than ever to join forces with the French, Dutch, and English corsairs sinking Spanish galleons. What would this mean for their relationship? He had suggested his absence would last a year, perhaps a little longer, but not two years. Would he be able to keep that promise; would he even wish to do so?

Rachelle sought the breezes by walking along the promenade. The mournful cooing of doves sounded from the top of the arbor.

Would Fabien be more willing to sponsor Nappier with that twenty-gun ship they had spoken about so lightly the night of the masque when on the little butterfly boat?

Maurice Beauvilliers might believe matters would quiet down and return to normal, but Rachelle was not at all inclined to agree. Everything had changed. What grief awaited the loved ones of those slaughtered at Amboise! Wives would not see their husbands again. Children would be without fathers. Would Madeleine and the soon-to-be-born enfant ever see Sebastien? And what would befall Andelot?

It was dark. Andelot did not stir from his cramped fetal position, his face at last dry of tears. He could not stop his trembling. His clothes were damp with sweat, and now as the chill evening blew against him he was cold. The guards had all departed and nothing stirred but the regal canopy flapping in gusts of wind like ghostly wings. For a long time Andelot did not move. All desire, except to escape through the sleep of unconsciousness, had left him.

The stars glittered cold and hard in the blackness. The flapping of the canopy continued. It began to rain. The drops at first came lightly and mingled with the bloody courtyard. Then the rain came still heavier.

He thought he heard footsteps once and his name whispered on the wind. The guards would find him at last, and he would be carried to the scaffold, to the blood-soaked block—

A quivering sob came to his parched throat, sounding inhuman, as a hand reached beneath the vine and touched him.

"Non! Non!"

"Shh! Mon ami, it is I, Fabien. I have been searching for you for what seems hours."

Fabien … Fabien …

"It is over. Quick! Come out. The cardinal looks for you. Charles has confessed everything. He admits bringing you here. We do not have much time. We must leave for Vendôme."

Andelot remained silent, still curled up.

"Nappier and Julot are at the postern gate."

Andelot felt Fabien grabbing hold and pulling him from beneath the cherubs.

Fabien shook him. "Can you understand me? Can you walk?"

He nodded, his teeth chattering, able to move, stiffly at first, stumbling to his feet with Fabien's help. Whereupon Fabien threw an arm around him and together they made their way across the wet courtyard, staying close by the wall.

Fabien whispered: "Do not look about you … I will lead, you follow. Make no sounds."

Minutes later they reached the low postern gate. The master swordsman Nappier hovered in the shadows with horses.

"He is overcome," Fabien warned in a low voice. "Be careful with him."

Julot emerged from the darkness. "Let me take him to a house on the quay, Marquis. The man there is reliable. I shall care for him until he can ride of his own to Vendôme."

"You can trust this man, Julot?"

"Most certainly. He has long been a friend."

"Very well then. I choose to ride on. When Andelot awakens, if he chooses to seek me, I will be at Vendôme."

"We will be there, Marquis." His dark eyes flashed with hate. "We will both come."

Nappier drew near to Fabien. There was an angry grimace on his sweating face. He formed a fist that struck silently but savagely into his other palm. "It is now, Marquis. Now. Let us get that ship and take to the waters of Florida. Let us smash the Spanish galleons that bring gold to Spain that pays for legates like the Guises to kill our fellow Frenchmen."

Fabien's own anger surged in his temples with each heartbeat. He had walked in streams of blood and had some of it on the hem of his cloak. He had seen the piled corpses in the river Loire — so many the Loire was dammed up and overflowing its banks.

He turned and looked up at the ramparts of Amboise. As though adding its own voice to echo their passion, the moon had come from behind dark rolling clouds. The moonlight fell on the hideous, headless corpses dangling from galleries, rooftops, and walls. Body parts were missing, the grotesque bodies of Huguenots would be left for days until the smell would force Catherine and the court back to the Louvre.

As Fabien stared up at the grotesque silhouettes swinging in the wind, groans came from Nappier and Julot. Fabien felt fingers tighten on his shoulder, and he turned his head to see Gallaudet. His usual composed face was contorted and his gray eyes were bloodshot and angry.

"If you go to sink the treasure ships that pay the taskmasters of Spain and Rome, then let me go with you, I beg of you."

Fabien looked over at Andelot. He was hunched over on his saddle, wet and looking as though he too had emerged from a torture chamber.

Fabien gave a determined nod. "We will get a ship. We will go to Florida as planned for Admiral Coligny and his colony. But we will also sink every Spanish galleon we come across on the Caribbean waters. We will send our own message to the Guises and to Philip. We will continue to fight for our freedom. If necessary, we will die fighting. We will never give up until every Frenchman has the right to choose his own faith in Christ — and read the Bible in French if he so wills."

"Ah ..." The sound of approval came from all, until it merged into one determined hum that lit the fires of passion within them.

Fabien walked over to Andelot and gave a squeeze to his arm. "I go to Vendôme, mon cousine. Rachelle is there safe. You are free to do as you will when you are stronger. I hear you have the possibility to return to Paris to the Corps des Pages. I am going to sea. When I return I will see you again. Au revoir, Andelot."

Andelot stirred. Fabien wondered if he had taken in what he told him. He was ready to turn away when Andelot's muffled voice murmured, "Au revoir, mon cousine Fabien. Godspeed. And — merci."

Fabien smiled, reached over, and tousled his damp hair. "Be strong, Andelot. Do not let the evil men who claim they speak for God destroy your gentle faith in the One who is faithful and true."

"I will try, Marquis Fabien ... I will do my best."

"Adieu, then."

Fabien left Andelot, walked into the dark shadows, and mounted. He looked up at the moon and tried to blot from his mind everything but the light.

Without another word he, Gallaudet, and Nappier rode off toward the road to Vendôme, a road that would eventually lead toward the sea, a ship, and St. Augustine, Florida.

You will show me the path of life.

After the sound of the horse hooves faded into the night, Julot mounted and rode up to Andelot.

"Come, Cousine Andelot, there is a safe house not far. There is dry clothing, hot broth, and a warm fire."

They rode off together into the night. *Tomorrow, Julot will ride to Vendôme, and I — I must take my own road*, Andelot thought. *A road to Paris, to the Catholic university, to the Corps des Pages.* His heart felt heavy, even empty now. There were no more tears to shed. *Would he meet Monsieur Fabien again? When would their roads merge as one?* He looked up at the starry sky, and his eyes were clear. He murmured, "Yes, God speed us all in the way we are to go. And one day soon bring us together again."

"Did you say something, ami?" Julot whispered.

Andelot glanced at him. "I am hungry for that hot broth you mentioned."

"Ah. You are recovering. Just a little farther, Cousine, just a short way down the road."

Down the road. The road of life … was he traveling the right path — the way of truth?

The path of the just is the shining light, that shineth more and more unto the perfect day.

GRANDMÈRE, who had just aided the physician in the delivery, lifted her first great-granddaughter into her arms. The bébé appeared healthy and of joie de vivre.

"Thanks to God our Sustainer and Redeemer for this precious gift of life," Grandmère said as she looked down at her granddaughter. Madeleine, with tears and sweat glistening on her face, received her first bébé.

"Her name is Joan," Madeleine said weakly, "named for the courageous and lovely Huguenot Queen of Navarre."

Grandmère leaned over and kissed her great-granddaughter. "And may she walk as courageously through life as Queen Jeanne."

Madeleine looked up. "Have we heard from Sebastien yet? He is expecting this birth."

Grandmère had not told Madeleine that Sebastien was missing from the Chambord Palais chateau. She had feared the troubling news would do her and the bébé injury during birth. Now, with the happiness shining in Madeleine's brown eyes, Grandmère still could not find the heart to spoil her glowing happiness with this dark omen.

Grandmère reached over and bathed her face with a damp cloth. "Not yet, Madeleine. Perhaps in a few days. Surely you can wait?"

Madeleine smiled. "I will wait another day or two to hear from him. If not, I will send a messenger."

"Yes, another day or two, ma cherie. Rest a little while longer. Let us consider our blessings and enjoy what is ours today."

"Grandmère? Was there not a gift from the queen for the night of the enfant's birth? A gift for both of us in red boxes?"

"Ah, I had forgotten. But yes, bien sûr. I shall go now and retrieve them, ma petite."

If ever there is a time of blessing to be grateful for in the midst of trial, we must seize the moment. Grandmère left Madeleine and walked through the appartements to her closet.

Sebastien is missing and he may even have been arrested, but did not their great God have all power and authority in heaven and on earth? It was possible that God would move in answer to prayer and return Sebastien to them.

Grandmère retrieved the two red boxes from her trunk and for a moment stood looking at them. She felt the smile on her lips slowly begin to fade, though she could not have said why. The very sight of the outwardly belle boxes brought the cruel, conniving eyes of Catherine de Medici to mind. Catherine and her pathetic Madalenna spying about on silent feet, reporting back to her mistress the secret things that brought death to the unsuspecting.

Why did Catherine give these gifts to her and Madeleine? And yes, to Rachelle as well?

You are too suspicious, Henriette, she drew her brows together. The gowns were most belle, so why would not Catherine wish to reward us? Even a cold, calculating woman such as the Queen Mother would take delight over a work well done.

Yes, too suspicious.

Grandmère forced her smile to return and walked with the boxes into her granddaughter's chamber. She handed a pretty red box to Madeleine and kept the other for herself. They exchanged smiles and opened their gifts, while the midwife sat with the enfant rubbing its tiny pink body with a fragrant ointment.

"Oh ... gloves," Madeleine sighed. "But how lovely they are."

"And how well made." Grandmère took out her own pair. "They are identical, are they not?"

"Yes, how pleasant."

Grandmère examined the outer material of both pairs, always enjoying the skill of the cut and the stitching of other couturières. She thought back to Rachelle's meeting with Catherine. How frightened Rachelle had been when she returned to the chambers after returning the key to the listening closet in the Queen Mother's chest.

Grandmère stood looking at the gloves, remembering ...

She laid Madeleine's pair on the bedstand, then walked into her closet and placed her own pair on the table beside her mirror. She would wear them tomorrow when she went to the fruit market.

Teach me thy way, O Lord, and lead me in a plain path, because of mine enemies.

At Vendôme, Rachelle pondered what her path should now be. She could return to the Chateau de Silk to work with Macquinet silk. Soon now, Maman and Père would arrive from Geneva. How she longed for them! How she wished to be enfolded in their arms, to pour out all that had taken place since their separation, the good things, and the evil doings of the Queen Mother and the House of Guise. Weary in soul, she longed for Bible exposition by the scholars from the theological academy who usually returned with her parents. She wanted to bask in hearing Père Arnaut praying aloud for each member of the family and for the edifying of Christ's body on earth. She knew their suffering as she never had known before, and her wounded soul needed spiritual balm. There was also a letter from Comtesse Claudine Boisseau, asking Rachelle to come and visit her at the Dushane estate at Orléans. Rachelle remained undecided.

She stood near the steps that led down to the parterre as the sun was setting golden, making the lake sparkle with a cascade of rippling gems. The breeze stirred her hair and cooled her feverish skin, quieting her restlessness. Her blue satin gown rustled. She looked up at the sky as an evening star was appearing. A smile tugged at her lips as her heart recalled the masque on the river when she and Fabien had strolled together beneath the same gleaming stars. She recalled his embrace, the precious promises.

I could not forget you, ever. Not even if I tried to forget.

He had kissed her, showing her he meant it, and she had clung to him, basking in the protection of his strong arms.

Cherie, I will return ... I will come back to you.

In her memory she heard his footsteps in the courtyard, heard them coming toward her until the sound became so real that she turned ...

"Fabien," she whispered.

She moved toward him in the silken gleam of starlight. In a moment he reached her, drawing her into his arms.

"Ma belle amour."

The setting sun splashed the vast sky with ruby fierceness. Soon twilight deepened and the jewels sparkled above, and somewhere a nightingale sang.

Two silhouettes stood in an embrace beneath the starlight, their lips meeting, reaffirming a promise that whatever tomorrow might bring, whatever distance in time and place might separate them, their hearts would forever beat as one.

End of Book One

Written on Silk

Book Two, 2007

Macquinet/Dushane/Dangeau/Beauvilliers Family Tree

(Fictional Characters)

Duchesse Xenia Dushane
(blood relative to Grandmère)

Claudine Dushane-Boisseau
(Comtesse, blood relative to Xenia)

Henriette Dushane (Grandmère)
(Grand couturière, Chateau de Silk, Lyon)

Bernard Macquinet
(cousin to Arnaut)

Arnaut Macquinet = **Clair Dushane**
(Comte) (Chateau de Silk, Lyon)

Louis Dushane
(deceased)

Francois Dangeau-Beauvilliers
(Comtesse, Sebastien's sister)

Sebastien Dangeau = **Madeleine**
(Comte) (in Paris)

Idelette
(grisette)

Rachelle
(grisette)

Avril
(12-yr-old)

Jean (baby)

Maurice Beauvilliers
(Comte, Sebastien's nephew)

Athenais Beauvilliers
(Comtesse, Maurice's sister)

Andelot Dangeau
(Messire, a serf, Sebastien's nephew)

The Royal Valois Family Tree

(Historical)

King Henry Valois II ═══ **Catherine de Medici**
(King of France) ⸺ (Queen Mother and regent during reigns of Francis II and Charles IX)

King Philip II ═══ **Elisabeth**
(King of Spain) ⸺ (oldest daughter)

Mary Stewart
(of Scotland)

Francis II
(the young king)

Marguerite
(princess, second daughter)

Charles
(future King Charles IX)

Henry of Anjou
(King Henry III after Charles)

Hercule
(forth and youngest son)

The House of Guise Family Tree
(Historical)

Anne d'Este ═══ **Duc de Guise (Francis)**
(Marshal of France,
persecutor of Huguenots,
blood uncle to
Mary of Scotland)

Cardinal de Lorraine (Charles)
(younger brother of Duc de Guise
and a leader of the French inquisition
against Huguenots, blood uncle
to Mary of Scotland)

Henry de Guise
(the love of Princesse
Marguerite Valois)

Three ways to keep up on your favorite Zondervan books and authors

Sign up for our *Fiction E-Newsletter*. Every month you'll receive sample excerpts from our books, sneak peeks at upcoming books, and chances to win free books autographed by the author.

You can also sign up for our *Breakfast Club*. Every morning in your email, you'll receive a five-minute snippet from a fiction or nonfiction book. A new book will be featured each week, and by the end of the week you will have sampled two to three chapters of the book.

Zondervan *Author Tracker* is the best way to be notified whenever your favorite Zondervan authors write new books, go on tour, or want to tell you about what's happening in their lives.

Visit *www.zondervan.com* and sign up today!

ZONDERVAN™

GRAND RAPIDS, MICHIGAN 49530 USA

ZONDERVAN.COM/
AUTHOR**TRACKER**